Sounds of Yesterday

A NOVEL

Celestial Seaside
PUBLISHING

Sounds of Yesterday

A NOVEL

Jacob Hubbard

Sounds of Yesterday
Copyright © 2024 by Jacob Hubbard
Cover Design by Monét Nyree Panza
Interior Illustrations by Doan Trang

Library of Congress Control Number: 2024910961

Published by Celestial Seaside Publishing
San Diego, CA, USA

ISBN (Paperback): 979-8-9908479-0-3
ISBN (eBook): 979-8-9908479-1-0

This book is a work of fiction. While inspired by real people and events, names, places, and dates have intentionally been changed to distance any resemblance between fiction and nonfiction counterparts. In addition, any dialogue and scenes inspired by true events are subject to the imperfection of memory and subjectivity of emotion. These words, this story, and the messages contained within are shared without malice or ill-intent towards any person.

Printed and bound in the United States of America

To Diana,

For without you, this book would not have come to be.
I wish you nothing but peace and happiness,
Yesterday, today, and tomorrow,
Wherever you are . . . .

*"Then a woman said, Speak to us of Joy and Sorrow.
And he answered: Your joy is your sorrow unmasked."*

— KAHLIL GIBRAN, "ON JOY AND SORROW"

Today

1

May 19, 2022

A fire broke out in my neighborhood.

Black smoke painted the afternoon blue sky in the distance. I deviated from my usual route, turning the corner to see firetrucks and my neighbors breathlessly watching firefighters run with hoses toward the house engulfed in flames. Some took out their smartphones and recorded the fire while others just stood to view it like a spectacle. I stayed on the opposite side of the street to watch, stopping directly across from the house. I took my Airpods off, watching firefighters try desperately to put out the fire as smoke came from the roof. All the surrounding houses remained unscathed.

Watching the fire became another chance to get my mind off the amount of grading I had to do, or thinking about being stuck living at home with my mom and my sister, or wondering where to take Ana for Memorial Day weekend. I watched the house burn. The roof soon collapsed, and I could see everything charred and covered in ashes through one of the windows. Out of habit, I took out my phone and opened up Snapchat.

I have to send this to Ana! I thought. I took a video of the firefighters putting out the fire and the small crowd watching, typed in the words, "This is insane!" and sent it.

I watched the house fire before noticing someone next to me taking pictures with her phone. "Excuse me, but do you know what happened here?"

"No idea," she said. "All I know is that they were doing some work on the roof and the next thing you know, you see all this."

"I hope everyone's okay."

I watched firefighters working to contain the fire and save what they could of the house. More people took more pictures as police taped off the area. I looked to my left to see an older man crying as two police officers put a blanket over him, trying to calm him down.

"I think that's the owner of the house," the woman, who I assumed was a neighbor based on her knowledge of the roof repairs, said to me.

I then looked back at the homeowner across the street before seeing a teenage girl filming the fire, only to have what I assume was her mother grabbing the phone out of her hand. "What's wrong with you, Jill?" she yelled. "Those people are having the worst day of their lives and you wanna film it?"

I checked to see if Ana received the Snapchat I sent her, but she didn't open it, something she would have done by now, but I figured since she was in Baltimore for her business trip, it probably didn't mean anything. I watched the fire a little bit longer before cutting my walk short to force myself to finish grading. Final grades were due tomorrow!

I got back to my house and went to work, my laptop and filled-out notebooks all set up at the outdoor dining table not too far from our swimming pool. Neither Mom nor Alicia were home, so I had the place to myself for the afternoon. Mom was probably at the casino again, and Alicia was likely somewhere out with her boyfriend. I sat down and got myself situated, looking up again to watch the smoke from the neighboring house fire swirl in the sky for a couple minutes before getting to work.

I logged into Canvas and saw all the student submissions I had to grade. Not exactly encouraging. I sighed, opening up my Spotify to put on Poets of the Fall again, a Finnish rock band I'd been a fan of for over a decade, putting their music on shuffle to grade.

As I graded, I began seeing myself *on a huge semi-circular thrust stage in a massive auditorium with hundreds of people in the seats. I have imagined being on this stage countless times before, but this time the audience cheered and clapped as Glenn Sawyer presented me with an award. By my side was Ana, smiling at me and holding my hand.*

"Welcome everyone," Glenn said to the audience. "Every year as chair, I present on behalf of the Rhetoric & Writing Department Teacher of the Year award to one of our esteemed colleagues. This year, we present the award to Robert Sullivan. Rob has been with the department as a lecturer since August 2017. I know from classroom observations and countless conversations I've had with Rob, he is a smart, hardworking, and dedicated teacher with a bright future ahead for him. At the start of the pandemic, so many of us struggled to adapt to what everyone has called 'the new normal,' but Rob stepped up to the challenge."

Ana held my hand and rested her head on my shoulder. I kissed her on the top of her head before looking back up at Glenn.

"When Rob started working for us," Glenn continued, "he started off with a 1-semester contract, only able to work for us during Fall semesters. This year, he was offered a continuing contract with us and is now an established member of our department. We sincerely believe Rob has rightfully earned this honor. He has gone above and beyond and put the needs of our students first, never once complaining. Outstanding teaching evaluations, valuable contributions to the department, and hard work and determination show why Rob deserves this award. With that in mind, I present our Teacher of the Year award this year to our colleague Robert Brian Sullivan!"

The audience cheered and chanted my name once Glenn finished his speech. Ana signaled for me to step up and give a speech. I shook Glenn's hand, grabbed the award, and turned to face the audience.

"Wow, this is an honor!" I said. "Thank you, everyone! I don't know what to say!"

I looked over at Ana who smiled at me, and then I looked back at the audience.

"I cannot begin to even thank you all enough for this!" I continued. "This means so much to me! This semester—no, this year, no, the last two years—have probably been one of the most challenging times of my career. But it feels so liberating to finally be moving forward in a career so many of my friends continually warned me would not be financially stable enough to live in San Diego." I cleared my throat. "Speaking of San Diego, can we all agree that it can be an economic hell for people like us?"

"Amen to that!" Someone in the audience shouted.

"So many of us are stuck living with our parents because of this economy! But now I'm at a point where I can finally build enough of my savings and move out of my mom's house!"

The audience gave a huge round of applause. I paused to let them finish.

"At the start of the pandemic, when I lost my job at the community college, I didn't know if SDSU was going to give me work, but you all stuck by my side and kept letting me do what I love."

I looked over at Ana again, who gave me a thumbs up and smiled at me. I smiled back, and then looked over again at the audience. "I remember how for the past five years, I had to take countless side jobs just to get by. Think about it. Now that I am finally here, it is unreal. But I have to be honest: I could not have done this all by myself. I wouldn't be here today if it weren't for my partner right here, Ana Kang!"

The audience clapped again. Ana smiled and blushed at the same time.

I cleared my throat. "This woman is amazing!"

The audience cheered again.

"I couldn't ask for a better partner here. But I don't want to just make it about me either. Ana here, she's moving up, too. She's a leader now. She's doing so many great things with her life, and I can't be more proud to see it first hand. Give Ana another round of applause!"

The audience roared in applause. I looked over at Ana before walking over. As I wrapped my arm around her, Poets of the Fall's "Sounds of Yesterday" began to play.

I looked into Ana's eyes. "I really mean it when I say this: I love you!"

The audience gave a big "awww" sound as Ana blushed again.

"I love you too," Ana whispered in my ear. As we faced the applauding audience, a giant spotlight shined on us and the ceiling opened up to a night sky filled with stars, flooding the entire auditorium in bright light.

"We can finally build a future together," I said, kissing her on the forehead. "We won!"

The daydream began to fade out of my mind.

It started to get dark and I knew I needed to call it an evening. I needed to take a break from grading and focus on making a list of things I could do to make this year's Memorial Day weekend special for Ana. I leaned back as it got close to 7 pm and looked up at the sky to give myself a mental break before hearing a *ding* from my phone.

It was a text message from Ana. I assumed she was going to ask me to pick her up from the airport tomorrow or the next day.

ANA:

> I've been thinking a long time and I hate to hurt your feelings but at the same time, I also have to put myself first. I realize that I prefer to be alone than be with other people and considering I don't want any relationship or commitment, I am going to enjoy some time by myself and planning my own future.

My heart sank as I read it multiple times. Was this real? Was this some kind of sick joke she was pulling on me? I raced to figure out what to say, typing the first thing that came to my head.

ROB:

> Do you want to take a break? Do you want space?

No response. My heart pounded as I called her, going straight to voicemail. "Hey Ana, it's me, Rob. I just received your text. Is everything okay? I just wanted to know if you were okay. I was hoping we could talk. Is something wrong? Please give me a call back when you get a chance. Love you! Bye!"

I hung up. I fidgeted in my chair, my heart thumping so heavily it felt as if it was going to jump out of my chest at any moment. I hustled through the house, out the front door, and ran toward the street corner. *This can't be happening!*

Just as I reached the corner, my phone rang. "Rob? Can you hear me?"

It took me a few seconds to muster up what I wanted to say. "Ana? I can hear you. How are you? I got your text. Is everything okay?"

No immediate response. I sat down at a curb, pressing my phone more firmly against my ear so I could hear her more clearly, as if that proximity could somehow bridge this distance between us. "Hello? Ana? Can you hear me?"

"Yeah, I can hear you."

"What's going on? Your text is scaring me!"

"I really am sorry for this. I just . . . I just couldn't figure out how else to tell you."

"Tell me what? Why are you doing this? None of this makes any sense!"

"Rob, this is not something that just happened overnight. I didn't just wake up one day and decide this."

"How long have you felt this way?"

Ana took a moment to answer. "A couple years now."

A couple years now? I thought. *What in the world is going on?*

"Wait, what? What do you mean 'a couple years now'?" I asked, suddenly breathless.

"I've been wanting to say something for a while," Ana said. "I just . . . I just didn't know how to tell you."

"Did I do something wrong?"

"No, you didn't do anything wrong. It's just . . . I don't like people. I realized that I don't like to be around people in general. I prefer to be alone. I didn't want to keep leading you on. I want my free time. I've been thinking a lot about my career, my future, and just what I want to do with my life. I've thought a lot about what it all looks like, and every time I look at what it looks like, I have to be honest with you. I don't see you in it."

"What do you mean you don't see me in it?"

As we talked, I imagined Ana on the other line sitting in her chair, no longer the sweet, adorable, and joyful entry level insurance agent one year out of college I met five years ago, but a cold and emotionless seasoned CEO having to make all the difficult decisions in a boardroom. I even speculated she was wearing her normal work attire at the insurance office: black dress pants and matching jacket, the utilitarian makeup. I could imagine her being the type of businesswoman firing countless people in a room without a second thought.

This was not something I thought she would ever do to me.

"We're not compatible," she finally blurted out.

What do you mean we're not compatible? I thought. *What the hell?* I struggled to come up with something to say.

"Again, it's not you. You've done nothing wrong. I've just thought about this for a long time. When I make a decision, I am firm on it!" She emphasized *firm* in a way that made me feel like an unwanted employee being let go, a sense of frustration in her voice.

I was still in a state of shock even as she said this.

"I've just been doing a lot of thinking, and I don't know if I can keep doing this. It's not you. You're so sweeeeet."

A moment of silence.

"But I have to . . . I have to be honest with you . . . I just don't see you in it."

"Is this why you have been emotionally distant for the last few months?" I blurted out. "Why every time I try to cuddle with you, you push me away? And why every time I come over over on the weekends you just want to sleep or be on your phone or watch your shows? Is this why every time I try to talk to you about something lately, you either tune me out or put on your Airpods? None of this makes any sense."

No response from her.

My heart pounded, forcing me to take deep breaths. Eventually, I spoke again. "Can I ask you a question?"

"Sure."

"Do you still love me?"

"I don't," she stated coldly. "I don't love you."

The second she said those words, I felt like she stabbed me in the chest. I instantly thought about the homeowner who cried to the point where two police officers had to calm him down. Was this the same feeling he had when he lost his house today?

"Are you still in Baltimore?" I eventually asked her.

"No, I'm back home now."

What the hell? I had driven her to the airport a week ago and expected to pick her up again. Why would she do this? Why would she keep me in the dark?

I caught my breath again. "So what's next? Do you just want to be friends?"

"I mean . . . we can try."

"What do you mean by that?" I desperately asked.

"I haven't been a really good friend," Ana said. I could sense distress in her voice, but I didn't know if she meant in general or just to me specifically.

"Don't say that!" I exclaimed. "Why would you even say that? Of course you're a good friend! What are you talking about?" I sighed as neither of us said anything for a moment. "Did we have a good five years at least?" I wearily asked.

"Sure, you can say that," she said. I couldn't tell by the tone of her voice if she meant it or if she was saying that to be nice.

"What about my stuff?" I slowly asked.

"I'll just go ahead and mail it to you when I get a chance."

"No, it's okay. I'll just come pick it up."

"Okay. I'll text you and let you know when you can come pick it up."

I hung up and just sat on the curb, watching all the cars drive by me. This did not feel real to me at all. I felt weird for feeling nothing. No sense of anger. No sadness. Just emptiness. The only thing I could do was watch cars drive by.

Instinctually, I logged onto Facebook and posted to everyone she ended it, making sure she could not see my status update. I knew final grades were due tomorrow, but I didn't care. All I could think about was what I could've done that made her end it after being together for so many years.

I sat on the curb for about an hour, even as it got dark, until I heard another *ding* from my phone.

ANA:

Your stuff is in the front by the mailbox in a red bag.

I sighed, sitting there for a while before getting up and walking away.

After getting home from picking up my stuff from Ana's place, I began playing my guitar in the front living room. My laptop sat on the coffee table with social media opened in the background. Next to the coffee table was the red bag full of my stuff I used to have at her place for whenever I would go there on the weekends. I already saw comments on my post from people expressing condolences over what happened, but I ignored them for the moment so I could focus on playing my guitar. I felt completely numb, continuing to strum my guitar in an effort to keep my mind off what happened over the past couple hours.

A half hour later, my phone rang. It was Ben. *Probably gonna talk my ear off again, isn't he?* I thought. I put down my guitar and answered the phone just to be polite.

"Hey Rob," Ben said. "I saw what you posted just now on Facebook and wanted to check up on you. I'm really sorry to hear about you and Ana! Are you holding up okay?"

I sighed. "I guess you can say that."

"Do you want to talk about it?"

"Nah, I'm good."

"Are you sure?" Ben asked, clearly confused by my response.

"Yeah."

"Ooookay. Well, I know I never had the chance to meet her, but I know you two were so close, so I'm just really sorry you're going through this!"

"It happens," I said meekly. "If anything, it's kind of freeing in a way."

"What do you mean by that?"

I readjusted myself in my chair, clearing my throat. "I mean . . . for some reason I . . . I don't feel anything. It's kind of weird, but at the same time . . . I feel somewhat of a sense of relief. At least I don't have to deal with her pushing me away whenever I want to cuddle with her, or her snapping at me from time to time, or her door slamming anymore! God, fuck that door slamming!"

"Door slamming?"

"Never mind. Forget I said anything. Point is that I'm doing fine."

"That's good, I guess," Ben said, though obviously still confused. "Sounds like you're taking this pretty well, all things considered."

"I can assure you I'm fine," I insisted, "But thank you for checking up on me anyway."

"Of course. If anything, stuff like this is why I've sworn off relationships! One minute they are there for you all lovey-dovey and making you food, and then the next minute they stab you in the back, like Ana did to you!"

"No, Ben, it's not like that she stabbed me in the back—"

"Of course she stabbed you in the back, Rob," Ben interjected. "What are you talking about? I was hoping this wouldn't happen to you, but it sucks that you had to experience this the hard way. I mean, I remember when I was with Claire all those years ago. That bitch never gave our relationship a real chance!"

Ben then rambled on and on about his ex-girlfriend Claire from his early twenties which turned into a massive rant about why relationships were bullshit. I began to mentally tune him out, knowing nothing I said would matter. The more Ben talked, the more worn out I felt. I didn't know how to politely get him off the phone, so I put him on mute and allowed him to say whatever he wanted for the next few minutes. After what seemed like an adequate amount of time, I finally took him off mute.

". . . and she still never gave me my favorite book back. Total bullshit! Anyway, sorry for all that!"

"It's okay."

"By the way, there's going to be a bonfire on Saturday night! Alex is having a going away party before he moves to Boston. You wanna come? Everyone will be vaccinated so you don't have to worry about getting COVID."

"Sure, I'll be there," I meekly said.

"Awesome! I'll see you there. I gotta go get ready for bed. You have a good night, Rob. Again, I'm really sorry to hear about you and Ana."

I hung up, thoughts of Ana and I appearing here and there as I played my guitar.

***

May 20, 2022

At around 3am I gave up on trying to sleep, so I sat at my bedroom desk hoping to submit final grades. I put on Poets of the Fall again to help get me in the headspace to grade, making sure not to make the music loud enough to wake up everyone else in the house. I finally finished grading, but then I had to submit them into the school's grade roster. All I could do was sit there and stare at the grade roster on my laptop screen, as if my body didn't want to do anything. Each passing moment, I felt an increasing aching feeling in my chest. I could not stop thinking about Ana. The last phone conversation we had kept playing in my head.

Do you still love me?

I don't; I don't love you.

It replayed in my head over and over again. I could feel the stab in my chest each time the track restarted.

"It's whatever," I muttered. "If you don't love me, then go. Go live your life without me. I don't need you anyway."

I felt another ache pierce my chest but tried to brush it off.

I pulled up my attendance records and began calculating but found myself not doing anything with it. I just mindlessly stared at my screen.

I eventually found myself on Facebook scrolling through my feed, seeing an endless cacophony of shallow inspirational pictures. I scrolled through them before finding myself looking at Ana's Facebook. *Looks like she hasn't unfriended me and that's good at least,* I thought. I was about to click out but instead looked at her profile picture which showed her holding up a wine glass at a winery with the caption, "Cheers to the weekend."

I clicked out of Facebook and hit my left hand over and over again to relieve stress. I put on my Airpods so I could turn the volume of the music up louder and stim.

After I found myself in a calmer space, I picked up the Airpods case and held it up in my hand. These were the same Airpods Ana got me for Christmas last year. As I looked over the Airpods case, I thought about the afternoon at Ana's place when we exchanged Christmas presents.

She sat across from me at her kitchen table as I opened the Christmas present from her to reveal brand new Airpods Pro. *Oh my god!* I exclaimed. *This is so awesome! Thank you!*

I know you like to use headphones all the time, so I thought these would be great for you, Ana said.

Now I can go on my walks or go to the gym and not get tangled! Exactly.

I keep looking at the Airpods Pro case as the memory of that

Christmas afternoon stayed in my head before fizzling out. I put my case away, but I didn't have the energy to do something as simple as updating attendance records. *Screw it*, I thought as I tossed the attendance records in the trash bin, calculated their final grades, and submitted them. *They all came to class anyway.*

I scrolled through social media again before finding myself going through my Google pictures. I saw collections of photos of Ana and I and what we've done over the years. Street fairs, cooking dinners, trips to Ensenada, Las Vegas, Atlanta, and the Grand Canyon—the digital montage of the life we'd lived together, proof of a love that had been very real for me. As I scrolled through them all, Poets of the Fall's "Sounds of Yesterday" started playing again.

I came across a selfie of us together at a Christmas lights festival outside of Las Vegas we took on New Year's Eve, a few months before the start of the pandemic. It was cold that night, so we wore extra layers of clothing so we could comfortably walk around and see all the different Christmas light exhibits. We sat down at a bench to rest our legs and before I knew it, she took out her phone and took a few selfies of us together. Looking at the selfies, I couldn't help but be mesmerized by her smile and embarrassed by my messy, curly hair. *I should have gotten a hair cut before we went on that trip,* I thought as I looked at the photo.

I went through more pictures and found an old video clip I took of Ana riding a green rental bicycle somewhere near a pier in Pacific Beach. In the video, Ana rode past me with the biggest smile I've ever seen, looking so happy and excited to be there. "Go Ana!" I shouted in the video. Each second I looked at photos and videos of us, I found myself having to take deep breaths here and there, trying to hold back tears each time I looked at each new photo.

After some time scrolling through my photo collections, I looked over at my bed and a memory of us cuddling came to mind. I remembered a November night five years ago when we had just gotten back from trying to attend the Comedy Store in La Jolla; we'd realized we just wanted to stay in for the evening. As we cuddled, Ana looked up at me.

I have something to tell you, she said.

What is it? I asked.

She looked at me and didn't say anything for a moment before out of the blue she whispered, *I . . . I love you.*

I took a moment processing what she said. This was the first time she ever told me she ever loved me. *I love you too,* I finally said before we shared a kiss. Five years later and now I could not stop thinking about her, remembering the first time she told me she loved me and the phone conversation we had yesterday at the same time, side by side. *I don't; I don't love you* repeated in my head again.

I could no longer hold anything back and began sobbing uncontrollably. I saw myself *on the same stage I imagined myself on earlier, this time Ana was ripped away from me by a supernatural force I couldn't see. Glenn grabbed the award out of my hands as the audience all booed me.*

"It's your fault Ana left you!" Half the audience shouted. "You're a complete failure!"

I stepped back, trying to come up with something to say before tripping into a bottomless black hole in the floor.

I started to breathe more heavily, my head on my desk as a stream of tears poured out as flashbacks of five years of memories rushed through my head like a movie.

Just then I heard Mom bang on my door as she tried to get in. "Rob, are you okay?"

I rushed over and sat back against the door. "Go away!"

"Rob, it's five in the morning! Please tell me you're okay!"

"Go away! LEAVE ME ALONE!"

I couldn't stop crying and hitting myself, drowning out everything else Mom tried to say before I could no longer feel her presence outside my room.

For the next half hour, I sat by the door, numb as I stared off into space until I looked up at the wall of posters above my desk, the majority of them Ana either helped buy or got for me as gifts. In the center was a painting of a moth Ana bought for me at the San Diego Art festival years ago.

I began remembering the day we bought the poster.

Isn't that your favorite band? Ana had asked when I pointed it out.

The painting of the moth was not just some ordinary moth. It was the iconic logo for Poets of the Fall, each member of the band standing side by side underneath it.

I went over to rip it off from the wall, but when I put my hands on the painting, I couldn't do it.

Oh my god, you are awesome! I exclaimed when she bought it. *Thank you!*

I took my hands off the poster, sitting at my desk.

"Ana, why did you do this?" I asked, unable to stop myself from crying. I looked up again at the poster, reliving in my head the day we bought the painting.

Yesterday

2

———

September 9, 2017

When Ana came over as usual for the evening, I couldn't help but notice her smile.

We had the house to ourselves, so we cuddled on the couch to watch a movie in the front room, putting on *Spider-Man: Homecoming*, the one Marvel movie neither of us had seen yet. Alicia worked a normal Saturday night DJ gig somewhere while Mom spent the weekend at Grandpa's house again, so we didn't have to worry about either of them bothering us. Ana smiled more than usual as the movie went on before halfway rubbed her hand alongside my leg before she kissed me, leading me in a deep, passionate kiss. We soon forgot about the movie as we hustled to my room, shredding our clothes and plunging into bed.

We lay on our backs, side pressed together when we were done.

"Damn, we both *really* needed that," she teased.

I chuckled, wiping sweat off my face. I caught Ana smiling as she met my gaze. She pressed in even closer and rested her head on my chest.

I watched her smile hold steady as I wrapped my arms around her. But I also couldn't help but remember how she reacted when I tried giving her a pair of earrings as a gift back in June in this very room.

I'm looking for companionship, she said.

Oh, I said. Ana handed them back to me, so I put them in the bottom drawer of my desk before going back to cuddling.

What does that make us? I eventually asked.

Friends.

With benefits?

You can say that.

It took me a moment to process all that, disappointed yet another relationship opportunity had dissipated before I shrugged. *I'm okay with that.*

A month later when grandpa asked me about Ana as I visited him some time ago, I told him I didn't really see her in my future and was considering other options.

What do you hope to do then? Grandpa asked.

Probably go for a PhD, I said. *Maybe travel. Work first and then go from there.*

I didn't tell him anything else. I've accepted it was up in the air what would happen between us once I figured out what next for me. At least I was getting laid for now. Since the house Ana was renting a room in up north in Rancho Peñasquitos didn't allow overnight guests, she would come over, business as usual, on Saturday nights so we could "watch movies."

I'd noticed the last few weeks, she would come over for extended periods of time, staying much longer than originally planned or spending the night and the next day with me. Yet here she was, acting like she didn't want to be anywhere else in the world.

Without thinking, I wrapped my arms around her and gently combed my fingers through her long black hair, but as I combed through her hair something about it felt weird. Is this something she is okay with? Are we still *just* friends? With benefits? Combing her hair made it feel like we were a couple, even though she'd made it clear we really weren't. I began to pull my hand away, but she grabbed it and guided it back to her hair.

We just enjoyed each other's company. "How are you feeling?" I finally asked.

"Good."

"How's work been?"

"Nothing new. Just my coworkers being children again."

"Again?"

"Yeah, so much gossip," Ana said, chuckling. "I feel like every time I come into the office, there is drama. Drama here, drama there. Feels like I'm in high school all over again."

"What kind of drama?"

"Oh you know, same as before."

I already had a general idea of what Ana was likely going to talk about, since it was not unusual for her to confide her work stories to me. "Anything different this time?"

"Well . . . one coworker is trying to get together with another coworker, even though it's against company policies. Another one is trying to get out of working at the office so she can pretend to 'work from home.' Lots of arguing and bickering and spreading gossip. It feels straight out of *Mean Girls*."

"So basically *Mean Girls: Hanmi Insurance Edition*?"

Ana chuckled. "That's one way of putting it. And then we just recently got this new employee. Oh my god! I've been trying to train her and it's like she can't even follow simple instructions!"

"Sounds like what I have to put up with."

"You're a teacher! College students don't follow instructions, especially *yours*!"

"Very funny," I teased. "Whatever you say."

"I mean, it's like she can't even do simple tasks, and she does not take the time to learn how to properly do her job. I don't even know why my boss continues to hire these people. I try to tell her that this new employee doesn't seem to know what she's doing at all, and my boss keeps saying that she will learn. But honestly, if I was in charge, I wouldn't have brought on that new hire in the first place."

"You just need to be patient, grasshopper."

Ana smiled. "First of all, I'm not a grasshopper, and no, I don't need to be patient. I need people who know what the hell they're doing."

"What you need are some tickles," I said, tickling her underneath the sheets.

"Oh my god, stop!" Ana shouted with laughter.

"But I'm the tickle monster!" I made her laugh again before we lay back in bed. I wondered if I went too far with the tickling, but she didn't seem to mind.

"Can you hand me my phone?" Ana asked. "It's in one of my pants pockets."

I reached down to the floor, pulled out her iPhone from her pants pocket, and gave it to her. She disengaged from my arms and began browsing social media, something she would normally do. I did the same with my phone, just watching random video clips or seeing people argue like idiots on Twitter. Ana showed me a funny meme on her phone to make me chuckle before she went back to browsing.

I could not help but sneak glances at Ana. I had seen her smile before, but for some reason something about her smile tonight seemed more radiant, more affectionate than what I was used to.

"Are you doing anything tomorrow?" Ana asked.

"Um . . . not really. I mean, I do have to prep for next week's class, but I can always do that later."

"There's this art festival downtown tomorrow. You wanna go?"

She showed me a Facebook advertisement for the San Diego Festival of Arts being held downtown by the waterfront.

"Sure, I'd love to," I said.

Ana clicked on the advertisement and went directly to the festival website.

"How much are tickets?" I asked.

"Don't worry about it."

"Wait! Are you *sure*?"

"It's fine. Don't worry about it."

I said nothing as Ana bought the tickets, and then we watched Netflix before going to sleep. I wondered the whole time if we were just friends or if we were something else entirely.

September 10, 2017

We carpooled in her Honda Civic to the festival. Since it was a relatively cool morning, I had on a black T-shirt, light blue jeans, and gray sneakers. Ana wore her usual blue flannel shirt, black yoga leggings, and brown boots. I rode shotgun as she drove.

"Do you want to stop and get breakfast somewhere on the way?" I asked.

"I'm good. There's probably going to be food there anyway."

I looked out the window as she kept driving.

"Are you okay with me playing Ariana Grande?" Ana asked.

"Um . . . sure?"

Ana changed the song on the radio to play "Into You." She normally wouldn't ask me if I cared what song we played, but I figured it was nothing.

But as we got closer to downtown, I couldn't stop thinking about last night. Why would she allow me to play with her hair? Why would she buy us tickets for both of us to attend this art festival? And now she was asking me if I was okay with her playing an Ariana Grande song? Why would she care? Where did we stand?

After Ana changed lanes, her phone rang. "Sorry, I have to take this," she said, putting the call on speaker and speaking Mandarin to the person on the other line.

The way Ana talked to her made me realize it was her mom.

For the next five minutes, I couldn't understand a single word they were saying to each other, but I could tell Ana grew more agitated the longer the call went on, as if she was trying to hold back profanities. When she finally got her mom off the phone, Ana let out a big sigh.

"Everything okay?" I asked.

"Yeah. She's just being difficult. That's it."

"Sounds like my mom."

Ana just shrugged and kept driving. I could sense something about that phone call bothered her but didn't press any further.

"There are way too many people," I commented after we got our event wristbands and water bottles and went through the festival checkpoint. Miles of booths lined up in a gridlike pattern on the grass, many close to the San Diego County Clerk's Office and others along the park with an open view of the bay. We checked out outdoor art galleries, looking at paintings of historic landmarks and famous people.

Ana seemed specifically fond of paintings of dogs and looked at them the longest.

"This cute one reminds me of my boss's dog," she said when we came across a painting of a Bichon Frisé laying on a purple fuzzy rug with a tennis ball.

It made me remember the time Ana pet sat for her boss's hyperactive dog while her boss was away on a business trip to Vietnam. I took a Snapchat of the painting, commenting on how cute I thought the dog was before taking a sip of water.

"Do you think you ever want a dog of your own?" I asked.

"I don't know. I mean, maybe, but probably not for a while."

"Considering how exhausting your boss's dog must've been, I don't blame you."

"They are cute, though."

"Like you?" I said playfully.

Ana looked straight at me, playfully gasping. "First of all, I'm *not* cute! Babies are cute! Kittens are cute! Puppies are cute! Do I look like a baby to you? Or a kitten? Or a *puppy?*"

I couldn't help but laugh as she gave me this "stern" lecture before she finally laughed.

We walked around and viewed more paintings before coming to

a festival tent selling necklaces, bracelets, postcards, and other small trinkets.

While viewing one of the San Diego Festival of Arts postcards at one of the tables, Ana went through a small sunglasses display rack, picking up a pair to try on before looking up at me.

Without a second thought, I lifted up my phone and took a quick photo of her.

"You going to get those?" I asked. "They look good on you."

Ana took off the sunglasses. "Not sure yet. I wanna look around some more first."

She walked around while I viewed the photo I took. The photo was nicely lit and I could clearly see myself holding up my phone in the reflection of her sunglasses, but I could also see her huge, radiant smile, front and center.

It was enough to make me feel like I had butterflies in my stomach.

You said you wanted to just be friends, but is that really the case? I thought. *Or do you actually want to be more than that?*

I looked at the photo more closely, wondering if I wanted something more than that too.

"Rob, you ready?" Ana asked from the register.

"Coming," I said as I put away my phone and caught up with her.

We walked around and saw more outdoor galleries. It started getting hot when we came across a huge art mural overlooking a small public spray fountain.

I started taking my shoes off.

"No, don't do it," Ana objected.

I ignored her as I pulled my pant legs up and dunked my feet in the fountain. "You don't know what you're missing," I exclaimed as I splashed my feet in the water.

Ana stood by the sidelines watching me, making it clear she had no intention whatsoever of following my lead. I splashed my feet in the water for a bit before putting my shoes back on and climbing up to look at the mural. The mural itself was bright blue with tons of small little designs and scribbles reminiscent of children's artwork, calling me back to simpler times.

"Let me take your picture," Ana said.

I stood in front of the mural putting my hands in my pocket to pose for her.

The butterflies in my stomach were gone.

In the distance behind her, a large art gallery of paintings of people from movies, TV shows, and major rock bands. There were even paintings of Mickey Mouse and Rey from the latest *Star Wars* movie hanging on the walls, standing out from everything else at the festival.

I pointed towards the gallery. "Let's check those out!"

We walked over and took our time looking at what the gallery had to offer. We separated to venture a little off on our own. I strolled around looking at artistic depictions of Walter White from *Breaking Bad* and Sheldon from *The Big Bang Theory* before regrouping with Ana staring at two watercolor paintings side by side of Steve Rogers in his Captain America uniform and Tony Stark in his Iron Man suit without his helmet.

"These are pretty cool," I said. "I really like the colors they used."

"I do, too."

"Steve still kicked Tony's ass in the movie by the way."

Ana chuckled. "Dude, Tony clearly beat Steve. You know it. I know it. The whole world knows it."

"As if."

"I rooted for Tony Stark to win in *Civil War*."

"We're not having this discussion again."

"I know we're not because I'm right and there's nothing to discuss," Ana teased.

"Oh god!"

Ana laughed until her phone rang and stepped away to answer it. I looked at both paintings of Captain America and Iron Man, hyper focusing on the similarities and differences. "But Steve did kick Tony's ass," I muttered under my breath.

A couple minutes later, Ana came back.

"Everything good?" I asked.

"Yeah, my sister just needed the password for the Hulu account."

We moved to look around other paintings until we stopped to look at a painting of Elsa from *Frozen*.

"How is Mary doing by the way?" I asked as we looked at the painting.

"She's good. She recently moved into the dorms and has been freaking out about what to expect her first semester. Keeps calling me about what to do."

"Well, you're the older sister! What do you expect?"

"She's always been like that, even when we were kids."

"Just like Alicia and Jason."

"I mean, there were times even when we were kids and she just wanted me to go out all the time and party. I always had to make sure she stayed out of trouble."

"That makes you a good sister *and* a good role model."

"Being a 'good role model' is so much work."

"I can relate."

"She can be feisty at times, but she means well. Maybe you'll get to meet her next time she visits San Diego."

I glanced over at Ana again. This was the first time she ever suggested the possibility of meeting *anyone* from her family. Is it normal for "companions" to do this? I thought she just wanted to keep things casual?

We moved on to check out another section of the outdoor gallery showcasing more paintings, but this time on posters instead of canvases. We skimmed over the posters hanging on another set of gallery boards until I saw one that immediately caught my attention.

From a distance it looked like a painting of a moth, but I knew instantly what it was.

The iconic logo for Poets of the Fall!

"Isn't that your favorite band?" Ana asked when I pointed the poster out to her.

I obsessively examined every detail of the poster, surveying its bright use of black and brown paint strokes of the moth. Each band member stood side by side underneath the moth. I didn't see any information about who made the painting, but I wanted to buy it anyway. The person running the gallery gave me a reasonable price of $50 for a copy of the poster.

I had to buy this poster. Now!

When I went to buy it, Ana stepped in. "Don't worry. I got this."

"Wait! Are you *sure?*"

"Don't worry. I said I got this!"

I said nothing as Ana pulled some cash out from her purse and paid for the poster.

"Oh my god, you are awesome!" I exclaimed. "Thank you!"

"It's nothing."

Without another word, we strolled off, spending the rest of the afternoon exploring the festival and then having lunch. During the entire time, I could not help but think about the intricate details of the poster and how excited I was to hang this on my wall above my desk.

But I also kept thinking how surprised I was that Ana paid attention to my love for Poets. I had recently started to worry I talked her ear off too much about the band, but she was willing to buy me this poster? I looked over at Ana and saw her smile at me and I smiled back.

At that moment, I still didn't know where we stood.

I just knew I would never forget her smile.

3

———

March 12, 2017

I looked at Ana's smile in her picture while sitting in my Mitsubishi.

Tonight was the first time we would meet in person. I wanted to make sure it was clear in my head what she looked like. In her Tinder bio, she only listed her name, age, and three pictures. In her main picture, she leaned next to a guard railing on a balcony walkway at UC San Diego wearing a dark blue windbreaker and glasses. I examined the picture multiple times to imprint in my brain who to look for at the restaurant.

We agreed to meet for dinner at Tofu House in the Convoy District. I've been through this type of routine with dating apps countless times before: match with someone, go on a date with them, and then never hear from them again when they don't return my texts. This time didn't seem any different, but the idea of meeting this new person still gave me a cold sweat. I parked a few blocks down the street and around the corner from the restaurant, having arrived two hours early to calm my nerves and verbally practice any dating scenarios in my head.

I needed to get out of the house early anyway since Mom and Alicia were fighting again. The yelling and screaming echoed in my head, making my breathing go in and out in short gasps until I began to hit my left hand over and over to handle the intensity. When I parked the car, I hit my hand some more before calming down, noticing my hand was redder than usual. *People think you're stupid for hitting your hand so much*, a voice in my head said. *Stop doing that, you idiot.* I sat there for a bit before putting on Poets of the Fall's "Diamonds for Tears" on repeat, flapping my hands around and twirling my fingers to the exciting rhythm of the music, one of my other forms of stimming.

I was in my zone until I saw a small group of people in my rearview mirror, forcing myself to stop so they didn't see what I was doing. I burrowed deep into myself, trying to be invisible to these strangers walking past my car so they wouldn't point and laugh at me.

Once they were gone, I took a deep breath and put the music back on, pulling up Ana's picture. I imagined *us sitting across from each other, coming up with countless scenarios in my head as to how our first meeting would possibly play out, many of which seemed to blend into one another. I saw myself in one scenario sweeping Ana off her feet for a romantic getaway in a flying race car and launching straight towards the stars. In another, awkward silence at the table, nothing happened until she left and I sunk into a blackhole as the audience laughed at me.* I pulled up our text messages and read them over again, trying to puzzle out how her texts would translate into her in-person personality.

I stopped thinking much about my upcoming date, giving myself a reality check: so many dates I had been on in the past either went nowhere or my dates would ghost me. Just last month, I went on a miniature golf date with a woman I met on Tinder (a date I thought went incredibly well), only for her to stop returning my texts and delete me from Snapchat. I scrolled through my phone to pass the time, skimming through photos of me with friends until I came across a picture of a young redhead girl standing in front of a bus, wearing a white snowcap, a dark leather jacket, and a study abroad program lanyard.

Kelly, I miss you, I thought. I couldn't stop looking at her photo.

I closed the photo and checked the time. I was supposed to meet Ana at the restaurant soon, but I figured this date would be no different from ones I've been on before. If I'm lucky I'd get two dates, maybe three, and then she'd ghost me like others have done. *That'll be okay*, I told myself. *She's not Kelly and never will be.*

I started the car.

July 15, 2006

I stood in the LAX airport lounge surrounded by nine other high school juniors and seniors from California, waiting for a ride back home to San Diego. But none of us could leave until we said goodbye to the students from Chicago one last time.

I had no choice but to put on a face so I didn't look like a freak to everyone else, but I barely kept calm. *Where's Kelly?* I frantically thought. *I have to tell her I love her!*

We waited a few minutes before a huge group of high school students came rushing towards us. It was the Chicago group! All twenty of them! My heart pounded, forcing me to take some deep breaths as kids around me cried and gave each other hugs. Was I supposed to hug? How do I know when I'm supposed to hug?

I then looked over and there was Kelly. Her long red hair and freckles made her stand out from everyone else, standing right there while looking at me. I walked over to her, seeing everyone else hugging goodbye. I hesitated to do so, not sure if she would even want a hug from me in the first place.

"Kelly?" I mumbled, holding my hand out thinking she would just shake it.

But she wrapped her arms around my neck instead and hugged me tightly, the smell of her perfume and the silkiness of her hair overwhelming my senses as I slowly hugged her back.

A tear dropped as we embraced, thinking about the last three weeks we spent together traveling overseas. My mind wandered to the moment I first saw her walking next to me as our travel group got off the airplane in Auckland. I thought about our epic snowball fight against each other in Christchurch, the laughs and smiles we shared as we gathered with the rest of our travel group to wage our little snowball war. I thought about the personal stories we shared and the conversations we had about comic books and our shared love of *Lord of the Rings* during long bus rides. I remembered when we climbed the Sydney Harbor Bridge and we waved to each other on opposite sides. *Hey buddy!* she had shouted out to me, so I tried to hide my massive fear of heights in order to stand up tall and wave back.

Now there she was hugging me goodbye before she had to go back home and we would never see each other again. *I love you so much*, I thought. I tried to say the words aloud but no words came. I just couldn't bring myself to say them. *I don't want you to go*, I thought. Then the flights to Chicago were announced, and we had no choice but to let go and walk away.

On the shuttle ride home, I couldn't stop thinking about her. I crossed my arms and buried my face in them as everyone else in the shuttle chatted away, hiding my exhaustion from having to put on a face and holding back tears.

4

───────

March 5, 2017

I picked Ben up and drove over to Spin City Sound, a new record store that recently opened in the area. It had been a few months since we hung out, so we made plans to spend some time there and get lunch. I agreed to proctor an online home exam he scheduled to take at home afterwards for a remote degree program he started not too long ago. Why he needed an in person proctor for an online home exam was beyond me, but I'd been wanting to check out Spin City Sound anyway since hearing about it on Facebook, so I figured why not.

We entered through the double doors of the store, in awe at the rows of vinyl records lined up on long tables in boxes, shelves filled to the brim with CDs and DVDs, and a couple sections dedicated to guitars and drums. The entire store felt like an open warehouse with dark gray walls covered in colorful paintings of musicians, bands, and concerts. Ben wore a white T-shirt with a black unbuttoned over shirt, glasses, khakis, and a baseball cap covering his sandy blonde hair. I wore my usual black zipped-up hooded jacket and jeans. We both looked like hipsters—perfect for the vibe of this place.

We spent time browsing one of the rows of vinyls. "Are you looking for anything in particular?" Ben asked as we browsed.

"I'm just hoping to get my hands on some old Don McLean stuff," I said. "Likely also get something for my grandpa."

"How big is your collection now?"

It took me a few seconds to recall the exact number. "Including ones that used to be my dad's, at least seventy, *maybe* a hundred," I said as I skimmed through a box of them, drawing out the maybe for emphasis.

"Damn!"

"What can I say? There's something about vinyl that's incredibly special"

"True," Ben said. "I just thought you didn't do well with loud sounds though. Vinyls can be pretty loud."

"Random loud noises I can't handle that well," I reminded. "At least with vinyl I can control the amount of surface noise that does happen."

"Fair point."

"And besides, even if there is noise, I have my headphones right here—" I stopped myself when I realized that my headphones were not around my neck. "Oh shit! I left them in the car!"

"Do you want to go back and get them?" Ben asked.

"Nah, I should be fine," I said. "We're not going to be here that long anyway."

We browsed the aisles, going through countless records as we caught up on what we had been doing for the past few months. Ben had been working on his Associate's in Psychology from this online school somewhere in Georgia, and I had been finishing my final semester of graduate school. I didn't ask him what he planned to do with the degree or what he was doing for work now.

"I had extra money so I thought I would give it a shot, and I have you to thank," Ben said.

"Me?" I said as I browsed more records. "Why are you thanking me?"

"Because unlike almost all the other kids at Schweitzer, you are actually doing something with your life and that's inspiring!"

"Good grief, dude. Do we have to talk about that place again? I get enough nightmares from that place as it is."

"I'm just saying so many of the kids we went to school with are probably still cleaning toilets and taking out trash somewhere while kissing up to their parents, but you—you are actually doing something with your life."

"I guess."

We browsed for the next ten minutes or so until we both found what we were looking for. I found a Don McLean album I could add to my vinyl collection, as well as a *Modern Marvels* DVD for grandpa I would give him next time I would see him. Ben picked up a couple of CDs and an Iron Maiden poster.

We got to the register to pay for our merchandise. More people walked into the store and strolled about, making the place more packed. I began noticing conversations from customers echoing here and there throughout the building. As Ben and I waited in a short line, I saw a mother trying to calm a screeching child next to a large drum set. The echo began to grow. I got more and more agitated the longer the noises went on. Instinctively, I reached for my head-phones, only to be reminded again I left them in the car. Only three people were ahead of us.

Then without warning, the child knocked over an entire drum set, the loud noise booming through the entire store like a bomb. I started to hyperventilate. I gripped my stuff so tightly my knuckles turned white. I placed my other hand over my mouth to control my breathing.

"Rob, you okay?" Ben asked.

I couldn't stop shaking and hitting my hand. In my head, all I could see in front of me was a kid acting like he was having a seizure.

"Rob?"

I didn't immediately say anything as the mother couldn't stop apologizing to everyone for her kid acting out. "I'll be okay," I said as soon as I felt calm enough. The loud noise still rang in my ears, but after some time, my ears started to hurt less. "Let's just go."

We paid for everything as a store employee helped the mother calm down her child.

***

After lunch, we went back to Ben's house so I could proctor his exam like I promised. "My mom is doing errands right now, but she should be home soon if you want to stay for dinner," Ben said after I parked the car.

When we got up to his room upstairs, I instantly noticed his room was barebones, having only his twin-sized bed, a small book-shelf, and a desk with just his laptop computer and a picture with him and his parents when he was ten years old. "Where did all your artwork go?" I asked.

"Took them down for now. Wanted to clear out space so I could get a new perspective on what I want to do with my life, hence why I'm working on this degree."

"I hope you haven't given up on your art."

"Nah, it's just temporary. I mean, look at all this space! Isn't it liberating not to have so much clutter?"

I shrugged. "I guess, but I don't know how this degree is going to help you with any career. I really think you should focus on your art."

"Listen, Rob," Ben said, picking up a stack of paperwork he wanted me to sign. "I appreciate you looking out for me. I really do, but I don't know if my art is worth anything so it's better to have a backup. I mean, didn't you once say that having a degree in anything is better than no degree at all?"

I sighed. "I guess." It was strange hearing my words used against me out of context.

"I'm glad you agree."

"At the very least, I hope you at least use this degree to inspire your art."

Ben shrugged. "I'll think about it."

After signing paperwork, Ben gave me his phone to hold on to so he wouldn't cheat, leading me into the adjacent room I assumed had been made into a secondary living room. "The exam itself shouldn't take me more than two hours. You can hang out in here, read a book, or watch Netflix."

I nodded as I sat myself on the sofa. "Sounds good to me."

Ben gave me the thumbs up and went to go take his exam.

I lay back on the sofa and found myself putting on (500) *Days of Summer*. Having seen it before, I watched about twenty minutes but soon got bored, letting the movie play in the background as I browsed my phone. Logging into Facebook, a notification popped up and alerted me to comments on a post I was tagged in last night in the Authentic Philosophy group.

I had been checking this group regularly since I was an under-grad, having connected with people I met online years ago. We used to engage in comment debates about philosophy on YouTube for fun before the platform's policy changes forced us to migrate over to Facebook. We saw ourselves as a small group of armchair philoso-phers constantly engaging in philosophical arguments, but we also talked about our personal lives and supported each other.

One of the group members, Chris, tagged me and five other people in a post about education, asking our opinions due to our experiences as teachers. When I first saw the post the night before, there were only a couple of comments, but my eyes widened as I realized there were close to a hundred comments. *What the hell?*

It was Vincent going at it with Chris about whether or not Cancel Culture existed. *There goes Vincent being Vincent again*, I thought. Vincent had always been the most outspoken of the group, and whenever anyone debated with him, he always had to have the last word.

I always respected Vincent, but this was not a debate I wanted to get involved in because people would always take his side regard-less of the merit of his opponent, so I turned off notifications and moved on.

I spent some more time browsing Facebook before logging into Tinder. I had gone on a few dates here and there with it, but they never went anywhere. The last Tinder date I went on was with a law school student named Sabrina who was not that much younger than me. She seemed nice, if a little pushy at first, but then after our second date, she sent me unsolicited nudes and sexually explicit text messages, so I ended it with her through text on Valentine's Day. I felt bad, but when she started sending me a series of "Fuck You" texts for the next couple days before finally stopping, I realized I dodged a bullet.

For the next hour, as the movie played in the background, I switched between scrolling Facebook and swiping through Tinder. During that time, I looked through profiles of different women between the ages of 21 and 35 living within twenty-five miles of San Diego. I periodically checked on Ben, and then went back to skimming profiles.

I swiped right on a woman named Jenny who seemed to be attending a wedding in her picture and indicated she loved reading and writing just like me, then I swiped left on a woman named Nora who had cute blonde hair but had nothing but Bible verses in her bio, making her too hyper-religious for my taste.

I lost track of time, strategically swiping left and right until I came across a profile of a young Asian woman with long black hair standing next to a guard railing on a balcony walkway, wearing a dark blue windbreaker and glasses.

I looked at the profile: *Ana* (22).

Nothing was written in her bio, so I just looked at her two other pictures. She had one selfie and photo of herself wearing a UCSD shirt and standing on a cliffside with a view of the ocean behind her. I couldn't help but be mesmerized by her smile. "She's cute," I muttered. I looked at her profile for a little bit longer, trying to decide if I should swipe right now or not. Despite the lack of description on her profile, something in my gut pulled me toward her.

"Might as well."

I swiped right.

I was ready to move on when I saw the words "It's a Match" pop up on my screen. My heart fluttered, unsure how to react. I opened my Tinder inbox and saw Ana in my matches. I tapped the speech bubble icon and stared at the "Send Message" screen. In the past, I've sent messages to matches only to not get any responses so I figured how would this be any different? Did I want to say anything at all? She had nothing written in her bio, so I had no idea if she was legit (but her pictures seem real enough).

After a few minutes, I decided to hell with it.

ROB:

> Hi there, Ana. My name is Rob. How are you today? ☺

I clicked "send," not expecting a response back. I swiped through different profiles until I ran out of Tinder likes as (500) *Days of Summer* played into its third act. I watched a couple of YouTube videos and read a Kotaku article before a notification showed up on my phone.

It was a message from Ana.

ANA:

> Hi Rob. I'm doing good. Nice to meet you. I'm just enjoying my day off. How about you?

Wait! She's actually talking to me?

ROB:

> I'm good. I'm at a friend's place right now just helping him with an exam. Other than that, not too bad. How about you? What are you doing on your day off?

It took her a few seconds to respond back.

ANA:

> I'm just at home watching Hulu. Nothing much other than that.

ROB:

That's good.

ANA:

Do you know anything about cars? I've been looking to buy a new car soon and trying to figure out where to buy a new one around here.

What a completely random question, I thought. *But she seems pleasant enough so I'll go along with it.*

ROB:

Well, I know plenty of dealerships around Convoy you could look into. There are even some good deals you can find on AutoTrader or Car Guru.

I cringed when I typed that. Outside of watching a few YouTube channels related to fixing cars, I didn't know a whole lot about them, and I didn't want to give this new girl *I literally just met* the impression I was an idiot.

I did not get a response so I quickly changed topic.

ROB:

So what do you like to do for fun?

Ana seemed much more receptive to this and responded back. For the next ten minutes, we texted back and forth, talking about what we liked to do for fun and what we did for work. She told me she liked watching Marvel movies and FBI-related crime shows, ice skating, traveling, and learning about the stock market; I told her I enjoyed hiking, playing video games, going to art shows and concerts, and listening to music. She told me she worked as an insurance agent in Mira Mesa, while I told her I taught writing classes at San Diego State while finishing up my Masters.

ANA:

That is really cool! 🙂 You must be super smart!

I smiled when I read that.

ROB:

Thank you! 😊

As we got to know each other better, we seemed to click a lot more.

ROB:

So what are you looking for on Tinder?

"Hey Rob, I finished the exam!" Ben shouted from behind me.

I jumped out of my seat. "Jesus! You scared the shit out of me!"

"Sorry about that. I just wanted to let you know that I finished the exam a little bit early."

"Cool, I hope you passed," I said unenthusiastically as I calmed my nerves.

"Me too," Ben said. I then noticed he was looking closely at my phone. "Say, who are you talking to?"

"Some random girl off Tinder."

"Oh that's cool. Can I see?"

I debated whether or not to show Ben, but ultimately I relented.

"Oh nice. You scored a cute Asian girl!"

I placed my hand over my face. "Dude, no!"

"What do you mean 'no'? She's cute, *and* she's Asian! What's wrong with what? Unless you think she's ugly or something!"

"It's not that! It's just I don't care!"

"You don't care if she's ugly?"

I buried my face in my right hand. "God, why do you have to be like this?"

"Like what?"

I shook my head.

"I heard Asian girls tend to make the best girlfriends," Ben said with a smirk.

"What the hell does that mean?"

"Oh you know. Loving? Submissive? Highly successful? I bet she would be amazing in bed!"

I looked straight at Ben. "Do you even listen to the bullshit that comes out of your mouth?"

Ben shrugged. "I'm just saying."

"I don't care if she's Asian. I really don't."

"Then what do you care about, Rob?" Ben asked. "What exactly do you want?"

"I want Kelly to be honest."

Ben rolled his eyes. "Besides that, you idiot! What exactly do you want?"

I sighed, taking a moment to figure out what to say next. "I don't know," I muttered. "Someone who could like me for me. Someone who could be at the same level as me. Someone I could spend the rest of my life with. I want to be with someone who can feel like they can be themselves and not feel like they have to serve me."

"Like I had with Claire before she dumped me like a hot potato?"

I grunted, looking away from Ben.

"Maybe this new girl can be what you're looking for," Ben said.

I shook my head. "I doubt it'll even last long. Not like it matters anyway. It's whatever. No one will ever replace Kelly."

"Don't you think it's time you move on from her?"

"How can I 'move on from her' if I never got closure from her in the first place?

"What do you mean?"

Before I could answer, the park bench scene near the end of (500) *Days of Summer* came on the TV where Summer tells Tom why their relationship was not meant to be. "Look there," I said. "Tom got closure from Summer. Why couldn't I have gotten something like that with Kelly?"

"That's Hollywood bullshit, Rob," Ben said.

I sighed. "I just wish I did a better job staying in touch with her and asked her when I had the chance. I would at least know why we couldn't have worked out."

"That's in the past, Rob. You should give this . . . uh . . what's this girl's name?"

"Ana."

"Ana! I think you should give this Ana girl a chance, Rob."

I sighed again.

"Anyway, mom told me she's on her way. You can still stay for dinner if you like."

"Sure."

"Cool. I'll be downstairs. We're having linguini. You can relax in the meantime."

I gave Ben his phone back, and he left the room to go downstairs. After he left, I checked my Tinder inbox to see Ana had responded.

ANA:

> I'm not sure. I'm not really looking for anything in particular. I'm just looking to meet new people, see where it goes. What about you?

I got myself oriented back into texting mode.

ROB:

> Same. I'm just looking to meet new people. See where it goes. I'm a go-with-the-flow kind of guy.

For the next hour, I went back and forth between watching Netflix and talking to Ana on Tinder. We talked a bit more about what we did for work, what places we've traveled, and whether we were cat people or dog people (her, dogs; me, cats). The conversation seemed to flow naturally, and I began to like how each time I would talk about something, she seemed to show genuine interest in what I had to say, along with uplifting emojis.

The longer the conversation went on, the more I grew to like her.

I took the plunge.

ROB:

> Say, I think you're really cool. I really enjoy talking to you. We seem to have a lot in common. I would love to get to know you more. Here's my number. You are welcome to text me anytime. 🙂

I sent my phone number. I felt a little excitement, but then reminded myself to keep my expectations as low as possible. Not like anything will come out of it, so what was the point anyway? I got up and went downstairs to check up on Ben.

After dinner, I went home and got to work on last minute PowerPoint slides for tomorrow's classes. I had YouTube play in the background, keeping the music level down so as to not draw attention from Mom and Alicia in other parts of the house. I stayed in the zone, doing final touches on the slides when a YouTube ad for a collective lawsuit stopped the music and caught my attention.

"If you're a parent of a child who has autism, you may be eligible for compensation . . ." the narrator of the ad said at one point. I watched a bit of the ad, cringing at the sappy music and the clearly paid actors crying about how their lives have been a struggle since finding out their children had autism before turning that shit off.

I sighed, irked at the YouTube algorithm for showing me such a stupid ad. It made me remember the call center job I had years ago when I had trouble dealing with the angry customer calling in from Tennessee.

Sir listen, I remember struggling to say. *I'm doing the best I can. I'm autistic so it's a little overwhelming sometimes. I'm doing the best I can. Can you be just a little patient, sir?*

Huge mistake!

Oh I see! The customer shouted. *Maybe you need to look into medication for that!*

I rubbed my eyes, took a sip of my apple juice, and went back to work.

Sometime later, I saw a notification on my phone from a 415 area code phone number I didn't recognize, followed by "Hey Rob" and a smiley emoji. I wasn't sure who it was, but when it finally clicked who the mystery texter was, I immediately responded.

ROB:
> Hey, is this Ana?

ANA:
> Yes.

ROB:
> Yay! How's your evening so far?

ANA:
> Going okay, just trying to fall asleep haha. How early do you start your Mornings?

ROB:
> I'm usually up by 7. You?

ANA:
> Wake up around 7:30 am so not too far off from you. When does your day end?

ROB:
> It varies. Tomorrow I'll be at school all day until 7. Usually I'm done by 2. I'm usually free on the weekends unless I have to grade a lot of papers. We can chat tomorrow if you're tired.

I didn't hear anything more from her, but that was okay. As I worked, I thought about our text exchange today. I did not want to get my hopes up, but something about her showed promise.

5

———

March 6, 2017

I woke up and began panicking when the clock read 7:47 am.

Shit, I'm going to be late!

I struggled to get out of bed, groggy from being up half the night working on my seminar paper and PowerPoint slides for a class I was teaching at 9 am. I hustled into the hallway to rush my regular morning routine, only to find I couldn't get into the bathroom.

I knocked on the door. "Alicia, are you in there?"

"You can wait, Rob!" I heard Alicia shout.

"Bullshit! You don't have class until noon! I have to get ready to leave *now*!"

"You can wait!"

I banged on the door. "Dammit, Alicia! Hurry up!"

"Fuck you, Robert! You can wait!"

"Stop fighting!" I heard Mom scream from the other room. "Just wait until your sister is done, Rob!"

"You can wait, asshole!" Alicia shouted.

I rushed back to my room, shutting the door behind me. I had to fight every urge to yell back when I started hearing Mom and Alicia fighting about how impatient I was.

"Tell your son to stop being so selfish!" I heard Alicia scream.

I sat on the edge of my bed, hit my left hand over and over to let out frustration before putting on my headphones to listen to calming music.

As I immersed myself in the music, I saw myself *walking among the clouds, looking down towards the earth. I jumped from cloud to cloud and then teleported into a helicopter directly onto the stage where students and faculty cheered me like a rockstar as I escaped the clutches of my sister's wrath. The audience went wild as I raised my fists in the air, ready to inspire the next generation of writers.*

I heard a *ding* from my phone, snapping out of it to see it was a "Good Morning" text.

It was Ana!

My heart leapt as I replied back.

ROB:

Good morning! Did you sleep well?

ANA:

Yes, I did. Are you heading off to school now?

ROB:

Yep. Got a long day ahead of me. Going to be going over visual rhetoric with my students today. I think that's exciting.

My sister taking too long in the bathroom no longer mattered. I lay back in bed, grinning as I sent one final text message.

ROB:

I'll text you later. Hope you have a good day.

I spent the entire day on campus, doing everything I needed to do. It was 8 pm when I finally got home, but Alicia decided all three of us would have Domino's for dinner. Neither she nor Mom called or texted me to ask if I wanted pizza. I would have been content with just having a quick bowl of steamed rice and vegetables to watch my calorie intake, but Alicia wanted Domino's and that was the end of that.

After we had our food set up at the kitchen table and Mom said the dinner prayer, Alicia and Mom engaged in banter while I mentally tuned them out, eating my pizza and browsing my phone. I heard glimpses of Alicia talking about her day at school and making plans for graduation. After an extended gap year, she was finally finishing her Bachelors in Music at San Diego State.

During dinner, I sent Ana a simple text, not expecting a response so I kept eating pizza and scrolled through social media. Mom tried to say something to me, so I lifted my headphones.

"What's that?" I asked.

"Rob, how many times have I told you not to wear those head-phones at the dinner table!" Mom exclaimed.

I took my headphones off. "Sorry. I forgot I had them on!"

Alicia snapped her fingers at me. "Mom was asking when was the last time you saw Grandpa."

"I saw him a couple weeks ago."

"You need to see him more often," Mom said, as if there was an edge in her voice. "He's not going to be around forever."

I begrudgingly nodded and took a bite of pizza. *There goes Mom guilt tripping me again,* I thought. *Better keep my mouth shut so neither of them start arguing at the dinner table.*

I kept eating while Mom and Alicia bantered on, with Mom bringing up a recent visit to see our brother for his 34th birthday last week up at Palm Springs Developmental Center. Jason had been locked up there for almost ten years, but it's anyone's guess how long he'll be there at this point. I got a colleague to sub for my classes and go with Mom on the two hour drive north to see him. Alicia was not able to get out of work to go with us.

"How's Jason doing?" Alicia asked Mom.

"He's doing fine," Mom said. "I keep telling him that he needs to be on his best behavior if he wants to be relocated closer to us!"

"Does he know yet about Grandma?" Alicia asked.

"Oh Alicia, I don't think he's ready to know," Mom said.

I was about to interject before Mom's phone rang. "Jason, we're having dinner right now," Mom said when she answered it. "No, I don't know when we're visiting again."

I started tuning everything out as Mom tried to assure Jason we would see him again soon before hanging up and continuing her conversation with Alicia. I slowly finished my pizza and when enough time passed, I put my plate in the sink and left the house without them noticing.

I spent the rest of the evening at Lestat's coffee shop in Normal Heights, trying to catch up on school-related work. Since the place is open twenty-four hours, I would come here once in a while to get work done.I ordered a cup of coffee and sat at a table by myself, opening my laptop to Blackboard and settling in for the evening. I worked for the next few hours, fighting off the drowsiness that always accompanied late night grading.

At 11:35 pm, I heard a *ding* notification from my phone.

It was Ana again!

ANA:

Hi Rob. Day went well. How was your long day?

After I read that text, another one popped up.

ANA:

Visual rhetoric. Is that like analyzing pictures?

I grinned, sipping my coffee and proceeding to engage.

ROB:

Mine was good. Just finishing up a Powerpoint. Doing a lecture on Martin Luther King soon. And kind of. Visual rhetoric is more like using images to make an argument.

ANA:

Nice! Is rhetoric what you're getting your
degree in?

ROB:

Yep. And I'm qualified to teach college level
rhetoric and writing.

ANA:

I'd love to teach someday but I don't know what
subject yet.

ROB:

What level would you like to teach?

ANA:

Probably college undergrad.

ROB:

Maybe you could teach biology!

ANA:

Nah, biology was tough enough. I need a subject
I'm more confident about haha.

ROB:

Fair enough. What subjects do you like?

ANA:

Right now, I like business and insurance. I'd
probably teach some uncommon course just
for fun.

ROB:

You could teach business!!! 😀

We texted back and forth for the next half hour. Talking about
our own experiences as college students; she showed genuine
interest in what I did as a grad student, so I shared teaching tips I
could give her and how I approached the writing class. I even texted
her a link to a Google Doc version of a syllabus I made last semester

loaded with silly memes and cartoons. I even boasted my high marks on RateMyProfessor, just so I could impress her.

ANA:

You must be a good teacher.

ROB:

Hopefully. 😅

The longer the exchange went on, the more I began to wonder what Ana was like in person. All of her text messages up to this point gave me an image of her being a sweet and friendly insurance agent straight out of college. My hope was that if we meet in person, that would actually be the case. God only knows how many Tinder dates I've been on where the person wasn't exactly who they said they were.

ROB:

So what are you doing up this late?

ANA:

I have a hard time falling asleep.

ROB:

You should sleep. 😴

ANA:

You should sleep, too!

ROB:

As soon as I finish this PowerPoint! Do you work tomorrow? I hope I'm not keeping you up.

ANA:

Nah, it's all good. And yep. Every weekday. I hope you're almost done with your PowerPoint.

ROB:

> Okay. Well I like talking to you, but if you need to sleep, you are more than welcome to chat with me tomorrow.

After I sent my text, it was 12:15 am. Ana didn't respond, but I figured she fell asleep anyway. I reread our texts over and over. The more I read them, the more I couldn't help but grin.

March 9, 2017

On and off for the next couple days, Ana and I exchanged multiple text conversations, many ranging from silly to mundane. I finished grading my students' papers late that afternoon. I had to do another seminar paper, but since it wasn't due until next week, I spent the rest of the evening playing video games.

I texted Ana earlier to see how she was doing, but didn't get a response until hours later. I paused my game and looked at my phone, my stomach full of butterflies. She told me she had dinner at Buffalo Wild Wings with a friend and now was just relaxing.

She texted me half an hour later.

ANA:

> Any weekend plans?

I paused my game again. Normally I'd be annoyed with pausing my game for people, but for her I didn't mind.

ROB:

> Nothing really. It's kind of up in the air. How about you?

ANA:

> Just going car shopping but other than that, not much.

I read her last text multiple times. Since I began talking to her, I grew more to like her, but I was still cautiously optimistic. God only knows how many times I've been burned from previous dates, enough to keep any expectations as low as possible.

But something about her made me think things would be different.

I took the plunge.

ROB:

> Well, if you are free anytime this weekend after car shopping, maybe we can get something to eat sometime. If you want, of course.

I clicked "send," staring at my phone's screen, excited but also nervous for what response she would give. Would she say no? Would she turn me down? Would she just not respond at all?

A few minutes later, she texted back.

ANA:

> I would love to. I'll text you later in the week about my weekend availability.

I smiled.

March 11, 2017

After visiting Dad's grave, I went to see Grandpa. His tool-filled garage was wide open as he worked on the engine of one of his cars lifted up on a ramp in his driveway. Despite being in his late 80s, he easily passed for someone in their late 60s or early 70s with the physique of an aging outdoorsman. When Grandpa saw me, he stopped to take his gloves off and give me a firm handshake.

"What are you doing?" I asked.

"Just replacing the alternator."

We talked about what we've been doing for the past couple weeks as I had been busy finishing the semester while he had been working on various projects for his church. After a few minutes, he invited me inside. I followed him through the garage to the kitchen where he grabbed a Pepsi for me from the fridge.

"Let me make you a sandwich," he said.

I already had lunch before coming over, but I made it a point to never turn down his food because I didn't want to ever hurt his feelings. He washed his hands and made us both BLT sandwiches before sitting across from each other at the kitchen counter.

"I got you this, Grandpa," I said, handing him the *Modern Marvels* DVD.

He read over the box and grinned. "Why, I'll be damned. You must be so rich to buy this for poor old me."

I shrugged. "It's nothing, Grandpa."

"Oh, it ain't nothing."

For the next half hour, we sat and visited. He told me a long rambling story about a job he did as a contractor in the 1970s, occasionally cracking a few jokes. I listened, not really trying to grasp every detail but just to make Grandpa feel heard. As he told his latest story, I couldn't help but look around the kitchen and be reminded when Alicia, Jason, and I would come over to have lunch with Grandma. As Grandpa began telling another story about him and Grandma traveling to Oregon, a random memory from when I was kid popped into my head. Grandma hugged me, and then prepared a slice of her famous banana bread for me. I then thought about her making me my favorite deviled eggs and cracking jokes and attending all my little league baseball games. I thought about the day she came to my college graduation and the presents she gave me over the years.

I still couldn't believe it had been six months since I'd been forced to watch cancer take her to the great unknown.

"When we got to the hospital, your grandma *insisted* she hold you in her arms," Grandpa said as he wrapped up his story about the day I was born.

"I remember that story," I said, having lost count of the amount of times I had heard it over the years. I looked across the counter to my right and noticed Grandma's old coffee mug still there, having never been put away. "I miss her."

Grandpa took a sip of his water.

"Dad is at least showing her around Heaven," I said.

Grandpa didn't show any emotion, but I could tell by his body language that he was trying to fight back tears. He took another bite of his sandwich.

"Is Mom still coming over tonight?"

"She is."

"That's good." I drank another sip of my Pepsi.

Neither of us said anything as we ate. "How are you and her getting along at home?" Grandpa finally asked.

I paused. "We fought yesterday," I slowly admitted.

Grandpa didn't respond. He just sat there, open to hearing what I had to say.

"We made up, of course," I said. "But she can be draining to live with."

"What happened?"

"The same old crap. She wanted me to help with dinner, so I did, even though I was tired and had a long day. She wanted me to help make the meat sauce, so I did. But she would not stop micromanaging me. *Do this! Do that!* She wouldn't stop, Grandpa! And then one thing led to another and I accidentally spilled an entire bottle of black pepper into the sauce, and she yelled at me about how I ruined dinner for everyone. And I . . . I felt overwhelmed. I then told her 'F You,' and that set her off."

"You should not have said that, Rob."

"I know! I regret that. She just . . . wouldn't stop! And then she told me to my face that something was wrong with me, and I needed therapy."

"You have to keep your mouth shut if you want to keep living there."

I shrugged. "I try, but it's hard. I mean, like I said we made up, but . . . I don't know. She always makes me feel like I have to walk on eggshells with her."

"She knows how to push your buttons, Rob. You can't let her."

I took a moment to take a breath. "I just . . . I just don't feel like I can ever talk to her."

Grandpa nodded. "Just don't let her get to you."

I sighed again. We kept eating our lunch and chatted some more. As we talked, I heard a *ding* notification from my phone. "Sorry, I have to take this."

I pulled my phone out and saw a text from Ana.

ANA:

Do you want to meet up tomorrow?

My eyes lit up. I let her know I would be up to meeting tomorrow and I was looking forward to seeing her. I sent the text and looked at Grandpa.

"Hey Grandpa," I said, grinning. "If I tell you something, you have to promise not to tell Mom, okay?"

Grandpa took his hand and zipped it across his mouth. "I promise not to say anything," he said playfully.

I paused for a moment. "I got a date tomorrow!"

Grandpa's eyes light up, followed by a bright smile. "Oh you got a *date*? Well I'll be damned."

I chuckled.

"Tell me more about this date of yours?" Grandpa asked enthusiastically.

I smiled as I began telling him all about Ana.

March 12, 2017

After parking the car near Tofu House, I texted Ana to let her know I was there. I didn't get an immediate response, so I sat back and took a few deep breaths. I took another look at her profile picture to remind myself what she looked like before Ana texted me back letting me know that she was stuck in traffic and would be ten minutes late.

ROB:

Sounds good. I'll see you soon.

I put my headphones on to immerse myself in a song to calm my nerves. I stared off into space, everything fading away until all that was left was me *standing backstage of a theater. I took a peak behind the curtain to see Ana sitting at a table placed in center stage. The audience filled up all the seats of this massive theater, each of them looking down waiting for the show to begin. I closed the curtain and began hyperventilating. I turned and saw a long table laying out a row of masks, all with different versions of my own face. Each mask had a nameplate in front of them with labels ranging from "happiness," "fine," "unbothered," and many others. I walked up to the mask with the nameplate "neurotypical." I glanced back at the curtain before picking it up, putting it on, and slowly walking out to the stage.*

I shoved my headphones into the glove compartment, got out of the car, and headed to the front doors of the restaurant.

There was already a wait, so I reserved a table for two and sat at a small bench next to the entrance. The plaza started getting more crowded as more people arrived. I fidgeted as different scenarios of this evening circulated in my head.

"Hi, are you Rob?" someone asked a few minutes later.

I looked up and it was a young woman with long black hair wearing glasses, a black jacket, and dark pants. "Yes! Are you Ana?"

"I am," she said. "Nice to meet you."

"Nice to meet you, too," I said. She sat next to me on the bench, apologizing for running late before I told her there was going to be a wait anyway. As we waited for our table to be called, neither of us said anything. I glanced over at Ana gazing out at the plaza as we sat on the bench, not really looking at me.

Neither of us said anything, creating an awkward silence.

"So . . . um . . . how was your day?" I finally asked.

"Good," Ana said. "Can't complain."

"You bought your new car today?"

"Yep. Bought it this afternoon."

"2014 Honda Civic, right?"

Ana looked up with a smile on her face. "I did! It feels nice to finally have a car that isn't a piece of junk!"

I chuckled. For the next few minutes, we talked about how glad she was to finally get rid of this run down 1996 Green Buick she bought for $1000 off Facebook Marketplace two years ago.

"It's nice to have a job that actually pays me money," she said. We chit-chatted about our day and what kind of food we both might order. She didn't initiate eye contact much, preferring instead to gaze at the parking lot while sitting next to me and talking.

So glad I don't feel pressured to initiate eye contact with this girl, I thought.

"I like your glasses," I awkwardly said at one point. "They're cute!"

She blushed. "Why thank you."

Our table got called and we were seated in a corner inside. Ana ordered Seafood Fried Rice with a cup of hot water while I ordered the Bulgogi House Special with a Diet Coke. We sat across from each other, both of us silent. I could not help but notice how quiet she was, something I was not used to based on past experiences with dating.

I scrambled to say something—anything—to break the silence.

"So what got you into insurance?" I eventually asked.

Ana cleared her throat. "Well . . . I think I told you this before, but I originally wanted to be a doctor, so I majored in biology at UCSD."

"You could make a lot of money as a doctor."

"I could, but my heart just wasn't in it, but I already had too many units in biology anyway to change majors, so I took this intro to business class as an elective and I liked it so much I made business my minor."

"You should've made it your major!"

"And take out even *more* student loans? Nah, you crazy!"

"But crippling, life changing college debt is *awesome!*" I joked.

This made her laugh, but in a noticeably reserved way. "You definitely crazy!"

As the waiter put our dishes in front of us and left, Kelly popped into my head again. I looked at Ana as she ate her food, and I couldn't help but compare her laugh to Kelly's. Ana's laugh seemed more reserved and whispering whereas Kelly's was more jovial and boisterous. We ate our food, not really saying much for the next minute or so. I didn't know what else to say to keep the conversation going.

"So what got you into teaching?" Ana asked.

"When my brother was in assisted living years ago, one of his workers wanted me to tutor him in writing. He liked my tutoring style so much he said I should become a teacher."

"That's cool," Ana said.

"Yeah."

"You said your brother was in assisted living? What's that?"

"It's . . . it's a long story. I'll tell you later." I drank another sip of my coke. "So anyway, after I tutored him, I was like 'let's go for it,' and next thing you know, I'm getting my Master's."

"That is so cool."

"I just like to help people learn."

Ana smiled. "You seem like someone who likes to help people."

"Well, you sell insurance, and insurance saves lives, so therefore, you like to help people, too."

Ana gave a mild chuckle. "I guess when you put it that way, that is true."

For the rest of the date, we lightly chatted here and there, but didn't talk much.

After Ana left and I got in my car, I put on my headphones to put on music, wanting some time to think before heading home. *She's definitely a lot more introverted than I expected*, I thought.

I replayed the date with Ana in my head, recalling all the

moments of silence between us. I took some breaths, as if I had just ran a marathon after forcing myself to come up with *anything* to talk about with her. *Are you normally this quiet?* I thought. *Why did it feel like I had to extract teeth just to get you to say anything?*

I then remembered Ben making those stupid comments about Asians last week. *Are you just embodying those stereotypes?* I thought.

But then I thought about the things we did talk about and she seemed pleasant and really kind. *But on the other hand you seem really sweet,* I thought. *And I do like the conversations we did have. But would you even be on the same level as me? Are you someone I actually even want to be with for the rest of my life?*

As I thought about these questions, Billy Joel's "Piano Man" began playing.

Whatever, I thought. *Won't last long anyway. You're not Kelly and never will be.*

As the music played, I found myself *in the front row of the auditorium seats by myself in the dark, looking up at Kelly standing on stage next to a grand piano waving to the audience.*

"Ladies and gentlemen!" an announcer shouted from the auditorium speakers. "Thank you for coming to our lovely show! We have a special performance for you tonight! There is no talent like her! Give it up for Kelly Dubois!"

The audience cheered, quieting down when Kelly took out a microphone.

"Thank you everyone for coming tonight!" Kelly shouted, her voice bursting with joy. "Tonight's show is going to be one of the best! I'm going to play you 'Piano Man!'"

The audience cheered again.

"But instead of being a 'Piano Man,' I'll be the Piano Lady!" Kelly joked, winking at the audience.

The audience laughed. Kelly sat at the piano, cracked her knuckles, and started playing one of the most beautiful renditions of Billy Joel's "Piano Man" I've ever heard, her voice filled with life in ways I feared no one could ever compare.

A few minutes into the song playing from my headphones, I received a text from Ana. *Probably going to tell me she didn't want to see me again,* I thought.

ANA:

Hey Rob, nice hanging out with you today 😊

I felt a sigh of relief as I read her text multiple times before telling her that I had a nice time hanging out as well, wishing her a good night.

I stopped the song and slowly started driving away, *witnessing the lights turn on in the auditorium. When the lights went on, the audience cheered as I leaned to my right to see Ana sitting right next to me. I briefly looked up at Kelly taking a bow before looking at Ana again.*

"Did you have a good time tonight?" Ana asked.

I didn't answer right away. I looked back up at Kelly as I held Ana's hand. "I guess I'll give you a shot, see where it goes," I said halfheartedly. "Won't last long anyway," I mumbled as I kept focusing on Kelly's performance on stage. "Not like it matters."

Today

6

———

May 21, 2022

For the past few hours, I practiced my cover of Don McLean's "And I Love You So" in the front living room.

I picked at the nylon strings and ran my hands along the fretboard to match the rhythm of the song. I worked to get better at the barre chords, overstretching my fingers to perfect them. The phone conversation with Ana the other day replayed in my head again while playing the song. *I don't; I don't love you.* Those words stung each time I strummed.

Just then, my phone rang, so I put my guitar down and answered.

It was Aunt Judy calling from Seattle. "I heard from your mom about you and Ana and I wanted to express my condolences."

I thanked her, randomly plucking another string from my guitar.

"Are you okay?"

"I'm fine."

"Are you sure? Your mom was telling me you've been taking it pretty hard."

I sighed. "To be honest, I don't understand why she would do this. None of it makes sense." I cleared my throat. "I mean, everything seemed fine. I mean, she seemed more distant than usual, but I just thought she had been stressed with work or that maybe it was just all in my head. I just . . . I just don't get it. Was she just not happy?"

"I don't know what to tell you, Rob, but I understand."

I stared up at the ceiling, a random memory of me sitting on Ana's bed and watching her sleep crossing my mind, remembering how distant she had been that day.

Alicia kicked the front door open, carrying her DJ equipment to her room, going in and out as I spoke on the phone. After bringing everything in, Alicia came back out of her room and told me not to forget to take out the trash, distracting me from the call.

"Rob, are you still there?" Aunt Judy asked.

"Yeah, I'm still here. Sorry about that."

"Well, buddy," Aunt Judy continued. "Just know that we all love you, and you're going to get through this. I know you can. You're stronger than you think you are."

"I just want her back, Aunt Judy. I really do."

"I know you do. Just give her time. You know the whole thirty days of no contact thing, right?"

"I do."

"Then just do that. Don't call her. Don't text her. Give her space, and then once enough time has passed, see if you two can have a sit down and talk things out, okay?"

I nodded, saying our goodbyes before ending the call. I sat back, staring up at the ceiling, closing my eyes to fight back small remnants of tears.

"Rob, the trash!" Alicia barked, coming back into the room.

"I'll get it in a minute."

"No, get it now! Don't make me remind you again!"

Alicia left the room as I forced myself to get up and to take the trash out.

Once I was done, I sat back down to play my guitar again. I kept playing, closing my eyes for everything to fade from the room until *I found myself standing on stage in front of a large audience. I played my song to Ana sitting in the front row, who looked up at me with her radiant smile. I strummed a melody until the lights for each section of the audience began to go out, one by one. I picked up a glass of water on the stool next to me, only for it to slip from my hands and shatter all over the floor. I looked up. Ana faded into the darkness.*

I stopped strumming, not having the energy to move. I looked up at the pool table to my right, where Ana and I played a game in our pajamas, cuddled, and ate pepperoni pizza together despite her distaste for red sauce.

Later on, Ben called. "Rob, you still on for the bonfire?"

It was a quarter to 5 pm. "Yeah, I'm still going. I'll see you soon."

I picked up everyone who needed a ride before getting on the freeway. Ben rode shotgun, and Nathan and Trent sat in the back. Nathan played his Nintendo Switch while Trent stared out the window. They bantered while I drove, mostly keeping to myself.

"When I was working on my Associate's years ago," Ben said at one point, "I learned a lot about psychology, specifically about applied behavior analysis. You guys heard of it?"

"Nope," Nathan said. I could see in my rearview mirror that he was clearly pretending to be interested as he played his game.

"You may find this interesting then," Ben continued, "I remember reading about it and I thought to myself, 'Wait a minute! This sounds awfully familiar!' So I went to Schweitzer's own website and sure enough, it's all *over* it! Rob knows all about it since he's the only one in this car besides me who has a college degree! Right, Rob?"

I feigned interest and nodded, keeping my eyes on the road.

"Remember how they treated us like babies?" Ben asked ecstatically.

"You mean kind of like how Ms. Merriweather always gave me praise for the most random shit?" Trent asked.

"Exactly!" Ben exclaimed. "It's all there! 'Catch 'em being good!' 'Evidence-based!' Maggie Richardson always reminded teachers and parents who attended our IEP meetings to focus on how 'good' we were doing. No wonder it was a shit school! They were using all that stuff to try and control us!"

"I mean, the school sucked ass, but aren't you sounding a tad bit conspiratorial, Ben?" Nathan asked.

"Not at all!" Ben insisted. "Think about it! Whenever we were 'out of line,' they would always—and I mean *always*—insist we did something wrong even when we didn't, give us the silent treatment, or put something in our IEPs against our will so they could make us act as neurotypical as possible! Not even treat us like real human beings! Disgusting!"

"Yeah, just like when Ms. Thompson sent me home for wearing 'inappropriate' clothing," Trent said.

"Dude, you got sent home because your shirt said 'I like cock,'" Nathan said. "No shit they sent you home, you idiot!"

"But there was a rooster on it!" Trent insisted.

Ben turned and stared at Trent in disbelief. "Aside from Trent and his cock shirt, the Schweitzer teachers were really controlling."

I started to tune out again as Ben started going on another one of his tired spiels about Schweitzer and I changed lanes to get off the freeway. As I drove, I looked over at the passenger seat and where Ben sat, I saw Ana. I remembered last Fourth of July weekend we went to the Grand Canyon, driving on a rural road in the pouring rain somewhere in Northern Arizona. Lord Huron's "The Night We Met" played as Ana held her phone to her face like she would usually do on long car rides.

I smiled at her. *We're two hours away!* I exclaimed. *Ready to see a big giant hole in the ground?*

Ana giggled. *Yep. Ready to see a big giant hole in the ground.*

I chuckled, reaching out to hold her hand. She held my hand back.

My mind eased back into the present reality of Ben ranting about Schweitzer. I dried my eyes and exited the freeway.

"So Ben, how many people are supposed to be at this bonfire?" Nathan asked.

"Oh a lot!" Ben said. "Alex knows plenty of people. Makes me wish we met him at Schweitzer. Would probably have made that experience less miserable."

"Will there be cute girls at the bonfire?" Nathan asked.

"Maybe I can find a cutie for myself!" Trent exclaimed.

"Maybe we can find someone for Rob," Ben said.

In the rear view mirror, I noticed Nathan and Trent looking at each other in confusion before turning back to Ben.

"Doesn't Rob already have a girlfriend?" Nathan asked.

"Yeah, Hannah, or something, right?" Trent asked.

"Well, actually her name is actually Ana."

"Ben, stop!" I grumbled.

"And no, they broke up!" Ben blurted out. "You didn't hear about it? It was all over Facebook."

I wanted to strangle him so badly but stopped myself when I remembered I was driving.

"Rob, is that true?" Nathan asked.

I nodded.

"Damn!" Nathan exclaimed. "No wonder you've been quiet tonight. I'm so sorry, Rob. That sucks!"

I stopped at a red light and changed the song.

"Why did you two break up?" Nathan asked.

"I don't wanna talk about it," I said.

"Why don't you wanna talk about it?" Nathan asked.

"You'll feel a lot better if you talk about it," Ben exclaimed.

"I just don't wanna fucking talk about it!" I snapped, "Is that so hard to understand?"

The entire car went quiet.

"You'll meet someone else," Trent eventually said. "There are plenty of fish in the sea. Just give it time, okay? I'll even let you borrow my cock shirt to pick up chicks."

The light turned green and I took a right turn.

"You guys are such assholes," I muttered under my breath.

———

It was sunset by the time we got to the bonfire in Mission Bay, on a small beach off Fiesta Island overlooking the water. There was no parking lot, so I pulled onto the beach next to a few other cars. A growing crowd of people began gathering around a giant fire pit.

"There's Alex," Ben said, pointing to a tall skinny guy with a mustache and goatee cracking jokes with two women. Several people threw wood and scraps into the fire pit while others placed beach chairs and blankets around the site.

Nathan and Trent got out of the car as Ben looked at me as he opened the passenger door.

"Ready to have some fun?" Ben asked, a big smile on his face.

"You go ahead," I said.

"Go ahead? Everything okay?"

"I'm fine," I assured him. "I just need a few minutes."

Ben patted me on the back before getting out of the car. I looked out where everyone gathered. It took me a few seconds to recognize this beach: Ana and I came to this place a few times before officially becoming a couple. I felt my pulse quickening as the sun set and more people walked towards the bonfire. Chatter from them grew louder. I rolled up my window and took deep breaths when I sensed an oncoming panic attack, putting on my headphones and playing Of Monsters and Men's "This Happiness" to calm myself down.

Surveying the beach, I thought back to the first time Ana met my Grandpa before we came here.

Yesterday

7

—————

November 4, 2017

Ana and I arrived at Grandpa's house around 12:30 pm. Ever since we went to that art festival back in September, Ana treated me less like a "friend with benefits" and more like an actual boyfriend. I noticed she often brought me boxes of pastries from H-Mart or 85 Degree or even made spontaneous plans for us to get Asian food up in Orange County on weekends.

Then out of the blue when we cuddled a few weeks ago, she expressed interest in meeting Grandpa.

For real? I asked.

Ana nodded. *Yeah, from everything you've said about him, he sounds like a great guy. Plus, with how much you talk about him, I want to meet the legendary Grandpa John.* She giggled while I cracked a smile.

I lay there pleasantly surprised, considering she told me she wasn't comfortable meeting him back in June. Now here she was expressing real interest. We then made plans to make a visit soon. I couldn't stop wondering for weeks where we stood but was too scared to ask.

I called earlier letting Grandpa know we were coming, so I rang the doorbell to let him know we were here, then entered. We strolled into his living room, Grandpa sitting in his favorite armchair watching *Modern Marvels*. He turned off the TV when he saw us.

"Oh boy! Is this Ana?" Grandpa asked enthusiastically.

Ana nodded. We both sat down on the couch adjacent to Grandpa's armchair.

"Well, I'll be damned," Grandpa said. "It's so great to finally meet you. Rob told me so much about you."

Ana blushed. In the eight months I've known her, it usually took her some time to open up to new people, so I wasn't surprised—albeit nervous—when she didn't say anything else at all to Grandpa. The lack of music in the room magnified the silence between us as we sat across from each other. I had to fight every temptation to put on my headphones.

"So Grandpa, this is Ana," I said in an effort to break the silence. "Ana, this is Grandpa."

Ana gave a short little wave.

"Nice to meet you, indeed," Grandpa said. He cracked a big grin, which told me he was about to make another one of his corny jokes. "I've heard so much about you, yet you never come over here. I was starting to think you didn't like me!"

Ana giggled. I rubbed my eyes to hide my embarrassment.

"No, it's not that, Grandpa," I assured him. "It's just . . . we've just been busy."

Grandpa took out a small cloth to clean his glasses.

"So what's been new with you?" I asked.

"Nothing much," he said. "Getting ready for your mom to come over tonight and then church in the morning." He finished cleaning his glasses and put them back on. "Are you two hungry? I can make you both something to eat."

I leaned over to Ana to ask her if she was hungry, but she shook her head. "I'm good, but thank you," she politely said.

"So you're telling me you come into *my* house to tell me you hate *my* cooking?" Grandpa joked again, feigning shock.

Ana chuckled, wringing her hands and looking down at her lap, showing hints of a smile. After a short silence, Grandpa asked us what we were up to today. I looked over at Ana again to see if she would say anything but still no response.

"Later today, we're going to check out Fiesta Island, and then get some pho," I said.

Ana kept wringing her hands and looking down at her lap. My heart began to pound, sweat slowly dripping from my face. *Oh my god she must not like him,* I began to think. *I shouldn't have brought her here. What was I thinking?*

Awkward silence.

You're a piece of fucking garbage for even thinking she would want to come here, a voice in my head said.

I cleared my throat. "I have to use the restroom. Be right back." I got up and went to the bathroom on the other side of the house, closing the door. I washed my face, trying my hardest to wipe away sweat. Drying my face, I looked in the mirror and *found myself on stage in front of an angry audience.*

"What the fuck were you thinking bringing her here, you bastard?" someone in the audience shouted.

"She wanted to come here," I said. "She said so herself! I swear!"

"Only because she felt sorry for your pathetic ass!" another audience member yelled.

"She said she wanted to meet my grandpa!"

"She won't even say anything because it's obvious she finds him weird and sees you as the pathetic, desperate moron you are!" an additional audience member screeched. "Why else would she act all quiet around your own grandfather!"

"She's just nervous!" I shouted, fighting back tears. "This is just her first time meeting him!"

The audience booed and started to throw stuff at me. "She thinks you and your family are pathetic now!"

I dodged a glass bottle.

"Kill yourself, you piece of shit!"

I splashed more water on my face, staring at myself back in the mirror again. I've lost count of the amount of times over the years I've fought those voices in my head.

I spent a few minutes calming myself down in the bathroom. I finished drying my face and went back to the living room, only to find Ana and Grandpa not there. *Where did they go?* I asked myself. Suddenly, I heard Ana's voice coming from the hallway.

"You were in the navy?" I heard her say. "That's so cool!"

I went into the hallway to see Grandpa giving Ana a tour of the house. They stood in front of a series of family photos hung up on the wall, Grandpa talking to Ana about a photo of his younger self when he was stationed in the Philippines during the Korean War. Ana seemed much more jovial than earlier, laughing at his jokes and asking questions about each photo. I went over to join them as Grandpa finished one of his stories.

"Who is that next to you?" Ana asked, pointing to one specific picture.

"That's my wife, Shirley." It was a photo of Grandpa and Grandma standing on a dock next to a boat in Monterrey. The picture itself was taken a year before the cancer diagnosis, long before it withered her away. Grandpa went on a long story about their trip to Monterrey that year, talking about the restaurants they ate at and the boat rides they went on for their fifty-seventh wedding anniversary.

"Let me show you an even younger picture of her," Grandpa continued. He dug into his wallet and pulled out an old, wrinkled photograph of Grandma when she was in her early twenties and handed it to Ana. I looked at the photograph from over Ana's shoulder. Grandma, at that age in this photograph, was stunningly beautiful with her black hair and beaming smile almost rivaled by her dress and high heels—*almost*.

It was at this moment Grandpa began his story about when he and Grandma first started dating, telling the story of their on and off again courtship in the 1950s not too long after he got stationed in San Diego. He talked about all the letters they shared back and forth and how uncertain they were of the kind of relationship they had before they both realized they really did care deeply for one another.

As Grandpa told this story, Ana glanced up at me from time to time. She lightly bumped my hand before looking back at Grandpa.

"This picture is a reminder of how I've tried to maintain that love for as long as possible," Grandpa said.

"That's such a sweet story," Ana said with affection in her voice.

Grandpa let out a huge smile. "You know, you look almost just like her, except way more oriental."

I put my hand over my face. *Oh my god why did you have to say that last part?* I thought to myself, fighting every urge to speak up so as to not make a scene.

Ana giggled. "Why, thank you," She said before handing Grandpa back his photograph. Grandpa continued giving Ana a tour of the rest of the house. "You have a lovely home," she said.

I began feeling more at ease as they continued their conversation further in the hallway.

We visited Grandpa for another hour before getting into the car to go to Fiesta Island. We chit-chatted about how the visit went before I started the engine.

"I really like your Grandpa," Ana said.

I looked at her and smiled. "That means a lot to me." I then immediately remembered Grandpa's comment about Ana looking more oriental than Grandma at her age. "I'm sorry, though, about the comment he made earlier about your ethnicity. I should've warned you he tends to say things that are not exactly politically correct."

"It's not a big deal."

"It doesn't bother you?"

Ana shrugged. "I'm sure it would have bothered my sister a little considering how big into politics she is right now, but honestly, I don't personally know many Asians who would outright be offended by it. It is what it is."

"That's good."

"He's obviously from a bygone generation. Many of the clients I've worked with talk similar to him, so I kind've expected he would."

Ana's comment made me relieved. I then remembered the panic attack I had earlier, fighting off the voices in the head. I wanted to tell her everything, but she seemed so happy I didn't want to ruin the moment.

"I can see where you got your upbeat personality from," she said as an offhand comment.

I blushed as we drove off to Fiesta Island.

We made it to Fiesta Island and walked along the sand before sitting side by side to take in the view of the bay.

"This is so nice," Ana said as she looked out to the water.

"Yeah," I said. I looked over at Ana, remembering the panic attack I had earlier at Grandpa's. I could not stop thinking about what happened. I struggled with whether I should actually tell her so she would know who I really am or keep it to myself so I didn't risk her walking away.

As we continued watching the bay, I thought about how a couple of years ago some bystanders stopped me from jumping off one of the eight-story parking garages at San Diego State, spending three days in solitary confinement at the nearest mental hospital. When the school therapist asked me why I tried jumping off an eight-story parking garage, I didn't have an answer—at least, I didn't know what answer to give him. I was officially diagnosed with clinical depression, prescribed antidepressants, and sent home.

I stopped taking them a few years ago, but I would still have to fight these voices every once in a while. I rarely ever talked about it with others, not even with Ben. Every time I tried to, people told me some version of *Suck it up* before walking away.

If I told Ana, would she feel the same way? If I told her, would she walk away?

We kept sitting in silence.

"I have something to tell you," I finally said.

Ana looked over at me. "Is everything okay?"

I sighed, my heart pounding at what I was about to tell her. "I don't tell a lot of people this, but I struggle with depression and anxiety. Sometimes pretty bad. Have for years."

Ana nodded. "If you ever need anyone to talk about it with, I'm always here."

"Thanks, I appreciate that."

She smiled and took my hand, giving it a reassuring squeeze.

I took a sip of my water. "I was so scared you weren't going to like my Grandpa and that you were going to think I was stupid for bringing you to meet him and think I was all these awful things that I had a panic attack."

I took a deep breath.

"I sometimes get these thoughts in my head," I continued. "Horrible thoughts, the kind of thoughts that tell me I'm stupid and worthless and I don't amount to much of anything and I'd be better off dead. Had them since I was a kid. I'm often afraid to tell people. I'm sorry I didn't tell you sooner. I was afraid if I told you, you would think less of me. I just wanted you to give me a chance."

I wiped away a few tears, expecting Ana to get up and tell me to take her home and that I would never see her again. Instead, she continued holding my hand while smiling up at me. "It's okay," she whispered. She wrapped her arms around me, telling me over and over again it was okay. I hugged her back as she kissed me on the head.

Today

8

———

May 21, 2022

The bonfire had been going for a couple hours now, everyone singing and dancing to music. I sat in one of the beach chairs, staring at the sand. *Why am I even here?* I thought.

Alex got on top of a chair in front of the fire, waving to grab everyone's attention. "Everybody having fun?" he shouted.

"Yeah!" almost everyone screamed in unison.

I said nothing.

Alex held up a Pepsi in the air. "You are all the best!"

The crowd started pumping their fists in the air. "Speech! Speech! Speech!"

Alex took a sip of his Pepsi and gave everyone the peace sign, causing everyone to cheer. "As we party tonight, we gather around the fire to celebrate something both scary but also exciting at the same time!"

"We're gonna miss you, Alex!" someone shouted.

I sighed.

"I'm moving to Boston not just to teach but to make a difference in people's lives, just like how everyone here at this bonfire made a difference in mine," Alex continued. "As we gather around this bonfire, we celebrate change for a better world. I'm sad to be leaving all of you, but I'm also excited to see what's in store for tomorrow!"

"That was cheesy but still awesome!" Trent shouted.

As Alex continued his speech, I put my headphones on so I could listen to music, before slowly getting up to sneak away while everyone wasn't paying attention.

I sat by myself at one of the cement picnic tables overlooking the bay not far from the bonfire, my feet resting on the grass. For a while, I stared out toward the shoreline, the stars and the moon illuminating the night sky. I could see the spot where Ana and I walked the afternoon she met Grandpa for the first time. We laughed and told jokes while strolling along the shore with a beach towel and water bottles to find a place to sit and watch the gorgeous view.

"Rob the Professor, how are you?" I heard Alex say.

I glanced up at Alex before staring at my feet again. I didn't expect him to come check on me, considering how many people came to the bonfire to celebrate his going away party. "Could be better," I muttered.

"Ben told me about you and Ana. I'm so sorry."

"Ben is such a blabbermouth."

"Yeah, he is."

I said nothing.

"But he does care about you," Alex said. "And I do too. I wanted to tell you I'm sorry you're going through this right now, and I'm here for you if you need me."

"Thanks."

"How long were you two together for, again?"

"Five years."

"Fuck, man! That's a long time! No wonder you've been more quiet than usual tonight."

I shrugged. "I didn't wanna ruin your going away party."

"You're not. You have nothing to worry about."

I looked up at Alex. "I appreciate it."

"I'm glad you're here though." Alex looked over his shoulder and then back at me. "Anyway, I'm going to go back, but I wanted to check up on you, see how you are doing, and all that stuff. Do you still have my number?"

I pulled out my phone to check. "Yep. Still do."

"Good. I wanna keep in touch. You've given me so many teaching ideas over the years I plan to use in Boston. I know you're going through a lot right now, but I'd like to hit you up from time to time if I need teaching tips. Is that okay with you?"

I gave Alex a lukewarm thumbs up.

"Awesome! Feel free to come join us again whenever you're ready."

Alex went back to the bonfire as I went back to staring at the water.

I kept thinking about that day with Ana, of getting pho at a place in Pacific Beach, the image of her smile replaying over and over in my memories.

Ben came and sat on top of the picnic table next to me. "Mind if I join you?"

I didn't respond as Ben made himself comfortable on the table.

"It's been a fun evening, hasn't it?" He asked.

I said nothing, trying my best to ignore him.

"Are you going to be okay, Rob? You've been pretty quiet all evening."

I kept looking out to the shoreline.

"Look, Rob. I've known you for a long time, and I know when you are not your usual self. You are not being your usual self right now. If this is about you and Ana, this will pass. You will find someone else."

I looked straight at him, flipping him off. "You know, Ben, you can be a real ass sometimes!" I snapped.

Ben looked like he was about to say something when Nathan called out to us asking when we wanted to head out. "Give us a few minutes!" Ben shouted. He turned to me again. "Dude, what's gotten into you?"

"What's gotten into me? You acted like a complete dick in the car on the way over here, egging Nathan and Trent on about wanting to find another girl for me at a bonfire I didn't even want to attend in the first place, and to top it off, you blab to Alex and only God knows who about what happened behind my back, and you're asking what's gotten into me? What the fuck is wrong with you, fucking asshole?" I took another deep breath, tears starting to flow again. "I'm sorry," I slowly said. "I shouldn't have snapped at you like that."

Ben didn't say anything before getting off the table and sitting in the seat right next to me. "No, you're right," he said. "I'm sorry. I really am. I just . . . I just remember how Claire ended things between us years ago and I didn't want you to go through what I went through."

I sighed.

"Do you wanna talk about it?" Ben asked.

"I don't know, man," I said. "I don't understand why she felt the need to end things. I still can't wrap my head around it."

"Sounds like what happened between me and Claire," Ben said. "Did she say why?"

"Her reasons don't make any sense to me," I asserted. I took a deep breath. "For the past couple of days, I've been thinking a lot about when me and her started seeing each other. I remember when we matched on Tinder and then had those first couple of dates all those years ago. I thought it would last at most two dates, maybe three. She didn't even make the best impression on me when I first met her, but I thought, 'might as well give her a chance because it's not like it was going to last long anyway.' It turned into five years."

"Hey, that's better than many of us on the spectrum," Ben said. "There are people out there similar to us who never have relationships at all, let alone ones that last five years, so consider yourself *really* lucky, Rob!"

"I guess."

"Sucks she ended everything over the phone though."

I sighed. "Like that makes any difference."

"Did you love her?"

I didn't answer right away. "I don't know, to be honest," I eventually said. "I'm still trying to figure that out. I just have so many unanswered questions. Part of me really does want her back. Maybe we could try again. But if she won't come back, I want to at least understand why. I just really hate the feeling of having unfinished business. Doesn't that feeling fucking suck?"

"I know what you mean."

"It would just suck so much if we couldn't at least talk it out and see why we didn't work out if it really is it. I can't have that sense of closure at all unless she tells me why."

"Have you reached out to her?"

"No, I'm giving her space for now. I need time to at least try to figure out what went wrong before reaching out."

"Still going on that trip you said you were going on?"

"Yeah. Will be leaving in June, so the timing couldn't be better. Go on that trip, use it to clear my head, and then go from there."

"Hey, you do what you gotta do."

I kept looking out to the bay.

"Ready to head out?" Ben asked.

"Give me a five or ten minutes; then we'll go."

"Sounds good. I'll meet you at the car."

Ben walked back to the bonfire to meet up with Nathan and Trent. I looked out to the spot Ana and I sat years ago again, remembering how after getting pho we tried attending a show at the Comedy Store in La Jolla, but it was sold out. We went back to my place to cuddle.

I have something to tell you, she said when we were cuddling.

What is it? I asked.

She looked at me and didn't say anything for a moment before out of the blue she whispered, *I . . . I love you!* It took a moment to process what she said. Did she really just tell me she loved me? For real? No one who I ever dated before ever told me they ever loved me! Smiling, I said that I loved her too, and we shared a long, passionate kiss.

I wiped away another tear as I looked at that spot again. I took a couple of deep breaths and put on my headphones to listen to some music to calm down before driving Ben and the others home. I put on Don McLean's "And I Love You So," my mind going along with the music while reflecting on my experiences with Ana years ago.

Yesterday

9

January 14, 2018

Ana wanted us to go to the Asian American Expo.

We got in her car and began the two hour drive up north to Pomona that morning after she spent the night on a Saturday, just as she usually would. I held onto the grab handle when she started speeding, something she did despite my attempts here and there to affectionately ask her to slow down.

An hour and a half later, we crossed into Los Angeles County.

"Have you ever been to this before?" I asked at one point.

"No, but my boss and her husband went last year and she said it's worth going."

Ana changed lanes to get off the freeway, taking a backroad. As I fooled around on Twitter, I glanced over at Ana, thinking about last week when she came over. During one of our random conversations, she showed me a Facebook ad for the Asian American Expo, an annual festival held every year in January at the Pomona Fairplex to commemorate the Lunar New Year. From the pictures and videos she showed me directly from their website, the event was massive: thousands of vendors, seven large exhibition halls, live stage shows, and tons of Asian food.

Do you wanna go? She asked.

Sure, I would love to go, I replied. I thought about asking if I should worry about it triggering some type of sensory overload, but I figure I'll just bring my headphones. She bought our tickets before watching a movie on my laptop, only for us to make out and have sex again halfway through.

We cuddled afterwards, and I gazed at her while her head lay against my shoulder, her eyes closed. *That feel good?* I affectionately asked. She grinned and nodded as I kissed her on the forehead.

Seeing her curled up next to me made me think about what we did together since I opened up to her for the first time months ago. She checked in on me more, sending me silly memes and funny texts. Once a week she would come over and sometimes surprise me with some of my favorite snacks. Over the holidays, we went to a winterfest light show at Qualcomm Stadium, losing track of the amount of times we heard Ed Sheeran's "Perfect" play on our car stereos. And I could not stop thinking about the flirty Snapchats she sent me when she visited her mom in San Francisco for New Year's.

We talked more about how our week went before the subject of how we clicked came up. It was that moment I finally asked her where we stood. She took a moment to clear her throat. *Will you be my boyfriend?* She asked, a hint of nervousness in her voice.

I kissed her and then enthusiastically answered yes.

I mentally eased back into riding in the car as I looked out the window and saw us pass ongoing traffic as we drove into Pomona. "I wasn't able to get any classes for spring."

"No? I thought you said you would."

"That's what I thought too, but then Megan emailed me the other day saying they didn't have enough classes to give any of the one-semester contract instructors."

"Megan's the schedule coordinator for your department, right? Can't she just pull some strings?" Ana asked semi-jokingly.

"There's only so much she can do though." I scrolled through Twitter again, reading tweets from writing teachers across the country about how shitty the academic job market has been lately. At the last minute, I got hired as a lecturer that fall not too long after grad school to meet a huge demand for classes. I held on hope I would get something in spring, but those hopes got crushed when Megan sent me the dreaded email: I would have to wait until next fall to get another contract. "It's why I've been doing all these food delivery jobs lately."

"You still have the community college job, right?"

"Yeah, as a tutor but it's only ten hours a week. It's better than nothing, but still."

Ana nodded. I checked my phone to see we were roughly fifteen minutes away from the Asian American Expo. When Ana stopped at a red light, her mom called, and she put her on through the Bluetooth speaker. For the next five minutes, Ana and her mom went back and forth in Mandarin about something. Whatever it was, I could tell Ana got more annoyed the longer the call went on. At this point, I could usually tell whenever Ana would be irritated by something her mom said, even if I couldn't understand what they were saying to each other.

"What did your mom want this time?" I asked once the call ended.

Ana sighed. "Nothing important. She just was having trouble setting up an appointment online with the DMV just to renew her license and wanted me to help right this minute."

"But you're driving!"

"She doesn't care. My sister wasn't picking up, and she just expects me to stop whatever I'm doing and help her whenever she's having trouble with anything related to technology. She's like, 'Pull over the side of the road if you have to! I need to make an appointment now!' So frustrating! I've already shown her countless times how to use the internet, and she still doesn't understand. I swear, this woman! She can learn how to send text messages on her phone but can't even do something as basic as navigating a government website."

"How's she doing with the iPad you got her for Christmas recently?"

"She only uses it as a clock," Ana said. "I should have gotten her a watch from Target instead. I would have saved myself $400!"

"You could've given me the iPad instead," I joked.

"No! Get your own iPad!" She teased.

We both laughed.

We parked close to Gate 17, got tickets, and made it onto the festival grounds. Large crowds moved in all directions, people lined up at all kinds of souvenir stands set up around the courtyard. Red and yellow Lunar New Year inspired decorations and banners everywhere, with many of them with Year of the Dog iconography on them. Everything here instantly reminded me of the fair I went to as a kid, with miles of attractions, fair foods, rides, and people going in and out of buildings to see everything.

As I walked with Ana through the courtyards, noises from people coming and going and music from the different buildings played out in every direction, but thankfully not at an overwhelming level.

I kept my headphones around my neck just in case.

"What do you want to check out first?" I asked Ana.

Ana stopped, a smile on her face. "I don't know. Let's see what they have to offer."

We passed countless people in the courtyard chatting amongst themselves or hurrying off to the next thing. We got close to one of the main exhibition halls where someone dressed up in a panda suit danced and waved around balloons as people watched and laughed.

We headed inside Hall 6.

The entire hall was filled with booths and tables from a variety of local and state-wide Asian businesses. In the middle of the hall was a tiny Hyundai showroom with a table where people could enter a raffle for a chance to win a brand new 2018 Hyundai Elantra. A cacophony of noises echoed throughout the hall, though I was still somewhat able to hear Ana. I followed close behind her, making sure not to get separated from her as more people filled the building.

We walked through an aisle until we came across a stand selling mochi ice cream. Ana asked me if I wanted any.

"What's that?" I asked.

"Just try it," Ana said. "It's pretty good."

"Sure."

We waited in a short line and she bought us a small variety pack of four mochi ice cream, eating it as we walked around the exhibition hall.

"Wow, this *is* pretty good," I said. I took another bite of my strawberry flavored mochi ice cream ball. "I like this a lot!" I glanced at Ana, both of us smiling as she affectionately held my hand. I gave her a quick kiss on the head as we walked past more booths.

We strolled around the eastern part of Hall 6, touring the aisles and looking at each of the booths before heading towards the other side of the building. I made a joke to Ana about the Hyundai Elantra being her next car.

"Nah, I'll stick with my Honda. But if I do win the Elantra, I'll sell it and make more money!"

I chuckled at her comment. "If you say so."

"Work smarter, not harder."

We kept walking past the Hyundai exhibit to look at more of Hall 6. I put on my headphones as it got louder. At first I worried Ana would be offended, but she didn't seem to mind. We strolled past more booths, many selling Asian themed merchandise and galleries of anime until we came to a section of the exhibition dedicated to Funko Pop figures. I grew excited, having started growing a Funko Pop figure collection of my own since last year.

We looked through Funko Pop figures to see what they had until we came across the founding members of the Marvel Avengers. I slightly moved my headphone cushions so I could hear better.

"Ana, look!" I said, pointing them out to her.

"Nice! That's so cool!"

"It's the original Avengers Team! All here together!"

Ana looked at the figures closely. "No, not all of them. Iron Man isn't here. Where's Iron Man? Where's Tony Stark?"

I looked at the figures again, hyperfocusing on the empty spot where Iron Man was supposed to be. "Oh my goodness, you're right!"

"So no, they are *not* all here together, dude!" Ana teased.

I chuckled. "Of course you would notice Iron Man isn't there. He's your favorite Avenger!"

"You have such a good memory."

We looked at the Pop figures, admiring how they had *almost* all the Avengers together!

"This reminds me of when I saw the first *Avengers* movie with friends when it came out during our senior year of high school right before I went off to college," Ana said.

"That's cool. Back up in San Francisco, right?"

Ana nodded. She talked about how she and her high school friends went to almost every Marvel movie that came out, followed by a trip to either Chinatown or Fisherman's Wharf to hang out. Other times they went to different Asian establishments for food or just to get Boba. "We went to those places so much, we used to always say we should start our own Pho business, call it the *Pho-One-Five*," Ana said, giggling.

"After the San Francisco area code?"

"The old one, yes. See, you're catching on!"

I chuckled. "That's cute." I momentarily kept quiet, suddenly remembering something I was curious about though admittedly nervous to ask. "What was high school like for you?"

"High school was high school. Nothing out of the ordinary. I took a bunch of AP classes and participated in some clubs here and there. I got to hang out with my friends all the time, so it was overall good."

"Did you have good teachers?"

"I would say so. One teacher I had, Mr. Chen, really encouraged me to pursue college early on, so I did. Now here I am!"

"That's . . . great," I muttered, stopping myself from tapping my hand.

"One thing about the high school I went to was that it was predominantly Asian," Ana said.

"Predominantly Asian?"

Ana nodded.

"So there were no white kids at your school? At all?"

"There were a few here and there, but most of the people I went to school with were Asian. I didn't personally know any white people who came to my school."

"What about now?"

"Other than this one guy at my work, you're the only white person I personally know."

I picked up the Captain America Funko Pop figure, debating whether to add it to my collection.

"You excited for *Infinity War?*" Ana asked.

"Yep. I'll be buying tickets in advance when they come out. You wanna go with me? Make it a date?"

Ana looked up and smiled at me. "I would love that!"

I smiled back, putting the Captain America Funko Pop figure back on the shelf. After a few minutes of exploring, we exited the building from where we came.

We walked straight through the courtyard and headed inside Hall 7. Rows of stalls lined the hall offering varieties of produce, meats, and countless specialty Asian foods. Aromas of hot foods and spices filled the air. Footsteps and chatter echoed throughout the building as we moved through crowds going in random directions.

"Reminds me somewhat of Chinatown back home," Ana said.

Following her lead, we slowly maneuvered around lines of people sampling hot food or waiting to buy produce. We walked past one vendor cooking spicy rice cakes on a flat stove while another sold Asian snacks such as sesame crackers, creamy wafers, sachima, and pocky.

We arrived at a table covered with large spiky fruits catching my attention. I asked the vendor what they were as I picked up one of them to examine it.

"Durian," the vendor said. "It's a tropical fruit from Southeast Asia. It's super delicious. We sell it unpeeled as a treat, as well as the fruit itself for only $8 a pound. Would you like to try?"

"No, don't do it!" Ana insisted. "You won't like it."

"What are you talking about?" I asked. "I'm always willing to try anything once."

"You won't like it!" Ana insisted again. "Trust me. Don't waste your money."

This was not the first time Ana had advised me not to buy something. Usually she would be right, but I *really* wanted to try this fruit, so I thought to hell with it: I'll prove her wrong this time! "I'll take one," I said to the vendor as I handed him my debit card.

Ana rolled her eyes the second the vendor handed me an unpeeled durian in a napkin. As we walked away, I could already smell the stench coming from the durian. Good grief it smelled like sewage!

"You're not going to like it!" Ana said again.

In an effort to prove her wrong, I took a big bite of the durian, expecting it to be similar to a banana despite the smell. Instead, the moment that abomination entered my mouth felt like I had bitten into vomit-flavored custard. I chewed for a few seconds before I spit it back into the napkin. "That was gross!"

"Dude, I told you you weren't going to like it!"

"Sorry."

"You do stuff like this all the time!" Ana snapped. "You always waste your money on things even after I tell you won't like it! It's like you don't listen to me!"

"I'm really sorry."

Ana let out an irritated sigh. "Let's just go!"

I stayed close to Ana as we looked around Hall 7 before heading to the exit, making sure to throw away the durian.

We strolled across the courtyard, looking at a few booths here and there along the way. Walking past Halls 5 and 6, I kept thinking about how she reacted when I bought and tried to eat the durian. *What does she mean I do stuff like this all the time? Why is she so annoyed about how I spend my own money?* I kept replaying that interaction in my head.

It's like you don't listen to me, I heard her say again.

When we stopped to look at trinkets, I suddenly remembered a couple months ago when we went out to eat, and I rushed to buy her a mango shaved ice she mentioned as being her favorite. But I forgot she mentioned already being full, and instead of her enjoying the dessert, she ended up pushing it away.

You're such a fuck up, a voice in my head said. *You should have taken the time to listen to her, you asshole! She definitely hates you now if she didn't before, Rob!*

"You ready?" Ana asked when she was done looking at trinkets. I nodded, struggling to ignore the negative thoughts that began to form in my head.

We walked past more outdoor booths before we went inside Hall 4.

Hall 4 had stalls for goods and services such as cosmetics and travel agencies, with bean bag chairs advertising AT&T laid out in the middle of a showroom floor for anyone to sit and relax. As we went down an aisle, it grew a slightly louder than Hall 6, so I put my headphones over my ears.

But I couldn't stop thinking about what happened in Hall 7.

Maybe if you weren't such a piece of shit she wouldn't need to snap at you, a voice in my head said. *She obviously thinks you're stupid so don't be surprised if she dumps you right now and leaves you stranded at this Expo! When that happens, throw yourself in front of a bus!*

I worked to calm my fluttering nerves as Ana turned to show me an adorable corgi figurine she found at one of the booths. "Isn't this so cute?" She said all gushy-eyed.

I smiled and agreed with her so I could better hide my ongoing anxiety attack. We strolled throughout the hall some more, taking time to see what different Asian businesses had to sell or witness mini demonstrations of appliances. I slowly calmed down as we walked around, Ana looking content with what we were seeing.

We made our way to the western end of the hall to sit down in two of the chairs laid out in rows in front of a large stage. This part of the hall started to get less crowded, clueing me in that it was getting less noisy so I could take my headphones off and just have them around my neck for now. We were the only ones sitting down in these chairs intended for an audience to watch a live show. Resting our feet, we sat back to watch a performance of three young women in traditional ancient Chinese garments doing a dance in front of a red and yellow banner, with paper cutouts of trees used as stage props in the background.

"Their dresses remind me of some of the things I used to wear during special events when I went to Chinese school," Ana said. "I never was too crazy about wearing them, but they are pretty. Just not for me."

"Chinese school? What's that?"

"When we were kids, my parents had me and my sister attend this school to teach us both Mandarin and Cantonese. They wanted us to make sure we never forgot where we came from."

"Is it because your parents are both from China?"

"Something like that."

"What was that like for you?"

"What was 'what' like for me?"

"Chinese school."

Ana shrugged. "It was good. I can't speak for the friends I made there, but I had fun. We had a lot of lessons on how to read and write in the Chinese language, but I really liked doing all the fun little art projects we got to do once in a while. It was such an innocent time. I didn't like having to wear a uniform at first, but I now see it as good practice for the workplace."

"I never have to wear a uniform for my line of work."

"That's because you're weird," Ana teased.

"Hey, you're the one dating me so who's the weird one?" I teased back.

"You think you are *so* clever."

We sat back in our seats and watched the performance, Ana resting her head on my shoulder. After a few minutes, I smiled down at Ana. She looked up and gazed into my eyes before we slowly embraced for a kiss, any intrusive thoughts slowly fading away.

We went back to watching the performance. "I'm sorry about earlier," I said.

"Sorry about what?" Ana asked.

"The durian. I should've listened to you about it instead of just rushing to buy it, and I definitely shouldn't have said how gross it was like that."

"It's okay," she softly said. "Don't worry about it."

I thought about asking if she really was sure but didn't dwell on it. We watched the show for at least ten more minutes before we headed out. We explored Hall 5, had a late lunch at one of the dining areas outside, and then made our way towards the parking lot.

As we got close to the exit, we came across a Hanmi Insurance agency booth we didn't see when we first came to the festival.

"Hi there," one of the insurance salespeople exclaimed. "Would you be interested in our new insurance plans?"

This immediately got Ana's attention, so we went to the booth.

"Hi! I work for Hanmi Insurance as well," Ana said as she pulled out one of her business cards. "I work for Stephanie Tran's Hanmi Insurance agency down in San Diego."

I let Ana do her thing as I looked at the brochures laid out on the table. Usually when we went to festivals or any type of community event like this, Ana would usually take advantage of any chance she had to network with other insurance agencies. I finished looking at the brochures on the table and noticed a large red and yellow prize wheel.

"Would you like to spin the wheel?" One of the salespeople asked us after they finished discussing networking opportunities with Ana.

I went first, spinning the wheel as hard as I could hoping it would land on a dragon image so I could win a stuffed animal for Ana, but instead, it landed on a pig and I won a keychain. "Your turn, Ana," I said.

Ana spun the wheel as hard as she could, taking a while to spin until it finally landed on a dog image.

"Congratulations!" the salespeople exclaimed. "You won a piggy bank!"

The salespeople handed Ana a piggy bank in the shape of a dog.

"That is such a cool piggy bank. You now have a cool little doggie you can save more money with."

"It is pretty cool," Ana said. She looked over the piggy bank for a moment before placing it in my hands. "Here. I want you to have it."

"Wait, are you sure?"

Ana nodded. "I'm sure," she said, smiling. "It's for you."

I looked at the piggy bank then gave her a huge smile. She affectionately grabbed my hand as we left to go home.

It was close to evening by the time we got back to my place. We would have gotten back sooner, but I grew really uncomfortable with her speeding. I had her slow down, something she tried to accommodate, but she still did it anyways. We went to my room, put the piggy bank on one of my bookshelves, and embraced each other.

"Did you have a good day?" I asked her, giving her a kiss.

Ana nodded, smiling. "I did." She kissed me back. "How about you?"

"Me too."

We kissed each other again. "Did you wanna stay a little longer?" I asked.

"Sure. I can stay a bit longer, but I do have work in the morning."

We kissed again, took off our shoes, and lay back on my bed. We were both too tired for sex, so we just cuddled. We talked about our favorite things at the Asian American Expo and how it compared to previous festivals we've been to. "Would you say the Expo lived up to what your boss said about it?" I asked at one point.

"Of course. Why wouldn't it?" she teased.

We then talked about her work and other random topics until Ana pointed to a picture hung up above my desk. "Is that your dad?"

It was an older picture of Dad in his early 40s. "It is. I found it when I was cleaning some stuff out of the garage recently."

"You look so much like him."

I've lost count of the amount of times people have told me over the years. "Growing up as little kids, he gave us so much love. He threw us so many extravagant birthday parties, took us on so many road trips, and took us to McDonald's so many times just for the toy. There was one time he allowed me, Alicia, and Jason to use cups as bowling pins because we wanted to play bowling in the backyard. It made Mom so mad!"

I chuckled at that last memory. As I told this story, I remembered Dad's beautiful smile and infectious laugh as he held my hand when I was toddler and took me to the park to play with the other kids. "I always told myself that if I ever had kids, I would give them the same kind of love he gave us."

"Awww, that's so sweet."

I wiped a tear from my eye. "I'm twenty-nine years old, and I still miss him. Every single day."

Ana put her hand on my shoulder.

"Do you think there's an afterlife?" I slowly asked.

Ana took a moment to respond, as if trying to figure out how to answer the question. "I'm not sure to be honest."

"I'm not sure either. But I hope there is one so I can see him. I hate to think that once we die, we will never see our loved ones again."

We said nothing for a few minutes, just laying there enjoying each other's company. "Are you close to your dad?" I finally asked.

"Not really."

"If you don't mind me asking, how come?"

"We're just not. He would work a lot at his construction job, and then he and my mom would constantly fight over the dumbest things. I remember lots of yelling growing up. They finally got a divorce when I was in high school."

"I'm sorry to hear that."

"It was for the best. I just don't really talk to him much, if at all. He was nice enough to come down here with my mom for my college graduation though."

"That's cool. Did you all take pictures?"

"We did. I'll show you." Ana pulled up her phone, scrolled through her Facebook photos, and then showed me one of her in her UC San Diego graduation gown standing with three other people. Next to her was a young teenage girl who also had black hair like Ana but slightly shorter.

"I can definitely see the resemblance," I said when Ana confirmed it was her sister, Mary.

On opposite sides of the picture apart from each other were her mom and dad, who both looked to be in their late 50s or early 60s. Ana's mom was short and skinny with long black hair and wrinkles similar to my mom. Her dad was taller but chubbier and had short, graying black hair.

"I can definitely see the resemblance," I said again.

"I get that from time to time."

"Did you all do anything special for your college graduation?"

"Dinner and a movie. That's about it. At least my mom and dad got along this time."

"But you don't talk to your dad that much?"

"It's just for the best that we don't talk that much."

"How about your mom? Since the divorce, I assume they don't live together anymore?"

"She moved into this small crappy one bedroom apartment in downtown San Francisco not too long after the divorce. Dad got the house because it was under his name."

"Shit! How is she able to get by? Isn't San Francisco insanely expensive right now?"

"Her only source of income right now, as far as I know, is working at one of the massage parlors over there. It's a miracle she's able to live off that over there right now."

I tried to process everything Ana was telling me. "Is this why your mom calls you all the time?"

"Not really. She calls me all the time but I've stopped trying to offer help because she would always say no when I do. She can be *really* stubborn! She would rather just call me for other reasons."

Sounds similar to my mom, I thought.

"I'm just glad to be on my own," Ana continued. "I would let you come over to my place, but my landlord at the house I'm staying at right now still doesn't allow overnight guests unless they're family."

"Maybe soon you'll get a place all to yourself."

"Hopefully in the next year or so."

We put on some music as we held each other, not really saying anything else. At one point she got hungry and wanted something from McDonalds, so I let her stay in my room while I quickly went to get her a small cheeseburger and french fries. I didn't get myself anything.

When I got back, she was curled under the sheets. "Your bed is so cozy," she whispered in a cutesy way.

I placed the McDonalds bag on my nightstand.

"Thank you," Ana said. "You're so *sweet*."

I lay next to Ana as she ate her food. She offered me some fries, which I accepted even though I wasn't hungry at all. She ate about half the food before putting it back in the bag.

"Would it be okay if I spend the night?" Ana asked. "I'm too tired to drive home. I'll leave in the morning."

"Of course. Stay as long as you like."

I got in the sheets with Ana and wrapped my arms around her. She held my hands as we continued cuddling.

"That painting is pretty," Ana later said.

"Which painting?"

"That one over there," Ana said as she pointed to a small, stylized painting of a red-haired girl above my desk blending along with the other posters.

"Oh that one? I got that one at an art show in Vista a couple years ago."

"It's really pretty."

As we looked at the painting, it made me think about Kelly, the image of us waving at each other from opposite sides of the Sydney Harbor bridge, the sound of her voice talking to me during our bus rides, followed by us hugging each other goodbye at LAX.

My heart ached a little as we looked at the painting.

We sat up and I leaned against the wall. "I bought it to remember a girl I fell for a long time ago," I slowly said.

"Oh?"

"It was. . . just some girl I met when I studied abroad in high school. My mom was so busy doing things for my sister and brother she never really did much for me. When I got a letter from this program to study abroad, she wanted to make it up to me so she convinced my grandparents to help raise money for it. I went on the trip thinking I would just take pictures and call it a day. I ended up traveling with kids my age from Chicago, who were the coolest people I've ever met."

Ana looked me in the eye.

"This one girl was my favorite," I continued. "She was this red-haired girl who had so much spunk and energy. When I first met her, I thought she wanted to kick my ass."

I chuckled when I said that last part. Ana smiled.

"But the more I grew to know her, the more I grew to like her, and by the time I realized I loved her, we were already saying our goodbyes." I paused, feeling a large ache in my chest. "The worst part is I never told her I loved her. I feel so stupid for never telling her. I feel so stupid for doing such a shitty job of keeping in touch. Now I have to live the rest of my life asking 'what if?' I'm just so stupid sometimes."

Ana rubbed my shoulder. "You're not stupid. You were only a kid. Don't ever cut yourself down like that."

"I tend to be pretty hard on myself."

"Don't be. You're a great guy." She kissed me on the cheek. We lay back in bed and cuddled, her warm embrace giving me a sense of calm and peace. As we lay side by side, I looked into her eyes, something I normally didn't like to do but felt safe doing so with her. As we embraced, Kelly's memory slowly began to fade.

"I love you," she slowly whispered.

I smiled. "I love you too."

10

April 1, 2018

I couldn't stop glancing at the clock.

I sat on my bed, fully dressed and ready to go, but Ana was still in the bathroom, fifteen minutes longer than she said she would be. We should've left over half an hour ago.

Why does she always take so long? I anxiously thought. *We need to go now!* I lightly hit my hand repeatedly, breathing in and out to the tempo of the music playing through my headphones.

I glanced up at the clock again. *Dammit, you're making us late again. I told you Grandpa is expecting us!*

I fidgeted before Ana finally came back into my room, forcing myself to stop, hiding my fidgeting from her as she sat at my desk to brush her hair in front of a portable mirror. Ana had made us late for things like this before, but she agreed to come to this Easter service and I told Grandpa we would be there right on time.

"C'mon, we gotta go," I gently said, trying to hide my frustration. "We're gonna be late."

"We're going," Ana playfully asserted, putting on makeup. "Relax."

I had the massive urge to nag at her for this. Making us late! *Again!* The last time she did this was back in late February when we went to see Jason at the developmental center up in Palm Springs. But as I watched her put on makeup, I suddenly couldn't stay mad at her—she was too adorable!

When it looked like she was almost done, I got up and wrapped my arms around her from behind, giving her a kiss on the cheek. "Ready to head out?"

"Yeah." Ana put away her makeup and zipped up her purse. "You said the service starts at ten, right?"

I glanced up at the clock again. *Shit!* "It's almost ten now! It's going to take us at least twenty minutes to get there!"

"Oh shoot. Can't you text your grandpa letting him know we're on our way? I'm so sorry!"

"He doesn't always answer his texts but I can try." I said as I texted Grandpa letting him know we were running late.

We got in my car and began the drive over, engaging in light conversation. "Sorry if I rushed you this morning," I said.

Ana simply played on her phone, not saying anything.

"I'm just one of those people that hates to be late."

"You are never late for anything," Ana teased. "I bet a million dollars when you go get breakfast in the morning at that little sandwich place you love, you're there even before the employees are!"

I chuckled. "Whatever you say."

"You know I'm right!"

I shook my head as I felt my irritation from earlier slipping away for now.

Every pew in the small sanctuary of the church was filled with what seemed to be every member of the congregation by the time we arrived. Our casual wear made us stand out in a church filled with people wearing suits and dresses. Pastor Daryl was in the middle of a sermon, so we tried to keep quiet. We saw Grandpa, Mom, and Alicia all wearing dress clothes as well, in a pew close to the back. Grandpa smiled at us, Alicia ignored us, and Mom looked at me but was clearly trying to pretend Ana wasn't in the room.

"Sorry we're late," I whispered to them.

Mom put her fingers over her lips to remind us to be quiet during the service. "We can talk after the service."

We turned to watch the sermon. As it went on, my heart began to beat faster as the thought of us being a half hour late began to creep into my mind. I quickly glanced over at my family sitting behind me, wondering if they thought Ana and I were irresponsible for coming in right in the middle of an Easter service.

You told everyone you would be here on time and you let them all down, a voice in my head scolded. *Idiot!*

I looked over at Ana who had her hands in her lap, listening calmly to the sermon. My heart pounded as thoughts swirled around in my head, catching only glimpses here and there of what the pastor said. "We remember the resurrection of our lord and savior and reflect on the grief and mourning that preceded the light of that Sunday morning," the pastor espoused as I looked at Ana. "But even in times of darkness we can look forward with hope because we can trust God's promises . . ."

My palms shook. *Please don't think less of Ana,* I thought. Ana kept her hands in her lap as my thoughts piled on.

"As it says in Matthew 5:4, 'blessed are those who mourn, for they will be comforted,'" the pastor said as I dwelled on what happened this morning.

Why was it so hard for you to be somewhere on time? I thought, remembering times in the past year when Ana would take so long to get ready to go out to movies or go to other events. The one event I couldn't be late for and she took way longer than she should have. *You take so long to do so many things, and it's so irritating!*

"When we reflect on the promises God gave to those who love him," the pastor continued in the background at one point, "he promises he will give us peace, for it says in John 14:27 . . ."

I kept dwelling on how aggravating it was that Ana made us late, but then I suddenly remembered: this was her first time here! Was she nervous? Did this place make her uncomfortable? Was that one of the reasons why she made us late this morning? I tried to think of reasons for this, going through every possible awkward scenario in my head of how everyone in this room would treat us once the service was over. Ana didn't know these people. Did it matter if they said something?

I reflected on how Alicia and Mom had treated Ana in the past year. I thought about how indifferent Alicia acted towards her: she wouldn't really even talk to her. Did it really matter if Alicia said something? Then I remembered how Mom stopped trying to have a mother-daughter relationship with Ana months ago simply because Ana didn't really spend much time with her and kept quiet. Did it matter if Mom said something?

I put my hand onto Ana's, and she lightly squeezed mine back.

"And before Jesus was ever born, God declared his love for his people," the pastor exclaimed. "As it says in Jeremiah 31:3, 'Love yesterday, today, and forever.'"

As the sermon continued, I thought about how Grandpa treated Ana in the six months since she first came over to meet him. She would only visit him with me on certain occasions, but they always got along so well and Grandpa always made her smile and laugh with his stories. When I would visit Grandpa by myself, he would always enthusiastically ask me how Ana was doing.

As Ana rested her head on my shoulder, I smiled and stopped caring that we were late to this service. What mattered was she was here with me.

We were the last ones to arrive at Grandpa's house after the service. I had to get gas on the way, and Ana wanted to return a DVD we watched last night at the nearest Redbox. When we got to the house, Mom and Alicia were already in the kitchen prepping the

Easter lunch while Grandpa read a magazine in the living room. Mom made a sardonic comment about us arriving late, something I tried to brush off as I offered to help with lunch prep. Neither Mom nor Alicia needed our help, so Ana and I went into the living to visit with Grandpa.

Sometime later, I went up to go to the kitchen to talk to Mom about this month's rent. Mom was making potato salad when Alicia said she had to get something from the store real quick and would be right back. After Alicia went out the door, I let Mom know I was going to be a day late with rent since I hadn't gotten paid from either of my jobs yet.

"I'm not worried about the rent, but I *really* want to talk to you," Mom said without even looking at me.

"Look, if it's about us being late this morning, that's completely my fault."

Mom looked up and prompted me to come closer so we were out of earshot for Ana and Grandpa. "I'm not concerned about that," Mom whispered. "I'm concerned about *her*," She said with a grunt as she pointed to the direction of the living room.

I could hear Ana laughing at one of Grandpa's jokes as it took me a moment to respond. "What are you talking about?"

Mom cleared her throat. "Last night, your girlfriend came over and she didn't even say hello. She just walks right past me."

"What are you talking about?" I angrily whispered. "You were on the phone with your friend. In the kitchen!"

"But this is not the first time she does this. Why wouldn't she go out of her way to talk to me or even say hello? Does she not like me or something?"

I put my hand over my face as Mom began to go on a short rant about how terrible Ana supposedly was, all for the times Ana would come over on weekends and not talk to her much. "Mom, stop!" I asserted.

"Stop what?"

I sighed. "Look. She's introverted. That's how she is. You can't expect everyone to be like you, and you were on the phone!"

"Well, she can make an effort to get to know me or something."

"What have *you* done to get to know her?"

No response. She just looked pissed off.

"Please, just do me a favor. Can you at least try to get along with her and not talk so much crap about her? Please! Do it for me!"

"Fine," Mom muttered as she went back to stirring the potato salad. "Whatever!"

I sighed again. "I'll get you your money tomorrow," I said before going back into the living room.

I sat next to Ana while Grandpa was in the middle of another one of his stories.

"So Mrs. Sutton was the one who handled all the accounting at that time?" Ana asked.

"Wait, what are we talking about?" I asked.

"I was telling Ana here about all these tiling jobs I had to do in the 1950s, and if it weren't for your grandma, I wouldn't have not been able to get my contracting business off the ground," Grandpa said. He took a breath and lay back deeper into his chair, closing his eyes momentarily. Neither I nor Ana said anything as Grandpa sighed, reached to his end table to take his blood pressure medication and washed it down with a sip from his water bottle. "Anyway, when grandma handled all the accounting, I was able to find out many people I hired had tried to financially screw me over, so I fired their asses."

Ana giggled.

"Grandma definitely knew what she was doing," I said.

"You bet like hell she did," Grandpa said.

"Lunch is ready!" Mom shouted from the kitchen. "Once Alicia gets back with the rolls, we can eat."

"Excellent!" Grandpa exclaimed.

I lay back on the sofa as Grandpa and Ana shared stories and laughed, relieved to see Grandpa really seemed to enjoy his time with her.

We all sat around the kitchen table, Grandpa having just finished the prayer and Alicia put rolls on our plates. I sat next to Ana, checking in on her to make sure she was comfortable and getting whatever food she wanted. Ana and I mostly kept to ourselves as everyone else engaged in chit chat about random topics. At one point, Alicia asked why Aunt Judy and Uncle Bill weren't able to come down for Easter. Grandpa mentioned they had to stay home in Seattle so Uncle Bill could recover from eye surgery.

As Ana made herself a small plate of salad, Mom raised the plate full of ham from across the table to Ana asking her if she wanted any. Ana politely declined.

"You don't want any ham?" Mom asked, the look on her face telling me she was offended.

"Mom, I told you beforehand she doesn't like ham," I whispered.

"What kind of person doesn't like ham?" Mom bluntly asked.

"Hey, don't be rude!" Alicia blurted out before asking Ana more kindly if she would like some ham.

Ana politely shook her head no. "I'm good, but thank you," she said.

"See," Alicia said. "If she doesn't want ham, she doesn't have to have ham."

I rubbed my eyes before I checked in on Ana, who didn't seem fazed by any of this.

"Well, I don't want to argue," Mom continued.

I made an exasperated sigh as everyone around the table kept putting more food on their plates. Thoughts of where Ana and I could go popped into my mind, making me wish I was anywhere but here. The conversation at the lunch table continued as Ana and I kept to ourselves and ate.

"Guess what?" Alicia said at one point. "You remember that music teaching gig I had an interview for? I got the job!"

"That's fantastic!" Grandpa exclaimed.

"I start next week."

"That is awesome," Mom said. "That means you can finally start paying rent, unless you really do need that money to move out or something."

Oh shit, I thought. *Not again!*

"What the hell, Mom?" Alicia asked. "Why do you always have to be *this* passive aggressive?"

"Alicia, I'm just saying that now that you have this new job, you can finally start paying rent," Mom said.

"Mom, stop!" Alicia asserted. "We already talked about this! Money is tight! I told you I would start paying rent once I get a stable job!"

Mom ignored Alicia as she turned to Ana. "Ana, you work with money, right? Do you think Alicia should pay rent?"

Ana leaned back and looked at me, clearly having no idea what to say.

"Mom, what are you doing?" I asked.

"Stop it!" Alicia asserted. "I just found this job! Why do you always have to be like this?"

Mom and Alicia bickered as I had no choice but to shut my mouth. Grandpa tried to get them both to stop, my palms shaking and my heart pounding as Mom and Alicia kept fighting.

Finally, Alicia got up. "I'm sorry, but I can't deal with this," she said before grabbing her jacket and storming out of the house.

I sighed. None of us said anything.

"I'm so sorry about my daughter," Mom said to Grandpa.

"I don't understand why you don't have the backbone to just evict her," he said. "Make her find another place to live."

"I don't understand why she has to be so difficult," Mom said. "I worry if I kick her out, I'll never see her again."

"I understand."

"I've lost my appetite," Mom said. "I need to go lay down. My anxiety is acting up again real bad."

"It'll be okay, Ruth," Grandpa said. "Go lay down. Me and Rob will clean up."

Mom got up and left the room. Grandpa turned to both of us. "I'm so sorry you had to see that," he said to Ana.

"It's okay," Ana said. "I've seen my sister fight with our mom like that before, so I understand."

Grandpa sighed. "Rob, you listen here. Your mom has been through a lot in her life. You have to be patient with her, and I know she can be a real pain in the ass sometimes, but you must be patient with her. Understood?"

I nodded.

"And I'm sorry again you had to see that," Grandpa said to Ana. "You handled that really well. I commend you for that. Rob is incredibly lucky to have you."

I closed my eyes as I struggled to calm my nerves.

"I'll be right back," Grandpa said. "Need to get some paper towels so we can clean up."

Grandpa got up to get an extra roll of paper towels from the garage. I took some deep breaths, desperately trying to stop my heart from beating so fast. *Don't be surprised if Ana hates you for having such a dysfunctional family*, a voice in my head shouted.

As I tried to calm myself down, I felt Ana hold my hand. I opened my eyes and looked at her, apologizing multiple times she had to see that.

"It's okay," she whispered. "It's not your fault."

I couldn't help but look at her. She was still here, smiling at me.

11

———

April 12, 2018

I finished doing my food delivery jobs for the day when Ben called to ask if I wanted to come down and do karaoke with Nathan, Trent, Alex, and Alex's girlfriend, Lydia. I didn't have to go tutor the next morning, so I agreed to come. I got to the bowling alley at around 7 pm and headed to the lounge to meet up with them. Thankfully, it was not jam packed full of people this time. Trent stood on stage singing Fleetwood Mac's "Landslide" while everyone else was at one of the tables drinking beers and talking.

"So what exactly is a, quote unquote, 'neurotypical?'" Alex asked Ben. "I don't understand what that is."

"A neurotypical is exactly what it's supposed to describe," Ben said. "It's someone who has a typical neurology."

"I *still* don't understand what that means," Alex said.

Everyone stopped their conversation and greeted me when I got to the table.

Ben took a sip of his beer and then looked up at me when I asked what they were talking about. "I was just explaining to Alex and Lydia here what neurodiversity is," Ben said before turning back to Alex. "What I'm saying is that if you're not autistic or you don't have other neurological differences that are outside of what society considers 'normal,' quote unquote, you are 'neurotypical.' Get it now?"

"Oh okay, that makes sense now," Alex said.

"So me, Nathan, Trent, and Rob here are all autistic, so that makes us *not* neurotypical!"

"Look," Alex said. "I won't lie: I never would have known any of you were autistic if you never told me. None of you guys look autistic to me."

Ben mockingly gasped at Alex.

Oh shit, I thought. *Another one of Ben's rants is coming!*

"Alexander Richard Flahive!" Ben exclaimed. "You, of all people, should know better than to say that! 'None of you guys look autistic to me!' Well, you don't look Mexican to me, white boy! Does that mean you're not Mexican?"

I could do nothing but sit there and facepalm. Nathan couldn't stop laughing.

"Alright, alright. Point taken," Alex said.

Ben drank another sip of his beer. "In today's society, if someone is autistic, is disabled, or is just not neurotypical, we get two extremes: we get the sappy, gooey, and disgusting inspiration porn that's clearly about how that random girl with 'special needs'—by the way, before I go any further, can we all agree the term 'special needs' is bullshit?"

"What's wrong with the term 'special needs'?" Lydia asked.

"'Special needs,' quote unquote, is a word designed to avoid calling what we are: Autistic! Disabled! *Neurodivergent*! But neurotypicals see all of that as bad, so they have to say we have 'special needs' instead, quote unquote!'"

I rolled my eyes at Ben's weird obsession with repeating that phrase. *We get the point already you idiot,* I thought. I began tuning out another one of his annoying rants as I just browsed Facebook, scrolling through my feed before checking to see what people were posting in the Authentic Philosophy Facebook group. I engaged in a thread within the group as Ben and Alex went back and forth, with Nathan backing Ben on everything.

"Take Rob here for example," Ben said at one point, immediately catching my attention. "He was told by all the teachers and all the school administrators at Schweitzer that he has 'average intelligence' and 'below average academic ability,' and he couldn't handle college. Now look at him! He has his Masters *and* he's a college teacher! That's amazeballs!"

"I'm just tutoring right now, not teaching until next semester," I quickly corrected him. "Look. Can we not talk about that place? I've had a long day. I just want to have a few drinks and do some karaoke, and that's the last thing I want to think about. Okay?"

"Suit yourself," Ben said. "But you really should be proud that you've proved those fuckers wrong!"

Ben's rant came to an end as soon as Trent finished his song and came back to our table.

"So Rob, how are you and Ana doing?" Lydia asked.

"We're doing good," I said. "We got plans to go row boating at Lake Murray on Sunday. She's never been. I'm excited to take her."

"She should come to karaoke sometime," Lydia said. "We would love to meet her!"

"Well, I've been trying to get her to come to karaoke for some time, but she works full-time during the week and the only times I can really see her are on weekends usually."

"Did you ever show us a picture of her?" Nathan asked.

"I thought I did, but let me show you," I said, pulling up a picture of Ana on my phone and showed up for everyone at the table to see.

"She's a cutie," Trent said.

"I know right!" I said ecstatically.

"She is beautiful," Lydia said.

"She really is, dude," Alex said.

"Duh! I could've told you that," I joked.

Everyone laughed and then engaged in conversation again as I went to put my name in the queue for karaoke. Alex and Lydia got called to go up on stage to do a duet when I got back to the table. As they prepared to sing Marvin Gaye and Tammi Terrell's "Ain't No

Mountain High Enough," I sat back to watch, suddenly receiving a funny meme from Ana via text, giggling as I sent funny memes back.

"I haven't seen you this happy in years, Rob," Ben said.

As Alex and Lydia performed on stage and Ben conversed with Nathan and Trent, I went back on my phone to participate in the Facebook thread I was in earlier.

After a while, I got so entranced in the debate thread I tuned out everything around me.

"Sharing love memes with Ana again, Rob?" Ben jokingly asked at one point. Nathan and Trent chuckled.

I stopped engaging the thread. "Oh no, I was just having a back and forth with some people in this Facebook group."

"About what?" Ben asked.

"Someone made a post about *March for Our Lives* and what started off as a simple discussion about gun control had turned into a drawn out debate."

"Isn't that just Facebook in general?" Ben asked, obviously trying hard to suppress laughter.

"Facebook just sucks," Trent said, making Ben laugh.

"Hold on a minute," I insisted. "This one is different."

"How is it different?" Ben asked when he stopped laughing. "Sounds like needless drama to me!"

"Here, let me show you," I said. I then held out my phone and showed them around the group itself. "The group itself is called Authentic Philosophy."

"Authentic Philosophy?" Nathan asked. "Don't you think that's a weird name for a group? I mean, what makes 'authentic philosophy' different from regular philosophy?"

"It's more of an inside joke than anything else." I then scrolled through the group's feed, showing them all the different threads, ranging from posts about absurdism versus nihilism to debates about free will over determinism. There were also random members venting about personal issues. "It's a small group because most of us have been friends online for years now, but we debate different issues and share stories about what goes on in our lives," I said as I handed Ben my phone to let him read the thread.

Ben held up my phone so Nathan and Trent could see the thread. As they read through it, the expression on Ben's face changed from skepticism to concern. "Are you sure these people are your friends, Rob?"

"What do you mean?"

Ben held up the phone higher so he could show me what he was referring to. "I mean, look. The guy who started this thread raised a valid question, and I see so many of these people dogpiling him rather than engage in discussion, for no good reason." He then pointed to a series of comments from someone whose profile picture had him wearing a casual buttoned shirt and a brown beanie and glasses. "This guy right here is doing most of it."

"Oh that's Vincent Smith," I said. "He just gets passionate, but in Google Hangouts, he's super nice."

"Are you close friends?"

"Not really. He's just some guy I know on the internet, but he does post stuff you might like, Ben."

"I don't know, man. Something about this group just rubs me the wrong way." Ben then handed me my phone back. "I would just be careful. That's all I'll say."

Just then, Alex and Lydia finished their song and came back to the table.

"Our next performer is Ben Tierney!" The DJ announced.

"Now if you excuse me. I got some singing to do!" Ben exclaimed before he hustled to the stage. I thought for a moment about what he said about the group before I brushed it off so I could enjoy the rest of my evening. I drank some more beer and engaged in conversation again with the rest of my friends as Ben sang Iron Maiden's "Wasted Years," the music echoed around the room until it faded into background noise.

12

———————

April 13, 2018

I got into my car after dropping off a food delivery.

I put my phone back onto my dash mount and checked to see if there were more orders. I'd been doing deliveries since early afternoon so I could stay on top of my bills; the aroma of pizza and burgers filled my whole car. I also wanted to make a little extra to take Ana out for dinner Sunday night.

I checked to see I had three more hours to go before my GrubHub shifts were supposed to end. I rubbed my eyes—what a long day. I just wanted to go home and sleep, but I was determined to stick it out. It was only three more hours! I wasn't getting any orders though, so I started my car to head to another area.

Just when I was about to drive away, Ana sent me a text.

ANA:

> Hey there. Are you free tonight? Do you want to hang out?

I stared at my phone, ignoring an order notification popup. I debated whether to keep doing deliveries and have Ana come over tomorrow like we originally planned or have her come over at such a last minute notice. *If you're ever just busy, don't feel like you have to stop whatever you are doing just to hang out,* I remembered her saying a few weeks ago.

I struggled to figure out what to say. Do I tell her I'm busy and hold off on seeing her until tomorrow? I didn't want to disrupt my routine; I needed the extra money.

Or do I say I'm free so she could come over, and I could hold her in my arms again? The thought of us cuddling filled me with joy. I wanted to feel her embrace and give her tons of kisses. I wanted to watch movies with her and talk about each other's work stories.

ROB:

I'm free tonight. I'm just doing a quick errand, but I'll be home in about fifteen minutes.

I canceled the rest of my shift and rushed home.

April 15, 2018

We rode out to the middle of the lake in a rowboat we rented for the afternoon, a light breeze keeping us cool as the warm sun shone directly above us in a cloudless sky. I took charge of paddling while Ana sat across from me. Several other people rode around on the lake in motorboats and kayaks while small groups went fishing on the pier.

"You wanna hear a joke?" I asked.

"Is it going to be one your dad jokes again?" Ana playfully asked.

"No no. It's not going to be one of my 'dad jokes.' I promise."

"Fine. What's your joke?"

"Here it goes." I cleared my throat. "Why did the football coach go to the bank? To get his quarter back!"

Ana smiled, shaking her head.

"Get it? *Quarter! Back!*"

Ana shook her head again. "You think you're soooooo funny! Do you tell these jokes to every girl you date?"

"Nah, just you," I said with a huge grin.

Ana let out a chuckle. "So I'm the lucky one who gets *all* your corny jokes?"

I bursted out laughing as Ana took a sip of her water. We had been hanging out since Friday night, having spent the entire day together yesterday on a day she would normally work. We watched movies and cuddled, with more rounds of sex than usual, before heading downtown to this new Brazilian steakhouse. I stopped rowing to take in the scenery, birds flying high over us and the boat slightly rocking back and forth. I smiled at Ana as she held her phone out in my direction to take my picture.

We sat back in the boat and enjoyed the view of the water surrounding us.

"My dad used to take me to this lake when I was a little kid," I said at one point. "He would take all three of us: me, Jason, Alicia. Mom would get worried about us getting sunburned, but he always made sure we had sunscreen."

"Wait, there was a time you *actually* wore sunscreen?" Ana teased.

"Wow! Ruining an intense, emotional moment simply for not wearing sunscreen today," I teased back.

"If your dad made you wear sunscreen when you were a kid, then surely you can wear sunscreen now Mr. 'I Don't Need Sunscreen'! But hey, if you want to be burned alive by the sun, that's your choice."

I noticed the sun got brighter, and I sweated more. "Alright, fine! I'll take some sunscreen."

Ana reached into her purse, grabbed the sunscreen, and poured some in my hand, so I could apply sunscreen to my arms and face.

"Anyway, what I was saying before I was *rudely* interrupted . . ." I jokingly said as Ana giggled.

I took a moment to gather my thoughts. "When we would come down here, we would all come here to fish or ride kayaks or swim in the lake."

"This seems like a fun place to visit as a kid."

"Yeah." I smiled. "I remember when Alicia and I used to have swimming contests at this lake, and even though Alicia was a *way* better swimmer than I was, she would let me win sometimes."

"I would've never guessed that based on how you two are often at each other's throats now."

I looked out across the water, letting out a sigh. "Me and her didn't always fight as kids," I said. "I mean, it's not like we don't have any good memories at all. When she used to have sleepovers, she would let me play with her friends and play board games with them. She even used to let me watch movies with her on movie nights during those sleepovers. I remember one time when we came here, we built a playhouse out of boxes. That was so much fun."

I sighed again as Ana took a sip of her water.

"But after finding Dad's body the night he died... she . . . How do I say this? . . . She stopped being as caring to me as she used to."

Ana's eyes widened. "Oh my god! That's awful!"

"Yeah," I mumbled, taking another moment to gather my thoughts. "Ever since then, she slowly stopped hanging out with me as much, and then me and her slowly kind've just . . . drifted apart. Lots of fighting over the years since. Maybe someday we could go back to the type of relationship we used to have, but I'm not counting on that."

"Still, that's awful," Ana said. "I feel bad for her."

I said nothing in response.

"Would you all still come down here after he died?" Ana asked.

"After dad died, Grandpa would take us here a few times, but it was never the same."

"Why do you say that?"

I shrugged. "I love my grandpa, don't get me wrong, but he's not my dad. He's just . . . my grandpa. That's how I always viewed him. My mom always tried to have me get Grandpa a Father's Day card, but I just couldn't do it. He's not my dad. I always viewed Father's Day as strictly for dads, and Grandpa is my mom's dad, not my dad."

Ana gave a small but acknowledging smile. "He's always been there for you, at least."

"I guess."

We looked out to the water again as a group of people rode their motorboat past us.

"Are your grandparents still around?" I asked.

"My grandparents on my dad's side still live in China while my grandma on my Mom's side lives in a nursing home in San Francisco."

"What about your grandpa on your mom's side?"

"He passed away when I was a baby, so I never got to know him."

"I'm sorry to hear that."

"It's okay. Like I said, I was a baby, so I never got to know him."

"Were you at least close to your grandma?"

Ana took another sip of water. "Not really. I mean, we got along, and I care about her, of course, but I wouldn't say we have the same relationship as you do with your grandpa."

"Did she just send you presents on your birthday or something?"

"Mostly phone calls. Sometimes she'll send a card."

"But not really presents? Not even a toy here and there?"

"I didn't have toys growing up."

I tilted my head when she said this. "Oh really? No toys at all?"

"No, not really."

"Any particular reason?"

"I just didn't. Mom never got me a toy, and dad definitely never gave me a toy. I just never had toys growing up."

I guess some people never grew up with toys, I thought.

"I never feel like I missed out on toys," Ana continued. "I had to watch Mary a lot since I was the older sister in charge."

"Well, surely you had some breaks from taking care of Mary, she's your sister, not your kid."

Ana just shrugged, looking out at the water as if she didn't want to answer.

We let the boat drift along the water, taking in the scenery once again.

"You said you were born in San Francisco, right?" I asked at one point.

Ana nodded. "That's right."

"Do you see yourself ever going back there?"

"Who knows. It's so expensive there right now. Way more than when I was a kid."

"It must've been so nice to have grown up next to the water," I said. "You probably got to go swimming so much!"

"Oh. I don't know how to swim."

My eyes widened in disbelief. "Wait! You don't know how to swim?"

"Nope."

I gasped. "You seriously don't know how to swim?"

Ana shook her head. "Never learned."

I sat back, my mouth wide open in playful disbelief. "Everyone should know how to swim! I can teach you how to swim!"

"Nah, it's okay. You don't have to."

I reached out and held Ana's hand. "But I want to! We have a swimming pool in my backyard. We don't even have to go to a public pool. We don't have to do it today, but next weekend you can come over, and I can teach you how to swim. What do you say? Will you let me teach you how to swim? Pleeeeeeeease!"

I gave Ana a massive puppy dog look.

"Oh alright," Ana finally said. "We can do it next weekend."

I pumped my fist in excitement, shouting "Yes!" as I did so.

"If I drown though, my ghost will come after you and kick your ass!"

I laughed as I snuck in a few photos of her with my phone while Ana gave me another huge smile.

April 22, 2018

The sun was shining on both of us as we stood in front the shallow end of the swimming pool. I only wore swim trunks while

Ana had on one of my black Marvel T-shirts I let her borrow since she forgot to bring her swimsuit. It was just us in my backyard that afternoon, no one around to bother us as I got more and more excited to teach her how to swim.

I stepped into the water on top of the pool step.

"Mmmmm, this feels so nice," I said. I then looked at Ana behind me. "You should come in. You'll love it!"

Ana just stood there, her hands behind her back. "It looks cold."

I smiled. "Nonsense," I playfully said. "The water is great. I'll prove it to you."

I jumped headfirst into the water, swimming like a triathlon athlete towards the other side of the pool before swimming back. I then dove underneath and did an underwater somersault before popping my head back up, making sure to rub water off my face. "See!" I exclaimed. "The water is amazing!"

Ana shook her head. "How are you not cold?"

"The water's not cold. I promise."

I swam back to the pool step and climbed back to the top step to reach my hand out. Ana stood there shaking her head.

"It's going to be okay," I assured her. "You can do this."

Ana stood there for a minute catching her breath before stepping into the water. "Oh my god! It is cold!" she shouted, shivering and vigorously rubbing her hands together. "You liar! You said it wasn't cold!"

I chuckled as Ana grabbed onto my hand. "It's okay, it's okay," I quickly assured. "Take a minute to adjust."

"How are you not cold?" Ana asked.

"It's okay," I assured her again. "Give yourself a minute to get used to the water."

Ana took a breath as she slowly stopped shivering. I patiently led her step by step into the pool, allowing her time to fully immerse herself into the water up to her shoulders. She wrapped her arms around me as we stood up within the shallow end.

"I can't believe you talked me into this," Ana said.

"I promise you it's going to be okay," I said. I gave Ana a minute to get used to water. "How are you feeling?"

Ana looked up at me. "Feeling good," she said with a smile. "Kind of scared though."

"It's okay to be scared. Don't worry. You got this!" We took another minute. I looked out to the other side of the pool, making a mental note of what areas of the water to bring Ana to and what areas to avoid. "You ready?" I asked.

Ana nodded. I let go of her, and I floated my body up closer to the surface of the water. "So when you are swimming, you have to be mindful of where you are holding up your body weight," I said. "See how I'm floating up like this?"

"Yes."

"That's because I'm making sure to keep myself up while lying on my chest, relaxing my body as needed. I then paddle with my hands and feet. Follow my lead, and I'll show you a simple swimming technique that even you can do. Ready?"

"Ready!"

I extended my right arm forward with my hand facing down along the surface of the water. "You wanna take your arm out and then move like this," I said as I moved one hand over the other to do a dog paddle.

Ana followed my lead. "So like this?" she asked as swung her arm over and pushed down on the water as she tried to move forward. She did a dog paddle for a moment before she lost her balance, letting out a yelp as her head fell halfway under the water.

I grabbed onto her torso so she could keep her entire head above water. "It's okay! I got you!" I exclaimed as Ana immediately wrapped her arms around my neck.

"I swear to God if I drown, my ghost will come and kick your ass!" Ana exclaimed before she let out a big laugh.

I chuckled. "You have to allow your body to float with the water, Ana," I said.

"I was allowing my body to float with the water!" Ana insisted.

I chuckled again before I kissed Ana on the forehead. "Let's try this then: I'll hold on to you as you swim. Once you feel like you are able to float, let me know and I can let you go. You wanna try that?"

"Only if we stay out of the deep end."

"You got it!"

Ana took her arms from around my neck and went back to the swimming position she was in before. I guided Ana around the shallow end as she did a dog paddle, making sure to hold her up by the torso as we swam around the pool. "Make sure to kick your feet as well," I said at one point.

We did a few laps around the pool before I checked to see if she was ready to swim without me holding her up. "You got this?" I asked.

"I got this!" Ana asserted.

I let Ana go so she could swim without my help. "I'm actually swimming!" She shouted as she triumphantly swam on her own for a few feet. She swam from one end of the shallow end to the other, kicking herself up from the floor of the pool as she did so as needed.

She got close to the center of the pool and lost her balance again, her head dipping halfway through the surface of the water once more. I grabbed on to her to help her regain her balance as she wrapped her arms around my neck like she did earlier. "You okay?"

"I'm okay," she insisted.

By this point, we both had our arms around each other, gazing into each other's eyes.

"You're doing great," I affectionately said. "You just have to keep practicing. That's all." As we held each other in our arms, I couldn't help but admire her warm, radiant smile. "I'm glad you're here."

"I'm glad you're here, too," she said back.

I placed my hand on her cheek. We drifted a little towards the middle of the pool, embracing each other as we kissed.

13

April 28, 2018

Ana got off work early so we could spend the evening together.

We planned to check out the Hillcrest Farmers Market in the morning before going to see *Avengers: Infinity War*, having bought advance tickets weeks ago. We hung out in the front living room, sitting across from each other as I showed her songs I could play on my guitar. "Let me play you this one song from Don McLean I've been practicing for the past couple weeks. It's called 'And I Love You So.'"

I picked the capo off the coffee table and clamped it over the second fret, double checking that the strings were still in tune. I strummed lightly, plucking at the strings to begin the song. I did it smoothly before messing up one of the bar chords and stopped.

"Sorry about that," I said before picking back up.

I played the rest of the song before ending with a long strum.

"That was good," Ana said.

"Thank you."

"Surprised you didn't sing any of the vocals. Have you thought about singing? You and your sister can sing together!"

I playfully shook my head.

Mom came into the room before I could play another song.

"Okay Rob," she said. "I'm going to Grandpa's. Watch the house while I'm gone." She unenthusiastically said "Hi" to Ana as she got to the front door.

"Will do," I responded, equally unenthusiastically. I was about to turn back to Ana when my phone started buzzing. I looked at the Caller ID and instantly recognized it. "Mom, Jason's calling again! Can you please call him back when you get the chance?"

Mom rolled her eyes. "I'll call him tomorrow. I'm not up to talking to him right now." Mom then opened the front door. "I'll see you later, Rob. Love you," she said before she went outside and locked the door.

Ana got up and sat next to me. "Why don't you call your brother back?"

I sighed. "I never really know what to say to him. Besides, he only bombards me with phone calls when he can't get a hold of Mom." I gave a frustrated shrug and plucked one of my guitar strings. "I mean, you met him. You know what he's like. He literally has the mind of a 7-year-old."

Ana nodded.

I had taken her to see Jason at the Developmental Center in Palm Springs in late February after she expressed interest in meeting him. We brought him Panda Express for lunch and spent time with him during visiting hours, playing board games suitable for toddlers and watching *Blue's Clues*.

"You probably got less phone calls from him when he was living here," Ana joked.

"Well, he did have this weird obsession with calling random phone numbers all the time when we were growing up."

"What do you mean?"

I sighed. "Every day he would spend hours on the phone calling every number he could find, just so he could talk to random strangers."

"What would he want to talk to them about?"

"Anything!" I exclaimed. "To Jason, the phone was a toy. If there was a phone, he would just call someone. He used to collect newspapers or copies of phone books everywhere he went in case he came across a phone he could call. Mom found it cute at first, but then it got to the point where he got so obsessive she would limit how long he could be on the phone. I'll give you an example: you know the tree stump next to our front lawn?"

"Yeah."

"Well, there was this one time Jason called a tree-cutting company all because he just wanted to call and talk to someone, and the next thing we know, someone came down and chopped down our tree. When Mom came home, she went ballistic. She was so pissed!"

Ana laughed. "Wow! That's crazy."

I laughed as well. "It's funny now, hindsight 20/20, but at the time, I never saw Mom so pissed off."

"I don't blame her. I would've been pissed too."

"The guy felt so bad for her that he decided to not charge her. And the funniest part is when Mom asked Jason why he had someone chop down our tree, he just said he wanted an orange tree."

"No way!"

"Yes way! My brother wanted an orange tree so he thought calling someone would just magically get him an orange tree!"

Ana chuckled. "That definitely sounds like something a little kid would do."

"Yeah, and it happened around the time I worked my ass off getting out of that hellhole."

I suddenly stopped myself. I stared into space, taking a breath and closing my eyes, harshly plucking a few guitar strings.

"You okay?" Ana asked.

I took a sip of water from a bottle on the coffee table and then closed my eyes. "I'm okay."

"Are you sure?" Ana asked again.

I didn't respond. I stared into darkness, thoughts racing through my head. The memory of coming home to Mom screaming hysterically at Jason played before it morphed into me sitting in a cold office as I faced a much older red haired woman behind a desk covered in stacks of paperwork giving me a lengthy finger-wag, random flashes of teachers at Schweitzer talking down to me like I was a child.

My shoulders tensed up. "I had another nightmare last night."

Ana looked at me expectantly, waiting for me to continue while she rubbed my shoulder. I quickly glanced at her, but I could still see kindness and patience in them. It suddenly clicked that Ana was listening to what I had to say.

I put my guitar to the side as the muscles in my shoulders began to relax. "I dreamt I was back at that place again."

"What place?"

"The place I went to high school growing up. I dreamt I was reliving that experience all over again." I sighed. "Do you recall when we went to the Asian American Expo, and I asked you about what high school was like for you?"

Ana took a moment to think before perking up. "Oh yeah, I remember. Why do you ask?"

I took another breath. "I won't lie. When you told me all that, I remember being a little jealous. Your experience sounded so much better than mine. I wish I had even an iota of the experience you had. I hated high school so much. I hated it so fucking bad that after I got my Master's last year, I dusted off my my high school diploma and ripped it up. Tore it to shreds! Stomped the pieces on the ground and threw them in the trash."

Ana kept listening, her eyes widening in surprise.

"It was that bad." I took another sip of water, gathering my thoughts. "I never told you this, but when I was three years old, I was put in Special Ed." I shuttered as I thought how gross those words made me feel. "We moved down here from Oregon in the early 90s so we could be closer to my grandparents, but there was no public school here that would take Jason. Long story short, Mom found this place designed for really mentally disabled people like my brother, but it was also for those who are 'high functioning,' so I ended up going there too."

"How did you end up going there?"

"Both me and Jason were non-verbal—Jason probably way more so—so the school had me assessed. They diagnosed me with Asperger's. I know today they would just call it autism, but they also diagnosed me with specific learning disabilities—whatever that means. That's how I got an IEP. That's how I went to this place my entire childhood. I thought I would eventually go to a regular school and never come back, but that all changed when Dad died."

I stopped and gazed out the window, gathering my thoughts again.

"After Dad died, Mom was left to take care of us all by herself. A single mom of three kids. Because of the way Jason is, she focused so much of her time and energy on him, it just seemed like I was left to fend for myself. I would go to school and deal with kids with severe medical and behavior issues. Some would throw tantrums and hit walls. Others would have seizures in the middle of class. I would see this and then come home to Jason doing the exact same thing. And this would happen almost every day. Every day! I've lost count of the amount of times I had to deal with this. It got so exhausting!"

I lay back, exasperated. The memories washed over me, causing me to sink lower into the couch. Ana moved closer and rubbed my shoulder.

I took another deep breath and continued. "I was hoping that I would finally go to a normal school and feel like a normal kid, like in so many TV shows and movies. Alicia got to do that. She got to go to a normal school and have a life I never had. I begged my mom many times to take me out of that place and let me go, but she kept saying no. When I finally started high school in 2003, Mom finally relented and put me in a regular, public high school. When I got there, I couldn't get away from the gangs who just made fun of me and tried to beat the shit out of me, and all the teachers who would make me feel dumb. I couldn't take it so I would just ditch all the time, just so I could get away from all of them."

I stopped for a moment as I choked up a little. Ana held my hand.

"After a few months, they pulled me aside and the next thing I know I'm back at that place. I didn't want to be there, but after what happened, it didn't seem like I had a choice. It was a place students would go to when no other school would take them."

"What did your mom say about all this?" Ana asked.

"Like so many parents, Mom looked to the program director of the school for guidance. Her name was Maggie. Maggie Richardson. If you took a less funny, watered down, more passive aggressive version of the Trunchbull from *Matilda*, that's how my friends and I saw Maggie. Mom just accepted, without question, any course of action she recommended."

"I see."

"Not like it mattered anyway. Mom didn't play much of a role in my IEP meetings other than follow along with everything they said since I wasn't as 'disabled' as Jason. Not like she had all the time in the world anyway, but I just stopped caring. I mean, what was the point? It's not like they saw potential in me anyway."

"Why do you say that?"

"For a long time, they saw me in the shadow of my brother. It didn't matter Mom had already taken him out of that school by the time I came back. To them, I was just 'Jason's younger brother Rob.' When the public school placement didn't work out, they made it seem like they were rubbing it in my face that I didn't belong anywhere else. I was a kid with quote unquote 'learning disabilities,' and I had no other place to go."

I cleared my throat, reflecting as Ana listened.

"The school just became a place I would go to during the day. I wouldn't have to deal with my sister yelling at me or my brother throwing another tantrum or my mom guilt tripping me to do things for her, but it also meant I would be dealing with the same shit over and over again. This time, though, it became much more noticeable just how so many of the teachers would talk down to us. Some of them even treated us like babies. Some of them even spoke to us in a cutesy little baby-talk voice whenever they would 'catch us being good.'" I made a crocodile hand gesture and chomped my fingers together to imitate babbling. "'Great job saying *thank you* to your classmate after they returned your pencil,'" I said in a mocking tone. "Little things like that. Praise for the most basic common courtesy. The most mundane shit. On a regular basis."

I stopped. I leaned back up, rubbing my eyes. *On a regular basis,* I thought, the words ringing in my head. I suddenly remembered all at once every teacher who either talked down to me as if I was a child or gave me the silent treatment. My heart pounded, forcing me to take a few deep breaths to calm my nerves. I thought about stopping, but then I looked over at Ana again.

"Much of what happened for the next few years feels like a blur to me now, but I will never forget how they gave a young kid like me with terrible social skills false expectations on how to prepare for the 'real world.' They never really sat me down and told me what I needed to do to finish school. I felt I wasn't learning anything I couldn't learn from the internet or from books or watching movies or playing video games. The teachers didn't teach me or give me guidance. Maggie didn't care. I was a fifteen year old kid who didn't think my life would amount to anything!"

I paused while Ana squeezed my hand and looked up at me. Even though I was still in the room with her, *I found myself on stage.*

As I stared out at the audience, I started talking to Ana again. "One day, that all changed when I get a letter in the mail. It was an invitation for me to study abroad. I still to this day don't know who nominated me to go in the first place. I showed my mom the letter and she asked my grandpa to take me to the informational meeting about it. My grandpa was so impressed by it since he and my grandma traveled the world and recognized immediately it would be worth the money to have me go. Mom wanted to make up for not always being there for me since Jason took up so much of her time after dad died."

On stage, I looked to my left and saw Kelly, standing next to me and smiling at me as she held my hand.

"When I went to the other side of the world," I said to Ana, "I thought I would just see cool sites, take pictures, and go home. That's it. Instead, I spent time with kids the same age as me who treated me like I was one of them."

On stage, I held Kelly's hand back, only for her name to be called by someone standing next to the exit stairs near stage left. Kelly let go of my hand and walked towards them. I proceeded to follow her but then felt something heavy around my feet, stopping me from moving further. I saw a heavy metallic band appear around my ankle and secured with a shackle, connected to a long metal chain nailed to the center of the stage. I attempted to pull away but couldn't move. "Kelly, come back!" I screamed out as she looked at me one last time, walked down the exit stairs, and disappeared into the darkness.

Back in the room, I looked at Ana again, taking a breather. "Those kids told me I had value. They told me that I was smart and funny. They told me I had the best smile and the best laugh. They told me that I had a bright future ahead of me. I was so ready to branch out into the world and join them in making the world a better place. I wanted to write books and play music and see more of what the world had to offer for someone like me. For the first time, I believed there was more to life than what I had been offered, and I have those kids to thank, but then I came home and realized how much the school wanted to hold me back."

Back on the stage, I desperately tried to pull the chain out so I could break free. "You're not good enough for Kelly, Rob," a familiar voice said. I turned around to see Maggie towering over me.

I looked over at Ana. "For years, they put me at high risk of falling through the cracks. None of them prepared me academically. They didn't help me advance in math so I was doing fifth or sixth grade math even when most kids my age would already be seniors in high school. They never helped me work out what type of future I wanted, or what life outside of this place would look like. Instead, they made me feel I was better off taking Voc Ed classes where I had to sweep floors, wash dishes, and clean trash cans and dumpsters."

I took another sip of water. "Behind years of a facade of niceness, they simply didn't care. They saw my autism but they didn't see me. They would smile and tell me and the few friends I had that we were smart, but then do nothing when we got dangerously behind because we weren't learning concepts the way they wanted us. I didn't even find out that noise canceling headphones existed until I went to college because they never allowed them in the classroom at all."

I stayed quiet for a minute before I continued.

"When I dealt with insomnia because of how bad my depression got, they just allowed me to sleep in rooms like it was no big deal. When my friend Ben struggled to pass chemistry for the fourth time, they blamed it on his ADHD. They wouldn't outright say it, but it was extremely obvious that's what they were doing. I could go on and on about how they treated so many of us, but if something went wrong, they would blame us. But we were kids! We didn't know any better!"

Maggie sternly stared down at me. With my entire body weight, I attempted several times to pull the chain out from the floor, but it would not budge. On the sixth attempt, I fell on my back, out of breath as Maggie lectured me in a booming voice about how I would never be good enough if I didn't finish my high school diploma.

"When I found many of the kids I traveled with were high school seniors, it suddenly dawned on me: why wasn't I graduating like them? I was the same age as them! That's when I found out a lot of the requirements I needed to finish high school, they never told me. They never sat me down and really told me what I needed to do, not even the time I came back to them when I was fourteen."

A large toolbox fell from the sky and landed next to me on stage as I caught my breath.

"So when they told me they were going to keep me there for two more years, whether I liked it or not, I decided to fight back," I said to Ana.

I reached into the tool box, grabbed a hammer, and began pounding away at my chain as a pile of math books rained from the sky landing on top of its anchor. Each time I pounded at my chain, the audience grew larger and more belligerent.

"I had to demand they give me homework because they never once gave me homework. I had to take extra classes at the community college and continuing ed classes at another school. I had to overwork myself, going to three schools at the same time, working a grocery store job I had just gotten, just so I could catch up on credits I didn't even know I needed. I spent the better part of my last couple years there trying to catch up on three years worth of high school math in one year. One fucking year!"

I stopped. I closed my eyes, *still pounding away at my chain.* "I worked myself day and night. I lost sleep. I didn't eat much. I stopped spending time with friends. I stopped doing the things I enjoyed. I became irritable—sometimes hostile—to teachers every time they would give me false praise or talk down to me or tell me that I didn't do enough. I burned so many bridges with them, but I didn't care. I've lost count of how many times I would go to Maggie's office and argue with her, only for her to constantly tell me it was all my fault."

I stopped again. *The audience started making jokes about me as I tried to break free.* I took some deep breaths, my heart pounded a little. Ana squeezed my hand a little tighter.

"I could go on and on about how embarrassed I was doing any of this. I remember once telling a coworker at the grocery store that I was in Special Ed and he literally laughed in my fucking face! I ended up lying to my boss where I went to school because of that. I felt like I was truly 'special.'"

I began to wipe away tears. "I'm sorry if I'm telling you too much. I'll stop."

"No, it's okay," Ana said as she rubbed my hands. "I'm listening. It's okay."

A small wave of relief washed over as my shoulders relaxed. I breathed in to ease my nerves once more. "You know, after a year of working to get out of there, I only come to find out that all the work I did—whether it be demanding homework, going to night school, taking more electives at the community college, or losing so much sleep trying to catch up and do what they wanted me to do—it was all for nothing."

"Why do you say that?" Ana asked.

I sighed. "After a whole year of doing everything I could, I had tried to work with the system to see if I had everything they asked for. Because I was now eighteen at this point, I didn't need my mom to set up an IEP meeting; I could do it all by myself. I thought I could negotiate with them. I thought they would finally listen and work with me. I thought I have enough to at least graduate in 2008 instead of 2009 or 2010 like they 'planned for me.' That didn't happen. Instead, they told me what I did wasn't enough. They claimed the school district wouldn't accept it, even though these incompetent assholes said they would." I then began to list everything off with my fingers. "The demand for homework wasn't enough. The night class at the continuing ed school wasn't enough. The work I did at the community college wasn't enough! I remember being so angry I screamed at them— " My voice slowly began to crack. "— Right . . . in front . . . of everyone . . . in the room."

My eyes began to swell up with tears. I pounded at my chain multiple times but I finally stopped. I put the hammer down and examined it: not even a single dent! I turned to the audience, all of them claiming I was worthless.

As I caught my breath, Maggie kneeled down to speak to me at eye level.

"I don't understand why you keep fighting this, Rob," she sternly said. "You brought this onto yourself. This is all your fault."

"You tell 'em, Maggie!" Someone in the audience cheered on.

"I hate it here!" I cried. "I don't wanna be here!"

Maggie put on an angry face. "If you hadn't ditched. If you hadn't slept in rooms. If you hadn't redone sixth grade math so many times—"

"Stop! Please stop!"

"You wouldn't be here now! This is strictly on you!"

The audience exploded in applause.

"You're not good enough, Rob," Maggie said. "Never have been. Never will be."

I slowly caught my breath. As I sat up, I turned to see Kelly at the edge of the stage. She stood there, looking at me. I tried getting up but the chain kept me stuck to the floor. I glanced back at Maggie. "Fuck you, Maggie!" I shouted before grabbing the hammer and pounded away at the chain again.

In the room with Ana, I tried regaining my composure as I worked to prevent myself from sobbing uncontrollably. I lay back into the couch, my head on the pillow as I stared up at the ceiling, imagining myself continuing to break away at my chain. Ana wrapped her arms around my stomach, her head resting close to my shoulder.

"I'm sorry," I mumbled.

"You have nothing to be sorry for," Ana softly said.

I breathed through my nose, rubbing my eyes before wrapping my arm around Ana.

I tuned out all the background noise as I slammed at my chain over and over. I then stopped for a moment turned over to look at Kelly, only for her to disappear into the darkness again. "Kelly, wait! Come back!" I shouted. I pounded at my chain harder and faster, giving it everything I got.

Back in the room, the tension in my muscles began to ease as Ana wrapped her arms around me. We cuddled on the couch for what seemed like an eternity.

After a while, we both sat up as I drank another sip of water.

"Thank you," I said. "I needed that."

Ana placed her hand on my shoulder again.

I took a deep breath once more. "After it became clear that nothing I did was going to be enough for them, I was like, forget it. I took a gamble: I told them in that meeting that the next academic year at that place was going to be my last, with or without a diploma. Since the community college at the time was allowing anyone eighteen and up to take classes, I chose to get a head start on my college degree. They objected of course, but I wouldn't budge."

"What would have happened if you didn't get a diploma?"

"I don't know. Maybe do adult school. Maybe take extra classes while I got college credits under my belt. I honestly had no clue. I just wanted out of there so bad. I didn't care. I could have just dropped out and did it, but I made a choice and stuck with it because I didn't know what else to do. I just didn't want to be a failure."

I sighed, *pounding away at my chain on the stage.* "It was at this point when Jason got in trouble with the law sometime after he got someone to cut down our tree."

Ana's eyes widened. "What did Jason do?"

"He went to a public park when Mom wasn't looking, dropped his pants, and exposed himself to a little kid."

"Wait? Are you serious?"

I nodded.

"That's awful!"

"Someone called the police and he spent the night in jail. They wanted to charge him with indecent exposure as a felony. The judge determined he wasn't mentally competent to stand trial, so he became a ward of the state and has been in developmental centers ever since."

I sighed again. "That, understandably, made Mom upset. That meant Jason would no longer be living with us. Mom didn't think they would take care of him as well as she would. If you ask me though, I honestly think he's where he needs to be right now."

Ana nodded. "He seemed pretty happy when we visited him."

"He's come a long way since then."

Neither of us said anything.

"Anyway," I finally said. "My last year at that school was miserable for me, and that's putting it mildly. I was taking four classes in Fall 2007, either at night or on Saturdays, just so I could get a head start on college. I spent the entire year just doing that. Many teachers just stopped talking to me or ignored me outside of class time because I burned so many bridges."

"Did any of the teachers care at all?"

"Maybe, at most, one or two, but even if there were more teachers that cared, it wouldn't have solved anything. The school itself just made going there toxic. There was, at one point, an attempt to provide counseling for me that year, but it was with a guy who had no previous counseling experience, and I didn't feel comfortable sharing *anything* with him. I mean, this is the same school that criticized me for using slang over the phone with my new boss at the grocery store, while she used slang with me! So much of what they did that year felt so self-serving. Too little, too late."

I pounded away at my chain again. I was about to give up when I made one more swing and one of the links made a dent. I pounded much harder, smashing into the dent several times until my chain finally broke in half.

"The weirdest thing is," I said to Ana in the room, "by the end of the school year, I learned the school district 'found' credits I needed to graduate that year."

"That's weird."

"It is. I still don't know to this day how that happened. There's a part of me that thinks it has something to do with people in the higher ups, including Maggie, realizing they were screwing up and didn't want to have me contribute to their high school dropout rate statistics, so they scrambled to find credits and conveniently they found them. That's pure speculation of course. I don't think I'll ever know for sure. What's important is that I finally finished and I could focus on college full time without having this place holding me back anymore."

"Well, you never have to think about it anymore," Ana said.

I shrugged. "I guess. I don't know. When I think back on it now, I just wish things turned out differently. . . . I guess when I think about it now, I wish Mom had been more proactive in dealing with them. I know Grandpa said weeks ago that she's been through a lot, and I have to be patient with her, which reminds me again—I'm so sorry you had to see that fight break out!"

"It's okay. It happens."

We had a moment of silence. "I was angry at Mom for a long time for putting me in that place at all. I've forgiven her for it. I know Jason took up so much of her time. I still feel ... resentment ... over it still, if that makes sense."

"She was a single mom though. Can you really blame her?"

I sighed. "I know that. I know she's not a bad person. I know she meant well. I know she really tried. I'm trying really hard not to blame her, but I wish she had done way more." I stopped myself. "If she tried more, maybe I wouldn't have had to fend for myself as much. It makes me wonder if dad were still alive, how long I would have actually stayed at that school," I whispered softly.

A long stretch of silence.

"Before he died," I finally said, "he hid a heroin addiction from my mom."

"Oh wow!"

"He got it from Vietnam. He saw so much awful shit there. Mom told me all the stories my dad told her growing up: seeing his buddies killed right in front of him, forced to shoot child suicide bombers on sight. He saw so much carnage. He once fell off the back of a Jeep and when he ran to catch up, everyone in that Jeep was gunned down. If he hadn't fallen off that Jeep, I wouldn't be here today. He took up heroin there as a way to cope with all of that!"

I took a deep breath.

"When she found out he was doing it again," I continued, "she had no choice but to divorce him. CPS would've taken us away from him if she didn't."

"I'm so sorry."

I thought of me at eight years old hugging Dad while he hugged me back before disappearing forever, leaving me all by myself in an empty room.

"I just know he tried so hard to get clean," I said. "He went to rehab. He got counseling. He tried to get clean. He really did. He wanted so much to be in our lives again that when he hit rock bottom, he knew he had to get help. A few years later when he was renting a room in Lemon Grove, they talked about getting back together. But then Mom and Alicia went to visit him when we hadn't heard from him, so they went to go see them only to find out he had a heart attack."

"Is that when your sister found him?"

"She was the first to find him, yeah." I took a deep breath. "I didn't go because I was sick. I wonder from time to time if I should have."

Ana rubbed my shoulder once more.

"Not like it matters. I just know I miss him so much," I softly said.

I stood up as the pile of math books and the chain I had broken free from evaporated. I surveyed the entire auditorium to find Maggie was nowhere to be seen. I looked up to the audience to see Kelly in the back row near the exit, smiling at me while everyone just stared.

I looked at Ana. "I feel better now. Sorry for dumping so much of that on you."

"It's okay," Ana said, smiling.

"I don't talk about all that with a lot of people," I said. "It feels good to let it all out."

"I'm glad you felt comfortable sharing that with me."

I smiled, a huge sense of relief lifting off my shoulders.

"You excited for *Infinity War?*" Ana enthusiastically asked.

"Hell yeah I am!"

Ana checked her phone. "It's starting to get late. Do you wanna head to your room?"

I picked my guitar back up. "Can I play you one more song before we go?"

"It's getting late—"

"Please! Just one more song. I promise!"

Ana paused, as if unsure whether or not to grant my request. "Oh, alright, but one more and that's it!"

I pumped my fist before I readied my guitar and got my hands and fingers in the appropriate position, doing a light strum.

"This next song is 'Carnival of Rust,'" I said, a giant grin on my face.

On stage, I looked out at the audience. Suddenly, the roof opened up to a sky full of stars. More lights went on throughout the entire auditorium as an acoustic version of Poets of the Fall's "Carnival of Rust" played through the auditorium's sound speakers.

As I looked out to the audience, I felt someone grab my hand. I turned to see it was Ana. "How are you feeling?"

I felt an immense sense of calmness and I smiled at her. "I'm feeling great!"

We looked into each other's eyes, both of us smiling as we held each other in our eyes and kissed, causing the audience to all shout "awww." After we kissed, we stood there on stage and hugged during the entire length of the Poets of the Fall song.

Once the song ended, I looked directly into Ana's eyes. "I'm so glad you're here," I said.

"I'm glad you're here."

"You ready for Infinity War? *You ready to fight Thanos?"*

Ana smiled again and stepped back. "I was born ready!" She shouted, now wearing Tony Stark's Iron Man suit without the helmet. "You ready to kick Thanos's ass?"

I saw I now wore Steve Rogers's Captain America suit and held his Vibranium shield. The music changed to a more action-heavy orchestral theme before Thanos appeared on stage, towering over both of us while he lifted his fist which wore the infinity gauntlet in the air.

Ana and I looked at each other again.

"More than ready!" I exclaimed. "Let's kick his ass!"

We fist bumped and rushed into battle with Thanos, the audience cheering as we worked together to defeat him.

14
___

July 15, 2018

I *still* couldn't believe it had been twelve years since I hugged Kelly goodbye.

She appeared in my thoughts again when I looked up and saw today's date on the TV while waiting in line inside a Shell gas station near San Clemente. Ana and I were on our way home after spending the weekend exploring Venice Beach. Ana pumped gas into her car while I went to buy a soda. I sent her a quick text asking her if she wanted anything.

I pulled up Kelly's picture again. I gazed at her smile and red hair, the memory of us waving at each other from opposite sides of the Sydney Harbor Bridge. *Hey buddy!* she shouted at me while I tried hiding my fear of heights so I could wave back.

I glanced out the window to see Ana put the pump away and get into her car. I looked at Kelly's picture again, the memory of that day on repeat.

As the line moved, Ana texted me to let me know she didn't want anything. I smiled at her text before looking at Kelly's picture one more time and clicking out of it.

I paid for my soda and headed back to the car, getting into the passenger seat and buckling up. "Ready to go?" I asked.

"Yep. Ready to go!" Ana said, smiling at me, and putting the car in drive.

Today

15

May 30, 2022

One by one, I tucked my clothes into a small suitcase on top of my bed. I always had a strict routine of how I packed: heavy pants on the bottom, shirts folded up on the right, socks and boxers on the left, and my *The Emoji Movie* toiletry bag on top. I'd lost count how many times I packed this way whenever Ana and I went on trips.

This time though I was going by myself, something I hadn't done in over a decade. A sense of emptiness washed over me while staring at my open suitcase, everything inside crammed together and lined up like they were supposed to be. I wasn't leaving for another two days, but here I was packing anyway.

I zipped up my suitcase and sat down, the phone call I had with Ana replaying in my mind. *No, I don't; I don't love you.* I picked up my guitar and placed it on my lap. I attempted to practice a few songs, but the only energy I could muster was plucking a few strings. Sighing heavily, I felt my phone vibrating in my pocket. I put the guitar down to answer it.

It was Ben. "Hey Rob," he said. "How are you? You busy?"

"Not really. Just finished packing."

"Did you have lunch already? If not, you wanna get something and hang out? I just got a big, fat juicy paycheck today, so it'll be on me."

I checked my phone to see it was a quarter after one. "Sure," I unenthusiastically said. "I have nothing else to do. I'll pick you up in a bit."

I ended the call, taking a few deep breaths and staring at nothing for a while longer.

***

The lunch rush at Red Robin had already slowed down by the time we made it to the mall. Ben insisted on this place because neither of us had been here since the start of the pandemic. Even with only a small group of people in the main dining room, we ate outside just to be safe. "Thank God we don't have to wear masks anymore," Ben muttered as we were escorted to a table.

We sat across from each other, Ben glowing with excitement as I blankly stared at the menu. "For someone who never went to art school, getting $250 just to design a book cover is awesome," Ben said. He took a sip of his water. "I know it's not a lot now, but I'm so happy this freelance stuff is finally starting to pick up."

"That's great, man," I said, numb to everything he said. "Good for you."

"Once things pick up, I'll be able to save up for a car and then get my own place!"

I continued staring at the menu until the waiter came to take our order.

"Again, it's on me," Ben reiterated. He ordered the Burning Love burger while I settled for chicken nuggets and a coke.

I rested my chin on my hand, gazing at the tabletop as Ben raved about the book cover job. I mentally tuned out the details as Ana's phone call repeated in my head over and over again. Thinking about the conversation, *I imagined myself in the center of a stage again, handcuffed to a chair at an interrogation table.*

" . . . And as I get more clients, I'll be at a place where I will have the type of freedom my younger self could only dream of," Ben said.

"That's cool," I muttered.

I gazed at the interrogation table.

"Is everything okay, Rob?"

"Everything's fine," I mumbled.

"You don't look fine to me. Are you sure?"

I shrugged.

The waiter came and placed our orders in front of us and left. Neither of us said anything as Ben took several bites of his burger while I twirled one of my chicken nuggets in ketchup.

"I was thinking a lot about what you said at the bonfire and I wanted to say I'm sorry," Ben said at one point.

"It's fine."

"No, it's not fine. You're grieving right now and I should've respected that. I shouldn't have tried to egg you on to find another girlfriend like I did."

I shrugged again as I bit into my chicken nugget.

"You're going through what I went through with Claire and it sucks to see that."

"I just don't get it. What did I do to make her leave?"

"You didn't do anything."

"That's what she said over the phone, but I must've done something."

Ben sighed. "Look, whatever the reason is, don't see it as a reflection on—"

"—do you think I'm sexually controlling?" I finally blurted out.

Ben leaned back. "What? Of course not! What the hell are you talking about?"

"Did Ana think I wanted to sexually control her or think I'm some sort of creep?"

Ben tilted his head. "What's gotten into you, Rob? Why would you ask that? *Did* you try to sexually control Ana?"

I shook my head, fighting back tears.

"Then why would you say this?"

I rubbed my eyes. *Back at the interrogation table, I struggled to break free from my cuffs.*

"Do you remember the first time Ana broke up with me?" I slowly asked.

Ben stared at me before it dawned on him. "I do remember. Then you two got back together over a month later as if nothing happened."

I sighed before sipping my coke.

"One thing I still don't understand is why she left you in the first place, and then just came back," Ben said. "I know it's none of my business, but I just find that weird."

"When she came over that night, she said she grew to like me but didn't know what to do. I didn't want to pressure her because I never ever want anyone to feel they have to be with me. But I begged her not to leave me and looking back on that now, I wish I didn't do that."

"I don't see how that makes you sexually controlling though."

I stopped to try to find the right words. "When she left, I got so upset I vented about it in that Facebook group."

"What Facebook group?"

I took a breath. "Do you remember that Facebook group I showed you years ago when we did karaoke?"

Ben scrunched his eyebrows together. "Were Alex and Lydia there?"

"Yes."

Ben rubbed his temple before his face lit up. "No fucking way!"

I reluctantly nodded. "After our first break up, I didn't contact her for over a month, but I missed her so bad I vented in the group multiple times. When I later reconnected with her and posted about it, Vincent tried forcing advice down my throat, and then started this whole drama where he somehow turned half the group against me."

"What happened?"

Yesterday

16

November 3, 2018

I woke up with Ana right next to me, the morning sun bringing light into the room.

"Give me thirty more minutes," she mumbled.

I cautiously combed my fingers through her hair as she lay her head on my chest.

It had been a month and a half since we broke up. I opted to give her space and focus on work. I made no contact besides a "Happy Birthday" text, but earlier in the week took a chance at hanging out as friends. We chatted over ramen the night before, then we went to my place to watch a movie. Now she was wrapped in our arms after a night of intimacy. Neither of us once brought up the breakup.

Later, I walked her to the front door. "Have a good day. I'll see you later?" I softly said.

She gave a sweet smile as we kissed each other goodbye.

I rushed back to my room and immediately called Ben after she left.

"That is so confusing," Ben said after I explained what happened. "Does that mean you two are getting back together?"

"I have no idea."

Ben sighed. "What do you plan to do now?"

"I don't know. I'm still trying to figure that out." I took a deep breath. "I guess I'll just be there for her if or when she needs me so I can focus on myself more. I just need to take some time, weigh my options, and work it out myself. Right now I just have low expectations."

"Could you still be friends with her even if it doesn't work out?"

"I hope so. If not, then I have no choice but to walk away."

"Whatever you decide to do, Rob, just be careful, okay?"

I thanked Ben for his concern and ended the call. I sat back against the headboard of my bed, thinking about last night. Did Ana still love me? Were we getting back together? Or would this be a one and done thing? These questions swirled around in my head as I took out my laptop, smiling as I played Poets of the Fall's "Dancing on Broken Glass."

I logged into Facebook after responding to a few emails. I went through my Facebook groups and clicked on Authentic Philosophy.

There was the usual activity, with Chris posting his regular musings about macroeconomics and Gabriel arguing back and forth with Jonathan and Peter on another thread about free will and determinism. But then there was a post Jennifer made about her struggle with depression and just needing to vent. Many members gave heart reactions and left supporting comments. I made similar posts grieving about Ana, expressing my desire to feel heard. I gave a heart reaction to Jennifer's post.

Feeling safe to muse like I did during the past month, I needed to just get my thoughts out of my head, so I shared my experience with Ana last night. "So an interesting development in my breakup story," I began writing, highlighting what I told Ben. I checked for grammar and clicked *Post*.

I browsed Facebook before being notified Jonathan liked my post. Gabriel warned me to be careful and keep my expectations low, something I acknowledged. I had a brief but polite back and forth with Peter about it before logging off and leaving the house to grade papers.

Throughout the day while grading at Lestat's, I couldn't stop thinking about Ana. The thought of getting to spend at least another evening with her made me smile.

But I had to accept the real possibility this could be short lived.

Would Ana text me tomorrow telling me it was a mistake? Would we just be friends? If we tried being friends, could I emotionally handle the idea of her sleeping with other men?

Later that evening when I got home, I sat at my desk, logging into Facebook on my laptop. I saw a notification: Vincent commented on my post, the first time he left any comments related to my breakup threads. Why was he commenting now?

VINCENT SMITH:

> This is a disaster! RUN for the hills! This is a nightmare waiting to happen and you deserve better than that!

The second I read it, my blood pressure shot up from his abrasive tone. *Why the hell are you telling me what to do?* I hit my hand repeatedly before stopping to reread my post twice, taking time to calm myself down. I tried to figure out what made him react this way, but I couldn't find where I hinted at wanting advice.

ROB SULLIVAN:

> @Vincent Smith, I don't find your pessimism here particularly helpful. I acknowledge it may not go well, but I don't think it means I need to "run." Right now, I'm just trying to work things out and then go from there.

I gazed at the thread, thinking about the many times he would just argue with people. Literally just argue. Back in April he argued with someone about gun control to the point it drove that person out of the group.

I didn't want to argue with him. People were going to side with him anyway, so what was the point?

I clicked *Leave Group*.

I put my laptop down and lay in bed, calming down to soft music gazing at the ceiling.

Ten minutes later, Vincent sent me a private Facebook message.

VINCENT:

Hey, I hope you know my comment was only meant to be honest advice from similar situations I've been in. But it's what I think given what you're saying. I think this will end badly and you deserve better.

I reread his message multiple times before responding.

ROB:

You missed the point. I prefer to work this out myself. I do not want to be told to "run." I accepted Gabriel and Peter's advice to "be careful." It's not like I haven't thought about it extensively. Hell, I dedicated an entire final 2 paragraphs about being careful and recognizing it could end badly. Did that get ignored?

I waited for a reply before realizing he likely went to bed. I forgot he lived in Wisconsin.

***

November 4, 2018

I woke up and logged back into Facebook to see Vincent's messages.

VINCENT:

I don't think I ignored anything. It's a bad situation and we're being honest that you should get out.
And then you left the group in a huff.

What is he talking about? I thought. I couldn't stop hitting my hand as I fumed at the mouth. I typed something but deleted it and took deep breaths. *Okay maybe I'm overreacting. Think before I say anything.*

ROB:

> TBH, I find that a load of crap. It's condescending to ignore everything I've said and just GIVE me advice like they were instructions, rather than suggestions. I find that rather insulting. I thought this over, slept on it, and that's the conclusion I've come to. I left the group because I knew I needed to cool down.

I pressed "Send," hoping he would take the hint.

No response, so I went and browsed YouTube. An hour later, he responded with a wall of text, causing my heart rate to skyrocket.

VINCENT:

> You should read between the lines on these posts, dude. You're paying lip service to the suggestion that this is a bad idea . . . .

I skimmed the rest, my blood boiling as I read through his entire essay of condescending prose. Reading it transported me *to the curtain of the auditorium, the stage decorated to resemble a Schweitzer classroom, an interrogation table appearing center stage. Two Schweitzer teachers grabbed me from behind and dragged me over to the table, cuffing my hands and ankles to a chair as I screamed in agony.*

Vincent stood on a large soap box as the teachers stood side by his side. "Part of you is hopeful but part of you is also worried," Vincent calmly lectured. "I'm telling you in no uncertain terms that you should only be listening to that worried voice!"

The spotlight focused on me as I tried to break free from my chains. Then in a flash, the entire stage decoration changed from a classroom to Maggie's office.

Vincent removed his beanie and glasses, revealing himself to actually be Maggie as she tossed her Vincent mask aside.

"You've said you can't handle the idea of her sleeping with other

people," she smirked, "but she has every right to do that! She doesn't owe you any explanations if that's what she wanted to go out and do."

The audience erupted in applause at what she said. "You tell 'em!"

"Why are you treating me like I don't already fucking know that?" I cried out.

"You clearly have to be told the obvious since you're so stupid!" The audience shouted, booing as they threw more bottles at me.

Back in my room, I hit my hand repeatedly while reading Vincent's entire message. Why is he still talking to me? I left the group and tried not to make it a big thing, but he just won't leave me ALONE! No one else felt the need to message me and bother me like he is, so why is he inserting himself into my life like this?

I wanted this asshole to go away!

I rushed to find something—*anything*—he wrote I could use to end this exchange.

VINCENT:

> . . . I know everything in your mind and body is telling you I don't know what I'm talking about and you're probably pissed at me . . . .

I stopped reading and typed the first thing that came to mind.

ROB:

> You bet your fucking ass I'm pissed at you.

No immediate response. A wave of guilt flowed over me.

VINCENT:

> Well listen, if I'm not getting through then I'll leave you alone and you do whatever you want. But again, if you can't handle a conversation with a friend about things going badly then you shouldn't be in a situation where things will almost assuredly go badly.

I was at a loss for words at his last statement. *What kind of asshole says something like that?* I thought. I fumed with rage as I quoted it before giving one last response.

ROB:

> Thanks for confirming my decision to leave the group. I was uncertain if I made the right choice, but you've just confirmed it. Fuck off!

I immediately unfriended Vincent, laying on my bed numb to everything.

Today

17

May 30, 2022

Ben's eyes widened in disbelief after telling him what happened. "Damn, man! Sounds like something a teacher at Schweitzer would do."

"What do you mean?"

"I mean, they would always tell us what to do, like their word is law. They wouldn't allow us to make our own decisions. It sounds like Vincent did something similar."

"He humiliated me in front of everybody in that group." I sighed. "He made me feel like the biggest piece of shit in the world."

"What I don't get is why do you care what some asshole from Wisconsin says? It's not like he has control over whether or not you graduate the way Schweitzer had on us."

"He wasn't just 'some asshole from Wisconsin,' he was someone I looked up to and saw as my academic equal. I respected him. He contributed so much for years to the group. I mean, he was getting a PhD in Psychology and posting about the type of work I could never do."

"I hear you."

"But then that happened and when I came back, I found out there was drama about me leaving. I wanted to apologize for lashing out, but I was so disgusted— *disgusted*—by how he tried to justify his bullshit! Publicly told everyone how he 'worried' I would not just hurt myself, but also hurt her! That I would hurt Ana!"

I took a sip of my coke, doing what I could to stop the swelling panic attack.

Ben stared at me, his mouth slightly open. "He said you wanted to hurt Ana?"

"He heavily insinuated it. Claimed that I might yell and scream at her. A person that I trusted telling others that I would yell and scream at her. That I wanted to 'sexually control her.'"

"Dude, that sounds like something a troll would say just to get a reaction out of you," Ben insisted.

"I know him enough and interacted with him enough for years to know that he meant every word," I asserted. "He wouldn't just say or do shit if he didn't mean it. That's what makes it hurt so bad. I still have access to the comments and messages on my phone. I can show you."

"I wanna see, but let's talk about it over ice cream. You wanna get ice cream?"

<hr>

We sat at a bench inside the mall as Ben savored his ice cream. I went through my phone, pulling up what he wanted to see. "Keep in mind this is not every comment and message but this should give you a general idea of what happened," I said as I handed it to him.

As he read through the comments, I was *on stage again, my hands and ankles cuffed to the interrogation table, the spotlight focused on me as the audience watched my every move. Vincent came out from behind the curtain, carrying a chair and sitting across from me.*

"What do you want?" I angrily asked.

Vincent straightened his beanie. "Hold on, Rob. I'm just here to talk. There's no need to get angry with me. I care about you. It just pains me to see you like this."

"I literally do not fucking believe you, you selfish piece of shit!"

Vincent held his hand up, chuckling. "Whoa! No need to use foul language with me. We're friends, right? Can't we just talk?"

I said nothing while trying to break free from my chains.

"Look," Vincent calmly said. "I saw the red flags you refused to see, so I reached out to you. I expressed concern. I messaged you privately so you can be more open. I tried relating my experience and expressing empathy to your mindset. But what did you do when you weren't hearing what you wanted to hear and people were honest with you? You throw a tantrum, rage quit from the group, and go back to a situation where things would go badly."

I tried again to break free from my cuffs as Vincent's lecture grew increasingly cold. "I've been open to communication since the start. I've never called you names. I've never spoken down to you. I wished you well even when you were telling me off. Now that things have gone bad—"

"Shut up!"

Vincent cleared his throat. "I told you that it wasn't a learning opportunity or a playful roll of the dice. Every sign was there that it was going to go badly and you admitted such an outcome would leave you hurt. Now it has and you've wasted five years of your life only to be hurt. Don't you wish you'd taken my advice? You would've been so much happier."

"I'd be happier if you would just shut up!"

"And I'd be happier if you didn't have to go through this pain."

"Shut up! This is my life, and I can make my own choices!"

"Isn't that what friends are supposed to do?"

"I would have been happier if you said nothing at all and minded your own business! Now get me out of these chains now!"

Vincent sighed. "Welp. If you can't handle a conversation with a friend about these things, then you shouldn't put yourself in that situation." He then pulled out a water bottle from his pocket, taking a sip and putting the bottle on the table. He then took out a microphone, tapping it to check if it worked before he faced the audience.

I was about to scream when suddenly a chain wrapped around

my body and duct tape got smacked onto my mouth by a pair of hands I didn't recognize.

"Be quiet and listen to what Vincent has to say, Rob!" someone behind me asserted.

Back in the mall, Ben's tone grew more agitated as he scrolled through my phone. "Holy shit, who does this guy think he is? Jesus Christ himself?"

I said nothing while staring at my feet.

"You have all these people arguing about you leaving, and he's going around painting you as if you're mentally unstable!"

People walked past us. *Do you really have to read it all out loud?* I thought.

"Someone posted a screenshot of something you wrote on Facebook and it started a comment war about how you were 'being toxic!' Vincent is making snarky jokes about the whole thing, and Nadine is claiming what Vincent did made her feel safe? What the fuck is wrong with these people?"

I sighed, numb to everything Ben was saying.

"What Vincent says here about you is *really* disgusting: 'What happens when all this goes south? Is he going to swear and scream at her? Is he going to become more controlling towards her? Is there going to be another outburst, potentially a violent one?' He's acting like you're Trevor from *GTA V* or something!"

I watched more people walk past us.

"Oh fuck me, this part makes me want to puke," Ben said. "'He's a big, strong, mentally ill person who wants to control the sexual behavior of this girl and that is not something we should ignore.'" Ben handed me back my phone. "I'm sorry, but I can't. If I wanted to read hateful lies like that, I would've gone to church."

"To be fair, there were a few people who stood up for me."

"Some of these other assholes here are just going along with everything Vincent is saying here, so no, definitely not enough!" Ben asserted. "Hell, one of them even misspelled 'mentally ill' with only one L! One fucking L! They couldn't even bother to proofread their own bullshit!"

"For the last few days, I've been replaying what Vincent did to me in my head over and over and over again, and it sucks so bad. I'm sorry I never told you before now. It's just—I remember how you reacted when I told you about this group. I was so embarrassed!"

Ben looked up at me, his mouth slightly downturned. "I'm not going to say I told you so because that would be a dick thing to say. I just wish you didn't have to learn the hard way that many neurotypicals can be such assholes. I don't know if Vincent is a neurotypical himself, but that doesn't matter; he's no different than them, and it's so obvious though he's trying to use his perceived power in the group to paint you as the bad guy."

"I just know that I was so pissed when he claimed I wanted to sexually control her. How does feeling unsure if I could handle her being with another man mean I want to 'sexually control' her?"

"That is such a leap in logic!"

"Why does everyone think I'm not capable of making my own decisions? First Maggie, now Vincent?"

"So . . . help me understand something," Ben said. "Maybe that will help me see better what was going through your head at the time. When Vincent kept bugging you, you said it started making you think of Maggie, right?"

"Yes."

"And Vincent, in your head, became Maggie? Is that right?"

I sighed. "I don't know. I don't know how to explain this. It just felt like he believed his opinion was the only one that mattered. Like his way was the right way, and me thinking there was any other way made me stupid."

"You're not stupid," Ben said. "Why would you say that?"

I saw myself *back on stage again. I turned to see who chained me to the chair and put duct tape on my mouth.*

It was Maggie. "You need to be quiet, Rob."

"Thank you, Maggie," Vincent said before facing the audience again. "Ladies and gentlemen, the signs were all there. I tried to warn him, but Rob here went back to a situation that's gone bad. Shark infested waters, mind you. And he's trying to make me the bad guy?"

The audience booed.

I tried to break free from my chains again.

"You saw all the posts!" Vincent shouted. "For weeks, he cried over this girl so he could gain sympathy points from us! And then he literally—and I mean literally—tells me to eat a bag of shit and gets angry when we try to be honest with him?"

The crowd cheered before Nadine stood up. "I would like to say something," she said.

Vincent walked to the edge of the stage, pointing his microphone at her. "Yes, Nadine."

Nadine cleared her throat. "I never commented on Rob's posts asking the group for relationship advice. But I read them all because Rob was my friend. It made me uncomfortable. He was getting all these sad reacts, like it was an addiction for him. You finally said something so he could stop hurting himself, yet you're treated like the villain when all you were trying to do was help him? That's not right!"

The audience cheered at what Nadine said.

"He was looking to his peers for approval of his feelings and behavior," Nadine exclaimed, pointing straight at me. "This is not something to handle with kid gloves!"

The duct tape stopped me from screaming to correct Nadine's bullshit.

"His inability to assess proper social interactions is no excuse for how he reacted!" Nadine shouted, causing the audience to boo me again.

Vincent gave a thumbs up towards Nadine. "That's right, Nadine," he said. "I don't think that someone has a right, when they post their own personal problems, to be shocked that someone is giving them advice they don't agree with."

The audience cheered as Vincent held his microphone higher up in the air to amplify their applause.

"Why do you say you're stupid, Rob?" Ben asked again.

"I demanded he take it back, but he wouldn't budge," I said. "He insisted we do a Google hangout. I didn't want to do it because I knew he would talk over me better in a voice chat than over text. When he refused to take anything back, I blocked him. Tried to forget about it, but . . . it bothered me for a long time . . . I kept it from her. I never told Ana, and I regret that. I'm so stupid. I'm just so fucking stupid!"

My eyes began watering.

Back on stage, Maggie instructed everyone to be silent before turning to me, holding up a plain white mask. "Rob, if you want to speak, you must wear this. You aren't allowed to speak unless you are wearing this mask. Do I make myself clear?"

I tried freeing myself from the handcuffs and the chains again before stopping. I glanced at Maggie, then Vincent, and finally the audience before staring at the mask.

The mask slipped away and all I saw was Ben's half-eaten ice cream cup.

"All my life," I slowly said. "I always felt I was never good enough. At Schweitzer, I often felt I had to hide my true self, like I had to put on a performance, just so teachers didn't think I was dumb or stupid. I just wanted to be normal, Ben. Was that so hard to ask for?"

"What do you mean?"

"All I ever wanted growing up was to feel like I was no different than anyone else, that I was just a normal kid who got to sit in a normal classroom with normal kids and have normal problems like you see in all those Saturday morning cartoons or after school specials. Yet I never got that. My sister did. Not me. That's why after I got the hell out of that place, I worked my ass off in college. I purposely chose to not use any of their 'special accommodations' services.'"

"You didn't need any of that away, Rob."

I took a moment to compose myself. "I just wanted so hard to prove these assholes wrong so I refused all of it. I thought, 'If I can get my college degree, that would show them I'm normal.' But I still always feel like I have to prove myself. I'm tired of it. Maybe that's why almost every time I'm lost in my own thoughts, I can't stop thinking I'm on some stage, judged by people like them as if they wanted to control me. At Schweitzer, if I didn't do what they wanted in the way they wanted, it wasn't good enough. It's why up until I met Kelly, I went through the motions. I didn't realize until it was too late they just allowed me to fall behind. I almost gave up. I lost count of how many times I wished I was dead back then."

I expected Ben to go on another tangent about Schweitzer like he usually would.

But this time he was quiet. "I know that feeling too well," he solemnly said.

I looked up at him. "What are you talking about?"

Ben gave a light chuckle. "Remember those stupid time-out rooms they used to make us be in whenever we acted out?"

"Don't remind me."

"I remember they made me stay in one of those rooms because I got angry and yelled at Ms. Mason for talking to me like a baby when I finished a chemistry lesson, and then staff watched me like a hawk until I went to the time-out room."

"I can't remember: was it you who punched a hole in one of the walls of one of those rooms?"

"Nah, that was Trent," Ben said. "I would just go there to lay on that comfy carpet and not do crap until they gave up because I knew they would write about that crap in my IEP anyway, so what's the point? The only thing those rooms had going for them was that the carpet was at least comfy to lay on. At least it was a temporary escape from a lot of crap I had to deal with."

"I used to just sleep a lot," I muttered.

"And that was your escape. They didn't care. I wish they cared." Ben sighed again, putting his ice cream cup aside. "Do you mind if I tell you a story?"

"Sure."

Ben cleared his throat. "When my dad was alive, he used to cut me down all the time. He was embarrassed by how 'retarded' I was, quote unquote. Got to the point that whenever I had a meltdown, he'd grab me by the shirt and smack me. Not enough to give me bruises, but enough to hurt. Told me I needed to stop throwing tantrums so I could 'be a man' someday. Asshole even tried to get me conserved once. Thank god my mom talked him out of it." Ben took his hat off, putting it on his lap before taking a deep breath. "When I was twelve, I lived next door to this autistic kid named David. I think I told you this before."

"I'm trying to remember," I said. "Wasn't he the kid who got shot by police back in the early 2000s?"

"That's right, but I never told you that I personally saw it go down."

I began listening, *the thought of me whether to put on the white plain mask lingering.*

"Me and David used to hang out all the time. We did little league, played Battleship, and drew cartoons together. We'd go to each other's houses all the time. He was the smartest and funniest kid I ever knew. But then one day I was in my front yard and police cars had literally—*literally*—pulled up in front of David's house and they went running in with guns. A few minutes later I heard *pop-pop-pop-pop!*"

"You witnessed the police actually running into the house?" I asked.

"Yes! That's what I'm saying. I found out later David had a really bad meltdown his mom couldn't handle, so she called the police not knowing what to do and the next thing you know, they came and shot him! Killing him instantly! They didn't even attempt to figure out why he was having such a bad meltdown. They just killed him! When dad told me what happened, he made it very clear to me that if I didn't stop having meltdowns, I would end up like David!"

I rested my hand on his shoulder.

"It's like I've said before, society only sees us as two extremes. Either we're inspiration porn or we're violent uncontrollable monsters." Ben and I locked eyes. "That's what Vincent did to you. Just like the police did to David. Just like my dad did to me. Vincent tried to put you in a box, just like Schweitzer did to us because it's easier to do that than to, you know, *understand* us. Nothing we did at that school was good enough. I've also had days where I wished I was dead."

"Why didn't you say anything?"

Ben shrugged. "I just didn't. Didn't see the point. After Schweitzer, I started going to therapy. My therapist helped me see that, yes I do have ADHD. Yes dammit, I am autistic. I am *me* and with a capital M-E, and that's nothing to be ashamed of. I know you've said before that you've struggled with the label 'autistic' because of what that school put us through, which I get, but she helped me see it's nothing to be ashamed of, that it's a part of who I am. She helped me realize the way Schweitzer treated me is not much different from what Dad did. He used David's death as a scare tactic so I would conform to his standards!"

"I'm sorry your dad was so awful. At least your mom is nice."

"She's come around. Plus she doesn't hit me, which is a bonus."

Both of us chuckled.

"Anyway, my point is that Vincent acts like he understands and cares, but in reality he's no different from them."

"What do you mean?"

Ben looked straight at me. "Robert Brian Sullivan! Were you not listening to anything I said? You have a Masters degree and you still don't see it?"

I said nothing.

"Hand me your phone. I wanna point out something Vincent said to you."

The plain white mask loomed in front of me as someone in the audience started shouting at Vincent.

It was Chris. "Vincent, your treatment of Rob has been abusive and you berated him so you can prove to everyone else how smart and above-it-all you were!" he shouted.

Everyone in the audience gasped.

"Excuse me?" Vincent exclaimed. "I never berated him! I never said he was a bad person or stupid. I never said anything that was

hostile or angry. I was direct, but I wasn't harsh and I didn't treat Rob unfairly!"

The audience started bickering as I tried pulling free again.

Ben scrolled through Vincent's messages until he found what he was looking for. "Take a look at what he said here: 'You describe it as being careful or not being too eager, but trust me when I say, having been in those situations, I know that mindset. Part of you is hopeful but part of you is also worried. And the worried part scares the crap out of you so you try to dismiss it. I'm telling you in no uncertain terms that you should only be listening to that worried voice.' Don't you see what he's doing here, Rob?"

I said nothing.

"He's trying to script you," Ben said. "He's trying to act like he knows you better than you know yourself. But because you didn't follow his script, he has to twist your words because he's projecting and doesn't realize it. Maggie and other teachers at Schweitzer did exactly that!"

"But what if he sincerely thought he was trying to help?"

"Does that even fucking matter?" Ben asked. "He's still doing what Maggie and the rest of the teachers at Schweitzer used to do to us! He's presenting himself as someone with 'experience' so he can tell us what to do with our lives."

"Why do you think he would do that?"

"If I had to guess, it's because he went through a breakup himself. He's assuming he 'knows your mindset' because he thinks what he went through gives him credibility to tell you how you're 'supposed to act.' But you're Rob! He's Vincent! There's no way he can ever 'know your mindset' because he doesn't even try to know what's actually going on in your head. It's all self-serving attempts at empathy because he's projecting his own experiences and his own insecurities onto you!"

I stood up to stop myself from crying as I tried pulling free from my chains again as Vincent argued with Chris in the audience.

"You have facts staring you in the face!" Vincent exclaimed. "A history of violent outbursts! An admission he can't control his feel-

ings! Posts about self-harm! Hints toward controlling this girl's sexual activity! Given all of that, there's a nonzero possibility he would've hurt himself and her. Do you not see the signs? I'm just putting together things he said!"

My eyes started watering as I began walking away.

"Rob? Where are you going?"

Ben rushed to stand in front of me, both of us in the middle of a walkway.

"I wanna go home," I said. "I don't wanna be here."

Ben put his hands on my shoulders. "Rob, look at me! You have nothing to be ashamed of. You did nothing wrong! You never would have hurt Ana! That's not the Rob I know! If you really were sexually controlling, why would she have stayed with you for an extra three years? You're a good person, Rob! He's just some asshole from Wisconsin who will never know you the way I do!"

Tears fell as I struggled to break free from my chains. Chris and Vincent kept arguing.

"So you're, what, his court appointed counselor?" Chris shouted. "You claim to perceive a potentially violent situation and then have some duty to be his psychotherapist? No wonder Rob is so pissed at you!"

"I know Rob's mad at me, Chris," Vincent asserted. "I know I was pushing him to address ideas he wasn't comfortable with. I know I lectured him. But these are sometimes necessary things we have to do. Particularly as men. When we see one of our friends showing warning signs of potential violence and abuse, we need to tell them to their faces that they can't be in those situations."

I couldn't stop sobbing as I hit my hand again.

Ben wrapped his arms around me. "Bro, it's gonna be okay. Let it all out!"

"Dude, we're in public. People are watching us."

"Stop caring what people think, Rob! Your mental health is more important than what strangers think!"

Tears flowed as I slowly hugged Ben back.

"I love you, man! I would be devastated if something happened to you!"

As I laid my head on Ben's shoulder, *I wrestled to break free. As Vincent and Chris argued, the handcuffs loosened.*

I pulled one last time. My hands were finally free!

I tore off my chains, ripped the duct tape off my mouth, and grabbed the mask from Maggie. I threw it at the spotlight, smashing the bulb as glass shards rained onto the stage.

Everyone in the auditorium gasped.

"THIS IS MY LIFE!" I cried out. "AND I CHOOSE HOW I LIVE IT!"

I took in my surroundings, the auditorium lights dim and the stage covered in glass shards. Maggie squeaked and ran to hide behind the curtain. The audience scrambled to process what happened. And Vincent just stood there with a deer in a headlights look.

I tried walking away but my ankles were still cuffed to the table. I was only able to move a foot before falling to the ground and laying there, sobbing.

"I was only trying to help," I heard Vincent meekly say.

Me and Ben hugged for what seemed to be eternity, ignoring bystanders glancing at us, before we sat back down.

"Feeling better?" Ben asked.

I slowly nodded, wiping my eyes. "A little."

Ben smiled. "It's going to be okay, Rob."

We stayed quiet as we watched people walk around the mall.

"I remember the night I told Ana about what I went through at our 'school,'" I finally said. "I felt like I could be myself. I felt like I was finally moving on. I felt like I could finally open up to people again. After Ana helped me no longer blame myself for what I went through at that place, the Facebook group really felt like a space for me to feel accepted and be open about who I am. I no longer felt like I had to hide who I was. But Vincent took that away from me, and I felt like I had to start all over again."

Ben nodded.

"A reason why I ended up never asking Ana why she left me in the first place is because by the end of the day, why she left wasn't important. The reasons didn't matter to me. I just didn't care. I guess a part of me also never asked because I was worried that I would prove Vincent right, so I've done everything I've could to move on and black it out of my mind."

"There is no way in hell he could predict that!" Ben insisted. "So no, her breaking up with you at any point would never prove him right."

I sighed.

"It just sounds like to me you gave that asshole way too much power over you to the point where it affected your relationship with her. He's just some asshole from Wisconsin, Rob."

I took a moment to gather my thoughts. "He was right about one thing though."

"What's that?" Ben asked.

I took a moment to think of the best way to phrase it. "I remember him saying that there were, quote unquote, 'little tells' I was scared. Well, to be honest, I was scared. Who wouldn't be? I decided to take a chance anyway. You wanna know why?"

"Why?"

"When Ana started coming back, I had no idea what to expect. But then I remembered saying goodbye to Kelly all those years ago. I had the chance to tell her how I felt but I didn't. I had the chance to stay in touch, but I didn't. When I worked my ass off to get the hell out of Schweitzer, I did it because I thought it would free me to go find her again. I was so naive."

"That explains why you were such a dick to teachers in the last year we were there," Ben said. "I'm so sorry you went through all that, Rob."

"For a long time, I always asked myself 'what if'? What would have happened if I had told Kelly how I felt about her? What would have happened if I wasn't at Schweitzer when I met her? What if I had let myself find out if I even had a chance with her? Once I got out of Schweitzer, I was too scared to try again. 'What if'? That still bothers me to this day."

"Couldn't you try again now?"

"Too much time has passed." I sighed. "When I met Ana, I had no idea it would last five years. After the first breakup, I later tried again. Vincent's right that I was scared, but what he doesn't get is I did it anyway because I don't ever want to have another 'what if' hanging over my head ever again."

Ben nodded. "I can see that."

We fell silent again. "I'm going to Chicago in a couple days," I finally said.

"Why Chicago?"

"That's where Kelly's from. I think going there, even if it's not to see her, will give me some catharsis. Closure should be about catharsis? A feeling of something, right? I think going there will help me see why it didn't work out with me and Kelly, which in turn can help me see why it didn't work out with me and Ana."

Ben shrugged. "I don't see how going to the city she lives in will do that, but I'm not going to pretend I understand. I just hope you get what you are looking for."

"Thanks."

We sat there for a little longer. "You ready to head out?" Ben eventually asked.

"Yeah. Let's go."

June 1, 2022

I sat in my room, waiting for an Uber to take me to the airport. It was 4 am, and I had on my Airpods so I could listen to music without waking up Mom and Alicia. I stared into space, beginning to twirl my hands before realizing I was holding my Airpods case, the one Ana gave me for Christmas last year. *I know you like to use headphones all the time, so I thought these would be great for you!*

I repeated the last phone call I had with Ana in my head. I

placed my Airpods in the case and forcibly shoved them into one of my drawers, reaching into another drawer storing the headphones I wore all the time before meeting her.

Waiting for my ride, I pulled up Kelly's picture again. I tried thinking about the time I spent with her, but felt nothing. I gazed at her picture, thinking back to the three weeks we spent together before hugging goodbye at the airport.

I clicked out of Kelly's picture and stared out into space again. Before I got lost in thought though, my phone pinged, letting me know my Uber arrived.

I took a breath. "I hope this trip's worth it," I mumbled to myself. I grabbed my suitcase and headed out the door, unsure what to expect when I'm finally in Chicago.

Yesterday

18

November 11, 2018

All I felt like doing was listening to Pink Floyd's "Wish You Were Here" on repeat.

I listened to the song for what seemed to be the millionth time that evening as I sat at my desk in my room, blankly staring at Facebook on my laptop. I should be grading, yet all I felt like doing was listening to the same song over and over. But I couldn't enjoy it like I usually would, a knot in my chest as I stared at my screen.

I had blocked Vincent a few hours ago.

I rejoined Authentic Philosophy after being gone for a week, posting a public apology when I found out my leaving caused drama. Many accepted it, but Vincent was noticeably silent, even after twenty-four hours. When I later saw all his horrible claims about me, I got filled with so much rage I engaged in a comment war with him to defend myself before telling him I would block him if he didn't take it all back.

VINCENT SMITH

@Rob Sullivan, But frankly, I just think you like playing the victim at this point. Block me if you want, but I hope you think about how disproportionate your responses have been.

For the last few hours, I repeatedly imagined myself *on stage as the audience hurled insults at me after I banished Vincent to behind the curtain.*

"Vincent is right about you and you know it!" An audience member shouted.

"Blocking Vincent makes you a cowardly piece of shit, Rob!" Another one blurted out.

I stared at my feet in shame as bottles broke around my feet, joining the sound of the audience deriding me as they hurled their glass missiles. I mindlessly scrolled through Facebook, the knot refusing to go away. Eventually as I scrolled, my thoughts shifted to Ana.

Over the past week, Ana would send me funny memes through Snapchat or share an amusing work story through Facebook Messenger. *Have you ever been to Universal Studios?* She randomly asked me the other day. As it got closer to the weekend, her text messages slowly grew friendlier than what I was used to from her, sometimes including a smiley emoji or a random cute puppy gif. I had to keep reminding myself this might not last though, even as I became more cautiously hopeful with each passing day.

I gazed up at the moth painting she bought me last year at the San Diego Art Festival. I replayed the day we attended the festival in my head again, remembering all the tiny gestures of genuine care and affection. I thought about her playful jab at me when we looked at the painting of the Bichon Frisé. *First of all, I'm not cute!* She exclaimed. *Babies are cute! Kittens are cute! Puppies are cute! Do I look like a baby to you? Or a kitten? Or a puppy?*

My mind drifted off to everything we had done in the past year before Pink Floyd's song played again. "I really do wish you were here," I mumbled.

I browsed social media until Ana, out of the blue, sent me a message asking if I had tomorrow off for Veteran's Day. Startled, I gathered my thoughts before I typed back.

ROB:

Yep. I'm off tomorrow. Going to honor our vets since they provide the best healthcare for our pets 😄 lol

We then talked about plans for Veteran's Day. Ana playfully vented about having to work tomorrow and drama going on between her and Mary, while I talked about visiting my dad's grave. I was about to watch another video when her next message grabbed my attention.

ANA:

Do you want to hangout tonight by the way?

My heart leapt, the knot in my chest completely gone. I took a breath before I answered.

ROB

Sure. You can come over tonight. 🙂

I tidied up my room, cautious about any noise since Alicia was in her room. I just was not in the mood to deal with her yelling again if I accidentally disrupted another one of her binging sessions of *The Golden Girls*. Mom was at the casino again and wouldn't be home for another few hours. Ana said she would be over around 9:30 pm, so that gave me at least an hour to make my room presentable.

After I cleaned, I lay on my bed, staring up at the ceiling before pulling up photos on my phone. I gazed at a kiosk portrait of the both of us at the Mob Museum in Las Vegas during Memorial Day weekend, my arms around her as we both smiled for the camera. But as I scrolled, I also found a photo I snuck of her playing on her iPhone that one time in July we went to Manna BBQ. I suddenly thought about *all* the times she would be glued to that phone, sometimes so quiet I wondered if she was ignoring me. *Do you do that on purpose?* I thought. Then I remembered, a few weeks before the breakup, our awkward road trip to Ensenada to see La Bufadora. During the trip she barely talked, a habit that constantly forced me to figure out what she wanted. *Why can't you just say what's on your mind?* I thought. *Why do I have to constantly feel like I have to find a way to knock down the walls you put up?*

Before I could dwell on it, a *ding* went off on my phone with a text message from Ana letting me know she was here.

Close to 10 pm, late as usual, but this time I didn't care.

I rushed to the front living room and opened the door. There she stood, holding her purse and a bag of snacks. "Hey there," she said.

I smiled back as we hugged. Everything that bothered me about her no longer mattered.

"I'm so glad you're here," I mumbled before we kissed.

We laid next to each other in bed, naked under the sheets as we cuddled. She rested her head on my chest as I combed my fingers through her hair. It was close to 11:15 pm, having started the evening with us watching a movie on my laptop before one thing led to another. I began questioning what this all meant as I combed through her hair, wondering if we were a couple again. *Should I ask her where we stand now?* I thought. I debated whether to ask her now, but she looked so much at peace I decided against it.

"Thanks again for the snacks," I said instead.

"You're welcome."

"You said you have work in the morning?"

Ana nodded. "Yeah, but my boss said I can be a little late. You have to grade tomorrow?"

"Yeah. Have about fifty papers left, but I can get them done by Wednesday. Gonna visit Dad's grave tomorrow like I told you earlier."

"That's so sweet of you."

Just then, I heard the sound of the front door of the house: Mom had just come back from the casino. I ignored it as Ana and I continued talking about how our week has been.

"Since you have work tomorrow, I guess you have to go home?" I asked.

Ana took a moment to respond. "Is it okay if I stay the night?" she mumbled.

I smiled before I kissed her on the head. "Of course," I whispered.

We had changed into sleep wear and were now laying in the covers. It was sometime after midnight, with the only source of lighting coming from Ana's phone as she scrolled social media. As I laid my head on the pillow, I held Ana's hand for a moment before kissing it. I then turned over to lay on my left side and face the wall to make myself more comfortable. Staring at the wall, my mind replayed the entire evening in my head again, wondering once more what it all meant. *Does she still love me?*

I was about to fall asleep when I heard shouting coming from the hallway.

"I just think you should move out," I heard Mom say.

It took me a moment to realize a fight between Mom and Alicia had started.

"How about you have your son Rob move out as well if you're going to have me move out!" Alicia screamed.

"Rob actually pays to live here!"

"Like what? $200 a month?"

I slowly started to hyperventilate, trying hard to subdue it. The argument escalated, with Mom defending me by pointing out I paid more than that a month before Alicia went on an angry tangent about how all she does is go to the casino, not giving a shit about anyone but herself. I didn't catch what started the fight in the first place, but as it went on, my eyes started to water.

As I tried to regain control of my breathing, I felt Ana wrap her arms around my chest from behind me, resting her head against mine. I held her hands, taking in some deep breaths as Ana kissed me on the head. She held onto me tight, not wanting to let go. As she hugged me from behind, Mom and Alicia's argument began to fade into the background. My heartbeat began to slow down as I held onto her hands. Any questions I had about where we stood as a couple were not important right now.

Ana didn't say anything, but she didn't have to.

I was just glad she was here.

19

December 12, 2018

Poets of the Fall were officially coming to America for the first time!

The band announced on their social media pages they were coming to ProgPower next September, tickets scheduled to go on sale Saturday. I was at Lestat's grading final papers for the semester when I read the news, barely able to stop myself from shouting at the top of my lungs so people wouldn't stare at me.

But there was a catch: the concert would be in Atlanta, Georgia.

I paused, staring at my computer screen when I read this. Would I even have enough money to not only buy tickets but also fly all the way to the other side of the country and have a place to stay? Just to see Poets of the Fall live? I argued back and forth with myself for several minutes. *Unless you want to bankrupt your entire life savings and go to Finland,* I thought, *Atlanta may be the only chance you will ever get to see them live!*

I thought about what to do before realizing my best option was going with someone to split the cost. I called Ben, but he said he couldn't come because he already had plans to attend a family reunion at that time. I then called Nathan, who answered on the third ring.

We exchanged the usual pleasantries before I told him all about Poets of the Fall coming to Atlanta next year, giving him the price of the tickets and the date.

"I would love to go, but I already have plans," he said.

"What plans do you have that are more important than going to this concert?"

"Twitchcon 2019, baby, yeah! It's gonna be so epic! I'll be the next Ninja!"

I rolled my eyes. *Great,* I thought. *Another one of his get-rich-quick schemes again?*

"Maybe ask Ben or Trent?" Nathan suggested.

"Ben already has plans, and Trent is constantly broke. No way in hell can I rely on him for money. You know that."

"Why not ask your girlfriend to go with you?" Nathan asked.

"You mean Ana?"

"Yeah, that's her name. You guys are back together, right?"

I took a deep breath before drinking some water. "I think we're still kind've working things out. I don't know. She still hasn't said why we broke up in the first place."

"Why not? Have you asked her?"

I sighed. "I don't know, Nathan. I want to ask her, but at the same time, I would rather she be the one to bring it up. I don't want to force her to talk about something she's not ready to talk about yet."

"Maybe this concert could be a chance to do just that."

I groaned. "What? No! There's no way she's gonna want to go."

"You don't know that!" Nathan insisted. "Think about it. You told me recently you two started seeing each other, are having a shit ton of sex I'm never gonna have, and you two go out to do things on weekends again. If you two have been doing all that lately, is she really your ex at this point? I don't know about you but it sounds like she's treating you like you're boyfriend material again."

I said nothing.

"I'll put it this way," Nathan continued. "If she says yes, it should be extremely obvious even for dumbasses like Trent to see that you two are back together."

"I guess."

"It's just something to think about," Nathan said. "Listen. I need to go. Getting ready to kick some more ass with my next Twitch stream. We can talk later, okay?"

I ended the call. I stared at the band's announcement on their Facebook page, a sense of crushing defeat. *Will I even be able to go?* I went back to grading for the next hour before browsing Facebook again. I commented on a few memes in my feed before I instinctually opened up a Facebook Messenger chat box to Ana, replaying the conversation I had with Nathan in my head, wondering if I should ask her.

As I stared at the chat box, I thought about the last few weekends when we spent time together, whether we checked out new restaurants that opened up on Convoy or went to the movies. I thought about all the times she checked up on me, sending me funny gifs again like she used to in the past. Finally, I thought about the night she came over and wrapped her arms around me when Mom and Alicia fought in the hallway outside my room.

I was about to type something in the chat box when Ana suddenly sent me a message.

ANA:

> Hey there. Are you doing anything Friday night? There's going to be a Nutcracker show at Spreckels Theater. Would you like to go? ☺

I read her invitation multiple times, smiling but also unsure if this was the right time to ask if she wanted to go with me to see Poets of the Fall on the other side of the country.

ROB:

> Sure. I would love to go with you! ☺ Aren't you supposed to be at work though? ☺

ANA:

I'm on my lunch break! Haha

We chatted about our day as I argued in my head whether or not I should ask her about the concert. By the time she had to go back to work, I ended up not asking her. *I think I'll ask her later,* I thought. *Better not wait too long though. Tickets will sell out quickly!*

December 13, 2018

I arrived at Grandpa's house at around 1 pm. It had been almost a month since I last visited him. I had been swamped with my workload at SDSU and focused on taking things slow with Ana as she gradually came back into my life. Grandpa was in his garage sanding a wooden stool when I pulled up into the driveway. He stopped what he was doing and waved at me, inviting me inside for lunch.

I sat at the kitchen table as he gave me a Pepsi and then made us both BLT sandwiches.

"Sorry I haven't been around lately," I said once he sat across from me. "I've just been really busy."

Grandpa playfully waved it off. "Don't be sorry. You're doing what you have to do. You're earning your keep."

I shrugged. "Not enough to get my own place."

"Don't you have work lined up next semester?" Grandpa asked.

"Not at State. I'll still have the tutoring job, but I won't be making enough." I sighed. "State really needs to give me a longer contract. I can't keep only working during Fall semesters my whole life."

"Just keep at it, Rob," Grandpa assured. "They're bound to give you tenure soon."

I don't get tenure as a Lecturer, Grandpa, I thought. *I've told you this so many times.*

I thought about correcting him, but felt it wasn't worth getting into another convoluted explanation with him again.

We talked about how we have been doing for the past month. Grandpa went into a long story about how he volunteered to build a new stool for his church. I talked about how work has been hectic but thankful everything has seemed to cool down ever since Mom and Alicia had their fight in the hallway last month.

"I heard from your mom that you and Ana have been seeing each other again," Grandpa said at one point.

"That's one way of putting it."

"Sounds like you two are working things out. Are your mom and Ana getting along?"

I shrugged. "Mom's kind've just been ignoring her lately. Mostly indifferent now. She stopped talking shit about her to me behind her back, which I appreciate."

Grandpa took another bite of his sandwich.

"I just wish she would stop wishing I dated girls who were more like her, when I would rather just date people I want to date, if that makes sense."

"It does," Grandpa assured me as I sighed and drank another sip of my Pepsi. "The thing you have to remember though is that you can't change your mom."

"I know."

"You've always said you would rather be more like your dad, so keep doing that and you'll be fine," Grandpa said. "Don't worry or care what she thinks. You've practically raised yourself without a dad anyway."

I sighed. "I miss him," I mumbled.

Neither of us said anything for a moment. "I miss him, too," Grandpa mumbled as well. We continued to eat our sandwiches and enjoyed each other's company for a while. "How is Ana?" Grandpa finally asked at one point.

"She's good. Mostly working a lot. We're planning to go see *The Nutcracker* at Spreckels Theater tomorrow night."

Grandpa smiled at this. "That sounds like fun."

I nodded. "I think we'll have a good time." I took another bite of my sandwich. "I did want to ask her something though and I want to ask for your insight."

"Oh?"

I pulled out my phone and showed Grandpa Poets of the Fall's Facebook ad event at ProgPower, explaining in detail about the band and how this would be a once a lifetime opportunity to see them live in America. "The only problem is that they will be in Atlanta, so I'm thinking of asking Ana to come with me to split the cost, but I don't know if I should."

"Hmmm. What kind of music do they do?"

"You wanna hear a sample?" I excitedly asked.

"Sure. Why not?"

I pulled my headphones out of my jacket pocket and handed them to Grandpa for him to put over his ears, opening up Spotify from my phone to play "Cradled in Love." He began listening to the song, nodding off here and there with his smile growing bigger as it went on. After roughly two minutes, he took the headphones off and handed them back to me. "That's a nice sound," he said. "Not something I care all that much for, but it's certainly better than some of the crap I've heard from next door."

"Thanks Grandpa. So do you think it would be a good idea to ask Ana to come with me?"

Grandpa looked straight at me. "You'd be stupid not to," he said with a chuckle.

My face lit up.

"Go ahead and call or text her or whatever you need to do to ask her." Grandpa insisted.

I pulled out my phone and sent Ana a long text, asking her if she would be interested in going to the concert with me next year, providing a link with the details of the event itself. No immediate response, but I figured she was at work anyway. "Done," I said.

"There you go. You feel better now that you asked?"

My heart began to pound. *What if she says no?* I thought. *What if she outright rejects the invitation?*

"Yeah, I do," I lied as I tried to hide my shaking hands.

We chatted for a while before I heard a *ding* from my phone, almost giving me a heart attack. I pulled up my phone, showing Ana's response to Grandpa's as we read it together.

ANA:

> Hmmm. Let me think about it and get back to you. Are we still on for tomorrow night? 🙂

I breathed an uneasy sigh of relief. Not quite a "no," but definitely not a "yes."

"That's still a good sign," Grandpa said. "You can ask her again tomorrow."

I nodded, responding in the affirmative to Ana's text before putting my phone away to continue my visit with Grandpa.

***

December 14, 2018

We sat in the second row on the right side of the auditorium as "The Waltz of the Snowflakes" began, getting close to the end of the first act of *The Nutcracker*. It was a full house, with everyone in the audience except Ana and I wearing formal attire and the entire theater covered in festive decorations. Both of us wore jackets to keep ourselves warm as we watched the ballet performers begin the dance number.

Throughout the entire show, I kept thinking about when to ask Ana again about the concert. We had a quick dinner at Chipotle across the street before the show, but I didn't take the chance to follow up before heading in to take our seats. Halfway through the dance number, I imagined myself *on stage where Ana and I stood facing each other as the dancers themselves surrounded us.*

"Do you wanna go to this concert?" I asked.

"No, I don't want to go to this concert with you," Ana said.

"Why the hell would you ask her that? What are you, twelve?"

Someone in the audience exclaimed. Everyone, including the dancers on stage, then burst out laughing.

I then saw Vincent in the audience. "What are you going to do now that she has said no?" he shouted. "Are you gonna swear and scream at her now?"

I tried to shake out the entire daydream from my head as I watched the performance. As the dancers moved along with the rhythm of the music, I looked over at Ana to my left as she slowly drifted to rest her head against my shoulder. When I put my hand on the armrest, Ana gently held it and rubbed it slowly as she absorbed the performance on stage, making me smile.

Once the dance number wrapped, the lights in the auditorium turned on and people either started chatting amongst themselves or got up to stretch their legs.

I looked over again at Ana. "You enjoying the show?"

Ana nodded. "Yeah, it's good. I like it so far. How about you?"

"I like it. Do you need to use the restroom or anything?"

"Yeah, I'll be right back," she said.

Ana got up from her seat and left the auditorium as I scrolled social media on my phone. I pulled up the Facebook post from Poets of the Fall about their show at ProgPower next year, fixating on the announcement. I read through the comments of people excited about buying tickets the second they go on sale. *I need to ask her again. I'm running out of time.*

I stayed glued to my phone until Ana came back and handed me a water bottle. "I got you this," she said before she said back down.

"Thank you!"

I took a sip of water before I put the bottle under my seat. We sat there in silence, looking up at the empty stage as intermission continued. I kept thinking if I should ask her now or I should wait until we got home later after the show.

"I forgot to ask you earlier," I said at one point to start a conversation. "How did you get tickets for this show?"

"My boss told me she got free tickets but had other obligations, so she gave them to me and said I could take whoever I wanted."

"That's cool. Thank you for inviting me."

Ana nodded.

"Hopefully work hasn't been too hectic," I said.

Ana shrugged. "It's the usual: more gossip. All my coworkers do is gossip all the time. We even had another person quit on us, right before the Holidays, too."

"Oh boy," I muttered.

"My coworkers invited me to go to this Christmas party tonight, but I had no interest."

"Because you'd rather spend it with me, which is so sweet of you," I said, chuckling.

Ana gave a smirk. I looked over at her, seeing how relaxed she was sitting there waiting for the show to start up again.

"So . . . I was wondering if you had a chance to think about the invite I sent you yesterday," I slowly said. I pulled up my phone and showed her the Poets of the Fall Facebook announcement. "It's in Atlanta and it's next year, so it would be more cost effective for me to go with someone. You know, to split the cost. Have you ever been to Atlanta?"

Ana shook her head. "Nope. I've never been there."

"Neither have I."

"You're willing to travel across the entire country just to see one band live? You definitely crazy," Ana jokingly said.

"Well, in a way . . . yeah. I am. Um . . . tickets go on sale tomorrow and I know for a fact they will sell out. Would you want to go? I'll understand if you say no, but it really would mean the world to me if you went with me. We can even check out some cool stuff that is in Atlanta besides the concert."

My heart began to pound as I felt a lump in my throat.

Ana looked up at me. "I've thought about it. Yeah. I'll go with you. It should be fun."

A sense of relief poured right through me. "Awesome! I'll buy the tickets and then you can Venmo me your half?"

"We can worry about all that when we get home."

We kept sitting there as everybody eventually came back to their seats once intermission was over. As the show went on, my heart elevated as a feeling of joy flowed through me. Any questions I had about where we stood as a couple no longer mattered. When Ana put her hand on the arm rest, I gently held it. "I love you," I whispered.

She held my hand back, staying silent for a moment. "I love you, too," she whispered back.

I smiled.

20

June 30, 2019

Today was the day I would help Ana move into her new place.

I was practicing another one of my guitar solos when Ana, out of the blue, told me last week through Facebook Messenger she was moving out of the room she was renting in Rancho Peñasquitos. *I'm moving to a new place starting July 1st!* she texted. *Finally my own place! It's even five minutes away from my office!*

The property manager was allowing her to move into the place a day early since the previous tenant had already moved out, so I offered to rent a U-Haul truck for furniture she would not be able to fit in her car. In the U-Haul, we went to La Jolla to pick up the furniture for the new granny flat attached to a house she would be renting in Mira Mesa. *She will only be fifteen minutes away from me now*, I thought. My forehead began to drip with sweat as we carried the heavy dining room table through the side gate and into the kitchen area of the living space. I didn't think about how miserably hot it was going to be when I offered to do this with her.

Once all the furniture was in place, I drank water and wiped my forehead before standing in front of Ana in the kitchen area, wrapping my arms around her waist and smiling down at her. "We did it!" I exclaimed.

Ana looked up at me as she wrapped her arms back around my waist, her mouth wide open and closing her eyes while making a playful gah sound before we kissed. We hugged for a bit and then looked into each other's eyes. "How does it feel to finally have a place to call your own?" I asked.

Ana smiled. "It feels so great. I am so glad I don't have to share a bathroom with an annoying roommate anymore."

"No one from the rest of the house can come in here, right?"

"Nope!" Ana assured. "The only way they can get in this part of the house is through the side gate."

"That means you can finally have me come over on weekends and they won't care?" I teased.

Ana chuckled. "Of course."

I kissed Ana on the head before we let go. Ana stretched her arms and got a water bottle from the mini fridge as I surveyed the kitchen area, admiring the hard work we put into furnishing the place with a long dining table, a shelf for boxes, and a folding table to put a rice cooker and a portable stove. As Ana drank some water, I looked over at the entryway between the kitchen and the bedroom and noticed something I didn't notice before.

"I just realized that you don't have a door here," I said pointing to the entryway.

"Yeah, the property manager told me they removed the door when they made this into a granny flat," Ana said. "I don't know why. It seems silly to me."

"Maybe you can ask them to install a door," I suggested. "You can get even more privacy that way."

Ana shrugged. "Maybe. A door would be nice. Probably not right now but hopefully in the future."

I didn't say anything else as I surveyed the room again, taking another sip of water. "I have to go take the U-Haul back. Would it be okay if I come back afterwards?"

"Sure."

I headed over to the sliding door.

"Oh, before you go, there's something you should know," Ana said.

"What's that?"

"I'm going to have a 'no shoes in the house' rule, so when you get back, make sure you leave your shoes outside."

I nodded. I then noticed a large box filled with shoes by the sliding door. "By the way, if I see a shoe rack, do you want me to get it for you?"

"If you want. You don't have to."

We said goodbye before I left to return the U-Haul.

I dropped the U-Haul off around 5:00 pm and sat in my car in the parking lot scrolling through Facebook Marketplace. I know Ana said I didn't have to, but I wanted to find a high quality shoe rack at a reasonable price on the way back to her place as a surprise for her. I stumbled upon one for $10, advertised by someone who lived in the same new neighborhood as Ana. I sent him a message asking if it was still available.

As I waited for his response, I began to think about the possibility of moving in with Ana. Would I even be able to afford to, considering how unstable work in general has been? Would she be open to the idea at some point? As these questions swirled in my head, Ana texted me.

ANA:

> I'm going to head to Vons real quick and get stuff for dinner. You want me to get anything specific for you?

Before I could respond, the person selling the shoe rack messaged me back. The shoe rack was available, so I told them I would pick it up in a bit before responding to Ana's text.

ROB:

Can you get me a Diet Coke and also some strawberries? We can have strawberries for dessert tonight. Also, I just dropped off the U-Haul, but I have to do a quick errand so I'll be over in an hour or so.

I then started the car, getting another text before I was about to drive away.

ANA:

Sounds good. I'll probably take a shower after I get food, but if you're not here when I get back, I'll leave the gate unlocked for you.

I grinned as I drove out of the parking lot.

I stopped at my house to take a quick shower, grab my pajama pants, and then drove to Mira Mesa to pick up the shoe rack before arriving back at Ana's place. She left the gate unlocked like she said she would. I left my shoes outside on the doormat in front of the sliding door like I promised. She opened the door for me, expressing gratitude for the shoe rack before placing it by the door and went back to cooking steamed rice and Chinese sausage. I sat at the table, making a comment about how the carpet under my feet felt so nice as she served us plates of food once it was ready.

Sometime after dinner that evening, we cuddled in bed as she opened up her laptop for us to watch a movie. As she scrolled through Hulu, I looked around the room itself, amazed at the wide open space. "You really scored with this place," I said. "How much do you pay a month, if you don't mind me asking?"

"It's definitely higher than what I was renting before. $1200 a month."

"Geez!"

Ana shrugged. "I prefer to have my own space, so I think it's worth it."

"Is that why you prefer not to have anyone wear shoes in the house?"

"Not really."

"Is it because you're Asian?" I teased. "I know not having shoes in the house is usually an Asian thing."

"Growing up, every Asian family I knew did not allow us to have shoes in the house," Ana said. "I don't really believe in any of the cultural or supposedly spiritual reasons for leaving shoes outside the house, but there are practical health benefits to doing so. No tracking in mud, not spreading germs, all that. That all makes sense."

I sighed. "Hopefully someday I can have a place like this." I then thought about asking her if she would be interested in me moving in or maybe living together, but decided since she had just moved in that day, it probably wasn't the best time.

"Did you get classes for fall?" Ana asked.

"I have four," I said. "I'm still waiting to hear from Megan if I'm getting a fifth one."

Ana continued scrolling to find something for us to watch.

"I don't know how long I can keep this up," I continued. "I tutor only ten hours a week and I only teach at State in fall semesters, and when I'm not, I'm wearing out my car delivering people food. State *needs* to give me a permanent contract."

"Hopefully you get that fifth class."

I sighed again. "It makes it hard to save. Even harder to contribute to my Roth IRA, which again, I can't thank you enough for helping me with that."

"Stuff like that takes time. You save as much as you are able to afford."

"I know. It's just hard."

Ana didn't respond as she found a movie for us to watch. "How about this one?"

"Sure. Whatever you want."

As she started the movie, I looked around the room again, suddenly noticing the small night stand in front of the bed and how it contrasted with the wide open space of the room. *That would be a good place to put a vinyl player*, I thought.

"You have work in the morning, right?" I asked.

"I do."

"Is it okay if I spend the night? I'll leave in the morning."

Ana nodded. "That's fine. Can you turn the light off for me?"

"Of course." I got off, turned off the light, and went back to bed.

We watched the movie for the next half hour or so before I found myself with my hand on her chest. I placed a few kisses on her cheek, and Ana gently grabbed my hand and let me rub her breast. We did this for a few minutes before she closed the laptop, put it to the side, and wrapped her arms around me. We made out for a while, slowly taking our clothes off before I realized something.

"Oh shit," I whispered right as Ana had just taken off her shirt. "I forgot condoms."

Ana wrapped her hands around my neck. "It's okay," she whispered, smiling. "I'm on the pill."

I was taken aback. "Wait! Are you sure?"

Ana nodded. "It's okay. I trust you."

I smiled. "If you trust me, then I trust you."

We kissed again and embraced for another evening of intimacy.

August 18, 2019

I started setting up my dad's vinyl player in Ana's bedroom as she cooked us spicy chicken ramen for dinner. It took time and gentle nudging, but I was finally able to convince Ana to let me bring it over just for one weekend so she could hear what music from a vinyl player sounds like. I had already placed the vinyl player on the nightstand in front of her bed when I began looking for the electrical outlet.

"Rob, dinner's ready!" Ana shouted from the kitchen.

"Be right there," I said as I plugged in the cord. Ana was already at the table eating when I came in. I made myself a bowl, thanking Ana for dinner as I grabbed a can of diet coke from the mini fridge, sitting across from her at the table.

"You're not going to have milk with that?" Ana asked when I sat down.

"I have my soda," I said as I held my can up.

"Dude, you're eating spicy ramen. It's going to be hot for you."

I shook my head. "I can handle spicy ramen."

"Just like how you were able to 'handle' that Carolina Reaper you tried at the street fair in Carlsbad we went to a couple weeks ago?"

"This one's different. Here, I'll prove it!" I took a couple of bites of my food. As I chewed my food, my eyes slowly started to water.

"You insisted on spicy ramen tonight, so don't say I didn't warn you."

I swallowed my ramen and took a big gulp of my soda. "See! Wasn't that spicy!" I exclaimed as I tried to hide how my mouth felt like it was on fire.

"I can tell by the look on your face you're such a terrible liar," she teased.

I drank my entire can of soda, then excused myself to grab the jug of milk from the fridge and pour myself a glass before coming back to the table. "I heard you talking to your mom on the phone while I was setting up the vinyl player," I said at one point. "Everything okay with her?"

"She's fine," Ana said. "Today's her birthday so she called to thank me for the gift card and then talk my ear off like she usually does."

"Oh nice. Happy birthday to your mom."

Ana took another bite. "She's been asking me about grandchildren again, and I keep telling her I'm not interested in having kids. She should bother Mary about it instead."

"Kids are expensive anyway, especially in this economy."

"I know, right? She's not getting any grandkids from me."

"There you go!" I exclaimed. "Tell her who's boss!"

Ana chuckled. "If I were to have a kid, I would prefer to have a boy. Easier to raise."

I nodded. "I can see that."

"Do you want kids someday?" Ana asked.

I took a moment to figure out how to respond. "I don't know, to be honest. I go back and forth on that. I don't care one way or the other. I guess for me, if I were to have kids, I wouldn't want them to go through some of the same things I went through growing up. I would want to be more proactive in their schooling, which I don't know I would be in a position to do."

"That makes sense."

"Right now, I'm more focused on trying to build a stable career. Fall semester starts soon, so I'm preparing for that."

"Any updates on classes for spring?" Ana asked.

"No, nothing yet. I'm hoping I get something in spring, but I'm not counting on it. We'll see, though. How about you? How's work been?"

Ana took a sip of water. "Work is fine. Been having to go to all these networking events lately, and it's so annoying. I hate networking."

"I do, too!" I exclaimed. "They should just magically make us all billionaires so we don't have to work anymore!"

Ana laughed. "Exactly!"

We eventually finished our dinner, and I offered to clean up for her as she went to the bedroom to change into her pajamas. After I finished cleaning up and putting the dishes away, I turned the kitchen light off and went into the bedroom. Ana sat at the edge of the bed as I went over to the vinyl player, picked up a vinyl disk that was next to my backpack, and put it on the turntable. "You ready to hear good quality music?" I playfully asked.

"If you say so," she teased. "What song are you going to play?"

I slowly placed the needle on the disk. "Something that makes me think about my dad every time I listen to it."

The vinyl player took a moment to load up before Don McLean's "American Pie" began to play. "You heard this one before, right?"

"I know of it," Ana said.

I sat next to Ana on the bed. "Now you get to hear it in its original glory!"

We held hands as we sat there, listening to the song. "Don McLean is great," I said. "This one isn't my personal favorite of his, but this one always makes me think about my dad. He loved this song, and he would always play for us when we were kids."

"It's nice," Ana said. "I like it."

I smiled as we lay down and absorbed the melody.

"Is that why you listen to so much old music?" Ana asked. "Is it because of your dad?"

I took a moment to think about how I wanted to answer her. "In some ways, yeah. In other ways, something about old music resonates with me so much. I love newer stuff, too—don't get me wrong—but something about older music speaks to me."

I squeezed Ana's hand tighter as "American Pie" kept playing.

"I started to appreciate older music more after I began community college," I continued. "I was still angry over what I had been through with my old 'high school,' if you even want to call that place a school. I majored in English because I loved writing, and I wanted to study literature."

"That explains why you have so many books in your room," Ana teased.

"As a kid, I loved writing, and I loved books. What can I say? Anyway, I was still angry over what I had been through with my old high school, but when I started taking guitar classes and listening to more music, I let go of some of that anger. I remember reading this one book in the library for a lit class I was taking, and I found this description of music that stuck with me for a long time."

"What book was that?"

"Don't remember, but the author described older music as the 'sounds of yesterday.' Then someone wrote in the margins that it made them think about what tomorrow had in store for them. I thought that was really interesting, but for a long time I didn't know what exactly it meant. But then one day it made me think about everything I've been through, and it suddenly clicked. The way I see it now, the reason I listen to older music is because when I take the time to listen to the sounds of yesterday, they make me remember the promises of tomorrow."

"What kind of promises?" Ana asked.

"The way I understand it, they're the promise of a better future, and the promise that everything will be okay, no matter what," I said, smiling.

We cuddled to the rest of the song, not saying anything as we enjoyed each other's company.

"I remember when I was a kid, I had dreams of making so much money so I could travel the world," Ana said at one point.

"What kind of places would you want to go to?" I asked.

"Paris. London. Different places in Asia: Japan, Vietnam, China."

"Have you ever been to China?"

"No.

"Not even when you visited Indonesia while Mary studied abroad last semester?"

Ana shook her head.

"Really? Not even to visit your relatives there?"

"Nope."

I playfully gasped at Ana, shaking my head in a teasing way. "You and your sister had the chance to explore the jungles of Indonesia, fight mosquitoes, and eat cheap fruit, but neither of you had the common courtesy to hop onto a short plane ride to China to see your relatives?"

Ana chuckled. "Yep," she sarcastically said. "We were too busy doing that to see them."

I tried my best to hold back laughter.

"We're not that close to them anyway," Ana said, "so I don't know if I'll ever have the chance to visit them."

"You don't know that for sure," I gently insisted. "I mean, all my relatives from my dad's side are up in Washington, but I have no doubt that they would be happy to see me if I were to go up there now. I'm pretty sure your relatives in China would be happy to see you and Mary if you were to go there right now."

Ana shrugged. "If you say so."

I said nothing else as the music kept playing. "How's Mary doing, by the way?" I eventually asked.

"She's good. She's back home now from Indonesia and just getting ready to start school again," Ana said.

"That's good."

"She's told me she plans to get a tattoo, but I'm trying to talk her out of it because Mom would lose her shit if she found out," Ana said with a grin, as if to hold back to laughter.

"What kind of tattoo would she even want?"

"She wants a tattoo of a skull on her butt," Ana said, laughing.

"What? Are you serious?"

"She's serious," Ana said when she finally stopped laughing. "She says it'll be so cool, but I'm trying to tell her that she'll regret it and Mom will disown her and tell her she's a disgrace to the family if she gets that tattoo, but she won't listen to me."

I shook my head. "You should just let her learn the hard way."

Ana shrugged. "I don't want her to make the same mistake I almost made."

"What do you mean by that?"

"I almost got a tattoo one time."

I looked straight at Ana. "You got a tattoo?"

"No! *Almost* got a tattoo!" Ana exclaimed, a giant grin on her face and clearly trying to hold back more laughter. "The key word is 'almost.' Gee, I thought you were an English teacher. You should have your degree revoked right now!"

Ana laughed as I chuckled at her joke. "I was about to say," I said. "You never told me this. When did this happen?"

"Well . . . during my first quarter at UCSD, I remember going out with a group of friends to PB. Most of us weren't twenty-one yet, so we were mostly sneaking around to bars and going to different parties with some people my friends knew. We were walking down Garnet at one point, and we found a tattoo parlor, so we went in and talked about getting cool tattoos."

"What kind of tattoos?"

"I don't remember exactly what my friends wanted, but I remember wanting to get this dragon tattoo I saw and having it on my leg."

"A dragon tattoo on your leg?"

"Yeah."

"Why a dragon tattoo?"

"I thought it looked cool."

"You just thought it looked cool? I thought it had something to do with you being Asian?"

"Nah," Ana insisted. "I just thought it looked cool."

"Hmmm. What stopped you from getting it?" I asked.

"Well . . . we were in line at the tattoo parlor and Mom out of the blue called me, and like an idiot I answered it and when she overheard one of my friends telling me we were getting tattoos, she freaked out so bad and demanded that I stop or that she was going to disown me. She would not stop yelling at me over the phone. After that phone call, I ended up just walking away and not getting the tattoo in the first place."

"Geez. That's . . . harsh!"

"It is what it is. I think my mom had a point, but . . . I don't know. Part of me wishes that like with so many things, Mom would be less judgmental."

"Are you thinking you should've gotten the tattoo anyway?"

"To be honest, I don't know," Ana said, a sense of hesitation in her voice. "I know she was looking out for me, but I also wish I would have gotten it anyway so I could show her that she had nothing to worry about. I wish I had stood up to her more growing up."

I nodded in acknowledgement.

"You remember how you've sometimes talked about how your Mom would yell at you over really small things?" Ana asked.

"Yeah."

"My mom can be like that, though thankfully now I only have to deal with that when she calls to check up on me once in a while. But when I think back on it now, I do wish she would just respect my choices a lot more. That's why there's a part of me that wishes that if I had gotten that tattoo then, I could've shown her that I would've been fine regardless."

"It's not too late to get a tattoo if you wanted," I playfully said.

Ana shook her head. "Nah, I changed my mind. I don't need one anyway."

"So you're saying you hate tattoos now like your mom?" I teased.

Ana looked straight at me with a smirk. "You know for a fact I never said that, you troll!" she exclaimed, trying to hold back laughter.

We cuddled for a while in silence when another song from the vinyl player began to play.

"It sounds like your mom can be a real pain in the ass sometimes," I said at one point.

"Growing up, I remember how we didn't have much," Ana said. "Mom always pressured me and Mary to make better lives for ourselves. She and my dad fought a lot. One of the reasons why I don't talk to my dad that much is because his temper was so bad. A lot of the times worse than Mom's, and he didn't always know how to control it. Sometimes he would just swear and scream at us."

I said nothing as I looked into Ana's eyes. All I could imagine in my head as I lay next to her was Ana holding on to Mary to protect her from the screaming coming from their father in the next room.

I slowly reached out and held her hand. "I . . . I hope you know that I would never do that to you," I slowly said.

"You wouldn't. You're not that kind of person."

"That's good to know," I mumbled.

Ana continued smiling. "As annoying as Mom can be some-times, I'd rather help her over Dad since Dad took the house after the divorce. I'll never forget all the fighting and the arguing, and with how little we had, I'd rather just not deal with that ever again. It made me dream that someday I would be in a position where I didn't have to worry about money."

"Not everything has to be about money," I said.

"Not the money itself, but what I could do with it," Ana said. "I saw how both my mom and dad struggled to take care of me and my sister. I saw firsthand how they were barely able to keep a roof over our head or put food on the table. I just remember so much arguing and so much fighting, a lot of times over money. Neither of them were ever happy. So I thought, 'Maybe I could be a world traveler or a multi-billionaire.'"

I chuckled. "Multi-billionaire?" I teased.

Ana chuckled as well. "I don't know I would want to be like that now, but I still think about how I wanted to do something in my life that would allow me to not have to worry about relying on others. Mom relied so much on dad to help support us, only for him to take the house when they divorced. Seeing all that made me want to be in a place where I didn't have to rely on other people for happiness or money. I wouldn't have to worry so much about what happens to me or my mom or my sister or anything like that. Where I could be in a position where I could go to my own special place and away from the pressures of the world."

"Maybe I could join you at your special place," I said, smiling.

Ana smiled. "You could."

I smiled back as we continued cuddling.

"I feel so blessed," Ana said out of the blue at one point.

"How so?"

Ana took a moment. "I may not have the dream job I wanted when I was a kid, but I have a growing career. I have a roof over my head. I have people who care about me. But most of all, I have you."

I gave a big smile as I placed my hand on her cheek.

"I love you," she whispered.

My eyes began to water a little as I kissed her on the lips. "I love you, too." We continued to cuddle for a while as another song from the vinyl started. "You ready for Atlanta soon?" I asked.

Ana nodded. "Yep. I got the day off that Friday. We should be ready to go."

I smiled again.

21

September 7, 2019

We flew into Atlanta late in the afternoon, settling into our Airbnb and exploring what downtown had to offer before getting ready for ProgPower the next day. When we checked into Center Stage Theater around 1 pm, we were each given a program. Ana looked through hers and asked me if I wanted to watch other bands like Demons & Wizards or Sorcerer since Poets of the Fall wouldn't go live until later in the day.

"These other bands don't interest me at all," I said. "I'm here for Poets and that's it. Plus I need to charge my phone anyway."

"You always let your phone die," she chuckled. We walked around the circular lobby looking for a place to sit. We stopped for a moment when someone opened the door to the auditorium and a loud scream pierced through the lobby before the door closed. Ana had a surprised look on her side but then shrugged it off; it took me much longer to recuperate. Once I calmed down, we kept looking around until we saw a long line for an autograph booth.

There wasn't anyone behind the booth yet, but my eyes were wide open when I saw the sign for which band was giving autographs: Poets of the Fall!

"Oh my god!" I exclaimed. "We gotta get their autographs!"

We went to stand in line to wait for the band members to come out and give out autographs. As we waited in line, Ana scrolled through her phone while I skimmed through the program I was given at the door. I came across a written interview with the band coupled with a group photo of them all wearing black ties and white dress shirts.

"Isn't this so cool?" I excitedly asked when I showed Ana.

"Is that what the band looks like?"

"Yep! That's right!" I then pointed to each band member to explain who is who. "This right here is Marko Saaresto," I said pointing to the guy in the middle with short blonde hair. "He's the lead singer and he has such a gorgeous voice!"

"He's one of the best vocalists of our generation," someone in front of us said.

"I know right?" I exclaimed before continuing with my explanation to Ana. "That right there is Olli Tukiainen; he does lead guitar. That's Markus Kaarlonen; he does the keyboards. That's Jani Snellman; he's the bassist for the band. Jaska Mäkinen here plays rhythm guitar—"

"How does that make it different from regular guitar?" Ana asked.

"Rhythm guitar sets the foundation for the rhythm of their songs, so it works in collaboration with the lead guitar," I said. "You can't have a good song without it."

"I see."

"And finally, this is Jari Salminen, the drummer!"

"You really do know so much about this band," Ana said.

"What can I say? They're awesome! Don't you have any bands you just love?"

Ana shrugged. "I mean, I really like Ariana Grande and Taylor Swift, but I don't really follow their personal lives like you do."

"I'm not obsessed. I just know a lot."

Ana playfully shook her head.

A few minutes later, the band came out and sat in the autograph booth. Security instructed everyone in line to not take pictures as they allowed everyone to take turns. I took out my program and got an autograph from each band member one by one. My heart pumped when I came face to face with Marko Saaresto himself!

"Oh my god, I can't believe it's really you!" I said as I handed him my program. "Your music means so much to me and has made such a huge impact on my life!"

Marko smiled. "You are so welcome," he said as he reached out and shook my hand, my other hand over my mouth as I could barely keep my excitement. Ana had Marko sign her program as well. She smiled up at me as we left the autograph booth and waited out in the lobby so I could charge my phone and wait for the show.

It was a quarter after 4 pm when we sat down near the middle section of the right side of the auditorium to get ready for the show. I looked around the room: the lights were still on as people slowly either went to stand in the orchestra pit or take their seats as we faced the stage.

I noticed Ana was on her phone again. "Whatcha looking up?"

"Seeing where we can go for dinner tonight," Ana said.

"Find anything?"

"This place looks good," she said, showing me the website for a Vietnamese restaurant ten miles away.

"That does look good. You wanna go there after the show?"

Ana nodded. "Yeah." She kept scrolling through her phone as I looked around the room in anticipation for the show.

As the auditorium started to fill up, I reached out and held Ana's hand. "I'm really glad you're here."

Ana held my hand back, smiling. "Me too."

"I'm sorry we had to wait so long in the lobby with almost nothing to do."

"It's okay," Ana assured. "There's not a lot of places within walking distance anyway."

"I hope you're having fun at least."

"I am," Ana said before browsing her phone while holding my hand.

"By the way, something funny you should know," I said.

"What's that?"

"This place is called 'Center Stage Theater.' The band has a song called 'Center Stage.' If they don't play it tonight, it will be a missed opportunity and a complete fail."

"Oh god," Ana giggled. "You and your corny jokes again."

"My jokes are not corny!"

Ana shook her head again. "I've come all the way here to Atlanta, to see a band that you are obsessed with, just to hear your corny jokes?" she teased.

Sometime later as the auditorium filled up, the lights dimmed. The spotlight shined on the backdrop with the band's logo and equipment on stage as people in the orchestra pit shouted out "Poets" over and over.

This is it, I thought. *The moment I've been waiting for!*

A few minutes later, the band finally came on and the crowd went wild. Marko stood with his microphone in hand addressing the audience. "Hello Atlanta!" he shouted, riling up the crowd. "Are you all ready for a great show tonight?" The crowd cheered. "Are you all ready for a great show tonight?" he asked again before he raised his microphone towards the audience, the audience cheering louder, though someone next to me had to apologize when they realized they screamed in my ear. "Then let's do this!"

The crowd continued cheering as all the band members took their positions while fluorescent lights illuminated the stage. They started with "Dreaming Wide Awake," setting the tone for the rest of the show. I couldn't help but absorb the atmosphere, feeling rejuvenated from the music flowing in my ears. All other noises faded away as their music put me in the zone. I looked over at Ana who had her phone up recording a short Snapchat video. We briefly held hands as we took in the first song being played.

The show went on for another half hour as the band played a catalog of their most popular songs. I occasionally looked at Ana, seemingly enjoying the performance even if she didn't directly say anything. Eventually, the band began to play "Late Goodbye," causing the crowd to scream in excitement when they started playing it.

Two minutes into the song, Ana tapped my shoulder. "I'll be right back," she whispered. "I have to use the restroom."

I gave Ana enough room to climb out so she could walk up the aisle. I glanced at her exiting the auditorium before going back to watching the show. I absorbed more of the performance, but something Marko sang in "Late Goodbye" gave me pause. I thought about the night we broke up last year. *Would she do that again? I* thought. *Would this be the last time we ever go to an event like this?*

Marko pointed his microphone to the audience to have them sing along to the chorus. I stopped dwelling on the thought, pushing it out of my mind for now so I could sing along with the crowd and enjoy the moment.

22

———————

February 9, 2020

For the first time since leaving Schweitzer, I was excited for the Oscars.

I couldn't remember the last time I actually sat down and watched something I used to love as a kid, having spent so much time and energy trying to get the hell out of that place. Now here I was, sitting back on Ana's bed watching a show from my laptop I never thought I would ever enjoy again while Ana put laundry away. "Ana, they're getting ready to announce Best Picture!"

Ana hung up a shirt. "Which one do you think is going to win?"

"It better be *Parasite*. If it doesn't win, I'll get in my car and drive all the way up to LA and give the Academy voters a piece of my mind!"

"You go do that," she teased. "Make sure you don't get arrested."

I looked back at my laptop screen as Ana finished putting her laundry away and came to sit next to me. I began rubbing my arm as the show went to commercials.

"Is your arm doing better now?" Ana asked.

"Getting there." I sighed as I rubbed it a little more. "I still can't believe that asshole just stopped all of a sudden. Didn't give me enough time to react."

"You shouldn't have admitted fault."

"What would've been the point? I would've had to go to court, and it was a 'he said, she said' anyway. It is what it is. At least I got a new car out of it."

"How's the new car driving?"

"I love my new Scion; it drives great. I know it's only been a week, but I love it so far!" I then grabbed Ana's hand and kissed it. "Thank you so much for taking me to get it."

"Of course," Ana said, smiling.

The Oscar ceremony returned from commercials. "Are you rooting for *Parasite* to win Best Picture?" I asked.

"I know it's popular with a lot of Asians. All my coworkers can't stop talking about it."

"What did you think of it?"

"I watched about thirty minutes of it on Hulu and fell asleep. Found it boring."

I made a playful gasp. "What? You fell asleep to one of the greatest movies ever made?"

"Since you put it that way, yes!" she teased as she grabbed her water bottle placed on her desk chair next to her bed. "I fell asleep to one of the greatest movies ever made!"

I giggled. "I can proudly say that I've seen all the Best Picture nominees so I can say with authority that *Parasite* is the best!"

"Why am I not surprised you've seen *all* the movies?" she teased again.

The Oscar ceremony went on, with Jane Fonda announcing the Best Director winner as Bong Joon-ho. "Hell yeah!" I exclaimed.

"That is pretty cool," Ana said.

"Now *Parasite* has to win Best Picture and all will be right with the world!"

"I doubt it will win."

"Why do you say that?"

Ana drank some water. "It's usually films by white people that win Best Picture. It would be cool if a movie made by Asians won, but I wouldn't count on it." She took another sip of her water before getting up to use the restroom.

A few minutes later into the Oscars, Jane Fonda began the announcement for Best Picture. "And the Oscar goes to . . . *Parasite!*"

"Yes!" I exclaimed as I pumped my fist.

A moment later, Ana came out of the bathroom.

"*Parasite* won!" I announced.

"Oh nice."

I put my laptop on the nightstand as Ana changed into her pajamas. I snuck a picture of her smiling as she sat at the edge of the bed and looked at her phone before getting into the sheets. I cuddled her from behind and wrapped my arms around her. She held one of my arms with one hand while scrolling through her phone with the other.

"My sister and I are planning to go to Vegas next month," Ana said at one point.

"You're going to Vegas again?" I teased. "We literally just went for New Years."

"I know, but it's my sister's spring break, and she really wants me to go."

"You are such a good older sister. I hope you have fun."

"Has the semester started for you already?" Ana asked while browsing her phone.

"I start work in the Writing Center at Mesa this week."

"What about SDSU?"

"I got nothing this semester from them again." I sat up and rested against the headboard while Ana sat up as well. "I can't keep doing this every spring."

"What about other colleges or even teaching high school?"

"I've sent applications for every community college I can think of, and don't even get me started on high school."

"What about GrubHub or Doordash?"

I sighed. "I'm so burnt out by all that. Every cent I make doing that just goes towards gas and car maintenance. I'm at the point where I just do the bare minimum and then go home. If I had an excuse to just not do any of it, I'd take it—"

"Oh my god!' Ana interrupted.

"What?"

"Another coronavirus case reported up in Orange County."

"Another one? Weren't there other cases reported up in LA? There are more cases now?"

Ana took a moment to respond. "This is starting to get a little concerning."

"Do you think it's going to come here to San Diego?"

"I hope not."

I sighed.

"Do you think it's going to become an epidemic?"

I looked over at Ana, thinking about what to say. "I remember when I was a sophomore in college, there was the Swine Flu. It was serious. Don't get me wrong, but life went on as normal. I'm not too worried. This'll likely pass."

"I hope you're right," Ana solemnly said.

Ana went back to her phone. I climbed off the bed and went into the kitchen to grab a Diet Coke, browsing Facebook on my phone as I drank. A few seconds after I logged in, a half-joking, half-serious post Alex made last week showed up in my feed again.

ALEX FLAHIVE:

So are we all gonna die from this virus or what?

I thought about what Ana said. *I hope I'm right too.*

March 18, 2020

It had been a week since the WHO declared COVID-19 a pandemic.

I sat in my car in the Vons parking lot, putting on music to calm myself down. I had just left the store not getting what I came for after seeing all the shelves empty and huge crowds causing excessive noise throughout the building. On Facebook, all Ben, Alex, and everyone else could talk about was the coronavirus. "Don't go to crowded areas, don't eat out, be concerned and start preparing if you haven't as this is only the beginning," one of Alex's friends posted.

I sent Ana an article about the Las Vegas strip being completely empty just as Aunt Judy called.

"Rob, I'm trying to get a hold of your mom," she said. "Have you heard from her?"

"I saw her this morning before I left. She likely didn't charge her phone again."

Aunt Judy grunted. "Not surprised. Is that woman ever going to join the twenty-first century?" She cleared her throat. "Anyway, I'm trying to call her to tell her that I don't think she should be seeing Grandpa for a while. This virus is really getting out of control, and with the way she goes out all the time and the amount of times she goes to the casino, I'm scared she's going to catch it and spread it to him."

"I know. But she's stubborn."

"Can you at least make sure she's staying safe? I'm stuck up here and can't just drive down where you're at and slap some common sense into my own sister."

"Sure," I muttered.

"Thank you! Anyway, sorry for unloading all that on you. How've you been? How's Ana?"

"Ana's fine. Her sister is in town for the week and spending time with her before she goes back home to Santa Cruz. They were supposed to go to Vegas this week, but they decided to cancel."

"Smart girl. Not safe to travel anywhere right now."

I sighed. "Mesa shifted all tutoring online and had my hours drastically cut again."

"Yikes! That's bad! I know you're not working at State right now, but are you still doing food delivery?"

I rubbed my eyes. "Barely. I'm sick of it! I don't know if I can keep doing it."

"Have you thought about applying for unemployment?" Aunt

Judy suggested. "My neighbor's son recently got laid off, and he had to file for unemployment. You could look into that. Food delivery is still 1099 work, right?"

"Yeah."

"Then do it! At least consider it."

We talked a little bit more before we ended our phone call. I then checked my messages to see Ana responded to my last text about the Las Vegas strip.

ANA:

> Yeah, in pictures it's so empty. Everything is shut down. Probably the first time in a long time it's been like that.

ROB:

> When we went there for New Years, it was so crowded. Never dreamed it would be so empty three months later. I'm glad you didn't go.

I came home and parked on the street sometime later close to the evening to see both Mom and Alicia's cars in the driveway, their trunks wide open and filled to the brim with grocery bags. As I approached the front door, Alicia came out and went to the trunk of her car. "Rob, come help!" She demanded as she grabbed groceries.

I picked up a couple of bags and headed into the house. In the kitchen, every single square inch of the floor was covered with grocery bags, stacks of soda cases, milk and juice jugs, extra spices, cans of ravioli and spaghetti-os, and piles upon piles of TV dinners. There were even three large packages of toilet paper on the counter.

"What the hell?" I shouted.

"Quiet, Rob!" Mom exclaimed, standing near the kitchen table with her phone to her ear. It was clear by the tone of her voice she was talking to Jason. "I keep telling you! I don't know! We just found out today the Developmental Center is not allowing visitors for a while because of this stupid virus. Don't you get that?"

"What's going on here?" I asked.

Mom ended the call. "Rob, the news said there's a major food shortage, so me and your sister rushed out and got $500 worth of groceries."

"You gotta be kidding me?"

"Rob, help us!" Alicia demanded again when she came back into the kitchen and dropped off a few more bags. I took pictures of the ocean of groceries and sent them to Ana, texting about what's going on and how insane this all was.

"Mom, before I forget, Aunt Judy called," I said. "She's scared you're going to spread this virus to Grandpa. She doesn't want you to see him until this whole thing blows over."

"She's being ridiculous! I'll call her back later about it."

I grunted. *This is pointless,* I thought. As I was about to get more groceries, Ana texted me back and we engaged in a brief exchange.

ANA:

WTH? Are they going to work from home now? LOL

ROB:

That was my reaction haha. At least I don't have to go out for food. We are prepared. WTH indeed! LOL

March 27, 2020

I sat in my car in a parking lot somewhere after I left Grandpa's and did food deliveries. For the past week, I'd used whatever I could find as a face mask: cooking aprons, bandanas, ripped up towels, and many others. I was lucky to get a bottle of hand sanitizer to keep in my glove compartment before it became impossible to buy. When Grandpa offered me an extra N95 mask, I rushed over to get it but made it clear he had to leave it outside on the front porch. *You're more vulnerable to this virus than I am,* I told him over the phone. *I don't want to come around and risk spreading it to you, but I'll still call you.* I had decided the best thing to do was limit face to face contact strictly to Mom, Alicia, and Ana.

I checked my GrubHub app and saw my earnings for the day. "This is a load of bullshit," I muttered. I turned off the app and put on music, giving myself time to stim before heading home. I browsed social media before I found myself opening my Facebook Messenger app to Ana, realizing it was Friday and I hadn't talked to her for the past couple days.

I texted Ana to check up on her, not expecting a response right away since she likely was at work. To my surprise, she messaged me back saying she was fine and was on her way home. We engaged in idle chit chat before talking about the lockdown.

ROB:

How long do you think this lockdown will last? I'm thinking at least two months at the rate we're going.

ANA:

IDK. Not going to be done anytime soon. USA has closed its borders, and the virus has a higher infection rate in the USA than China. I think China is lying lol.

ROB:

I wouldn't be surprised. China lies all the time.

ANA:

😂 No way they only have 80k infections, whereas a small country like USA and we still have more infections. Now I don't allow anyone within 6 feet of me. I'm trying to be super cautious.

ROB:

Same.

ANA:

> This is crazy. I even wipe down my packages now since idk if it will live on the surfaces of the packages. Our office has limited Clorox wipes too. It's impossible to buy them right now.

ROB:

> That's crazy. I'm glad you're staying safe.

ANA:

> I don't think it's a good idea that you come by my house until this thing dies down. I don't want you to get sick and I don't want anyone to infect me either.

My heart sank when I read her last text. I took a breath before I texted back.

ROB:

> 😢*hugs* I don't blame you. I want this to be over.

ANA:

> If possible, I would rather not go to the grocery store lol. People touch everything there.

ROB:

> Do you want me to deliver your groceries for you? Lol

ANA:

> No, it's fine. I don't need much groceries. I already stocked up.

ROB:

> If there is anything you need that I can get for you, let me know.

ANA:

ROB:

I can't wait for this to be over. I want to see you. ☹

I put my phone away. "Fuck this virus!" I shouted as I began driving home.

March 30, 2020

I woke up and read my text messages with Ana from last night. We had played hangman and watched a movie together through the Netflix Party extension. I couldn't help but smile as I read our last part of our exchange.

ROB:

I love you! ☺

ANA:

🖤 I love you, too.

I reread the exchange multiple times. *I can make this social distancing work with her*, I thought as I got ready to do GrubHub. I only tutored online on Tuesdays and Thursdays for two hours at a time, so it seemed like a good idea to make food deliveries worth it today. After I showered and got dressed, I went outside expecting to do my normal routine, only to begin to fume with rage the second I saw what had happened.

Someone had hit the rear end of my car and pushed it over onto the sidewalk!

I let out a stream of obscenities as I screamed into the air.

I spent most of the day on the phone with my insurance company going through the headache of having to file a claim to deal with the mess. I lost count of how many times I hit my hand over and over so I could avoid having a meltdown in front of my neighbors. Police came a couple hours later to investigate so I could file a report before my car was towed away to be assessed for damages. I dropped all my GrubHub shifts and stayed home, helping my mom clean the house before taking a nap in my room.

Later that evening during a break practicing my guitar, I sent Ana pictures of the crash telling her what happened.

ANA:

> OMG, people have to drive normally. Just because less cars are on the road doesn't mean they can drive recklessly. Have you taken it to the repair shop or are you waiting for insurance?

ROB:

> They had it towed to assess the damage. They'll let me know by tomorrow.

ANA:

> What are you going to do in the meantime?

ROB:

> Well, since we're under quarantine and stuck at home, it's not like I need to go anywhere.

ANA:

> Exactly! If I didn't have a car I wouldn't be too bummed out since it would give me more reason to stay home. Have you filed for unemployment?

ROB:

> I haven't.

ANA:

> If I were you, I would do it. Might as well.

ROB:

> I don't know what I'm going to do with my time.

ANA:

> Maybe do more writing. Play your guitar more or
> go on walks.

I thought about her suggestions for a moment before I sent her one more text.

ROB:

> Off topic, but I heard my sister cough and I
> thought it was the virus but saw she was just
> smoking her bong. I never thought I'd be glad to
> see that lol

ANA:

> LMAO. Stay away from her!

ROB:

> Oh me and her stay away from each other anyway
> so it's not like it makes a difference lol

ANA:

> Now is the time to stay far away. Continue the
> distance LOL

I laughed before putting my phone away and practicing my guitar.

March 31, 2020

No students came for tutoring, so I logged out fifteen minutes early. I still hadn't received a call from the repair shop about my car. At 11 am, I suddenly thought again about what Ana suggested last night about going on walks. *That's actually not a bad idea*, I thought. I changed my clothes, plugged my headphones into my phone, and grabbed my mask before going outside, putting on "Yesterday Once More" by The Carpenters to start my walk.

I walked down the sidewalk away from the house and towards

the park. Barely any cars drove by as I walked for some time before having to cross the street and continue my walk, strolling on the sidewalk next to the park and heading towards the main street. I took in the light breeze as the sun warmed my neck.

I crossed the other side of the park and began going past the parking lot of a church while Simon and Garfunkel's "Kathy's Song" played in my ears. Staring at the lot as I strolled, it made me remember the one time Ana had me pick her up at this spot after she hired someone to detail her car here. "Still can't believe you paid $150 to have that done here," I said out loud as I kept walking past the church.

I arrived at the four way intersection and pressed the crosswalk button. The main road would normally have plenty of traffic at this intersection, but it was now an empty landscape, with only two or three cars at the red light and nobody else for miles. A weird sight to see, the only thing missing were rolling tumbleweeds. I looked around at the strange new world, waiting a long time before the light finally turned green so I could cross the street.

I crossed over the bridge extending over the 805 and kept walking until I was in the Convoy District. Along Convoy Street, almost no cars drove on the street as I took a left turn. I passed by a car dealership and some Korean BBQ restaurants, all with empty parking lots. When I saw Tofu House in the distance, I stopped for a moment and walked toward it, crossing another lot to stand next to the restaurant. A "Take Out Only" sign plastered on the front door of the restaurant with not a single customer inside.

Ana and I had our first date here, I thought. *It's so weird to see this.*

I looked around the empty strip mall again and then took pictures, texting them to Ana when I saw she was online.

ROB:

This feels straight out of The Walking Dead!

I put my phone back in my pocket and looked at the front entrance of Tofu House for a bit thinking a lot about my first date with Ana before I went back to my walk. I walked around the strip mall and then continued down Convoy Street, passing more empty parking lots and other restaurants and closed down non-essential businesses. I stopped in front of a Wendy's when I heard a *ding* from my phone, thinking Ana had texted me back.

Instead, it was the repair shop calling me about my car.

"Good news is that it is covered by your insurance," they said after they explained what they found in their inspection. "But it is going to take about three weeks to fix."

"Three weeks? How much damage did they do?"

"About $5000 worth."

I gasped. "You're kidding me?"

"Afraid not." For five minutes, the repair shop went over my options about car rentals. I reluctantly told them I would pick up the rental tomorrow afternoon.

"I'm filing for unemployment," I muttered after the call.

Ana still hadn't texted me back even when I got back home two hours later.

April 4, 2020

For the past few days, walking around the neighborhood slowly started becoming part of my daily routine. Since it was Saturday, I would normally be getting ready to go to Ana's, but we were still under lockdown.

I was an hour into my walk when I went past a house near an elementary school, stumbling upon a multicolored chalk drawing in the middle of the sidewalk. Surrounded by flower designs, it depicted the words "April Distance Brings May Existence." Every word was written in a different color, like colors of the rainbow.

I stared down at the drawing, smiling as I took a photo of it and shared it with Ana. She sent me a laugh emoji a moment later.

ANA:

I totally agree. April will be worse though.

ROB:

It will be. 🙁 At least we're staying safe at home. I can't wait for it to be over.

April 5, 2020

I walked late into the afternoon, two full hours of walking before my phone started dying. I sent Ana a funny meme about the pandemic, but no response. *Probably napping again,* I thought. I bought a portable charger and went home to play video games.

April 6, 2020

I went on another walk, making sure I had my portable phone charger. I didn't talk to Ana and instead focused on walking. I was ready to take on the quiet world, step by step.

April 7, 2020

I held my regular tutoring hours on Zoom before walking again for three hours. I sent Ana another meme but no response until later that evening. We chit-chatted before she fell asleep, making me wonder if I was messaging her too much.

April 8 & 9, 2020

I alternated between taking naps and doom scrolling. Constant news about massive death tolls all over the world appeared in my social media feeds. Hospitals everywhere were overwhelmed. Reports of morgues running out of body bags. I couldn't get it out of my head. I didn't talk to Ana. I gave her more space so I didn't feel like a burden to her.

April 10, 2020

I excitedly told Ana I would get unemployment and made her a Spotify playlist. She sent me a thumbs up and a smile emoji.

April 11, 12, 13, & 14, 2020

For four days straight, I did nothing but walk, play guitar, or play video games. On and off, Ana and I would chat through Facebook messenger or share random memes about the pandemic. At one point, I shared a drawing Ben made. It was a more polished, professional version of a children's artwork of a dog he posted on Facebook.

ANA:

OMG that dog is so cute!!

I had smiled at her message, imagining us *on stage side by side dressed up as Iron Man and Captain America, ready to face an army of COVID clusters while the audience cheered us on.*

April 22, 2020

I started my routine walk with Radiohead's "No Surprises." I walked past the park, crossed the bridge over the 805 freeway, and went down Convoy Street again, something I've done countless times. More people were around than last week, so I kept my mask on just in case. I arrived at a bus stop and sat at the bench to rest for a few minutes. I changed the song and drank water from a bottle I brought with me.

I was about to stand up when Ana sent me a frantic text.

ANA:

OMG, I drove behind a person who pulled out a gun and shot it into thin air. No idea what he was firing at but I was shocked.

ROB:

OMG! Are you ok???

ANA:

I'm fine. He wasn't aiming at me. I'm back home, but this was maybe 10 minutes ago.

ROB:

That's terrifying! Why the hell would he do something like that?

I hyperventilated, taking several deep breaths and drank more water to calm down. I needed a few more minutes of rest before I went back to my walk, so I scrolled through social media again. *She's going to be okay!* I thought repeatedly. I started calming down until a news story from CBS showed up in my feed about a man kicking an Asian woman wearing a mask while riding the subway in New York City, calling her a "diseased bitch."

Ana is going to be okay, I thought. *She's safe. No one's going to hurt her!*

I tried to get it out of my head as I crossed the street and onto another strip mall. As I walked into the parking lot of a Target, a large group of lockdown protestors stood near the entrance with banners and signs. "End this Lockdown!" One sign read. "Tyranny is Spreading Faster than the China Virus!" read another. None of these protesters wore face masks. I stood twelve feet away from them keeping my face covered, unsure what to do next.

If these assholes had it their way, this pandemic will go on forever, I angrily thought.

I began walking towards the other side of the parking lot when an Asian woman and her young daughter wearing face masks walked in my direction, going around me and past the protestors. As they went into the Target, I suddenly thought about Ana again, *my headspace placing me on stage decorated to look like Ana's kitchen. We were eating lunch, chatting, telling jokes, and laughing when a trio of lockdown protestors barged onto the stage.*

Two of the protestors held me down while the third one grabbed Ana as she screamed. "You diseased bitch!" The protester shouted as he pushed the table out of the way and opened a trap door in the middle of the stage. He then grabbed Ana and jumped down through the trap door, the other protestors following behind.

"Ana!" I shouted.

Back in the parking lot, I looked at the group of the protestors. Without thinking, I gave them the finger. "You are all pieces of shit, and I hope you all fucking burn in hell!"

I squirted water in their general direction and ran as fast as I could. One protester gave chase before giving up when I hid in an alley. I sat down against the cement wall, trying to catch my breath. I pulled out my phone again and looked at my messages from Ana, debating whether or not to send her a text to double check if she was okay. Ana didn't respond to my last text.

As I debated whether or not to message Ana again, *I jumped through the open trap door and fell in a dark abyss for what seemed to be an eternity until landing flat on an empty stage.*

I lay there before picking myself up, the audience shrouded in darkness.

But then I heard Ana's voice behind me. "Hello!" her voice echoed. I turned around to face five tall mirrors surrounding me in a semicircle. Ana stood in each mirror, each one a different version of herself I've known since the day I met her. "Hello," she said again, echoing throughout the auditorium. "Hello," she said again.

I stared at the mirrors, unsure what to say as Ana's "Hello" echoed multiple times.

This thought lingered in my head as I stared at my text message exchange with Ana from earlier. Still no response. I began to type something, but then stopped myself. I didn't want to burden her more. "Fuck this virus so bad!" I cried.

April 25, 2020

I was playing video games that morning when Ben called. We talked about being stuck at home and how glad I was to get my car back. When I told him Ana liked his artwork, he expressed gratitude and asked how we were holding up since we are not quarantining together.

"It's hard," I said. "Really hard. Trying to stay connected with her through text is not the same at all as being with her in person. Can't cuddle or be intimate online. COVID has ruined our sex life."

"At least you were having sex before all this went down," Ben chuckled.

"Oh shut up! The point is it feels like I'm in a long distance relationship, and it sucks. I miss her like crazy, Ben!"

"What about calling her?"

"You know I'm not much of a phone person and neither is she," I said.

"You're talking to me over the phone right now!" Ben exclaimed.

"You're different! Not everyone loves the phone like you do." I let out an exasperated sigh. "I'm just hoping things will die down soon so we can get back to the way things were."

"Don't you get it, Rob? There is no 'going back to the way things were.' COVID has changed everything!"

"So what are you saying? That me and Ana are never going to see each other in person again until this stupid pandemic is over?"

"I'm not saying that. I'm saying with the way things are going, whatever 'thing' we are going back ain't going to be the same as it used to be."

I sighed again.

"There is some good news though," Ben continued. "Based on

the current trajectory, it's likely things will get a little bit more under control by either early or mid May. Did you hear that they've opened up COVID testing this week?"

"No. Where?"

"Let me send you the website." Ben texted me a link to the COVID Clinic website. "The closest location to you is downtown. If I were you and I wanted to prove to the girlfriend that I'm not having sex with right now—wink, wink—that I don't have COVID, this is your best bet. Test negative and you two can start boning again."

I cringed at Ben's comment, clearly said without a hint of irony or sarcasm. "You are definitely something else."

"Just something to consider, Rob."

I ended the call with Ben before I looked through the COVID Clinic. It was legitimate, though a huge downside was it would cost $125 just for a single PCR test. "Shit," I said when I saw the price. I thought about not going through with it, but then I thought about what Ben said about proving to Ana that I was not infected.

I took out my credit card and pre-registered for my PCR test tomorrow morning before texting Ana a link to the website, telling her all about it.

***

April 26, 2020

A nurse thrusted a swab up my nose when I went to the drive-thru COVID Clinic. Having that swab hurt like hell. I then went home afterwards to take a shower. Looking at myself in the mirror after I showered, my hair was long and wild. Makes sense, considering I hadn't been to a barber in almost four months. All the barber shops closed when I realized I needed a haircut.

I grabbed a pair of scissors and trimmed my hair, cutting off all of my curls, staring at myself in the mirror, numb to the terrible job I did.

April 29, 2020

Ana and I didn't text at all for a few days, so I did nothing but play video games and practice my guitar. When I received an email my COVID results were in, my heart raced. I nervously opened the email, sighing with relief after I read them.

I texted Ana.

ROB:

I got my COVID results today. I'm negative. 🙂

Twenty minutes later, Ana sent me a thumbs up emoji and nothing more.

April 30, 2020

I walked for four hours straight, avoiding everybody. When I came home later, I sat on the curve and wiped sweat from my face and uncontrollable tears from my eyes.

May 1, 2020

When I called Grandpa to wish him a happy 89th birthday, he convinced me to come over and celebrate with Mom and Alicia when I told him I tested negative for COVID. "You're not going to spread the virus to me," he said, assuring it would just be him, Mom, and Alicia with her new boyfriend Dale. They also all tested negative. "I trust you!" he reiterated.

We had steak and birthday cake, everyone excited except me. I snuck a Snapchat photo of Grandpa and posted "Happy Birthday." Five minutes later, Ana responded to my snap.

ANA:

> Happy Birthday, Grandpa John! ☺

I couldn't help but give a weak smile when I saw her response.

May 3, 2020

I started my walk close to 11 am with Coldplay's "The Scientist." I had a short text exchange with Ana an hour before I left, talking about being stuck at home. Before leaving, I made another Spotify playlist for Ana and sent it to her. She expressed appreciation.

As I walked, I suddenly had the desire to hear Ana's voice again. Since it was Sunday and she was likely to be home, I debated whether or not to just call her out of the blue. When I got to the corner, I texted her again.

ROB:

> If you're up for it, I can call you later. I miss hearing your voice ☺

I put the exchange out of my mind and walked. Ten minutes later, she responded back.

ANA:

> You can come over if you want.

I immediately stopped, trying to process what I read.

ROB:

> Wait! Are you sure? Is it safe to come over?

ANA:

> Up to you.

I had my hand over my mouth, trying to control my excitement.

ROB:

Only if you feel safe. I'm free atm.

ANA:

Ok. You can come over now.

I took a deep breath, texted Ana I would be right over, and rushed home to get to my car.

———

I drove to Ana's place as fast as I could. Ana told me she left the gate open for me, so I parked my car across the street and let myself in. I could see Ana through the sliding door cooking lunch with the portable stove and the rice cooker as I left my shoes outside.

I opened the door and walked into her kitchen for the first time in months.

"Hi," Ana meekly said when she saw me.

I smiled at her, feeling her carpet underneath my toes before I went to give her a hug.

"I missed you so much," I mumbled as we hugged. *My Iron Man*, I thought, holding back tears. I kissed Ana on the forehead, both of us hugging for a moment before letting go.

"Did you eat already?" Ana asked as she went to flip the spam.

"I have not." I offered to help with lunch, but Ana said she was fine, so I sat at the kitchen table at the spot I usually sat before the pandemic started. Sometime after Ana finished cooking, we made ourselves plates of food and sat across from each other. I looked over at Ana, unsure what to say.

"How are you?" I asked, trying to start a conversation.

Ana sighed. "I'm okay," she said, not looking at me as she took another bite.

I sighed as well. Neither of us said anything else to each other as we ate.

Today

23

June 1, 2022

I landed in Chicago and grabbed an Uber, keeping my mask on as I sat in the backseat. We drove on the highway as I took in the view of the moving city until we got off at an exit. I stayed lost in thought until the Uber driver asked me where I was from and what I did for a living in an effort to start a conversation. I kept looking out the window as we talked.

"What brings you to Chicago?" she asked.

"Personal reasons. I have the whole month off, so I thought, 'Why not?'"

"That's cool. Hope you have fun."

The conversation died down as we stopped at a red light. I stared out the window, looking around the city again. I saw a billboard of an Asian American woman smiling while holding up her iPhone, instantly reminding me of the night Ana sat by her bedside smiling and scrolling through her phone during the Oscars. *She loved that phone more than she ever loved you,* a voice in my head lectured.

Fuck that phone so much.

I made myself at home at my Airbnb that evening, sitting up on the bed as I looked through photos on my phone. My room was on the third floor of a house in the Northside of Chicago, with nothing but a TV, mini couch, and a large window overlooking a neighborhood that could have come straight out of a Norman Rockwell painting. I stopped to cough before I scrolled again, only to pause and look at one particular photo. It was a photo of Ana and I smiling next to each other on a bench while attending a Christmas lights festival at the College of Southern Nevada in Las Vegas. We both looked so happy.

The date of the photo read December 31, 2019, right before the pandemic.

I stared at the photo for several minutes before putting it away, turning the lights off so I could sleep. Staring into space, I couldn't stop thinking about how long Ana and I were apart when the pandemic first started. I couldn't stop thinking about all the times Ana either barely talked to me or didn't talk to me at all. *Did the pandemic kill my relationship with her?*

I thought about the billboard I saw on the way over here. As I thought about how it made me think of Ana, my eyes began to water.

"Why wouldn't you talk to me?"

I sobbed, crying for a full minute before I coughed uncontrollably until it was completely gone. I drank from a water bottle sitting on the nightstand before laying back down, slowly drifting into an uneasy sleep.

Yesterday

24

───────

April 15, 2021

Grandpa was ecstatic when he told me he was cooking chicken curry for the first time. "Come over hungry," he insisted. "I'm making your favorite!"

I parked in front of his house when I saw Aunt Judy and Uncle Bill's RV in the driveway, completely forgetting they came into town recently. Aunt Judy told me they were road tripping around the country and planned to stay for Grandpa's 90th birthday before heading back home. As I lunged my backpack over my shoulder and walked up the driveway, Uncle Bill stopped washing the RV to greet me, engaging in friendly chit-chat before telling me the front door was open.

As I let myself into the kitchen, Grandpa stirred the chicken and rice while Aunt Judy and Alicia talked at the table about when they all got vaccinated. "I finally was able to get mine," Alicia proudly said. They stopped talking when Aunt Judy saw me and got up to give me a hug. "Rob, I'm so glad to see you," she said.

"It's been a while," I said. "Is Mom here? She said she was coming over today."

"She went to go get cigarettes, but she'll be right back," Aunt

255

Judy said. She then turned to Grandpa. "Dad, your grandson's here."

Grandpa kept stirring the food, not looking up from what he was doing.

"Oh shoot, he forgot his hearing aids," Aunt Judy whispered to me before turning to Grandpa. "Dad, Rob's here!" she shouted.

Grandpa perked up. "Hi Rob!"

I sat at the table and put my bag by my feet.

Alicia began heading out, saying goodbye to Grandpa and Aunt Judy. "I can't stay for lunch. I have to meet with a friend. Love you Aunt Judy. Love you Grandpa." She grabbed her stuff, not saying anything to me as she walked out the front door.

I caught up with Aunt Judy since we hadn't seen each other since the pandemic started.

"I finally was able to get spring classes at State," I said at one point.

"That's awesome, bud."

"It's only two online classes though. Kinda sucks, but ... at least I'll qualify for a one year contract."

"You're still moving on up though. What about Mesa? Will they hire you back once this pandemic is over?"

I sighed. "I wouldn't count on it."

We kept chatting before Aunt Judy's phone went off. "Shoot, I have to take this," she said. "Dad, you and Rob can get started on lunch. I'll be right back."

Aunt Judy went into the living room. Grandpa served chicken curry and rice in bowls at the table so we could eat together. "I made this special just for you, Rob," he said. "Let me know if it's like that Indian restaurant we go to."

I took a bite, slowly chewing it to give Grandpa the impression it was the best chicken I've ever eaten.

"Well, what do you think?" Grandpa asked. "Did I do good or what?"

"You did great," I meekly said.

"How's Ana?" Grandpa asked as he usually would every time I came over. "She hasn't come around as much as she used to."

I shrugged. "She's good. She's just been working a lot lately, so it's hard for her to find time. We've been talking about going to the Grand Canyon this summer. We just haven't figured out when yet."

"I haven't been there in over thirty years," Grandpa said. "It's gorgeous!"

"I've never been."

Grandpa took another bite of his food. "Well, I hope you two have fun."

We kept eating, not saying much.

"So what have you been up to lately?" Grandpa eventually asked. "Busy as usual?"

I took another bite of my food. "I went to Dad's grave today."

"Yeah?"

"Yeah," I mumbled.

Sitting there, I found myself *on stage standing in front of Dad. Multiple TVs were mounted high up on the walls of the stage playing video clips of me with my dad either fishing, going bowling, or him telling me a bedtime story at seven years old. I walked up to Dad and gave him a huge hug, crying as I did so.*

"I wish he would come back," I said, getting the daydream out of my mind.

"I know," he muttered before taking another bite of his food. "If it means anything, he would have been very proud of you."

I sighed before taking another bite. "I just wish he was around to see it." I sighed. "Don't get me wrong, I love you to death, Grandpa, but you're not my dad. It's not the same thing. It's never been the same thing."

Grandpa looked at me, a faint disappointed look on his face. "I understand."

"I do love the curry you made here," I politely said.

"I'm glad you do," Grandpa solemnly said. "If you want the recipe, let me know."

"Thanks."

"Don't wait too long. I won't be around forever."

"Oh Grandpa," I chuckled. "Don't be silly! You'll be around for at least five more years."

Grandpa sighed. I took another bite as Aunt Judy came back into the kitchen, talking about a phone call with a friend who had an emergency with her dad, while Grandpa got up and fixed her and Uncle Bill some food. I excused myself to attend a planned Zoom meeting with a student, grabbing my bag before going into the living room to set up my laptop to take the call.

April 23, 2021

I had barely woken up around 9 am when Mom pounded on my door. "Rob, get up!" she screamed at the top of her lungs. "Grandpa had a stroke!"

Wait! What? I frantically thought.

I quickly got dressed and grabbed my face mask, phone, and keys. I rushed past Alicia's room, her door wide open as she desperately looked for her keys, and ran outside to see Mom getting in her car parked on the driveway. "We gotta go!" she exasperatedly demanded when she saw me. "Rob, are you riding with me?"

"I barely know what's going on!" I shouted.

"We have to go!" Mom shouted back, on the verge of tears.

"I'll take my car. What hospital is he at?"

"He's at Kaiser. You can follow me, or I'll meet you there."

Alicia ran past me, telling me to move as she got to her car while Mom frantically drove out of the driveway. I got in my Scion, trying to process what the hell was happening.

I parked in one of the parking garages and ran to the hospital entrance, only to stop when I saw Uncle Bill and Alicia sitting on the benches outside. Alicia talked on the phone with who I assumed was her boyfriend, repeatedly trying to assure herself everything was going to be okay. Uncle Bill stayed silent until he saw me and then me waved over.

I sat next to him, talking about how he was doing before I asked him what happened.

"I woke up around seven and made my morning coffee," he said, "but instead of going in the house to have coffee with Grandpa like I usually would, I had it in the RV. When I went to go check on Grandpa, he had been on the bathroom floor for two hours!" Uncle Bill paused to compose himself. "I panicked when I saw him just laying there. He kept saying over and over, 'I think I had a stroke.' Your aunt and I picked him up, got him dressed, and rushed him over here as soon as possible. God, I'm so stupid! Why didn't I check on him sooner! What was I thinking?"

"He's going to be okay, Uncle Bill" Alicia nervously said. "You said it yourself that the doctors were able to catch the clot early. He's strong. He'll pull through!"

"Where's Mom and Aunt Judy?" I asked.

"They're inside," Uncle Bill said. "They're only allowing two family members at a time right now because of stupid COVID restrictions. We're all vaccinated! This is absolute bullshit!"

I sighed, not sure what to say. I briefly called Aunt Judy, who told me they were still running tests and would let me know more once she received more information.

We all waited for a while, doing anything to pass the time. *Everything is going to be okay,* I thought repeatedly. *They caught the clot early. He'll be home and everything will be okay.*

Later, I checked my phone to see it was sometime after 11 am. "I'm gonna call Aunt Judy back." I dialed her number and gave Uncle Bill and Alicia space.

It took a minute for Aunt Judy to answer my call before I asked how she was doing.

"Well, not great. I don't know what else to say. Your mom is having a really hard time keeping herself together. They just finished examining him."

"Grandpa is going to be okay, right?"

There was a long pause before Aunt Judy finally answered. "Rob," she slowly whispered, as if trying to fight tears. "It's not looking good."

My heart sank as Aunt Judy began to tell me the grim details of what the doctors found when they tried to treat him. Each horrifying detail she gave started to blur in my head. None of this felt real. I ended the call, keeping my distance from everyone as I tried to take in everything.

I didn't see Grandpa until hours later. Mom refused to leave his side, so Aunt Judy compromised by having us each take turns being in the room with mom. I made sure to wear my face mask as I went through the hospital checkpoint, took the elevator to the fourth floor, and went down the hallway to his room. Grandpa slept on his back in the large bed. A nasal cannula pressed into his nostrils, IV lines connected to both of his arms, and medical equipment monitored his vital signs—it was a scene from every medical drama I'd ever seen.

Mom sat on a couch by the window with her Bible in her lap, praying with her eyes closed. A nurse stood in front of Grandpa's bed jotting down notes on a clipboard, greeting me when he saw me come into the room.

I told him I was family before asking him how Grandpa had been doing.

"He's been sleeping on and off, but otherwise, stable right now."

I looked over at Grandpa, noticing the large purple bruises on his left arm and a side of his face slanted. "What happened there?" I asked, pointing to his arm. "Was that from the fall?"

"That was from the fall," he confirmed.

"What about his face?"

"That's where most of the clot happened. Emergency surgery

was attempted, though I'm afraid because of all that plaque buildup in the brain—"

"Don't say that!" Mom shouted. "You don't know that!"

I let out a brief sigh. "Sorry about my mom."

"It's okay," the nurse affirmed. "I get it. I probably shouldn't say anything else. My mistake." The nurse wrote something else on the clipboard. "If you want to discuss your grandfather's condition, it may be a good idea to talk to Dr. Chudzinski."

The nurse wished us well and left the room. I went over to Mom to ask her if she was okay.

She looked straight up at me. "Do I look okay to you?" she angrily yelled, tears coming down her face.

I kneeled down to wrap her arms around her. She hugged me back, kissing my head and crying. "I'm sorry," she said in between tears. "I didn't mean to yell at you."

"It's okay," I mumbled. We hugged for a while before we let go. I grabbed a box of tissues and handed her one so Mom could dry her eyes.

"On her deathbed," Mom said at one point, "Grandma told me to look after Grandpa. Every weekend I spent time with him because that's what she wanted. I did it for her because I wasn't close to him like I was with Grandma. But the more I got to know him, the more I got to like him. I didn't just love him because he's my dad. I grew to like him."

I rubbed Mom's shoulder as she dried her eyes.

"Rob, I know I've not been the best Mom. Trust me, I really tried, but if there's one thing I hope I taught you, I hope it's how important it was to spend time with your Grandpa because he isn't going to be around forever. I know he's not your dad, but I hope you at least got to see how much of a dad he has been—not just for me— but also for you for a long time."

I glanced over at Grandpa again, comforting Mom for a bit longer before I saw him open his eyes. I went over to his bedside, Mom giving me the go ahead to spend time with him.

"Grandpa? It's me, Rob."

When he looked up and saw me, Grandpa tried to speak but couldn't move his mouth.

I gently held his hand. "It's okay, Grandpa. You don't have to talk. I'm here."

For the next hour, I stayed by his side. I didn't say much other than a few things here and there to keep Grandpa company, even when the nurse came in to rearrange his pillows and help him drink water through a straw. As it started getting dark, I suddenly thought about Ana. *I don't know how I'm going to tell her.*

I held Grandpa's hand one more time. "Ana's doing good," I said. "She recently got promoted to manager and is practically a boss now. Like you were! I know you are so proud of her!" I took a few breaths to compose myself. "I definitely will tell her you said hi." I got up, told Mom I needed to get sleep, and looked at Grandpa. "I'll see you tomorrow. Okay?"

Grandpa slowly gave me a thumbs up before I went home.

April 24, 2021

Everything Dr. Monika Chudzinski said felt straight out of a horror movie.

Aunt Judy asked me and Alicia if we wanted to meet with the physician. Mom and Uncle Bill stayed by Grandpa's side while the three of us were escorted into a small room next door, reminded to keep our masks on before sitting at a roundtable where Dr. Chudzinski and the nurse from yesterday laid out paperwork.

I sat next to Alicia, my elbows on the table and hands on my head, completely silent, lost in thought, and only able to grasp bits and pieces of what everyone was saying.

"As you saw already, he has further deteriorated," Dr. Chudzinski said. "We believe the chances of him surviving this is growing more and more unlikely by the day."

"There's gotta be something that can be done!" Alicia frantically said. "We don't wanna lose him! Please tell us that something can be done!"

"I'm afraid there is too much plaque build up in his arteries . . ." Dr. Chudzinski said.

Bits and pieces of the conversation began to bleed into my *thoughts as I found myself on the theater stage, Grandpa himself standing on a platform in the center, his hands in his pockets as he faced me. The theater speaker system broadcasted the conversation with Dr. Chudzinski.*

"This can't be happening!" Alicia exclaimed through the loudspeaker.

I tried to reach out to Grandpa, only for the platform to slowly rise up the closer I walked to him. "Please don't go!" I shouted. "I don't want you to go!"

Each step I took made the platform rise further, only for it to stop when I stopped.

The conversation with Dr. Chudzinski continued from the loudspeaker. "Even if we tried any life saving measures, I'm afraid he would be paralyzed from the chest down and never be able to use his left arm again, and there's no guarantee those measures would work anyway."

"He wouldn't want that," Aunt Judy said. "He has it written in his healthcare directive that if something like this were to happen, he would not want any of that done for him."

I stared up at Grandpa on the platform. "Is that true, Grandpa?" I asked him.

"Where does it say that?" Alicia asked.

"It says right here," Aunt Judy continued. "'I, John E. Sutton, being of sound mind, willfully and voluntarily make known my desire that my life shall not be artificially prolonged under circumstances set forth below, and do hereby declare . . .'"

As Aunt Judy read the rest of the healthcare directive, my palms shook. "Why would you do that?" I shouted. I ran over to the platform, Grandpa now high above the stage close to the rafters. The platform stopped rising when I reached it. "I don't want you to go!" I cried as I pounded my fists against the platform as hard as I could until they were battered and bruised.

The audience booed. "You are one selfish piece of shit, Rob!" they shouted as I slowly leaned against the platform, sobbing. "Let Grandpa do whatever he wants! Let him die!"

"When was this signed?" Alicia asked.

"November 22, 2016," Aunt Judy said.

"That's not too long after Grandma passed away," Alicia said.

In the room, I stared at the surface of the table. Alicia began sobbing as she leaned her head on my shoulder, something she hadn't done since we were kids. I allowed her to do so, giving her a short hug before putting my elbows back on the table and my hands on my head.

"He likely has, at most, a week if we are lucky," Dr. Chudzinski said.

I tuned out the rest of the conversation, tightly holding my hair as I saw myself *on stage sobbing uncontrollably.*

"Rob, are you okay?" Aunt Judy asked.

I kept completely quiet as I couldn't help but pull my hair as it started hurting my scalp.

"Crying makes you a wimp," an audience member lectured. "Don't you dare cry in front of them."

Aunt Judy wrapped her arms around me when she saw me pull my hair.

"I think the best thing you can do right now is to spend time with your loved ones," Dr. Chudzinski said. "Mrs. Pearson, you have your husband Bill. Do your niece and nephew have someone they can be with right now?"

I stayed silent as I thought about Ana.

Ana sat on her bed talking on the phone when I came to her place late in the evening, having already texted hours earlier about Grandpa and asking if I could come over. I stood at the entrance way to give her time to end her call before laying next to her, putting my head on her lap as I sobbed uncontrollably.

Ana gently rubbed my hair and kissed my forehead.

I took some breaths. "He really liked you," I finally said in between tears. "Every time I would go over there, he would always ask me how you were doing. He would constantly ask me, 'How's Ana?' He told me many times he always enjoyed your company and he would tell me how happy he was to get to know you!"

I took another breath and saw Ana had tears in her eyes. I sat up and put my hands on her shoulders. "Don't cry," I said, my voice trembling. "It's going to be okay!"

"Why do you have to make me sad?" she asked, trying hard not to cry but clearly was. I wiped a tear from her eye before we wrapped our arms around each other and lay in bed for a while, one thing leading to another before slowly undressing each other.

Sometime later, we cuddled naked under the sheets before Ana pulled away, looking up at the ceiling. We chatted about random topics for a while before laying in silence. "Shouldn't you be with your family right now?" she asked at one point.

I sighed. "I'm gonna go see them tomorrow. They said he'll likely be sent home so he can receive hospice care. It's what he would want. Not to die in some cold hospital room."

"Yeah," Ana wearily said. "He should be home with his family."

Ana moved to lay on her side away from me. I sat up, numb to everything as I gazed off into space before I glanced over to see Ana with a melancholic look staring at the wall.

May 1, 2021

I sat on Grandpa's couch, close to 8 pm as I watched him lay in a hospital bed set up in his living room. Mom and Alicia stood by his side wishing him happy birthday and reading him a Bible story while Uncle Bill pinned up birthday decorations around the room. "You made it to 90," Alicia said, trying hard not to cry. It had been a week since Aunt Judy collaborated with the hospital to have Grandpa be sent home surrounded by his family. We made sure he was as comfortable as possible while receiving hospice care, neighbors and most of his church congregation coming and going to pay their respects.

Ana texted me earlier in the afternoon asking if I was free to come over tonight. *It's possible he's going to go either today or tomorrow and I have to be there for my mom and aunt as support*, I told her. We talked about drama going on with her boss yet again to pass the time before she had to go back to doing errands, wishing Grandpa a happy birthday and telling me to let her know if we needed anything.

I observed Grandpa for the past few hours, numb to everything while lost in thought. Uncle Bill went outside to have a drink and talk with a next door neighbor who came over while Mom tried to help Grandpa drink water. "It's going to be okay, Dad," Mom said as she rubbed his head.

A few minutes later, Grandpa began to snore here and there as he pushed the nasal cannula out of his nose with one of his fingers.

"Grandpa, don't do that," Alicia said, quickly readjusting it back into his nose.

"What's going on?" Aunt Judy asked when she came into the room.

"He keeps taking the thing off," Alicia said.

Aunt Judy rushed over to Grandpa's side next to Mom. "You okay, Dad?" she asked. Grandpa snored louder before thrusting the nasal cannula out of his nose again.

"I don't know why he keeps doing that," Alicia said as she put it back in.

"Let me call the doctor real quick," Aunt Judy said, moving to the side to give everyone space while she went to make a phone call.

I took out my phone and pulled up Ana on Facebook Messenger. I began typing something, but then stopped halfway. I deleted the incomplete message and started over, only to delete it again.

The audience began to lecture at me. "Why would you tell Ana this part of what's going on with Grandpa, Rob? Stop being a burden to her!"

I put my phone away.

A few minutes later, Aunt Judy came back. "I talked to the doctor and they said if it's causing Grandpa discomfort, it's not a good idea to keep making him wear it."

Grandpa began to snore more softly for a bit before pushing the nasal cannula out of his nose again, drifting in and out of sleep. For the next hour, everyone gradually would come and go around the house, meet with neighbors who would stop by or have snacks in the kitchen.

I stayed in the living room most of the time.

At one point, I was the only one in the living room with Grandpa. With everyone in other parts of the house, I got up to sit by his side, looking over him as he lay there. Sitting there, I saw myself *on stage again, like I've done many times before. Grandpa stood in the center of the stage, looking straight at me.*

"Why did this have to happen?" I asked, trying not to cry. "I don't want you to go."

Grandpa didn't answer. High up, a TV appeared and started broadcasting a clip of me at the lake with Ana years ago. "I love my grandpa, don't get me wrong, but he's not my dad," I said in the clip. "He's just . . . my grandpa. That's how I always viewed him."

"You're a terrible grandson, Rob!" they shouted. "Even on his deathbed, he's ashamed of you!"

Back at Grandpa's bedside, I kept looking over as he slept. "Happy Birthday, Grandpa," I said, holding back any tears. "You're 90 now. Ain't that great?"

Grandpa softly breathed here and there.

More TVs appeared up high on the stage, all with countless clips of me with Grandpa throughout my entire life. One clip had one of me at thirteen and Grandpa taking me fishing. Another one had Grandpa teaching me how to drive. "Take your time, Rob. There is no rush," he said in the clip where he was teaching me how to parallel park. In one clip, Grandpa taught me how to operate a tile saw in his garage, while in another he helped me out when I accidentally got my Mitsubishi stuck over a curb in a parking lot near Lake Murray. In that clip, a crowd had gathered and cheered him on as he connected a chain from my car to his truck and pulled it off the curb. There were even some clips where we had strong political disagreements but reconciled.

Next to his hospital bed, I gently held Grandpa's hand. "I know you can't talk right now, and that's okay. I've done a lot of thinking this week." My eyes began to water. "Ever since Dad died, I never felt like I had a dad. Everyone else had dads but I didn't. But the truth is I actually did. You were there when my own dad could not be, and I'm so sorry for not seeing that much sooner. I am so sorry. I hope you'll forgive me."

Tears dripped from my face as I tried to compose myself. I took some breaths before feeling a hand. Looking down, I saw Grandpa squeezing it.

On stage, we gave each other a tearful hug. "It's okay. You can go," I said.

May 2, 2021

At around 1:15 am, I texted Ana.

ROB:

He's gone 😔

ANA:

I'm so sorry to hear 🙁 God has gained an angel

ROB:

He has 🙁

ANA:

He lived a good life 🙏🤍💕

ANA:

I'm glad you and your family were by his side during this week and the incredible part is that he will rest in peace knowing all the love he gave and received. It's a blessing in disguise to be able to peacefully pass surrounded by loved ones in the comfort of your own home.

ANA:

Sending you so much love! I love you so much! 🤍 🤍🤍🤍🥺🥰

ROB:

🤍🙂

May 25, 2021

For weeks, I went back and forth about inviting Ana to Grandpa's funeral. I didn't want to burden her, the audience in my head claiming repeatedly she wouldn't want to be there at all.

But here she was, sitting next to me as we attended a small military service for him with no more than fifteen to twenty people from Grandpa's church there with us. We were the only ones in the audience wearing face masks.

We sat in the front row on the right as Mom, Aunt Judy, and Uncle Bill sat on the left, and Alicia was with her boyfriend behind us. Navy personnel stood on each side of a podium and a small table covered in flowers and candles with a large tabletop collage of pictures of Grandpa. In the center of collage was a picture of him standing outside his house, smiling while wearing a suit, with "John E. Sutton, Rest in Peace (May 1, 1931 - May 2, 2021)" written underneath.

The service began with an opening prayer from Pastor Daryl before Alicia came up to sing hymns. As she sang "Saints Lift Your Voices," I couldn't help but glance at Ana and how tired she looked. During Alicia's hymn, I kept seeing myself *on stage with Ana, while*

Grandpa stood on a platform several feet away from us. Ana stood next to me stoic and numb, so I held her hand and told her over and over it was going to be okay.

Pastor Daryl came back up after Alicia sang the song and began his sermon commemorating Grandpa's memory. "We gather today to remember John Sutton. A loving father, grandfather, husband, friend, and man of faith …"

As he talked, I found myself lost in thought again. I glanced at Ana again, noticing how numb she looked, a weariness in her eyes that her face mask could not cover up.

On stage with her, Ana and I saw Grandpa standing next to Grandma on the platform.

Pastor Daryl's sermon broadcasted through the theater sound system. "We remember Shirley," he said. "His wife of over sixty years."

Grandpa whispered something to Grandma before stepping off the platform, walking towards us as Pastor Daryl talked about Grandpa's relationship with Grandma through the speakers. Grandpa stood in front of both of us, smiling before he shook my hand and faced Ana. Because of his height, Grandpa had to get down on one knee to hug her. Ana hugged him back, sobbing.

They said their goodbyes before Grandpa walked back, climbing onto the platform to stand right next to Grandma.

"Now he gets to be reunited with her," Pastor Daryl said through the speakers.

Ana knelt to sit down on the floor, wrapping her arms around her knees and having them pulled to her chest. I stood next to her, the ceiling high above the platform opened up, a bright light shining directly above my grandparents. They hugged, transforming into their younger selves as the platform rose up towards the heavens.

"Say hi to my dad when you see him," I said. They waved at us as the platform continued to ascend. I looked back at Ana as she sat on the floor, her eyes completely closed.

As Pastor Daryl's talk drew to a close, I looked over at Ana again, reaching out to hold her hand but stopping myself when she folded her arms.

Once the service ended, everyone got up to get ready to leave, many who planned to attend the reception at Pastor Daryl's house. I checked up on Ana to see if she was okay before we both got up.

"Rob, is that you?" someone said. I looked over and it was one of Grandpa's congregation members who had known me for years, but I couldn't for the life of me ever remember her name. We chatted before she noticed Ana. "Is this your girlfriend?" she asked.

Before I could respond, Ana answered. "Yeah," she said, her voice dripping with exhaustion.

"Well, it's so nice to meet you," she said. "Grandpa has told me so much about you. I hope to see you at the reception."

As people continued to pack up and leave, I quickly told my mom and Aunt Judy I would see them later and headed over with Ana to her car.

Once we got inside her car, Ana just sat there.

"Do you wanna go to the reception?" I slowly asked.

Ana didn't respond right away. "Sure," she unenthusiastically muttered. She pulled out her keys and started the car, as if she was going through the motions. I couldn't help but notice her blank stare, as though she wasn't fully there. I reached out to touch her shoulder, but quickly pulled away when she flinched as she pulled out of the parking spot of the cemetery.

I could sense something was off, but couldn't tell if it was the funeral or something else. We spent the rest of the car ride not saying anything to each other.

25

____

August 20, 2021

I stopped to collect the mail before going into the house, only to freeze at the front door when it sank in that the Phoenix Police Department sent me a speed violation. "You gotta be kidding me!" I shouted when I saw multiple black & white photos of my Scion going through an intersection with the captured speed of "53." I reread the notice multiple times to make sure it wasn't a joke.

I immediately rushed to my room and called the information line.

"Hey there," I said once someone finally picked up. "My name is Robert Brian Sullivan, and I'm calling because I literally just now received a speeding violation notice. Here's the problem: I live in California! I can't drive all the way to Arizona just to get this taken care of!"

"Can you provide me with the notice number so I can look up your case?" the operator asked.

I gave the operator the number before she put me on hold. I glanced at the date and time given: July 5, 2021 at 11:33am. Looking at the photos, it clearly was my car. _Was I driving or was it Ana?_ I carefully looked at the photo of the driver's side, blurry and difficult to decipher, until I finally made out who it was.

There was no doubt in my mind it was Ana!

Shit!

"Mr. Sullivan, are you still there?"

"I'm still here."

As the operator summarized the contents of the notice, I remembered Ana and I going through Phoenix on our way home from the Grand Canyon. I wanted a break from driving, so Ana took over when we made a pit stop outside of Flagstaff. *Can you please slow down?* I asked Ana from time to time.

"I'm looking at the photo and it looks like my girlfriend was driving," I said after the operator finished speaking. I stopped when I realized it probably would make Ana hate me if I explicitly said it was her for sure. "At least I think it was," I said to save face. "I don't know. I don't remember who was driving. We were just passing through on our way home."

"I understand," the operator said. "Something to keep in mind is that it's not a summons to appear in court. All it is, like I said, is a notice that a vehicle registered under your name has been documented as committing the violation as listed."

"What am I supposed to do then?" I asked. "I'm not driving all the way to Arizona just to take care of a traffic ticket."

"Right now, there's not really much you can do," the operator said. "The traffic courts here would have an interest in identifying the driver of the vehicle, but if that can't be determined, then they may not pursue the case, but that would be up to the courts. You would have to wait for a follow up, and even then, you may not even get a follow up at all."

"So basically just wait is what you're saying?"

"Like I said, there isn't really anything you can do at this point except wait."

I thanked the operator for their time and ended the call. I put the phone down and hit my hand repeatedly. "Fucking bullshit!" I shouted. "Why do you have to drive so fast all the fucking time?" I stopped hitting myself. *It's not her fault*, I told myself over and over. *She didn't mean to.* I took several deep breaths before I took pictures of the notice, waiting until I was completely calm before sending them to Ana, venting.

> **ANA:**
>
> I am looking at the photo now online. I think it's me 😢😭

> **ROB:**
>
> Oh no! ☹ I'm sorry.

> **ANA:**
>
> It says if you are not the driver you may identify but under no obligation to do so. Arizona is so freaking annoying. My boss also got a ticket there too one time!

> **ROB:**
>
> I'm worried this will affect my insurance.

> **ANA:**
>
> Call on them on Monday and ask them what would happen if you don't respond. Don't mention my name when you call. Let me know what they say when you ask them those questions. And ask it exactly the way I typed it, okay? 😄

> **ROB:**
>
> Okay. You got it! Another reason not to move to Arizona haha

I put the phone down, realizing I didn't tell her I already called the information line. *Dammit, I fucked that up!*

August 21, 2021

Ana texted me to let me know she would be taking a nap, but left the gate unlocked so I could come whenever. *Is she ever going to give me a key again?* I thought while driving to spend another weekend with her. It was close to dinner time, so I stopped at Meet

Fresh on the way to surprise her with an icy grass jelly, one of her favorites. I got myself a milk tea with boba. When I arrived at her place, I put her dessert in the fridge and stood at the entryway to her room to see her napping on her bed, just like she said she would.

I couldn't help but help but smile. *You are the most adorable woman in the world.* On the floor in the middle of the room was her futon covered in her laundry again, something she started doing when Mary came down last year in June for a couple weeks. *I wonder if I'll ever get the chance to meet her,* I thought. *Will that ever happen?*

I considered putting Ana's clothes away, but I didn't want to risk misplacing anything.

Not wanting to disturb her, I spent the next hour on lesson prep for the new semester starting soon. I drank my milk tea and helped myself to snacks she often got at 99 Ranch Market.

I later checked on Ana to see she was awake, laying in bed and glued to her phone. I cuddled behind her and wrapped my arms around her stomach.

"Hey there," I said, kissing her on the cheek while she stretched.

"Hey!"

I gave her another kiss on the cheek. "Did you have a good nap?"

"I always have a good nap," she playfully said. She gently grabbed my fingers with one hand and scrolled through her phone with the other for a while before putting it down so we could cuddle. "I'm getting a new door tomorrow."

"Oh nice," I said. "How does it feel to finally get privacy?"

"I thought I already had privacy."

"But now you have more privacy!"

Ana giggled as I kissed her again on the head.

"I have to do some errands tomorrow morning," Ana said. "Can you be here for the handyman?"

"How long are you going to be gone for?"

"Only a few hours. I have to go to Costco, drop off something at my boss's house, and get my car washed."

"You got it."

We cuddled for a while before having sex, our normal weekend routine.

August 22, 2021

I woke up before Ana did, making us both breakfast while she took a shower. I toasted our usual everything bagels and made sunny-side-up eggs, making hers into a sandwich and putting it at her spot at the table. I sat across from her spot, my laptop open so I could work on my Google Slides and browse social media while eating. At 9:15 am, Ana came into the kitchen, ready to do errands.

"Thank you," Ana said when she saw food for her on the table, sitting down to eat.

I told her it was no problem as I checked Facebook. "What time did you say the handyman was coming again?" I asked.

"Sometime between 9:30 and 11," Ana said. "I shouldn't be gone too long."

"Cool."

We both ate, not talking much as we did our own thing. I put on my headphones and listened to music as Ana ate half her breakfast bagel and put the rest in the fridge, picking up her purse from the table before leaving out the sliding door. Ana waved to get my attention. I took my headphones off again.

"Did you want anything from Costco?" Ana asked.

"Nothing off the top of my head," I said.

"Text me if you need anything then," she said before leaving.

I put my headphones back on and continued what I was doing, plugging in my phone to charge it. For the next half hour, I went back and forth between working on a Google Slideshow and browsing Facebook. A thread from Authentic Philosophy showed in my feed, but I scrolled past it. I hardly ever participated ever since Vincent humiliated me in that group years ago. *I hope that asshole got hit by a bus,* I thought.

The handyman came around 10:15 am and got to work installing the new door. I finished my Google Slide presentation before going back on Facebook to see Alex's Facebook memory post of his graduation from Chula Vista High School. I gave it a "like" and moved on. But I got curious and clicked the Memory Feature to see what I had posted on this day.

I opened up to a private post I made on August 22, 2010:

ROB SULLIVAN:

Kelly Dubois, I miss you so much!!!

Underneath were links to YouTube videos of songs from musicians like Radiohead, Sufjan Stevens, and Neutral Milk Hotel. All my comments expressed grief, but one stood out:

ROB SULLIVAN:

March 4, 2017, I'm pathetic to still have this old status up. I miss you so much. 😢

The day before I matched with Ana on Tinder.

"Door is done," the handyman said.

I looked away from my laptop, thanking him before he packed up and left. I tested the new door myself, happy with his work, before sitting back down. Returning to the post again and its comments, memories of that trip with Kelly flooded back in. The conversations, the laughs, the places we saw, the final goodbye at the airport. I expected that to hurt again.

This time, however, it didn't.

I smiled, lost in a thought before I began typing:

ROB SULLIVAN:

August 22, 2021, 15 years later and things are a little different. I still miss you, but I am healing. It doesn't hurt as much as it used to. I have Ana Kang in my life and she is amazing and makes my life better . . .

I typed out the rest of my long comment, only stopping briefly to give my phone permission to update its OS. I went into detail how all the hard work I did trying to get out of Special Ed would lead me to her, but instead led me to something else.

ROB SULLIVAN:

> . . . If I had not met you, I know my life would be different now. I probably would not have realized Schweitzer was hurting me and my life was going down the gutter. My love for you motivated me to make my life better. You helped me grow up, Kelly, and I will always be grateful for that! I love you, and I wish you a happy and fulfilling life. 🩶

I clicked out of the window, my phone slowly updating its OS as I went to take a shower.

A half hour later, I opened up my laptop in the kitchen to a voice message through my laptop's iMessage.

"Rob, pick up your phone!" Ana exclaimed in the voicemail, clearly agitated. "I need your help getting stuff in! Why do you never charge your phone?"

My heart began racing. *Not again!* Before I could do anything, I saw Ana behind the sliding door carrying a large box of groceries from Costco, struggling to open it. I instantly got up and opened the door for her. "I'm so sorry," I nervously said. "I was in the shower and my phone was charging . . ."

Ana just put the box on the floor. "Just help get some stuff in," she said before going back to her car. I let out an exasperated sigh as I followed behind.

After lunch, we sat at the table in our usual spots doing our own thing on our laptops again. Ana watched one of her FBI shows on Hulu while I browsed YouTube for music videos. I tried apologizing again for missing her call earlier but dropped it when she said nothing.

Halfway through her show, she took her laptop into her room, nonchalantly shutting the brand new door behind her loud enough to make noise. I looked at the door, confused and irritated.

Did she really need to slam the door like that? I thought.

I went back to browsing YouTube, putting it out of my mind.

26

———————

September 5, 2021

Ana stayed glued to her phone again while we waited for our seats at Garlic and Chives.

We spent the day in Orange County, checking out an Asian market Ana wanted to see before heading over to the restaurant. We hadn't been here since COVID started. A large crowd gathered outside, so Ana put our names on a waitlist. I tried to initiate conversation, but she looked so entrenched in her phone I listened to music instead.

Once our names were called, the host reminded us to wear our masks until we were seated before escorting us to our table. We took our time with the menu, Ana settling on stir-fried eggplant and pork and a cup of hot water, while I opted for chicken garlic noodles and a coke.

We began talking about work after the waiter took our menus.

"I swear I work with some of the dumbest people in the world," Ana said.

"Uh oh, what happened this time?"

"So I told you about how my boss continues to hire all these incompetent people, and I have to train them, right?"

"Yeah."

"My boss hired this new girl named Chloe, and already she comes up with excuses for not coming into work."

"What kind of excuses?"

"The typical ones." Ana cleared her throat. "'I have a family emergency!' 'I can't get a ride!' 'I caught my husband cheating on me and I'm too distressed to come in today!' But even when she does come into work, she just sits at her desk and gossips or plays games on her phone, and she hasn't even been here for a month!"

"Sounds like she's taking after your other coworkers," I joked.

"My boss is way too nice. She gives them way too many chances and because of that, they act like children."

I stopped smiling when I noticed Ana's exasperated expression on her face. "Sounds like work has been draining you again."

"It's typical. At least there's one guy who comes in and actually does work. Because everyone is either Asian or Hispanic, he's the only white guy there." Ana then chuckled. "I like to think of him as the 'model minority.'"

I giggled. "'The model minority'?"

"Yep. The model minority."

We both laughed.

"Are you still thinking about finding another job?" I asked.

Ana sighed. "I don't know. I keep going back and forth on it. We'll see."

We talked a little bit more about work before the conversation died down, and Ana went back to her phone. The waiter came back with only my food but told us Ana's was coming up. I began eating, quickly taking bites.

"Don't eat so fast!" Ana snapped.

I stopped.

"Why do you constantly eat like that?" Ana asked, sighing as she went back to her phone.

I put my fork down, staring off into space, my heart pounding before calming down.

"Are you okay?" I asked.

"I'm fine," Ana mumbled.

But I could tell by her tone of voice she was not fine. I thought about checking in but stopped when, without warning, I saw myself *on stage tied to a chair with Vincent standing in front of me with a baseball bat.*

"Rob's a big, strong, mentally ill person who wants to control the sexual behavior of this girl and that is not something we should ignore," Vincent shouted to the audience before swinging the bat against my head.

I snapped the thought out of my head. *I refuse to prove you right,* I thought. I didn't want to force Ana to open up, so I kept my mouth shut.

Ana's food came and she started eating while still on her phone. I didn't do anything until I noticed her playing a familiar game. "Are you playing Jenga on your phone?" I asked.

"Playing with my sister," Ana said as she moved a piece from one spot to another. Judging by the amount of holes in the Jenga tower, it looked like it would fall at any time.

"I played that game a lot as a kid," I said. "Didn't realize they have apps for it now."

"That's because you're old," Ana joked, albeit in a mumbled, tired way.

I playfully rolled my eyes. "I'm going to pretend you didn't say that." I finally felt comfortable taking another bite of food. "Did you ever play Jenga as a kid?"

"I never had toys growing up. So the only time I ever played it was when I was with friends."

"Did you play it a lot with friends?"

"Not really. At most maybe once or twice. They would have the game at the parties my friends in college would make me go to, but I went a few times and that was enough for me."

"You were never really into parties?"

Ana shrugged. "Never really cared for being around people."

The Jenga tower on her phone crumbled.

After dinner, we got in Ana's car and got ready to go home. I scrolled Twitter again, coming across an ad for *Shang-Chi and the Legend of the Ten Rings*, something Ana previously expressed interest in seeing. "Oh, *Shang-Chi* just came out this weekend," I said.

"Nice."

"We haven't been to the theater since *Frozen* 2. I was thinking we could go see it tonight. Maybe somewhere around here so we don't have to drive that far."

"What time is it now?"

I checked my phone. "It's about 8:20. Let me check showtimes."

"Check to see if there are any showtimes back home," Ana insisted.

"But it will be late by the time we get back."

"We can go to a late show."

My eyes widened. "Wait, are you sure?"

"Yeah. I'm sure. I don't work tomorrow so it should be fine."

I checked showtimes back home. "There's a showing at 9:45 pm in La Jolla AMC."

Ana started the engine. "We can make it. Let's go." She drove out of the parking lot and got on the freeway, going over 30 miles over the speed limit. I wanted to tell her to stop speeding again but held back as I firmly held the grab handle, silently praying for Ana not to kill us both.

September 6, 2021

Ana was already awake scrolling through her phone when I woke up. We got back last night after the movie around 12:30 am. Both of us enjoyed the movie, a nice throwback to how we used to go to every Marvel movie in theaters before the pandemic. Since it was Labor Day, neither of us had to go to work so we could do whatever we wanted.

I reached out to put my hand on Ana's hip. "Did you sleep well?"

"No, not really," she muttered. "You snooore!"

I instantly took my hand off her hip, my heart racing as I tried to hide my nervousness.

"I'm sorry," I mumbled, but Ana didn't respond as she kept scrolling through her phone. I lay back against the headboard as Ana got up to go to the bathroom, carelessly slamming the door behind her.

I could do nothing but let out an exasperated sigh.

I spent the afternoon in Ana's kitchen preparing a Google Slideshow for tomorrow's class while Ana watched Hulu. Sometime after lunch, Ana picked up her laptop and went into her bedroom to watch her show, slamming the door behind her.

Did she *really* need to slam that door?

I finished my Google Slides presentation and scrolled social media for the next hour before going into Ana's room. Ana lay on the bed under the sheets, her laptop on the desk chair as she watched an episode of *FBI: Most Wanted.*

I got under the covers and lay next to her from behind, gently placing my hand on her hip and watched the show with her. She gently held my hand so we could cuddle.

"Would you ever want to become an FBI agent?" I playfully asked.

"I would have to go to the gym, get buff, go to the police academy," Ana said with a weak smile. "Too much work."

"But you would be perfect as an FBI agent!" I excitedly said. "Defusing bombs, beating terrorists, rescuing hostages! Doesn't that sound like something you'd want to do?"

"It would be exciting, but . . . I want financial security without the fear of getting kidnapped and murdered."

I chuckled, but stopped when I saw how less vibrant Ana looked.

"Did you want to go anywhere tonight?" I asked. "Maybe get dessert or something?"

"I'd rather stay in tonight. I have rice and Chinese sausage."

"I can get that started soon."

"That would be great. Thank you."

I felt a sense of relief as we cuddled while watching the show.

<hr>

September 7, 2021

I lay in bed after work, immersing myself in Pink Floyd's *The Wall* before remembering to call Aunt Judy about recommendations for snoring medications.

"What do you need snoring medication for?" she asked.

"Ana has started complaining about me snoring."

Aunt Judy chuckled. "Oh Rob, that's something I've dealt with your uncle for years. You could start using a CPAP machine like he does, but you're too young for that. Just get regular nasal strips and you'll be fine."

I shrugged. "If you say so."

"Other than the snoring, how are you and Ana? I haven't seen her since Grandpa's service."

I shrugged. "Things are fine, I guess. She's been rather moody lately, but I don't know if it's just her work causing her stress or something else. It's like she's been putting up walls again, and I can't figure out how to get her to knock them down like I used to."

"Didn't you tell me one time she's really introverted?" Aunt Judy asked.

"She is."

"Well, just be patient with her. Introverted people tend to have a hard time opening up. When the time is right, talk to her about it. Let her come to you. I mean, you've done that many times before, right?"

"Yeah," I mumbled.

"Then try that and see what happens."

I sighed again. "I don't want this snoring to become a problem, you know? I've been thinking about asking her if we could move in together sometime next year once my finances are in order, and I have real job security."

"How does your mom feel about you moving out?" Aunt Judy asked.

I sighed. "I don't know. Me and her don't really talk much. She gets overbearing, and it's like walking on eggshells with her. I feel like she's gotten worse ever since Grandpa died, so I go to Ana's every weekend just to get away from her. If it wasn't so expensive to move out, I would do it right now."

"Well, let me offer you this: if it gets to the point where you feel you really need to move out, me and Uncle Bill are more than happy to help put a down payment for your first apartment."

"Wait, are you sure?"

"It's just something to consider."

I told her I would think about it before ending the call.

September 14, 2021

My birthday fell on a weekday, so I met up with Ana in Escondido after work to have a small get together to get food at Tacos El Gordo and boba at a small Asian supermarket next door.

On the way there, I thought about what she did for my birthday for the last couple years.

I thought about the time six months before the pandemic when she surprised me with a chocolate cake from 85°C and a Captain America Funko Pop figure for my 31st birthday. *You did that for me?* I remember asking, hands over my mouth and fighting back tears of happiness as she lit the candles and placed the cake on the table. It made me wonder what plans she had for this year.

We arrived and had tacos before walking over to get boba.

When we sat down at one of the tables to have our drinks and chat, it dawned on me Ana was wearing formal business attire, as if she was going to a corporate office meeting.

"You look nice," I said.

"Thank you. I'm meeting with my boss later to go to a networking event, so that's why I'm dressed like this."

"Well, you look nice," I said again. We talked about how work has been for both of us as we drank our boba teas. But as we talked, I noticed how distracted she seemed, periodically checking her phone as if she was in a hurry. I went back and forth in my head whether I wanted to say something, but decided not to, figuring she had a lot on her plate.

At least she took time out of her busy schedule to see me, I thought.

We drank our boba tea and headed out to Ana's car.

"Happy Birthday," she said before opening her door.

As she drove out of the parking lot, I went back to my car, conflicted.

September 22, 2021

I was in between classes when Ana texted me asking if I was free later to help set up an Ikea shelf she bought. It was overcast and lightly drizzling by the time I arrived at her place. Ana was at the table reading an instruction manual before looking up when she heard me enter. On her kitchen carpet was the IKEA box for the shelf, the pieces all laid out and organized, with the smaller pieces on the table and the bigger parts on the floor.

We briefly talked about how our day has been before we got to work.

Halfway through putting together the shelf, I began having a difficult time following the instructions. "Do they make these instructions suck on purpose?" I asked, annoyed.

Ana gaffed. "You're a writing teacher and you can't even read the instructions?"

I chuckled. "As an official master of the English language, I can objectively say that these instructions suck and Ikea sucks and they should be sued for writing terrible instructions!"

"Good luck with that," Ana said. "Hope you win your lawsuit."

As I pulled up a YouTube tutorial on my phone, I glanced out the window and saw it now raining hard, completely dark outside. "I'm gonna have to be careful driving home tonight."

Then we heard thunder, causing Ana to scream and grab my hand.

"You okay?" I asked.

Ana hugged me tightly, her head on my chest. "Can you stay over tonight?"

I hugged her back. "Of course." I kissed her on the head.

"I love you," I heard her mumble under her breath.

After we had a late dinner, we lay next to each other in her bed and talked about how our day went at work before she pulled up her laptop.

"Did you want to watch anything?" I asked as Ana pulled up Netflix.

Ana nodded as she scrolled through the selection, both of going back and forth as to what we wanted to watch before one movie caught my attention.

"Netflix has *Rain Man*?" I asked.

"I remember watching it when I was in high school," Ana said "It's really good."

"I never saw it."

Ana looked straight at me all surprised. "You never saw it?"

I shook my head.

"Really? I thought you've seen all the movies," she playfully said.

"I mean, I know of it. I just never got around to watch it."

Ana clicked on the *Rain Man* icon to pull up the film description. "I think you would really like it," she said, smiling. "I can watch it with you."

I chuckled. "I thought you said you never watch movies more than once."

Ana playfully shrugged. "I can watch it with you. I think you would really like it a lot."

I reluctantly agreed to watch with her before she put on the movie and put the laptop in front of us to watch. I had heard about the movie for a long time but had been hesitant to watch it because of how it would portray people like me, but I didn't want to say that so I didn't hurt her feelings. *It's the thought that counts*, I said in my head.

As the movie played on for the next hour or so, I found myself liking the movie but also put off by how much the movie focused on Raymond Babbitt's gifts. *I wish I could perform all those numbers and calculations*, I thought as the movie went on. *I wouldn't have been forced to do three years worth of math in one year to get out of that bullshit school.*

Near the end of the movie, I looked over at Ana to tell her I liked the movie overall despite some issues I had with it, but then realized she was asleep. I looked over to see it was close to midnight before looking over at Ana again.

I smiled. *It's the thought that counts.*

As she slept, I logged onto my Facebook through on phone and wrote a post only I could see:

ROB SULLIVAN:

She wanted me to stay so I stayed.
#EpicQualityVagueBooking

October 2, 2021

I brought over a mango cake from Tasty Bakery for Ana's birthday. Since she had to work on Monday, her actual birthday, celebrating it over the weekend made sense. Ana left the gate open for me as usual, so I placed the cake and a birthday card on the kitchen table and went into her room to see her lying on her bed watching Hulu while on her phone.

I cuddled behind her and put my hand on her hip, like I usually would.

"Did you have a good nap?" I affectionately asked.

"I always have a good nap," Ana playfully said, with a strong sense of tiredness in her voice.

I watched a little bit of her show as I lay next to her, my hand still on her hip.

"I brought some mango cake for your birthday, so if you want to have some either tonight or tomorrow, we can."

"Thanks," Ana mumbled.

I later reached to wrap my arm around her, but Ana immediately moved it off and put it back on her hip while glued to her phone. I sighed. She had been doing this a lot lately and I couldn't figure out why.

"Did you already have dinner?" I asked.

"No," Ana muttered. "But if you're hungry, there's some leftover spring rolls in the fridge you can have."

I said nothing for a bit before kissing her on the forehead and going into the kitchen. I gently closed the door behind me, setting up my laptop to sit at my usual spot at the table. I did some grading while waiting for Ana to come out so she could have her cake. *She'll probably come out in about ten or fifteen minutes*, I thought.

It turned into two hours.

During that time, I checked on her a couple times to see her asleep. When it came close to 9 pm, Ana finally came into the kitchen to sit at her usual spot. I had already put a slice of cake on a plate and her card on the table for her.

"You're so sweet," Ana softly said. "Thank you."

"Happy Birthday," I said.

Ana picked up the card and opened it, giving a light smile as she read it. "Aw, it's a doggie photo . . . and you got me a $27 gift card for Target?"

"You're turning 27, so you get a $27 gift card."

"So your plan every year is to give me money?" Ana joked. "I better wait until I'm 100 so I can get $100."

I chuckled. "That's my plan."

Ana looked amused, but I could still sense so much tiredness in her voice. She put the birthday card to the side and had cake. We didn't say much for the rest of the evening as we ate a late dinner, had routine sex, and went to bed.

October 3, 2021

Ana was still asleep when I woke up, so I took a shower, got changed, and made us both breakfast, making the usual Everything bagels with sunny side up eggs.

As I checked the eggs, I heard Ana calling me from the other room.

"You left water on the bathroom floor again!" she said loud enough for me to hear. "Can you please make sure you clean it up whenever you are done with the shower!"

I felt a lump in my throat. "Sorry! My bad!"

Ana didn't respond.

Shit, I thought. *Not again! Dammit!*

After I calmed down, I put the bagels and eggs on separate plates. I browsed online looking for events going on in San Diego as I ate my food, Ana coming in to sit at her usual spot with her laptop, thanking me for breakfast before putting on Hulu.

I found an ad for a street fair going on in Encinitas. "Did you want to go to this street fair today?" I asked as I sent Ana the link to the ad. "It looks pretty cool."

Ana briefly looked at it and shook her head. "No, it looks like every street fair we've been to, and it's all the same. I don't see the point."

I sighed as Ana went back to her show. For most of the morning, we stayed in her kitchen doing our own thing before Ana got up with her laptop to go into the other room, slamming the door behind her.

Why does she keep doing that?

I spent most of the late afternoon in the kitchen creating another Google Slideshow for tomorrow's classes as Ana napped for a couple of hours again. I checked on her occasionally in between watching Netflix episodes. Close to dinnertime, I checked on Ana again to see her awake and glued to her phone again. I crawled onto the bed behind her, asking her if she had a good nap.

"It was good," she mumbled, a tired smile on her face.

I nonchalantly placed my hand on her hip, just laying next to her before slowly moving my hand so I could wrap my arms around her waist, but she gently moved my arm off.

I pulled away, still laying next to her. I sighed. *Probably not in the mood,* I thought. I took my hand off and sat up, scrolling through my phone. A few minutes later, Ana answered a phone call, talking to the person on the other line in Mandarin while getting up to take the call in the other room, slamming the door behind her.

I waited a couple minutes before getting up to peek through the door, hearing enough to piece together she was talking to her mom again, the tone in Ana's voice more agitated the longer the call went on. When she hung up, Ana slumped in her chair, her eyes dulled as if all the energy had been sucked completely out of her, like she couldn't even bring herself to cry over whatever she was feeling.

I closed the door and dug in my bag for my headphones. I plugged in my headphones into my phone and sat on the bed, staring towards the door, the thought of Ana sitting there with that look on her face swirling my mind. *How much do I really know about you and your mom?* I thought. *I hope everything's okay.*

I sighed, laying on my back to engulf myself in Death Cab for Cutie's "I will Follow You Into the Dark."

27

December 25, 2021

On the way to Ana's place, I listened to countless versions of "Silent Night" back to back. After an awkward Christmas morning with Mom and Alicia with her boyfriend, I needed it to get in the mood to celebrate with her.

I stopped to get gas on the way before parking the car outside. I brought in a bag of mint cookies and a Christmas bag I purchased from Target and went through the gate, unlocked like Ana said it would be. I could see Ana sitting at the table watching Hulu on her laptop through the sliding door. I waved to Ana before taking off my shoes and coming in.

I went up behind Ana and kissed her on the head. "Merry Christmas," I said as I placed the cookies and Christmas bag on the table.

When I sat across from her, I noticed a decently sized Christmas present on her right side. "Merry Christmas," she said as she handed me the gift.

"What's this?"

Ana didn't say anything as I opened the present.

It was a brand new Airpods Pro!

"Oh my god!" I exclaimed. "This is so awesome! Thank you!"

"I know you like to use headphones all the time, so I thought these would be great for you," Ana said.

"Now I can go on my walks or go to the gym and not get tangled!"

"Exactly."

I smiled again as I encouraged Ana to open her present. Ana reached into the bag and pulled out a large green wool blend sweater. "Awww, this is cute."

"Now you have a nice, wool sweater to keep you warm for your naps!"

"But I already have a nice, wool sweater."

"But now you have one in green!"

Ana lightly chuckled. "You're so sweet."

But the look on her face told me so many conflicting things. I looked at the AirPods Pro box and began wondering if I should have gotten Ana something nicer than a $30 sweater from Target. I was trying to save money this year, considering how tight finances had been lately.

"Did you have a good Christmas with your mom this morning?" Ana asked.

I sighed. "This year has been hard for her. This is the first Christmas without Grandpa. An argument almost broke out between her and my sister, but thankfully it didn't go there. Other than that, okay. So . . . yeah. I don't know what else to say about that."

Ana didn't say anything, as if she didn't know what to say either.

"How about your mom?" I asked. "How's she doing?"

Ana shrugged. "She's okay. She called me this morning to complain about her landlord and why she wasn't a grandma yet, but other than that, not much."

I gave a faint smile. "Any plans to see her again soon?"

"Nothing definitive right now."

"Maybe we could plan a trip to SF once COVID has died down more," I suggested. "I've always wanted to meet your mom."

Ana stayed silent.

"Just an idea," I emphasized.

"I'll think about it," she said before going back to her show.

We didn't say anything else as Ana put the sweater in the bag and I opened up my new Airpods. I played around with them for a bit as I connected them to my phone's bluetooth before putting on Christmas music to try them out.

***

After dinner, Ana suggested we check out Christmas lights in her neighborhood. We put on our jackets and locked the gate behind us before walking around the corner, going down a street with houses covered in Christmas lights. With the exception of a few cars slowly driving past us, hardly anyone was around. I put on Christmas music again on my phone and put it in my jacket pocket, making it loud enough for us to hear.

We took our time looking at each house. One house was covered in multicolored Santa and Rudolph the Red-Nosed Reindeer decorations, whereas another had a large Nativity set on the front lawn with the words "God is Love" written on the roof in white lights. "This is so pretty," I would say, or some variation of it when a house would stand out, all reminding me of the first time we went to the Winterfest light show at Qualcomm Stadium together years ago, something we used to do. *I wonder if we are going to go back to that once COVID is officially over.*

We walked around for a while marveling at the Christmas lights and having a pleasant evening walk until we came across a bench and sat down to rest our feet, chatting about how our night was going and how nice the Christmas lights were.

"So are you done with grading now?" Ana asked.

"Almost. I should be done soon. Then I have to start prepping for spring. Oh, I forgot to tell you: I got four classes lined up next semester!"

"Oh nice."

"It feels so unreal to finally be moving up." I took a breath. "You know, when Mesa let me go before Fall semester started, right before COVID, I thought that was it, that my career was over. But then State pulled through for me, as if all the pieces started coming together. Now, I'm at a place where I can be something to someone in a way I didn't have when I was at that miserable excuse of a high school. I won't have to stress so much about job security anymore. I can keep my focus on helping those who like me. My hard work's paying off."

"Does that mean you'll get tenure?"

I chuckled. "Well, like I used to tell Grandpa, I don't get 'tenure.' I would need a PhD for that. What I get as a Lecturer are longer contracts, and when I can get a three year contract I can renew forever, that will be the closest I will get to tenure."

"When do you expect that to happen?"

I smiled. "Next year!"

"That's so cool," Ana said, but her tone seemed more polite than excited.

I checked my phone to see it was late, so I assumed she must be tired. "Things are picking up," I said as I looked at Ana again. "Thank you for being there for me."

Ana didn't respond as she looked out at the Christmas lights.

"So what's new with your work?" I asked.

"Nothing much. Busy managing a bunch of children again, but at least some of them are finally starting to quit."

"I bet if you had the power, you would fire all of them," I joked.

Ana giggled. "Of course I would."

"Do you see yourself taking over for your boss or starting your own business?"

"To be honest, I don't know. I mean, Stephanie has been in the business for over twenty-five years, and I don't know when she's going to retire. She's talked about me possibly taking over, but I'm not so sure. It seems like a lot of work, and I don't know if I'm ready to be the main boss right now."

"Baby steps," I playfully said. "I think you would be an awesome boss. I mean, you have the patience of a saint to deal with children who attend Hanmi Daycare!"

Ana laughed. "Hanmi Daycare! That's the perfect way to describe these idiots. I'm running a daycare."

We both laughed.

"If you were to be your own boss, would you be staying in San Diego?" I asked.

"Ideally I would like to stay, but it will all have to depend."

"Depend on what?"

Ana shrugged. "Wherever work takes me."

Would I still be part of that? I somewhat nervously thought. I considered asking what she meant but didn't want to ruin the moment. We kept sitting back taking in the view, Frank Sinatra's version of "Silent Night" playing on my phone.

"Do you wanna head back?" Ana eventually asked.

"Yeah."

I lay in bed browsing social media on my phone while Ana took a shower. I blew her a kiss when she came out, telling her how cute she was and wishing her a Merry Christmas. After Ana put her pajamas on and crawled into bed, I showed her a funny meme I found on Twitter of a cat's reflection in a Christmas tree ornament with the words "The Last Thing a Christmas Ornament Sees Before it Dies" plastered at the top.

Ana gave a big grin when I showed it to her. I scrolled through my phone again looking for memes to share with her.

"Did you wanna watch a Christmas movie?" Ana asked.

"Sure."

Ana opened her laptop and put on *Love Hard*, a recent Christmas rom-com from Netflix. I cuddled with her to watch the movie, though we both ended up ignoring it about an hour into it and individually browsed our phones.

I showed Ana another Christmas related meme, this time of the kid from *Home Alone* setting up a trap, the words "You can mess with a lot of things, but you can't mess with kids on Christmas" written around the edges.

Ana giggled. "Yep! You don't mess with Kevin."

I chuckled. "I know you said in the past you didn't want kids, but if you were to have a kid, would you want a kid like Kevin?" I playfully asked.

Ana paused for a moment. "A kid like Kevin? Maybe. I feel if I were to have kids, it would have to be when I'm at a point in my career where I can actually afford to do it."

"So you're not completely closed off to the idea of kids?"

Ana shrugged. "I go back and forth."

"Me too. What about marriage?"

"I don't believe in marriage."

"Neither do I."

"There are tax benefits to marriage, but honestly, I don't know if it's worth it."

"I can see that." I held her hand as she scrolled her phone with the other. "You know," I nonchalantly said. "I'm not saying this would happen, but if you ever decide you wanted to have a kid or something, I would be open to it."

Ana looked at me, silent as if not sure what to say. I stopped smiling, feeling a lump in my throat. "Nevermind," I quickly muttered. "Forget I said anything."

Ana went back to her phone.

A few minutes later, I got up to go to the bathroom to brush my teeth and wash my face before staring at my reflection in the mirror. *What were you thinking asking her that?* I thought. I stayed in the bathroom for the next fifteen or twenty minutes, working to gather my thoughts. *I hope that didn't ruin the Christmas mood.*

Once I felt composed, I came out of the bathroom, hoping to cuddle with Ana more, only to see her fast asleep with her laptop still on. I gently put another blanket over her to make her extra warm and cozy. I crawled onto bed and sat next to her. I then put my Airpods on to listen to more Christmas music, looking over at Ana to watch her sleep as a piano version of "Silent Night" began playing in my ears. "Good night," I mumbled, faintly smiling. "Merry Christmas. Love you."

I lay on my back and stared up at the ceiling, taking a breath before closing my eyes to engross myself in the music.

28

January 30, 2022

I flipped through a box of comics near the back of the store before noticing Ana staring at a graphic novel on the shelf.

"Is that what I think it is?" I asked. I held it up for both of us to look at what it was: a complete edition of Marvel's *Civil War*, Captain America and Iron Man front and center on the cover! "This inspired the last Captain America movie! You remember that movie?"

"Yep."

"This is the comic it's based on!"

Ana smiled. "Let me guess. You've already read it cover to cover already?"

"Actually, I have not."

Ana gave a playful gasp. "You mean you haven't read all the comics? I'm shocked!"

"I mean, I've been wanting to read this one, but I never got around to it."

I looked more closely at the book. It had a variant cover of Captain America and Iron Man at war, sparks flying as they clashed against each other in their epic fight. "Imagine if that were us?" I joked.

"If that were us, I would win!" Ana teased.

"No way. I would reign supreme!"

We looked at the graphic novel a little longer.

"I'll get it and let you know how it compares to the movie," I said.

"You do that."

"Did you see anything you wanted?"

"I'm good."

I skimmed through the book before heading to the register.

It was dark when we got back to Ana's car. We had dinner at one of the food vendors at Liberty Public Market before checking out the shops, the comic book store being the last place we explored. I began reading *Civil War* as soon as I sat in the car and Ana turned on the ignition.

"Did you want to get boba on the way home?" Ana asked.

"Sure."

Ana's phone rang as she was about to back out. "What now?" I heard her mutter under her breath. I saw the word "Mom" on her dashboard screen before she hung up the call.

"You could have answered it if you wanted to," I said.

Ana shrugged. "It's fine. I'll call her later."

But I could tell she seemed drained. "Is everything okay?"

"Everything is fine. She probably just wanted something from me again." Ana backed out of the parking lot. "I'm so glad I don't live with her."

"Your mom?" I asked.

Ana nodded. I thought about asking her what was going on between them now but held back. I kept reading as we left Liberty Station and made our way to Convoy.

February 5, 2022

I went over to Ana's at around 5 pm, the gate unlocked for me as usual. I checked on Ana to see her taking another one of her naps. I wanted to write up a lesson plan for Tuesday's class and watch YouTube, so I made myself at home in the kitchen. Sitting down, I noticed both her table baskets began to overflow, her mail piling up in one and snacks stockpiling in the other. I reorganized them so her table looked much cleaner.

Ana usually kept her kitchen table tidy over the years, but lately I've noticed she would take more time to get it back in order. I figured she had been incredibly busy lately so she was probably stressed. I worked on my lesson plan for an hour before going to the cupboard to see what she had to eat.

Opening the cupboard greeted me with ants crawling next to the soup cans.

"Shit, not again," I muttered.

I grabbed a washcloth and wiped up all the ants. *I thought she said she was going to call an exterminator!* I cleaned up the washcloth and left it in the sink.

I dried my hands and checked up on Ana, still napping.

An hour later, I checked to see her laying in bed browsing her phone. I crawled up to lay next to her, meekly greeting each other and asking how our day had been before she went back to her phone, a fatigued expression on her face.

"So Ana," I said to get her to smile. "Why did the football coach go to the bank?"

"To get his quarter back," she said. No smile from her. Emotionless. Glued to her phone.

I sighed. "That's right," I mumbled.

"Did you already have dinner?" Ana asked.

"I did. What about you? Did you want me to make you rice or anything?"

"Yes please."

"You got it," I said, kissing her hand. I got up to go into the kitchen to get the rice cooker set up, washing the rice before getting it ready to cook. The rice cooked while I made spam and corn, something she had been having a lot lately whenever we didn't go out. I kept wondering if Ana was okay as I made dinner.

When Ana came out, she thanked me for the food and sat down to eat, not really saying anything else. I watched a couple of YouTube videos as we ate.

"Did you want to do anything tomorrow?" I eventually asked.

Ana shrugged. "I don't know. I'm fine with just staying home."

"Maybe we can check out Old Town? We haven't been there in a while."

Ana continued eating, not responding to my suggestion.

I reached out to hold her hand. "Is everything okay?"

Ana shrugged. "I'm okay."

I tilted my head. "You sure?"

"I'm sure," she mumbled.

But I wasn't so sure.

It was close to 11 pm when Ana took a shower as I lay in bed reading *Civil War*. When Ana came out, I blew her a kiss, causing her to smile at me as she dried off and put on pajamas. I flipped the page of my book as she crawled into bed and under the sheets.

"If superheroes were real, would you ever want to become Iron Man?" I asked.

"Maybe."

"You would be an ultra tech billionaire, have a suit of armor, kick ass. Wouldn't that be awesome?"

Ana chuckled. "You still reading *Civil War*?"

"Been taking my time with it. So far it's good." I then showed a page where Tony Stark stood next to Peter Parker after he revealed his secret identity to the public. "Look at how amazing the artwork is!"

"That's pretty cool. I really like how Spider-Man is drawn."

"I know, right? Don't know if it's better than the movie yet, but I'll let you know."

We talked a bit more about the artwork before Ana went to scroll her phone.

On stage, we dressed up as Captain America and Iron Man, Thano's lifeless body behind us as we stood together waving to a cheering audience.

I put my book down, getting up to turn the light off and going back to bed.

In bed, I laid my head on my pillow and reached to cuddle with her, only for her to push my hand off her hip. "Stop," she muttered.

I took my hand off and turned to face the wall, sighing.

Rejected again.

February 6, 2022

I woke up and checked my phone to see it was 3 am, the room mostly dark as I looked over at Ana. I attempted to change positions to make myself more comfortable, accidentally getting too close to Ana. "Move!" she shouted before falling back to sleep.

I immediately pushed my whole body against the wall, my heart pounding. I turned to face the wall again, calming my nerves as I saw myself *on stage again as Captain America while Ana was Iron Man. Instead of standing side by side, we faced each other from opposite sides.*

"I'm so sorry," I said. "I didn't mean to do that."

Ana didn't respond. The audience began cheering for us to fight each other.

"I'm really sorry. Please forgive me."

No response from Ana again as the audience grew louder.

I tried hard to fall back asleep, lost in thought in the complete silence.

We slept past 9 am. Neither of us brought up what happened last night as we slowly cuddled and had routine sex, like we'd done countless times. As soon as we finished, Ana immediately turned to her side and went back to checking her phone.

I sat back against the headboard, letting out a frustrated exhale. "You hungry? Do you want breakfast?"

"I'm not hungry."

"So you are just gonna starve?" I teased.

"Yep. I'm just gonna starve," she teased back before looking at her phone again.

I stared at her bifold mirrored closet door across the room, our reflections in two separate panels.

We stayed in bed until Ana got up, picked up her laptop, and went into the kitchen, shutting the door hard behind her.

That fucking door again!

I found everything Ana wanted me to get at Target, texting her to see if she wanted anything else. We planned to make grilled cheese and caesar salad for dinner that night, so I volunteered to get them while she watched Hulu. I also got bananas and a special brand of peanut butter she had been craving.

I stopped at the greeting card aisle, noticing the Valentine's Day section filled with rows of pink, red, and white cards neatly lined up, having completely forgotten it was next week. *Might as well since I'm here.* I walked down the aisle to see what I could get for Ana. I picked up a red card with a cute puppy drawing and hearts and placed it in the cart.

But as I began to head out, I thought about the last few weeks. I thought about the times Ana acted grouchy or ignored me while on her phone or just napped. I thought about how I accidentally interrupted her sleep last night.

On stage still in my Captain America uniform, I looked at Ana, in her Iron Man suit, staring down at the floor.

"Can we talk?" I asked. "Are you okay?"

Still no response as the audience kept cheering us on to fight.

I surveyed the entire shelf until I came across a section filled with friendship cards. "Maybe one of these will cheer her up?" I mumbled. I looked at each card until I found a green one with mountain scenery on the front cover with the words, "You are the best!" written inside.

I then heard a *ding* from my phone.

ANA:

Could you go to Starbucks and get me a mint frap? I have a coupon.

I didn't immediately respond. I read the card multiple times before putting it in my cart.

ROB:

You got it.

Ana was eating rice and spam when I came back, encouraging me to help myself to the lunch she had made for both of us. I put food I bought from Target and the Starbucks mint frap on the table, hiding the friendship card behind my back so she couldn't see. When she wasn't looking, I gently hugged her from behind, giving her a kiss on the head as she held my arm.

I placed the card next to her plate. "I got this for you."

Ana opened the card and smiled. "Awwww, thank you."

"I love you and you *are* the best," I said, giving her another kiss on the forehead.

"I love you too," she responded quietly.

I gave her one last kiss before I went to sit at my spot at the table so I could browse social media. We chatted extensively about current events for a while based on things I saw on Facebook before she went back to watching Hulu. *She seems much better*, I thought at one point.

Two hours later, she got up to watch her show in her bedroom, slamming the door behind her again.

I sighed.

February 12, 2022

I double checked to make sure I had my Valentine's Day card and my box of See's Candies ready to go before heading over to Ana's. She had to work Monday, so it made sense to celebrate it over the weekend. Ana was napping again, so I put her gift on the kitchen table, sitting down to make room for my laptop so I could watch YouTube.

I then noticed a bag of chocolates and a white envelope with my name on it. I felt a sense of relief as I opened the envelope and read Ana's card addressed to me. *She does still care.*

I put the card down as Ana came into the kitchen. I held my hand out to her. "You're awake," I affectionately said.

Ana held my hand back.

"Thank you for the chocolate," I said.

"Of course," she said warmly. She let go of my hand to sit at her usual spot at the table, her face glowing when she opened her card. "Awww, look at the puppy!"

"Happy Valentine's Day."

Ana closed her eyes and smiled. "You're so sweet."

I scrolled YouTube as Ana browsed her phone. "Did you have dinner already?"

Ana didn't immediately answer, instead pulling up a website and sending me the link to a Vietnamese Restaurant off Mira Mesa Boulevard. "Let's do this place tonight."

I brought the food back an hour after Ana placed the order over the phone. Over dinner, she placed a slice of her Vietnamese crepe on my plate while I split egg rolls for both of us, telling her about my hectic week at work. "So many conferences with students back to back," I said. "No one comes to office hours early in the semester but the week before the final draft of a paper is due, students come running."

"How many students do you have this semester?" Ana asked.

"Around hundred and twenty, and I had to conference with all of them!"

"At least you can do it through Zoom now."

"Thank god for that! That's the only good thing to ever come out of COVID."

I told her about my busy schedule at State, how we all had to wear face coverings in the classroom, and red tape I had to deal with to get a long-term contract. "But honestly," I emphasized, "it feels so good to finally be in a position where my career is starting to take off."

"That's so cool."

I nodded before taking a few more bites of my food. "Anything new at work?"

"My boss has been talking about starting a new insurance company after Hanmi Insurance and wants me and a few others to come on."

"You should do it."

Ana shrugged. "Maybe. I'm not a hundred percent sure yet."

"What would you be doing otherwise?"

"Stay-at-home work. Other insurance agencies."

"In San Diego?"

"Most of them in San Diego, but also some back up in San Francisco. Some in LA or Orange County. I saw one in New York, but I doubt I'd get it."

My heart began racing. "But you would stay in San Diego?"

"Likely, but we'll see."

I took another bite. "Well, whatever you decide to do, I support it a hundred percent," I nervously said.

Ana didn't say anything else. I sighed, putting on my Airpods.

February 13, 2022

We spent most of the afternoon in Orange County attending a street fair, stopping by Porto's on the way home to buy pastries for us and for Ana's workplace. It was close to 8 pm when we got back, so I took a shower while Ana put stuff away.

After I dried off and put on pajamas, I came out and saw Ana laying on the futon she had left on the floor for almost two years now. "Getting comfy down there?" I teased.

Ana shrugged.

"So do you like laying on that thing?" I asked.

"Sometimes."

"Doesn't it hurt your back?"

"When I was in college, I sometimes slept on the floor when I didn't have a bed, so it's not that big of a deal. As long as I have a pillow and a warm blanket, I'm happy."

"Okay. I'll be on the bed watching a movie, but you're welcome to join me anytime to lay on your cozy bed that you refuse to lay on!"

Ana mildly chuckled while scrolling her phone. I picked up my laptop and sat down on the bed to watch Netflix, expecting Ana would eventually come to bed.

She slept on the futon for the rest of the night.

February 14, 2022

I woke up around 8 am, getting ready to leave since Ana had to work. I didn't have to teach until tomorrow, so I planned to spend the day at Lestat's lesson planning. After getting dressed, I noticed Ana still on the futon but now scrolling her phone.

I kneeled down by her side. "Happy Valentine's Day," I said as I tried to kiss her on the forehead goodbye.

But she shoved me back. "Stop," she grunted before going back to her phone.

I instantly pulled away, nerves shaking as I stood up and looked down at Ana. I took a moment to calm myself down. "Sorry about that," I muttered under my breath. I put on my backpack. "I hope you have a good day at work," I said, defeated.

I went outside and got in my car. As I drove away, *I stood across from Ana, both of us still in our Captain America and Iron Man costumes. My palms shook as the audience cheered us on to fight.*

"Stand down," Ana ordered as she pointed her fist at me.

"Ana, please I'm sorry," I exclaimed. "Let's talk—"

Ana fired a beam at me. I lifted up my Vibranium shield to deflect it.

The audience roared with applause.

February 19, 2022

Ana was already napping when I came over. I did nothing but grade papers or mindlessly scroll social media in the kitchen. I kept her door closed so I didn't disturb her, slowly accepting I would be alone for hours.

February 20, 2022

We spent time together in her kitchen, eating lunch before she went into her room to watch her show, slamming the door behind her once again.

Does she not realize how fucking irritating that is?

February 22, 2022

Not feeling like grading, I mindlessly scrolled through Facebook while holding office hours. My colleague Beth came into our shared office space and greeted me before sitting at her desk at the opposite side of the room to meet with a student.

I scrolled before stopping at a vacation photo of my friend Rachel and her family posing in front of the Bean, the Chicago skyline in the background. I liked the photo, but I couldn't stop looking at the skyline, Kelly appearing in my thoughts again. I suddenly remembered a bus ride we had two weeks into the trip, engaging in random banter.

So what part of Chicago are you from? I nervously asked.

Meadowville, Kelly said.

Where's that?

Small town an hour outside Chicago, so technically not in Chicago, but I just say I'm from Chicago because it's easier to explain.

I then thought about the day we said goodbye at the airport before replaying the entire trip in my head. *Why am I thinking about you again?*

I turned to see Beth had finished meeting with her student, so I asked her how the semester had been for her before going into what I wanted to talk about. "I hope you don't mind me asking, but do you recall when your ex-husband became emotionally distant from you?"

"Near the end of our marriage he barely talked to me," Beth said. "But that wasn't why we got divorced. Why do you ask?"

"I told you about Ana, my partner. I've noticed lately she's been . . . distant. I know she's an introvert, but even for an introvert, something seems off. I don't know how to explain it."

"How long have you two been together?"

"Almost five years now."

"That's a long time. Have you tried talking to her about it?"

I cleared my throat. "That's the thing. Every time I ask her if everything is okay, she keeps telling me everything's fine. I don't want to accuse her of being a liar."

"Right."

"But something in my gut is telling me something's wrong. Hopefully it's just in my head."

I sighed as I went back to Facebook, seeing a message from Ana.

ANA:

10c off gas at Shell now till Friday.

I nodded as I heart reacted to Ana's message.

February 27, 2022

Laying on my side of the bed, I scrolled through Expedia looking at plane ticket prices while Ana took a shower. *Maybe if I go to Chicago I'll get that feeling of closure about Kelly*, I thought. *And if I bring Ana with me, it could get her out of this emotional rut. Two birds with one stone!*

Ana came to bed sometime after her shower and turned on Hulu.

"Do you have any plans for Memorial Day weekend?" I asked.

"Not at the moment."

I showed Ana the average plane tickets to Chicago on my laptop. "Well, I was thinking we could take a trip to Chicago. I've never been and I always wanted to go."

"When would you want to go?"

"It would have to be after the semester is over, so maybe for Memorial Day weekend?"

"I have a business trip to Baltimore in May, and I don't want to do flights back to back."

"Oh. Maybe some other time then?"

Ana shrugged. "We'll see."

I put my laptop to the side and tried wrapping my hand around her stomach, only for her to gently move it away. "Stop," she muttered, like she's done so many times recently.

I gave up on trying to cuddle with her for the night. I watched the show for an hour before facing the wall to sleep.

March 1, 2022

I finished a meeting with a student in the office before going back to looking at plane ticket prices again, playing around with the arrival and departure dates.

Staring at my computer screen, I saw Ana and I facing off against each other, the audience cheering for us to keep fighting. Ana shot more beams at me, forcing me to dive for cover behind a boulder near the end of the stage.

"Ana, stop! I don't wanna fight you!"

"Why do you have to be such a burden to me?"

The audience cheered. "You tell 'em, Ana!"

"How have I been a burden to you?" One of her beams flew straight past my head. "Ana, I'm begging you! Stop! We can work this out!"

Ana flew around the auditorium and shot more beams at me and destroyed my cover, forcing me to run around the stage and hold up my Vibranium shield to deflect the beams.

I took a breath as the thought of the battle eased out of my head. I played around with the arrival and departure dates and found tickets at a price I could afford, talking to myself out loud to figure out if I should go through with it.

"I can finally move on from Kelly, and I can send Ana so many pictures. She would like that." I breathed a sigh of relief. "Yeah, that's a good plan."

Ten minutes later, I ordered plane tickets for the first week of June.

29

———

March 28, 2022

I struggled to figure out if the way Ana acted lately was all in my head.

Spring break started, so I drove over to isolate myself in my office after leaving Ana's place hours earlier. I graded several papers before googling "When to end a relationship," countless search results showing up but contradicting each other while "Black Hole Sun" played through my AirPods.

I logged onto Facebook and saw Rachel texted me a funny meme through Messenger. I chuckled and sent a laugh emoji, hesitant to tell her about Ana.

But then I typed two full paragraphs telling Rachel what had been going with Ana for the past month.

RACHEL:

hugs I remember you telling me before she works a ton of hours. She might be stressed. That's a possibility.

ROB:

That's what I'm thinking, too. But I'm starting to worry. I mean, last night she was checking her phone while we were having sex.

RACHEL:

Yikes! 😬

ROB:

I found it weird, so I googled what that means and people can't agree on what that means. Relationship advice on the internet sucks! It's like people think they know what they're doing but they really don't. Reminds me of the time Vincent tried to shove advice down my throat.

RACHEL:

Who's Vincent?

ROB:

Nobody you know. This only happened last night and I don't think it will happen again.

RACHEL:

Are you sure? I really would talk to her about it.

ROB:

If it happens again, I'll talk to her about it.

RACHEL:

As you should.

ROB:

I hope it's all just in my head. She did take me to a street fair recently and we've had moments where we cuddled and watched movies. Maybe she just has been stressed and I'm just being paranoid.

I sighed, thanking Rachel for letting me vent before scrolling my feed. I found a funny meme about Vin Diesel and sent it to Ana, who sent me a laugh emoji in response.

ANA:

How's your day going?

I felt a sense of relief reading her simple message.

ROB:

> Good. I have the whole office to myself, so I'm grading papers.

I looked around the office and noticed artwork on the wall above Beth's desk, her workspace nicely organized and colorful. I took a picture of it with my phone and sent it to Ana.

ROB:

> Look at how pretty my colleague's workspace is!

ANA:

> That looks so cool. You should do something similar to your desk.

ROB:

> I should. When I have my desk fully decorated, I'll send you pics!

I smiled when Ana sent me thumbs up. I graded papers until I saw Poets of the Fall's social media pages announcing their new album *Ghostlight* coming out by the end of April. I hit my hand in excitement, sharing the news with everyone on Facebook.

April 3, 2022

Ana walked a little faster than me as we checked out a street festival up in Orange County. "Wait for me," I said, hustling to catch up as small crowds moved past us in different directions. We skipped several vendors until Ana stopped at a Geico booth to do her usual networking routine. I tried to hide my irritation at the awful amount of time she took talking with the agents and exchanging business cards.

There she goes ignoring you again, a voice in my head lectured. *It's obvious she thinks you're a stupid piece of shit, Rob.*

I'm . . . I'm not a stupid piece of shit!

Yes you are! The voice argued back. *Why does she care more about these strangers than you? It's because you're a piece of shit! Kill yourself already and stop being a burden to her!*

I browsed my phone to try and tune out these thoughts.

"You ready?" Ana asked once she was done.

"Yeah."

We explored the festival further, not saying anything for long stretches of time. We came across the food court once we saw everything the place had to offer.

"Do you wanna get something to eat here?" I asked.

"Too expensive and the food doesn't look that good."

I sighed. *Always shooting down my suggestions,* I thought. *Why do I bother?*

"Let's go here," Ana said, sending me a link to a Pho restaurant in Irvine.

Ana turned on the ignition when we got in her car to head down to Irvine. I put on my seatbelt and winced when I looked out and saw golfers on the nearby golf course lifting their masks off to cough.

"Did you see that?" I asked.

"See what?" Ana asked while backing out of the parking lot.

"They just took their masks off and coughed! What is wrong with people? That defeats the whole point of masks!"

"They're stupid, but they have all the money in the world and can afford to do it."

"I hope your coworkers don't do that."

Ana chuckled. "They're children, so I stay away from them." She said nothing else as she got on the freeway, speeding as usual while changing the station.

I didn't know what else to say as I looked out the window.

You can't even hold a proper conversation with her, the voice in my head scolded. *What's wrong with you, Rob! You might as well get out of this car and throw yourself into oncoming traffic!*

I watched the ongoing traffic while looking out the window, seeing *Vincent towering over me as I kneeled on the stage floor.* "I told you in no uncertain terms that you should have listened to that worried voice. Now you are in a relationship that is going so badly right now!"

"Fuck off!"

"You're telling me that because you know I'm right. How about you break up with Ana right now before she breaks up with you like she did last time!"

Someone in the audience threw a bottle at me, glass shattering when it hit my skull. I wiped blood from my forehead as the audience laughed at me.

I went back and forth between looking over at Ana driving and looking out the window, *suddenly running as fast as I could on top of a tall parking garage and jumping headfirst towards the ground twelve stories below.*

I began hyperventilating.

"You okay?" Ana asked.

"Yeah," I quickly mumbled. I went back to looking out the window.

"So you refuse to even tell her the honest truth?" Vincent scolded. "This is just a bad situation with every sign pointing to the fact it's going to go badly, and you've admitted and demonstrated that such an outcome is something that would leave you hurt. If you'd listened to me, you wouldn't be in this situation and you wouldn't be having these thoughts of killing yourself!"

"You tell 'em, Vincent!" the audience shouted.

I drank water and looked over at Ana again. "You doing good?"

"I'm good. We should be there soon."

I played calm music through my Airpods to make the thoughts go away. *Maybe I am a stupid piece of shit for having these thoughts.*

I sat on Ana's bed reading Marvel's *Civil War*, peering over my book at Ana as she lay on the futon browsing her phone. I looked over at Ana's Alexa device on her desk and asked for the time, telling me it was 11:35 pm.

"You coming to bed?" I affectionately asked Ana.

"I'm too cozy," Ana playfully answered.

I gave a bittersweet smile. Ana indeed looked so cozy, but I was really hoping she would come to bed with me. I got up and leaned next to Ana by her side, holding her hand and giving it a kiss. "Do you want me to turn the light off?"

"Yes please."

I went and turned the light off, looking at Ana as she laid her head on the pillow. I covered her with a blanket. "Good night," I whispered. "Love you."

Ana didn't respond. I lay on her bed, staring up at the dark ceiling until I fell asleep.

April 4, 2022

Ana was still sleeping on the futon when I woke up. My phone told me it was close to 7 am, so I read a little bit more of *Civil War* until her alarm went off.

"Alexa, snooze!" Ana shouted.

She had to be at work by 9 am, so I put *Civil War* away and took a shower, later coming out to get dressed. While putting my socks on, Ana got up to go to the bathroom, slamming the door behind her again as usual.

Then Ana screamed as I heard her slip.

My heart pounded. I forgot to clean up water from the floor after my shower!

"Ana, are you okay?"

"I'm fine!" I heard her snap from the other side. "Just go!"

I grabbed my backpack, hustled out the door and put my shoes on before jumping into my car. I hit my hand repeatedly to prevent a meltdown before starting the ignition. "I'm so fucking stupid!" I shouted as I drove off. "I'm so sorry! Please don't hate me!"

As I drove away, *Ana and I were in our Captain America and Iron Man suits fighting again on stage, the audience cheering for Ana to kill me.*

She shot more beams at me as I deflected them again.

"Ana, please stop!" I pleaded. "It was an accident!"

Ana threw a punch. I held up my shield to block it, sparks flying as the audience roared in applause. I ducked another swing, moving back and forth as Ana threw punches at me.

"I hate you!" Ana screamed. "Why do you have to leave water on the floor!"

"Ana, stop!"

"Why do you have to be so impulsive?"

"I'm really sorry!"

"Why do you have to throw all your problems on me?"

Ana punched me in the face and knocked me to the floor. Lying on my back, I stared up at the dark ceiling as Ana stood above me with a disgusted look on her face.

I pulled over and began typing on my phone.

ROB:

> I feel sooooo bad about what happened this morning. Are you okay? I should've been more careful and I wasn't, and I'm so sorry. I love you and I hope you have a good day at

I stopped, deleting everything before getting back on the road.

April 7, 2022

I had the whole office to myself again, no students coming as usual. I googled "Signs Your Relationship is Failing" again. *This has to be in my head,* I thought.

I skimmed through some of the articles that appeared in my

search, growing more frustrated as I read them. I finished reading one when Ben called to check on me, asking if I was free this weekend to hang out with him, Nathan, and Trent.

"I'm going to Ana's again, so some other time."

"I totally get it. You gotta make her happy. Some other time then. How are things going between you two?"

I took a moment to compose myself. "Everything's fine. She's been stressed with work but other than not much."

"Glad to hear."

I sighed as I went back to reading the advice articles while tuning out Ben going off on a tangent about something Nathan did recently he found annoying.

I stood on stage again facing the audience.

"So you're just going to lie to Ben?" The audience shouted.

"I don't have to tell Ben everything!"

Vincent stood up in the audience. "Just like you never told Ben about how you treated me because I told you things you didn't want to hear?"

"I never told Ben because I don't ever want to go through what you put me through ever again!"

"Why don't you just admit already after all these years that you want to sexually control Ana, Rob?" Vincent asserted.

I grabbed a chair and threw it at him. "I hope you die of cancer, asshole!"

"Are you still there, Rob?" Ben asked.

I composed myself, trying to get the thought out of my head. "Yeah, I'm still here."

Ben and I talked for a little longer before ending the call. Without thinking, I then unblocked Vincent on Facebook, typing him a message.

ROB:

> I unblocked you not because I've forgiven you but because I wanted to let you know directly that even after all these years I still fucking HATE YOU!

> How dare you try to force your advice down my throat and then try to tell others that I wanted to hurt and control the one person in my life that I care about. From the bottom of my heart, FUCK YOU! I hope you die of cancer and you never treat others the way you treated me! I WILL NEVER FORGIVE YOU, you piece of

I stopped myself and deleted everything I wrote. *What's the point?*

April 9, 2022

I found a ring box when I started rearranging my drawers.

Ana told me she would be free around 8 pm, so I cleaned up my room. I wiped the dust from my desk so I could reorganize my workspace. When I found the ring box at the bottom of the drawer, it didn't immediately click what it was until I opened it to find the earrings I tried to give Ana years ago.

I replayed the memory in my head as I looked at the pair of earrings.

I'm just looking for companionship, she said when she handed them back to me.

I sighed as I started thinking again just how distant Ana had been lately. Would she even want this now?

I then heard a *ding* from my phone.

ANA:

> I'm free now. The gate should be open so come over whenever.

I let her know I would be on my way before looking at the pair of earrings for a bit longer. *She didn't want it then,* I thought. *Would she even want them now?* I took a moment to decide before putting the ring box in my backpack. *I think she'll appreciate it,* I thought as

I left the house to go to Ana's place. *I just hope to God it's all in my head!*

———

I placed the ring box on Ana's side of the kitchen table when I came through the door. She was taking a shower when I got there, so I sat on her bed to grade and played music. Sometime later, Ana came out of the shower and dried off so she could change into her pajamas.

I blew her a kiss. "You're beautiful."

She gave a light smile. "Thank you." She finished putting on her pajamas and went into the kitchen. I stopped grading and stared at the entryway, relieved she didn't slam the door this time. I suddenly began to feel a lump in my throat at the thought of her finding the earrings in the kitchen. I put my laptop to the side and went over to peek inside the kitchen.

I could see Ana at the table looking at the earrings.

"Thank you for the earrings," she said. "They're lovely."

I went into the bathroom, closing the door behind me and stared at my reflection in the mirror. I couldn't help but think again about the months of distance she showed up to this moment, tears starting to drip as I tried to prevent myself from hyperventilating.

You can see she does still care, one voice in my head said.

She's only saying that to be nice, Vincent said. *Dump her before she dumps you!*

I tried to ignore the conflicting thoughts about Ana. Once I felt calm, I flushed the toilet to give Ana the impression I used the bathroom and went into the kitchen.

I hugged her from behind and gave her a kiss on the head. "I hope you like them."

Ana put the earrings to the side and held my arm. "I'll wear them later."

"Sounds good. Did you have dinner?"

"I ate already, but there's some spring rolls for you in the fridge."

I gave Ana another kiss on the head. "Thank you."

Sometime later, we embraced in each other's arms in bed, cuddling to Poets of the Fall.

"Has everything been okay with you?" I asked.

"Everything's been okay," Ana muttered.

"Yeah?"

We cuddled before disengaging, sitting against the headboard.

"I'm sorry about last weekend," I said. "I should have been more careful about the water, and I wasn't." No response as I held her hand. "Anyway, I just wanted to say I was sorry."

She held my hand back. "It's okay," she meekly said.

But the look on her face looked drained. "You sure you're okay?"

Ana sighed, letting go of my hand. "A friend of mine's brother had a stroke recently."

"Oh no! Is he okay?"

"He was released from the hospital, so he's home. But my friend is struggling with it all."

"Was it the same type of stroke my grandpa had?"

"Thankfully no, but he's on crutches right now and has to have physical therapy for one of his arms, and he has to be taken care of for the rest of his life. It's so sad."

I stared out across the room, unsure what to say. "How's your friend taking it?"

"Not great. That's for sure. I wouldn't know what to do if I was in her shoes."

I looked directly at Ana. "What about you?"

No response.

"Ana?"

Ana looked drained as she sighed and looked away.

"For what it's worth, I'm here if you need anything," I said.

Ana turned her side, staring at her phone. I tried to cuddle with her again, but she gently pushed me away.

I stared up at the ceiling, thoughts swirling for hours as I tried to sleep.

April 16, 2022

I stood at the entryway to her room when I came around 5 pm again, numb but also disillusioned when I saw her napping. *Why am I here if you're just going to nap?* I thought for a bit as I watched Ana sleeping, exhaling as I went and sat alone again in her kitchen, mindlessly scrolling through YouTube as she napped for hours.

April 23, 2022

Ana asked me to pick up food from Lucha Libre Taco Shop, since she was in the mood for Mexican food for dinner. A little out of the way but I went over and got it. She was watching Hulu in the kitchen when I arrived, so I placed the bag of food on the table and gave her a hug. "How's your day been?" I asked as I kissed her on the forehead.

Ana gave a light smile, kissing my hand. "Good. Thank you for bringing the food."

"Of course."

Over dinner, we talked about how our week had been and shared funny memes with each other. On my laptop to the side, a news story about Russia's invasion of Ukraine appeared in my feed. "How long do you think this stupid war is going to last?"

Ana shrugged. "I don't know."

"Why don't they just assassinate Putin and get it over with already?"

"He's too powerful. It would just be better if the United States continued to arm the people of Ukraine so they can keep pushing them out."

"Amen to that," I said before taking a bite of my burrito.

"We've been getting clients who have family members in Ukraine, so we try to demonstrate solidarity with them."

I pulled up my phone and showed her my Facebook profile pic with the Ukraine flag banner. "You mean something like this?"

Ana nodded. "Something like that. The one white co-worker we have—"

"The one you call the 'model minority'?" I teased.

Ana laughed. "Yep. That's the one. Half of his family is from Ukraine, and he has been working on making our company show solidarity with Ukraine with the website. Says it would bring in more clients."

"Has it?"

"It has, actually."

"So basically, more wars equals more opportunities to make money!" I joked.

"Yep! Exactly!" She put a pepper on my plate and took a bite of her taco. I couldn't help but notice Ana seemed less distant for the first time in a long time. *Maybe it has all been in my head.*

"Any plans for Memorial Day weekend?" I asked.

"Not really."

"Do you want to do anything for Memorial Day weekend?"

"Sure."

"With me?"

Ana gave a forced chuckle. "Suuuuuure," she muttered.

But something about the way she answered made me feel a bit uneasy, but I brushed it off as I went back to scrolling Facebook and eating my burrito.

I sat on her bed reading the last several pages of Marvel's *Civil War* as Ana lay on the futon scrolling her phone again. I finished the book and put it aside, looking over at Ana and noticing she was about to fall asleep.

Another night of her sleeping on the futon.

She thinks you're a burden, a voice in my head said. *You are an absolute burden to her!*

I stopped myself from breathing too hard, getting up to go turn the light off before laying down on the bed, facing the wall. I took out my phone and texted Ana.

ROB:

> I really do hope I'm not a burden to you 🙁

I stared at my screen until accepting I wasn't getting a response when I heard her snoozing.

April 24, 2022

I slept past 10 am, stretching my arms before realizing Ana was no longer in the room. I climbed off the bed and opened the entryway door to see Ana sitting at the kitchen table typing something on her laptop.

I went over and hugged her. "Good morning," I said as I kissed her on the forehead.

"Morning."

I made myself a bagel and sat across from her. "Did you sleep okay last night?"

Ana shrugged. She typed away before putting her hand on the table.

I held her hand. "I'm sorry about the text last night. I'm better now."

Ana didn't say anything right away. She held my hand for a bit before letting go. "I have to get some groceries," she said. "Did you want anything from Costco?"

I stopped to think before responding, wondering if her lack of response about my text from last night really meant she thought I was a burden, or if her holding my hand was her way saying it was okay. "Nothing off the top of my head."

Ana let go, grabbing her keys and purse before going to the sliding door. "I'll text you, so make sure you keep your phone on."

I sighed as Ana left, so I browsed Facebook and finished my bagel.

For the next hour, I fooled around on social media and graded. I had Ana's place all to myself, feeling liberated to have the music play as loud as I wanted. I put on "It's Too Late" by Carol King, getting me in the mood to grade. I graded papers on Canvas until noticing one was missing, only to remember one student requested they submit a physical copy as part of their classroom accommodations.

I went back into Ana's room and pulled out the paper from my backpack, but realized I didn't have anything to write with. I went over to Ana's desk to see if I could borrow one of hers. No pen or pencil on her desk, so I opened the left drawer to see it empty except for two cards.

They were the same cards I bought for Ana before Valentine's Day!

I stared at them, trying to figure out why she would leave them in an empty drawer like this. On top of her desk were pictures of her with her family but nothing from me.

Staring at the cards all by themselves started making me see myself *across from Ana pointing her fist at me ready to shoot another one of her beams.*

"I'm breaking up with you," she said.

"Please, no! Don't do this!"

I dodged Ana's beam and jumped at her, both of us tackling each other on the floor as the audience screamed for Ana to kill me.

I immediately closed the drawer. *This has to all be in my head, I* thought.

We didn't do much when she came back from grocery shopping. Ana spent most of the afternoon watching Hulu while I graded papers. At some point, she went into her room with her laptop, slamming the door behind her, perhaps out of habit. By dinner time, I checked on Ana to see her still watching TV while in the sheets.

I climbed on the bed to cuddle next to her, only for her to gently move my hand away when I tried to wrap my arms around her. "Stop," she muttered.

I sighed, laying on my back. I checked my phone to see it was around 6:30 pm. Since Ana was glued to her show, I sent her a text.

ROB:

> If you want to go out tonight, I would love that, but if not, I'm okay just spending time with you.

I peered over at Ana still watching her show and not looking at her phone this time. For the next fifteen minutes or so, I just lay next to her, my hand on her hip.

Sometime later, when I tried to cuddle with her again, she gently pushed my hand. "Stooooop," she mumbled once more.

I lay on my side, facing the wall with a sense of uneasiness.

She clearly doesn't want you here! A voice in my head claimed. *Just go home!*

But if you go home tonight, she'll break up with you and you'll live to regret it! Another one argued.

Ana got up and went into the bathroom, slamming the door.

I grunted at the sound. *Does she even want me here?*

I sat up and looked across the room, seeing the clothes piled up on the futon and then my reflection in the mirror on the closet. I saw my backpack by her nightstand and packed up. I sat on the edge of the bed. *She doesn't want me here.*

A few minutes later, Ana came out of the bathroom and started folding laundry on the futon. I couldn't help but notice her blank expression, as if drained.

"Do you just want me to go home?" I bluntly asked.

Ana looked up at me. I half-expected her to say I could stay if I wanted to, so I could get something—*anything*—to confirm everything was all in my head.

Instead, she perked up. "Sure. You can go home if you want."

My heart sank as I sat there for a second to gather my thoughts and throw my backpack over my shoulder. "I'm gonna go home then." I went over to Ana and put my hand on her shoulder as she stood on the futon trying to fold a shirt. "Will you be free next weekend?"

"Yeah," Ana mumbled.

"I love you," I muttered as I kissed her on the cheek. "I'll see you next week."

Ana said nothing as she kept staring down at the floor while folding the shirt.

I felt drained as I reluctantly left.

I rushed home and sat on the couch in the front living room to call Ben.

"Ben, I just left Ana's. Something's wrong! Something's really wrong!"

"Whoa, slow down! What's going on?"

"I think she's going to break up with me!"

"Break up with you? What are you—"

"I've noticed it for months now! She's been so distant. She naps all the time, she ignores me every time I go over there—"

"Sort of reminds me of how Claire—"

"Shut up! LET ME TALK!" Tears flowed as I tried to gather my thoughts. "I'm sorry for screaming at you like that. I just don't know what to do!"

"Are you going to be okay?"

"I hope so. Sorry for bothering you."

I hung up on Ben and lay down, seeing myself *fighting with Ana again on stage in a climactic battle. She punched me in the face hard enough to knock my Captain America helmet off as I thrusted my*

Vibranium shield into her Iron Man suit chest. We knocked each other backwards onto the stage floor, both of us covered in sweat and bruises.

I couldn't stop crying.

May 7, 2022

We hadn't spoken much since leaving her place early two weeks ago.

I didn't go to her place last week since I had to catch up on grading projects in time for finals but told her I would be free this weekend. She left the gate open for me, so I let myself in.

I stood at the entryway of her bedroom to see Ana lying in bed, browsing her phone. I put my backpack by her nightstand and lay next to her, slowly wrapping my hand around her waist to cuddle with her.

Ana allowed me to cuddle her.

"You excited for Baltimore?" I asked.

"I am," Ana softly said.

"If you need a ride to the airport, just let me know."

"I'll let you know."

"What did you say you were going there for, again?"

"There's a conference I'm attending with my boss, and then I'll be seeing a friend."

I smiled. "I'm so proud of you," I muttered.

Ana said nothing.

"How does it feel to be on the path of being a multi-billionaire?" I teased.

Ana giggled. "I doubt I'll ever be a multi-billionaire."

"But you're 'on the road' to being a multi-billionaire."

Ana giggled again. "If you say so," she teased.

We continued cuddling.

"I may not ever be a multi-billionaire," Ana said out of the blue, "but I'm happy that I'm close to a point in my life where I don't have to worry about relying on others. I can travel, I can see the world, I can invest in things that make me and my sister happy. I'm close to being in a position where I can go to my own special place."

"I thought this place was already your own special place."

Ana said nothing.

"Anyway, I'm very proud of you."

We cuddled, talking about how work had been for both of us. She told me about how she felt proud of her advancements in her career while I told her about a formerly incarcerated student struggling in one of my classes. I even showed her a copy of his paper from my phone and how he's been really improving in my course. "That's so cool," Ana said. "I hope he gets an A in your class."

"He will."

Ana pulled up her laptop. "Do you want to watch a movie?"

"Sure."

Ana pulled up Disney Plus to find us something to watch. "Oh just so you know," Ana said. "I have to go somewhere tomorrow night, so I won't be free."

"That's fine."

Ana scrolled through Disney Plus.

"Oh, did I tell you that I finished the *Civil War* comic?" I asked.

"Nice."

"Do you want to hear about the differences?" I enthusiastically asked.

"Sure."

I started telling her about the main differences between *Captain America: Civil War* and the *Civil War* comic itself.

As I told her the differences, *I lay on the stage floor still in my Captain America suit. I rubbed my bruised eye before looking over at Ana on her back, knocked out unconscious with her Iron Man suit battered. I crawled over to her, laying next to her and putting my hand on her chest, hugging her.*

"I'm so sorry," I said. "I don't wanna fight anymore. I hope everything's okay now."

I hugged her tighter, tears flowing as Ana hugged me back.

May 14, 2022

I parked outside Ana's side gate at around 7 am, sending her a text letting her know I was here to take her to her 8:30 am flight. I got my Spotify ready to play Poets of the Fall's *Ghostlight* so Ana could listen to their new album on the way to the airport.

Ana put her suitcase in my trunk and sat in the front passenger seat.

"Ready for your trip?" I asked.

"Yeah."

"I hope you have fun."

Ana began browsing her phone as I started driving. She wanted to stop at Cali Baguette on the way and get sandwiches. "Do you want anything?" she asked as she placed an order through the phone.

"I'm good," I said. "I'm not hungry."

We picked up food from Cali Baguette and headed to the airport. I vented about another student for one of my classes, but I dropped it when Ana put on her earphones. She stayed quiet during the entire car ride.

I eventually arrived at the airport, parking in front of one of the terminals.

Ana started getting out.

"Have a fun and safe trip," I said. "We'll do something for Memorial Day when we get back."

Ana waved goodbye, got her suitcase out of my trunk, and went inside. As I began driving away, "Sounds of Yesterday" started playing.

I think it's going to be okay, I thought as I got on the freeway.

Today

30

—————

June 4, 2022

"What are you doing in Chicago, Rob?" Alex asked me over the phone.

I had been lying in my bed at the Airbnb all morning, staring at Kelly's picture and pulling up directions to Meadowville when he called. Alex settled into his living space in Boston and wanted my teaching tips for the school he would be working at. We talked about pedagogy before going into my reasons for coming to Chicago.

"You have family there or something?" Alex asked.

"No, just here to get closure for something."

"Closure for what?"

I exhaled. *Might as well tell him.* "Ben told you all about our time at Schweitzer, right?"

"When has he not talked about it?" Alex chuckled.

I didn't laugh. "Right. Well, when I was a kid going to Schweitzer, I went on a summer study abroad trip. I met a girl from Chicago . . ."

As I told Alex everything about Kelly, the memory of me and her on those long bus rides popped into my head again, the thought of all the conversations we had and the jokes we made and the stories we shared. "I never even told her I loved her. And I feel so bad for that!"

"Damn," Alex said. "And you were seventeen when that happened?"

"I know, pathetic."

"Not at all. I get it. Have you tried reaching out to her? Does she know you're coming? Maybe you could hit her up. Catch up on old times."

I sighed. "It's not that simple."

"Why do you say that?"

"The shitty part is when I got back home and Maggie Richardson told me the school was going to keep me there for two to three more years, I was so embarrassed that I worked my ass off to get out of that place, and over time, I just lost all contact with her."

"Maggie Richardson was the program director for Schweitzer, right?"

"Yes."

"Gotcha. Was this around the time you said you did three years worth of math in one year?"

"Yeah," I slowly muttered.

"Ohhh! Now I understand why you did all that!"

As we talked, a memory of being in Maggie's office popped into my head. I sat in the chair, my head down with my arms folded as Maggie gave another one of her lectures after I got in trouble for opening my mouth and arguing with one of the teachers when they treated one of my classmates unfairly.

What's gotten into you? She barked. *We gave you extra homework like you insisted! We've allowed you to take college classes in the afternoons! We've even gotten you counseling! Yet this is how you've treated us? What's wrong with you? Why do you have to be such an ass?*

I remembered fighting back tears, refusing to even look at her as I thought about Kelly.

"So if you don't intend to see her, how would going to Chicago help you?" Alex asked.

I sighed. "To be honest, I don't know. I'm hoping it will give me some sense of catharsis. Maybe enlightenment so I can feel something! I've spent the last few days checking out the city itself and then today, I'm going to see if I can go to the part of Chicago where she lives. There's a part of me that hopes I'll run into her and we can have our own version of the park bench scene from that movie (500) *Days of Summer*. You've seen that movie?"

"Yep. Great movie!"

"Yeah, so I'm hoping to find something as close to that as possible. I originally wanted to bring Ana, but you know how that turned out."

"Interesting," Alex said. "Well, I hope it works out for you, man."

But I could tell by the tone of his voice Alex didn't seem so sure.

"Thanks," I said. "How are you and Lydia doing?"

"We're taking a break right now. She's starting a PhD program in New Mexico soon and we may pick things up again, try the whole long distance relationship thing, but she wants to focus on her degree and I want to respect that."

"That makes sense."

We chatted for a bit before ending the call. I stared at Kelly's picture again.

I picked up my rental car and began the hour-long drive to Meadowville. Looking at the Google images on the way, it looked like a small rural town with only a few businesses and lots of farmland and open space. *Would she still be here?* I thought. I drove for the next half hour, avoiding toll roads and long stretches of traffic.

I got onto a long road where I saw nothing but miles of empty fields. The GPS said Meadowville was only twenty minutes away.

My heart began to beat the closer I got there. *Fuck, what if I do actually run into her?*

As I kept driving, a memory began playing in my head of me

sitting across from Kelly on the carpet of a large cabin somewhere in Christchurch, New Zealand. Our travel group gathered in front of a tour guide where he instructed us about the importance of journaling, each of us holding a notebook in our laps.

You are on a once in a lifetime trip to the other side of the world, the tour guide said. *But because our memories are fallible, over time our memories will start to fade, so it's important to write them down!*

Kelly and I looked at each other, getting ready to play a game with our notebooks before the memory faded away.

I wish I never lost that notebook, I thought.

I stopped at a red light, letting a car cross the intersection before driving.

Another memory flashed in my head: me walking over to Kelly as she played a piano in the cabin while the other kids socialized.

You're really good, I nervously said.

Thank you, she said.

As I drove by more farmland, I turned up the volume when Billy Joel's "Piano Man" started playing. As the song began, I saw myself *on stage with my guitar. I looked over to my right to see Kelly sitting at the grand piano, singing the same song. I tried to play backup guitar to Kelly's rendition of "Piano Man" but stopped when the audience booed. I put my guitar down and sat on the stage floor in a cross-legged position, my hands under my cheeks.*

"Rob?" Kelly exclaimed.

I looked up, Kelly standing right next to me.

"How are you, buddy?" she asked as she sat down. "It's been a long time."

"I know."

"What brings you out here?"

I took a breath before looking at Kelly. "Ana Kang broke up with me."

Kelly stopped smiling. "Oh. I'm sorry to hear that."

"She broke up with you because you're a piece of shit, Rob!" the audience shouted.

I looked at my feet again, trying not to look at the audience as I tried to hide my shame.

Kelly put her hand on my shoulder. "I usually ignore them. They tend to be assholes."

I let out a deep breath. "You've always been so kind." I looked up at her. "You were the first person outside of Schweitzer to ever be kind to me."

"I didn't know that."

"Remember that trip we went on so many years ago?"

"Of course."

I cleared my throat. "I never told you, but I was in Special Ed. I didn't tell you because I was afraid you and everyone else would think I was weird or stupid and that I was a freak. That I wasn't good enough."

"That's because you weren't good enough!" Maggie shouted in the audience.

"Fuck you!" I screamed.

Maggie wagged her finger. "If you hadn't ditched. If you hadn't slept in rooms. If you hadn't redone sixth grade math so many times—"

I stood up, grabbed my guitar, and threw it at Maggie.

Maggie and everyone around her jumped out of the way as the guitar smashed into pieces. The audience continued to boo me as I lay on my back, staring at the ceiling.

Kelly lay next to me.

I started crying. "I'm so sorry you had to see that."

"It's okay. I understand."

The audience booed, shouting every single horrible insult imaginable about me.

"Just ignore them," Kelly said. "Remember, they're assholes. I wouldn't let them have any control over you."

I slowly started to calm down. "Thank you."

Neither of us said anything as we looked up at the ceiling turning into a sky full of stars.

"I've thought about you for over sixteen years," I finally said.

"Yeah?"

"Yeah. I thought I had moved on from you when Ana came into my life, but now that she's gone, I'm here because I thought I could come here and make sense of why we couldn't work out. I hope coming to the place you live would give me a sense of your world so I can move on. I can't wait for that feeling of relief!"

"If you find me, I would love to hang out," Kelly said. *"Catch up on old times."*

We both smiled at each other.

I snapped out of the daydream and checked the GPS. I was less than three minutes away!

I parked in front of a general store with a closed sign in the window along the main street. I stepped out of the car and looked around, the entire town itself surrounded by miles of empty fields while hardly anyone walked the wide open streets.

Kelly, do you really live here? I thought.

I looked in both directions of the main road before I began walking, stopping at a corner to take in my surroundings. *Shouldn't I be feeling something right now?*

I continued walking down the street, trying my best to take in the feel of this small town. I kept walking until I saw a BBQ restaurant up ahead. I was starting to get hungry so I thought I would get lunch.

I made my way inside.

"Welcome," the hostess said. "Feel free to sit wherever you like."

I thanked the hostess and surveyed where to sit, the entire restaurant giving a 1980s southern BBQ vibe with an arcade and a jukebox in the corner.

I sat at the bar, an older woman handing me a menu. "Here you go, hun," she said as she poured me a glass of water. "My name is Carmen. I'll be your server today. Make yourself at home, and let me know when you're ready to order."

I thanked Carmen and skimmed over my options before looking around the restaurant. Not many people here except for a couple at one of the blue picnic tables. I looked out the window to my left, viewing the empty streets, wondering if Kelly was walking them somewhere.

"Are you ready to order?" Carmen asked.

"Gimme a few minutes, please."

"You got it," she said before starting to walk away.

"Wait! Sorry, I do have a question!"

"What can I do for you?"

"This is going to sound strange and random, but do you or anyone here know a Kelly?"

Carmen tilted her head.

"Her full name is Kelly Margaret Dubois. She told me a long time ago that she's from here. My name's Rob. An old friend."

"Hmmmm, the name sounds familiar."

I pulled up a picture of Kelly from my phone and showed Carmen. "This is what she looked like."

Carmen scrutinized the picture. "She looks familiar. I can't quite put my finger on it." She faced the kitchen. "Hey Nancy! Do you know if a Kelly Margaret Dubois lives here?"

"What does she look like?" Nancy yelled from the kitchen.

"Redhead. Freckles. A little buff."

"That sounds like that might be Daniel Dubois's kid, but I don't know if they still live here or not. I haven't seen them in ages."

Carmen turned to me. "Yeah, I don't know what to tell you."

I sighed. "It's okay. Was worth a try."

"Of course. Are you ready to order?"

"Gimme a few minutes."

Carmen walked away as I stared at the menu, feeling drained.

I drove aimlessly around Meadowville, not seeing much except houses and mom-and-pop stores. Almost an hour later, I parked next to a pick-up truck in the gravel lot of a small saloon on the outskirts of town. I turned off the ignition, giving myself a moment to breathe.

I called Ben. "Hey, how are you? Do you have a few minutes?"

"Hey, Rob. How's Chicago?"

I let out a huge cough. "Sorry about that." I took a moment to gather my thoughts. "I don't know why I'm here."

"What do you mean?"

"I thought I could come here and feel something. I walked around the place she lives in. I had lunch and even asked one of the locals if she was still around. They of course don't know, but I prepared myself for that possibility. But I thought, 'That's okay. I'm just here to get that feeling of closure.' But I don't feel anything! Why am I not feeling anything? Did I really waste money traveling two thousand miles away from home just to feel nothing? I feel like a fucking moron!"

I hit my hand repeatedly for a moment before stopping. Neither of us said anything as I took some deep breaths.

"For what it's worth, Rob, you've done more than I would have done if I was going through what you're going through."

"I guess."

"But have you considered that maybe going there wasn't exactly the best idea in the world? I mean, what does walking around looking at buildings accomplish?"

I said nothing.

"I've been trying to get this through your head for years, but I really do think it's time for you to move on from her," Ben continued. "When you and Ana were a thing, I thought you finally did that, but now that she broke up with you, I guess I was wrong."

"Why do you say that?"

"You live in the past too much, Rob."

"And you don't with that piece of shit 'school,' Schweitzer?"

Ben sighed. "Look, the point I'm trying to make is that the Kelly you fell for all those years ago, she's likely not the same Kelly she is now. Even if you had somehow magically run into her, would you still even recognize her?"

I grunted.

"Don't fucking grunt at me like that!"

"Sorry."

I pulled up Kelly's picture as Ben took a deep breath.

"I'm sorry," Ben said. "I didn't mean to lash at you like that."

"It's okay."

"Well, I'll let you go. We can hang out and grab some tacos if you like when you get back and talk about it. That sound good?"

"Sounds good to me."

I ended the call and stared at Kelly's picture. I replayed the phone conversation I had with Ben in my head. *Of course I would recognize her,* I thought. *What is he talking about?*

As I gazed at her photo, *I stood on stage across from Kelly.*

"Ben thinks I wouldn't recognize you," I said. "Isn't that crazy?"

"That is crazy," Kelly said.

"I mean, what I know about you is that you're smart, you're kind, you have the most awesome red hair, you tell great jokes, you're a fantastic conversationalist, you're a lovely singer, you're amazing at the piano, you have a great way with animals, you know so much about Lord of the Rings, you . . ."

I stopped, drawing a blank at what to say next.

"Rob?"

Still nothing.

"What is it, Rob?"

I then looked up at Kelly. "I . . . I don't know you."

Kelly said nothing.

"You were there for me when I really needed someone like you. I will always treasure that. I thought I knew you, but . . . I can't think of anything else I know about you. Do I even really know you at all?"

No response. We looked at each other before Kelly slowly began walking away, exiting the stage.

I clicked out of Kelly's picture and lay back in my seat. *Is this what closure feels like?* I thought. *Nothing at all?*

I took time to gather my thoughts, mindlessly browsing through my Facebook, looking at random memes and statuses before receiving a notification from my photo library. "You Have a New Memory with Ana Kang," it read.

I opened the notification to a photo of Ana with a huge smile, wearing sunglasses with a reflection of me holding up my phone to take a picture.

This was when we went to that art festival, I thought.

I looked at the photo more closely. I couldn't remember the last time she smiled like that recently.

You going to get those? I remembered asking. *They look good on you.*

I might, Ana had said when she took off the sunglasses. *Not sure yet. I wanna look around some more first.*

I stared at the photo, the memory of us attending that art festival flooding right back in.

I put the phone away, turned on the engine, and began driving back to Chicago.

31

———

June 13, 2022

I still couldn't believe I had gotten COVID.

I had not been able to stop coughing or throwing up since getting back from Chicago. I kept a bucket on hand as I locked myself in my room, too tired to get out of bed.

I tested myself again today twice. Both positive.

How the hell did I get COVID?

I lay on my side, giving myself a sideways view of piles of dirty laundry in the corner.

I feel worthless.

I drank ginger ale and stared at my messy space, different parts of the room making me remember all the times Ana and I spent together here. Looking at the desk, I remembered the time we ran late to Easter church service with Grandpa.

C'mon, we gotta go, I had gently said. *We're gonna be late!*

We're going! Ana playfully asserted while putting on makeup. *Relax!*

I replayed the morning in my head again, thinking how stupid I must've been for panicking about us being late. We cuddled in this room and watched movies and talked politics and current events so many times, wishing I could have those moments with her again.

I remembered her teaching me how to say "Hello" in Mandarin while cuddling.

So how do you say "I love you" in Mandarin? I asked.

Ana giggled. *You'll have to figure that one out on your own!*

I typed "I love you" into Google Translate on my phone and showed her the results, making her laugh and smile.

I coughed again, drinking more ginger ale. I ignored a call from Ben, texting him I had a sore throat before scrolling Facebook.

I saw the same mindless crap on Facebook. Unfunny memes. Selfies. People bickering over stupid shit. A thread from the Authentic Philosophy Facebook group appeared in my feed where Chris was arguing with Vincent about something.

I completely forgot I unblocked Vincent months ago.

I read a sample of their argument, not paying attention to what they were arguing about.

CHRIS NORDHOF:

> @Vincent Smith, don't you ever admit to being wrong about *anything*? God, you can be such a jackass sometimes!

VINCENT SMITH:

> @Chris Nordhof, look, I don't always know everything. I could be wrong. I don't think I'm wrong here, but if I am, I'll admit fault and apologize.

Yeah right, I thought. *You never apologize for shit! Why should anyone believe you?*

I went to Vincent's profile to block him, only to stop. *What's the point?*

I clicked out of his profile, liked all of Chris's comments refuting him, and moved on. I couldn't be bothered with this asshole.

I eventually looked at Ana's profile.

She thankfully never unfriended me, but she hadn't posted anything in months, not even to change her picture.

I suddenly thought of the night of the first break up.

I don't know if I'm the right girl for you, I remembered her saying.

I looked at the spot in the room where she said that years ago. *Then why the hell did you come back for three more years?* I asked myself.

I pulled up Ana's phone number in my texts, staring at the empty chat box unsure if I should reach out to her again right now.

Why the hell did you do this—again?

I started typing a text to her, but stopped halfway.

Whatever. I'll just wait until I'm COVID free. She'll come back if this is a pattern for her.

I put my phone away and fell asleep.

July 11, 2022

Nathan called after I finished a Zoom meeting. We talked about how we've been lately before he invited me to a birthday party planned at his mom's house this upcoming Saturday.

"Sure. I have nothing better to do anyway besides grading."

"You still don't have COVID, right?" Nathan asked.

"Oh no, I'm negative now. Still a little groggy, but I'm not contagious if that's what you're worried about."

"Okay good. Just wanted to be sure."

"Who's going to be there?"

"A bunch of local Twitch streamers, as well as people from our old school we haven't seen in a while."

"Like who?"

"Oh you know. John. Heidi. Even Maggie's coming!"

"Oh hell no!"

Nathan laughed. "I'm just messin' with you, Rob. I think Ben and Trent will be there, too, but I haven't heard back from them yet."

I grunted. "Let me guess. They need a ride, right?"

"No idea. You would have to ask them."

I logged off Zoom to end office hours for the day.

"Oh by the way," Nathan said. "If Trent does come and you pick him up, can you remind him to bring the money he owes me?"

"Again? *Really?* Doesn't he work at McDonald's?"

"Not anymore. He got fired. Now that dumbass is trying to get back on SSI. Last time I ever loan him money."

I shook my head. "Why am I not surprised? Stop loaning that idiot money."

I ended the call and lay in bed, watching YouTube for the next hour.

I later logged onto Facebook, checking Ana's profile. She still hadn't posted anything in months. I pulled up her number in my texts. *Should I reach out again?* I double checked the date, enough time having passed since she ended everything.

I imagined us *in center stage, hugging things out and getting back together before morphing into us sitting on a park bench, the audience watching us come to terms with why we couldn't have worked out.*

I kept going back and forth in my head between both scenarios.

I started typing a long text.

Here goes nothing, I thought as I pressed "send."

Hours later, I still hadn't received a response from Ana, so I went to see the new *Thor: Love and Thunder* movie. I got bored halfway through and looked over at the seat on my right, where Ana sat whenever we went to the movies

She would always sit here, but now it was empty.

I walked out of the theater, my heart beating faster the longer it took for my phone to turn on. I wanted so badly to check if Ana responded. *What will she say?*

It finally booted on, allowing me to see if she texted me back.

Nothing.

I sighed. *Maybe later tonight or tomorrow?*

July 12, 2022

I turned on my phone when I woke up, growing impatient as it took forever to turn on. My heart raced again, scared of the endless possibilities of what she would say.

Nothing again.

I stared at the text I sent, wondering if she would respond to it later tonight before putting the phone down and going on with my day.

I played guitar after a long day of grading. At 10 pm, I stopped to check my phone again.

Still nothing.

I put the phone down and kept strumming.

July 13, 2022

I woke up and checked my phone again, hoping—praying—she would answer.

She still hadn't gotten back to me.

I felt a lump in my throat as I began fearing the worst.

I isolated myself at Lestat's to grade papers. I took a break to check my messages.

Ana still hadn't responded.

Without thinking, I texted her through Facebook Messenger asking if everything was okay since I didn't hear from her.

ROB:

You're probably busy, but I would love to get together sometime for lunch and chat, but if not no worries. I understand. Hope you're doing well.

I went back to work, not expecting a response right away.

I sat on the couch in the front living room when I got home later and checked Facebook.

Still no answer. But then I noticed underneath my Facebook message I sent her earlier a small version of her Facebook profile picture.

She left me on read.

I felt a notch in my stomach. I put my phone down and lay on the couch, staring aimlessly at the coffee table as Alicia came into the house, slamming the door behind her.

Every memory of Ana slamming her door suddenly flashed all at once in my head.

I clenched my jaw.

July 16, 2022

Everyone else had spread out in Nathan's backyard as it started getting dark. No one seemed to be using the empty fire pit in the corner, so I sat next to it by myself as people socialized, drank beer, or danced to music in front of a boombox. I stayed glued to my phone, scrolling Facebook or watching YouTube as I faced the partygoers.

I opened up my texts, reminded that Ana never responded. I reread what I sent her, trying to figure out if I said something wrong.

I put my phone away, trying to take in everything. I looked over at the boombox across the yard when I heard it play "Into the Unknown" from *Frozen II*.

I started remembering Ana and I cuddling to this song after we saw the movie.

Do you think it lives up to the original? I asked.

Of course, she teased. *I wouldn't have paid money to see it if it didn't.*

We laughed as I told her jokes and talked about the housing market. *Hopefully we can buy our own house or condo someday*, I said.

That would be so cool, she said.

I turned away when someone changed the song and watched people talk amongst themselves. Over at the refreshments, Nathan gave Trent shit for wearing his "I Like Cock" T-Shirt while Ben went around catching up with people from Schweitzer.

My heart leapt when I saw someone with long black hair just like Ana's, only to reveal someone I didn't recognize when I saw her face. *Probably one of Nathan's friends*, I thought.

I glanced at the house's backyard door when I heard someone slam it shut while coming outside. Again, every memory of Ana slamming that damn door slammed into me. I hit my hand and then cracked my knuckles.

"Hey Rob, how's it going?" Nathan asked when he came up to me.

I gave him a so-so gesture. "Could be better."

"Is the music too loud?"

"No, it's fine. Just a lot on my mind right now."

"I hear you. You wanna beer?"

"I'm good. Happy Birthday," I muttered.

"Thanks, man." Nathan drank a sip of his beer. "You know, it feels so great that you are all here now. Not just my Twitch buddies but also you and people who survived that bullshit school we went to . . ."

I started tuning him out when he went on a long tangent about his growing Twitch career while saving up to move out, pretending to listen as I people-watched.

I overheard some partygoers near the fire pit talk about *Thor: Love and Thunder.*

"Oh my god, it was such dogshit," one of them said.

"You should've walked out then if it was bad," said another.

"I know, but it was such a disaster!"

"You should've got the hell out of there and got your money back!"

They laughed, causing me to feel an ache in my chest as I thought of all the times Ana and I went to Marvel movies together.

I imagined *myself wrapping my arm around Ana in movie theater seats, the audience laughing at us as I covered Ana's eyes to shield her from seeing them.*

"This is a disaster!" they screamed. "You should've run, Rob!"

My heart pounded as Vincent stood up in the front row and pointed at me. "It's a bad situation and people are being honest that you should've gotten out!" he shouted.

I closed my eyes and tilted my head down.

I looked away from the party goers.

"So anyway," Nathan continued. "You sit back and chill and we can chat later. Glad you're here, Rob."

I shrugged as Nathan joined the rest of the party. I checked a *ding* notification from my phone, half-hoping it was Ana, only to see a spam message. I people-watched until I noticed Ben talking to Heidi as they drank beer. I hadn't seen her since Schweitzer.

They talked about what they've been up to since the start of the pandemic before Heidi said something to trigger another one of Ben's rants about Schweitzer. I was about to tune it out when I heard Heidi's response.

"Look Ben," she said. "I know you have this weird hate boner for Schweitzer, but they did help me!"

"C'mon, Heidi. Do you really not remember the way they treated us?"

"Treated you, maybe, but Mr. Johnson inspired me to read more and if it weren't for him and that school . . ."

They went back and forth about Schweitzer, making me remember the times teachers there talked down to me or made me feel ignored.

If you don't have a high school diploma, then you would have no choice but to work at McDonald's, Mr. Johnson said, as if to make a joke but only making me feel stupid.

"What about Maggie?" Ben asked. "Can we at least agree that she's awful?"

Heidi shrugged.

It just made me remember my arguments with Maggie in her office when I worked my ass off so hard to catch up in credits, not telling her why I was doing it to get the hell out of this godforsaken place.

Rob, you brought this onto yourself. If you hadn't ditched, hadn't slept in rooms, hadn't redone sixth grade math so many times . . .

I couldn't help but try to hide tears.

You need to do this if you want to get anywhere *in life!* Maggie exclaimed.

I just sat there in her office feeling trapped forever in that hell hole, too ashamed to tell Kelly as the hope of connecting with her again began slipping away.

I think you're a cool guy, I remembered Kelly telling me on one of the bus rides.

I looked at Heidi, irritated. *I guess you think I have a weird hate boner, too.*

"We're just going to have to agree to disagree," Ben said.

I went back to people watching.

"Oh hey, Rob," Heidi said, waving at me.

I politely waved back, not saying anything as I people watched.

I stayed by the fire pit before Ben came over. "How are you holding up, Rob?" he asked, giving me a fist bump and sitting next to me.

"Eh, still a little groggy, but okay. Could be better."

"I hear you. At least you're feeling better?"

I shrugged.

Ben put his beer bottle on the ground. "You look like something's bothering you. You okay?"

I sighed. "I tried reaching out to Ana again this week."

"Oh?"

"I thought maybe enough time had passed where maybe we could talk things out. But she didn't respond. She won't even talk to me, and I don't know why."

"What did you text her? Did you say something that might have made her uncomfortable?"

"I hope not."

"Can I see what you wrote? Maybe I can give some insight."

"No, I'd rather not," I said, my voice choking up. "I'd rather keep it between me and her. No one else. I don't want to go through what I went through with Vincent ever again."

Ben nodded. "Understood."

"Right now, I'm just so mad at her. I mean, I've been replaying the last five years in my head, and I still don't understand why she did this. Why couldn't she have tried to talk to me? Why couldn't she tell me something was wrong? Then all of a sudden she tells me over the phone she doesn't like people and prefers to be alone? That just seems so random to me!"

"Sounds like what I went through with Claire."

"I knew something was wrong in the last couple months, but I couldn't figure it out because each time I would check in on her, she would just tell me she's fine—but her body language told a completely different story."

I talked in great detail about how Ana slowly became more distant in the past year, repeating patterns of behavior I couldn't understand.

I sighed. "I lost count of the amount of times she would say no. So many no's to this, no's to that. It's like she lost enjoyment in all the things we used to do. Never even got the chance to meet her sister or her mother like she said we could. There was one point it started feeling like she became a ghost or something. Lost count of the amount of time she would shut herself off from me in the past year."

Trent came up to us. "Mind if I join you?" he asked. There wasn't another empty chair so he just stood next to Ben drinking a Pepsi. "What are you guys talking about?"

"We're just talking," Ben said.

I cleared my throat. "Part of me thinks either since COVID started, or maybe when Grandpa died, something happened that caused her to start acting the way she does, but I don't know. Maybe it's when we installed that new door of hers. God, why the hell does she have to slam that door?"

"She sounds like she has issues," Trent said.

"Shut up, Trent," Ben grunted.

I gave Trent the side eye before continuing. "I hated that door slamming. I hated how she would sleep on that futon. I hated how she wouldn't really talk to me all that much. I hated how ignored I felt. Sometimes I would go to her place and she would be napping and I'd think to myself, 'Why am I even here?' It gave me so much anxiety in the past year."

Ben buried his feet in the grass, letting out a deep breath. "Rob . . . I . . . I don't know how else to say this, but as your friend, I have to be honest. She wasn't treating you very well."

I looked at Ben, unsure what to say.

"She was not communicating with you, hiding things from you, maybe even lying to you. Pushing you away without explanation. This is the same kind of shit Claire pulled on me!"

"Ben, stop—"

"You deserve so much better than that!" Ben exclaimed. "I can't fucking believe her! The nerve of her! That pisses me off and she's not even my ex!"

"Reminds me of how Claire never gave you back your book," Trent said.

"You remember that?" Ben asked. "This is so similar to that!"

Ben and Trent started talking as if I wasn't there. I stood up and faced them. "Both of you need to stop!" I asserted. "I am mad at her right now, but I'll deal with it myself."

I started walking away.

"Where're you going, Rob?" Trent asked.

"I'm getting a drink."

"Just remember you're better off without that bitch, Rob," Trent said nonchalantly.

I looked straight at Trent, dumbfounded by what he said. "What did you call her?"

"You deserve someone way better than that bitch, Rob! Don't you see—"

I punched Trent straight across the face, knocking him to the ground.

Everyone stopped what they were doing and stared at us. Ben sat there shell shocked while Trent lay on the ground holding his face and crying in pain.

"What did you do that for?" Trent shouted.

"Don't you ever call her a bitch, you fucking asshole!" I screamed at the top of my lungs.

"What the hell, Rob?" Ben cried out.

"You don't get to be mad at her! Not you! And not you! Only I can be mad at her!" I turned to face everyone at the party, hitting myself as I no longer could control my unfathomable rage. "And that goes for everyone here, too!"

Everyone stopped what they were doing to stare.

"Why do you assholes think it's okay to talk shit about someone you don't even fucking know? Why should people tell me how I'm supposed to fucking feel? So many of you think it's fucking okay to tell someone like me about how we're supposed to think, feel, and react? Like we're fucking robots?"

I grabbed a Pepsi can from a nearby chair and threw it on the ground. People just stared, unsure what to say as I fumed at the mouth.

"What's wrong with all of you?" I screamed. "That's the kind of bullshit Schweitzer tried to force down our fucking throats when we were kids! That school should not only be shut down, it should be burned to the fucking ground!"

"What's gotten into you, Rob?" Heidi shouted.

"None of you are allowed to be mad at her! Not you! Not you! And not you! No one—and I mean no one—can be mad at her! Only *I* can! You understand that? Only *I* can be mad at her! I should have the right to think and feel how I feel, without any of you pieces of shit being mad for me and telling me how I should feel! And if you want to stay my friend, you respect that! If you can't do that, you can fuck right off!"

I stopped, catching my breath as everyone just stared at me. I looked at Trent crying on the ground before surveying the yard, everyone frozen.

I felt a lump in my throat. "Oh my god, what have I've done?" I mumbled, sobbing.

I ran through the side gate, hurrying to my car.

I threw everything Ana gave me over the years into a plastic bin the minute I got home.

Flashbacks of all the times she went over the speed limit popped into my head when I found a postcard she bought me when she traveled to Indonesia, shoving it into the bin. "Fuck your speeding!"

I grabbed every single trinket she bought me I could find and threw them in the bin.

I grabbed the Funko pop figure of Captain America off my bookshelf, remembering all the times she slammed that door. "Fuck your door slamming!"

I looked up the wall of posters above my desk and began taking each one done, one by one. All the times she made me feel ignored flooded my thoughts as I began taking down a painting of Chris Cornell. "Fuck you for ignoring me!"

I dropped the Chris Cornell painting to the side and took down another one of Captain America, remembering all the times she would be glued to her phone. "Fuck that phone!"

I took down another one until the last one left was the one of the moth, the painting she bought me at that art festival years ago, remembering the time we went to see Poets of the Fall live, remembering the times I shared with her their music.

I couldn't bring myself to take it down the night she ended everything.

I started pulling the push pins off the edges of the painting, remembering all the times she would just sleep. "Fuck your naps!"

I dropped the first push pin on the table, moving to take another off. But as I started taking it off, I suddenly thought about her crying in my arms.

I stopped. I sat down, staring up at the wall, the thought replaying in my brain.

She could not stop crying.

Yesterday

32

―――――

Mid (??) 2018

We held a toast with our margarita glasses after the server brought tacos to our table.

"To tacos," I said, smiling.

"To tacos," Ana said, smiling back.

We giggled before clinking our glasses and sipping our margaritas at the same time. Live mariachi music and chatter from other people filled the Mexican Cafe restaurant in Old Town.

"You having a good time?" I asked.

"Yep," Ana said. "Now that I have my tacos, I'll have an even *better* time."

I chuckled before we started eating.

"Oh, I don't know if I told you, but my sister recently made the dean's list," Ana said.

I gave a thumbs up. "Right on! That's awesome!"

Ana took a bite of one of her tacos. "And now she's working on becoming vice president of her sorority."

"Has she decided her major?"

"Not yet. She still has to finish her G.E."

"Makes sense."

"Mom's pressuring her to major in something that's going to

make lots of money and bring pride to the family, whatever that means."

I chuckled. "Yeah, but that's just how moms are, right?"

Ana looked like she was about to say something before she stopped. She shrugged before taking another bite of her taco as we continued our meal and chatted about current events.

We left the restaurant after dinner and began walking down the busy Old Town main street, making our way towards my car. "Shall we head out and fight crime, Ms. Kang?" I joked, a huge grin on my face as I looked at her.

Ana chuckled. "Only if I have an iron suit."

"You're Iron Man, remember?" I pretended to hold up a Vibranium shield. "And I am Captain America!" I said as I threw a fake punch in the air.

Ana shook her head, fighting back laughter. "You are something else."

"I can do this all day," I teased. "We're a team."

Ana laughed as we passed the Whaley House and stopped at a crosswalk, waiting for the light to turn green. I pulled out a $5 bill and dropped it in an open guitar case of a sideshow musician.

As we waited at the crosswalk, we grabbed each other's hands as I kissed her on the forehead. "I'm glad you're here with me," I whispered.

Ana looked up at me. "Me too," she said, smiling.

I smiled back. "I love you."

"I love you, too."

We kissed, right before the light turned green. "Shall we cross, Iron Man?" I joyfully asked.

Ana chuckled.

Up ahead, I saw an ice cream cart across the street. "Oh my god, we have to get ice cream!" I exclaimed.

Once the light finally turned green, I rushed across the street and headed to the ice cream cart, only to then notice the "Cash Only" sign.

I scrambled through my pockets. "Dammit, I'm out."

Ana playfully shook her head. "That's what you get for giving your money away like candy," she teased. "Karma."

"Oh god!" I playfully exclaimed.

Ana pulled out her purse. "What flavor do you want?"

"You sure?"

"You can Venmo me later."

I said nothing as Ana paid for our ice cream.

We arrived back at my place and headed to my room, having the entire house to ourselves again. Ana placed her purse on my desk, taking something out before going into the bathroom across the hall and slamming the door shut. *Careful with that door, I thought.*

I remade the bed and reorganized the bedside, too lazy to do it since Ana spent the night previously and I wanted to focus on spending time with her over anything else. I double-checked to make sure I had condoms in the bedside drawer and the floor was clear of any junk. I pretended to scatter roses on the floor before putting on some soft romantic music from my Google Home. *Mmmm, sexy time is coming!*

Once everything was ready, I stared at my handy work.

I imagined us in each other's arms under the stars. *This evening is going to be so great!*

I glanced through my open door, the bathroom across the hall still closed to tell me Ana had been in there for the past five minutes. Shrugging it off, I sat at my desk, put on some cologne, and checked my email and browsed Facebook.

I blew Ana a kiss when she came out of the bathroom five or so minutes later, giving me a light smile before sitting at the edge of the bed. I finished responding to an email and got up to sit next to her, gently holding her hand. "Did you have a good time tonight?" I asked.

Ana slightly nodded. "Yeah."

I went to give her a kiss on the forehead but stopped when I noticed her somber facial expression while she stared down at her feet.

I looked at her face a little closer. "Are you okay?"

Ana rubbed her eyes. "I'm okay," she answered quietly.

I kept looking at her facial expression, a tiny tear in her eye. "Are you sure? You don't look okay."

Ana rubbed her eyes again. "I'm okay," she said, clearly trying to smile. "You don't have to worry about me."

I held up her hand, holding it tighter. "Ana, I know you. Something is clearly bothering you. What's wrong? Are you okay?"

Ana tried to smile as her eyes started to water more. "Can't I just be sad by myself in peace?" she said, trying to pass it off as a joke. "I'll be fine. You don't have to worry about me."

I put my hand on her shoulder. "Well, for what it's worth, I don't think it's a good idea to bottle up whatever is bothering you. You'll feel so much better if you talk about it. Let it out."

Ana closed her eyes.

"I don't want to pressure you. If you don't want to talk about it, you don't have to talk about it. But I know you, and I know you enough to know when something's wrong."

I continued holding her hand as Ana looked down.

I took a deep breath. "Ana, it's okay to—"

"My co-workers have been treating me like trash!" Ana blurted out.

I looked straight at her.

Ana cleared her throat. "Ever since I started this job, I've seen so many people come and go. Always gossiping. So many of these people are always talking crap about the job. Talking crap about me. They act so entitled that they can't even do their jobs. And when I try to get them to actually do their jobs, they would have an attitude with me."

I held Ana's hand tighter.

"They would consistently disrespect me. They would not take me seriously and listen to my instructions, but then actually do it if a male manager came around and told them to do it. They would talk shit about me behind my back!"

"What would they say about you?"

Ana's eyes started to water more. "They would call me a bitch! They would call me all these horrible names! They would call me cold and mean and how I deserve all these awful things to happen to me! And this is not just a one time thing. This has gone for months. Almost a year at this point."

Ana pulled out her phone and put on a black and white video clip. "Let me show you something."

She started playing the video and put the phone in my hands so I could watch.

"What's this?" I asked.

"It's surveillance footage of the office. I grew suspicious of their behavior, so I requested access to it. This was taken the other day during after hours."

In the footage, two people in an empty office were looking for something as they argued.

"Oh my god, I can't believe the nerve of that fucking bitch," said one of them. "Telling us how we're not doing our jobs. Tell us this, tell us that! What's wrong with her?"

"You're talking about Ana, right?" the other one asked.

"Yes! Her! She's on such a power trip! I wish I didn't have to work with that cold, manipulative bitch! Clearly has a stick up her ass!"

The people in the video kept going on and on about how horrible Ana was before the clip ended. Ana took her phone back and put it by her side of the bed.

"How often does that go on?" I asked. "Does that go on all the time?"

Ana took a breath. "On and off, but yes."

"Why don't you do something about it? Can't you report it to your boss?"

"And do what?" Ana's voice started to choke up a little, taking a moment to compose herself. "Not like my boss will do anything about it."

I rubbed Ana's shoulder.

Ana sighed. "My boss means well, but there are times when she doesn't do anything or doesn't do enough."

She stopped for a moment to calm herself down.

"I've had times when she would get mad at me for being late for work even though she would be late herself. Lately, when things have gone wrong, she would call me into the office and make me feel humiliated in front of everyone there. Sometimes she would even criticize me in the conference room in front of everyone. 'Ana, do you see what happens when you do this?' 'Ana, do you see how you're supposed to do this?' Do you see how you're supposed to do that?'"

I rubbed Ana's shoulder again.

"Up until recently, I had one friend named Cheryl. I met her when I started working for them. I thought we were friends. I thought we had each other's backs. But then she would keep taking my commission. Then I found out she would spread these rumors about me, like that would somehow help her get what she wanted in the company. It's why my boss would often call me to the office to chastise me for things I didn't even do because Cheryl would exaggerate or make up lies about me. She had even written these terrible things about me on Facebook all while trying to present herself as the model employee."

I took my hand off her shoulder as Ana took a moment to compose herself again.

"I've tried doing so much for them. I've tried making sure work can actually be done. But nothing I do feels like it's good enough. There have been many times where I've dreaded going to work. Dreaded finding out what it had in store for me."

"Why don't you just leave and find another job?"

"I don't know," she muttered. "I've debated that, but there are times I've felt . . . trapped there."

I reached to my desk and handed her a tissue.

She used it to blow her nose before dropping it to the side. "Many times I come home from work, and I feel the urge to sleep. Not doing anything because what's the point? People are so cruel."

I rubbed Ana's hand. "Reminds me how I was treated at 7-Eleven so long ago."

Ana sighed.

"Just know that you have me," I said, trying to cheer her up. "I'll always be there for you."

Ana laid her head against my chest. "That's the thing. I like you. I really like you. But I'm scared."

"Scared of what?"

Ana took a moment before responding. "My whole life, my mom has always been so demanding of me and my sister. It's like anything she didn't have where she grew up, she wanted us to strive for much more. She's always trying to pressure us to have kids and have high paying careers so that it would make *her* happy. She's always hoping either of us would date a doctor or a lawyer or someone who makes a ton of money or of high status because it was something she didn't have growing up in China."

I kissed Ana's forehead.

"I'm scared of what would happen if I were to have her meet you. Scared of how she would treat you. Would she see me as a disappointment? Would she say terrible things about you? Growing up, she would always have standards for us that I couldn't always meet. I love her, but I'm glad I don't live with her. But even though I no longer live with her, I'm always worried that she's going to do something that will cause her to complain again."

I put my fingers on one of Ana's cheeks as I looked into her eyes.

"It's like what I do is never good enough for her," Ana mumbled, choking up as she talked. "Am I just not good enough?"

"Why do you care what she thinks?" I asked, trying to put on a smile. "It's your life. You can live your life however you want. You're an adult. We're both adults. We have freedom."

Ana said nothing as she laid her head against my chest. I wrapped my arms around her as she slowly started crying. "It's okay," I whispered. "Let it out."

Ana cried in my arms, neither of us saying anything for the rest of the evening.

She could not stop crying.

Tomorrow

33

———————

July 17, 2022

I had locked myself in my room for hours practicing Don McLean's "Till Tomorrow."

My Spotify played the song on repeat as I listened carefully to the tempo, my fingers repeatedly messing up the chord progression as *I stood center stage with my guitar.*

The audience coldly stared at me as I tried to play the song properly but couldn't.

"You're garbage, Rob!" one audience member shouted.

"No wonder Ana left you!" shouted another. "You just aren't good enough!"

I stopped playing as the audience booed, someone throwing a bottle at me as it smashed against my head.

I snapped out of it, stopping to stretch my fingers and breathe. "Maybe I'm not good enough," I mumbled. I tried the song a few more times before resting the guitar in my lap. Looking up at the wall above my desk, the moth painting was all that was left, the rest of the posters under my bed.

Staring up at the painting, I began thinking about Ana again.

I thought about the day she ended everything. *I don't like people,* I remembered her saying over the phone.

I plucked a string before a memory of us cuddling one day popped into my head.

I learned a new word today, Ana said.

What's that? I asked.

Misanthrope.

So you hate humanity! I joked. *Humanity sucks so I agree!*

Were you actually serious, Ana?

I kept looking at the painting as I thought about the night she cried in my arms for the first time.

Many times I come home from work and I feel the urge to sleep because what's the point? she stated. *People are so cruel.*

I thought about the times I went to her place and lay next to her as she slept for hours, as if she no longer wanted to be alive.

I thought about the first time we broke up.

. . . but then I grew to like you! Ana muttered while sitting on the edge of my bed, choking up slightly. *I want to focus on my career . . . I want to focus on my mental health . . . I just . . . I don't know what to do . . .*

I remembered begging her to not leave before she walked out.

I thought about the night I left her place back in late April.

I love you, I muttered as I kissed her on the cheek. *I'll see you next week.*

I visualized Ana's face when she said nothing and stared down while folding a shirt, presented in my head side by side with her somber look the night she cried in my arms years ago.

The look on her face was exactly the same!

I suddenly saw myself *looking behind the curtain to watch Ana stand center stage as she looked down at her feet, her hands covering her face to fight back tears while the audience yelled and screamed at her.*

I looked up at the painting again, deep in thought. "Ana, have you been going through what I've fought my whole life?" I mumbled. "Is there a Maggie or a Vincent on your stage you've never told me about? Is there an entire auditorium of people telling you all these horrible things about you, too?"

July 18, 2022

Ben cooked us grilled cheese and tomato soup for lunch in his mom's kitchen as I sat at the counter and told him, in detail, about the night Ana cried in my arms.

"So that's why you punched Trent," he said as he flipped one of the grilled cheeses.

I said nothing as I folded my arms and looked down in shame.

"You never told me Ana went through all that."

"I never told anyone."

"You still shouldn't have punched Trent, man. Not that I blame you, but still."

"I feel bad about that."

"You're just lucky he's not pressing charges," Ben said before placing the grilled cheese on separate plates for us. "After you stormed out of the party, Trent was so upset that me and Nathan had to calm him down and then explain to anyone who cared what the hell happened. What a shitshow!"

"I'm really sorry," I mumbled.

Ben put the grilled cheese and tomato soup in our spots at the counter. "Just imagine if you did that at Schweitzer," Ben said as he stirred his soup. "Maggie Richardson would've sent your ass to jail. Imagine if you did that in front of any neurotypicals outside of that party. Prison! Fox News or some shit would be going on about how autistic people are monsters and Autistic Moms out there would be scared shitless of their kids growing up to be like you."

"I know—"

"Imagine if Vincent Smith saw you do that in person. Would have confirmed in his head that you would've been violent with Ana."

I sighed.

"I'm just looking out for you. I know you've been through hell for the past few months."

"Tried apologizing to Trent over the phone. He's not talking to me right now."

"Probably not ready to forgive you yet. Give him time."

"Thank you for being there for me," I muttered.

"Of course. I get it."

I bit into my grilled cheese before staring out into space. "I guess for me, I still don't understand why she had to end everything. Still don't understand why we couldn't have worked things out."

"I mean, based on what you've told me, it's possible that she might be going through something she didn't want to burden you with."

"I'm not a psychologist. I don't want to diagnose her, but it honestly wouldn't surprise me that she struggles with whatever invisible war she fights in her head. Maybe it's not exactly that. Maybe it's something else, or I'm imagining it. Maybe it's a combination of things in her life I don't know about. Maybe I'll never know, but maybe it's okay I'll never know. I just know whatever has caused her to feel like she had to end it, I hope she finds peace and happiness."

Ben didn't say anything as he poured himself a drink.

I started choking up a little. "The thing that makes me angry though is when people tell me to just 'move on,' like it's that fucking easy. I tried that with Kelly sixteen years ago and it didn't work! It took a long time to finally let go of her. When people tell me that it was 'not meant to be,' or how it was not meant to be 'long term,' or that I supposedly 'deserved better,' I grow to resent them really bad. 'Ana didn't treat you well,' you all say, as if I couldn't try to work that out on my own. People take the things they learned in therapy, and then use that to act like they know me better than I know myself. Pisses me off to no fucking end!"

I stopped to compose myself.

"I didn't mean to make you feel that way at the party," Ben said. "I'm sorry if I did."

I took a breath before taking another bite of my soup. "I guess for me, whenever people do that, they make me feel like what I experienced didn't matter. But if it didn't matter, then why the hell does it feel like she died?"

Ben shrugged, not saying anything for a moment. "Well . . . in a way, maybe she did."

I went back to eating.

"Can I ask you something random?" Ben asked.

"Sure."

"If you had to relive those five years with Ana all over again but not have the ability to change the outcome, would you do it?"

I took another bite of my soup. "Um . . . let me get back to you about that."

"Oh, a reason why I wanted to hang out today," Ben said. "I have something to tell you."

"What's that?"

"I'm moving up to Portland next month. Landed a job there."

"Oh." I put my spoon down, unsure what to say. "That's, uh, great."

Ben smiled. "Found out yesterday. I'm so excited!"

"I'm . . . I'm very happy for you, man."

"Mom is happy for me too. Will be a big change for her, but thankfully I have a cousin up there who'll help me get settled in. Nice to finally get out of San Diego!"

I shrugged. "I wish you luck," I said in a lukewarm way.

Ben finished up his grilled cheese. "Since I'll be moving soon, I want to show you something really cool I've been making on and off."

After lunch, Ben led me to the garage to show me what he was talking about, opening the garage door to get some light in.

"When's your mom coming home?" I asked.

"Not for another couple hours," Ben said as he went over to one of the walls where something leaned against it was covered in tarps.

"What did you want to show me?" I asked.

Ben slowly pulled off the tarps to reveal a large easel displaying a watercolor painting of a woman with brown hair and freckles wearing a pearl earring and glasses.

"Holy crap, did you do this?"

"I did," Ben proudly said. "When COVID started, I was stuck at home and my stupid Associate's degree wasn't able to get me any work, so I just started painting. Working on art of every kind to pass the time."

"Like you did when we went to Schweitzer."

"You can say that."

I gently felt the edge of the painting, carefully looking at the portrait of the woman.

"I've been working on this one on and off for the past two years now. Didn't tell anybody because I didn't want to show something unless I was absolutely sure it was ready. Probably redone this one countless times at this point because I couldn't get it exactly how I wanted it until recently."

I kept looking at the woman in the portrait. Something about her looked familiar.

"You like?" Ben asked.

"This belongs in an art museum, dude."

"Nah, I'm a nobody. I just did this for fun. Helps me with my drawing."

But something about her still looked suspiciously familiar. "Ben?"

"Yeah."

"What's Claire's last name again?"

"Rodenbo. Why?"

I typed "Claire Rodenbo" in the Facebook search bar from my phone, pulling up the first profile to come up. I examined the painting, looked at the profile, and then looked at the painting again.

They were practically identical! "You never got over Claire, did you?"

"What? Don't be ridiculous! Of course I'm over her. Why would you say that?"

"Dude, look at your own painting!" I held the phone up next to the painting so I could show him. "Don't you see it?"

Ben started acting uncomfortable. "It's just a painting of a woman," he said with a hint of anger in his voice. "It's supposed to be my take on *Girl with a Pearl Earring*. That's it! It has nothing to do with Claire!"

I kept my phone up by the painting. "If that's the case, why do they look identical?"

Ben tried to say something, but clearly was at a loss for words as he looked at both images next to each other. He took his hat off and stepped closer to the painting.

"Is this why you've always talked shit about her for so long? Is there something you don't want to admit, not even to yourself?"

Ben placed one of his hands gently against the portrait.

"Ben?"

Ben took a deep breath. "I was with her for three years," he slowly said. "Two wonderful years and a shitty third year. We argued a lot. She would ignore me many times. She would always be lukewarm about what she wanted. We would constantly disagree, so I was kind've relieved when she ended things out of the blue."

"Did you ever ask her why?"

"No. Didn't see the point. But before all that, I remember so many things about her. She was the first woman outside of Schweitzer to accept me, for me. We went to plenty of art shows, cooked great food, and played board games. Sex was badass too, but she always knew how to make me smile and make me laugh. In many ways, she made my life so much better." Suddenly, Ben's voice started cracking. "But then things went downhill and the awesome things we did slowly faded away until she was gone. Gone! I hated her for so long, but I . . ."

I put both of my hands on his shoulders.

"I still love her!" he screamed. "I miss her so baaaaaad!"

I wrapped my arms around him as he cried. "It's okay. Let it out."

Ben cried for what seemed to be an eternity before calming down and letting go.

"I'm . . . sorry," Ben said. "I didn't realize I felt all that."

Both of us looked at the painting again.

"What now?" he asked.

I didn't know what to say.

July 19, 2022

I tried playing "Till Tomorrow" again in my room that morning, my fingers still messing up the chord progression. *This song's hard*, I thought. I wanted to get some practice rounds in before going with Mom and Alicia to visit Jason at the developmental center.

I stopped playing when a Facebook Messenger notification popped up on my laptop screen, my palms shaking when I saw who it was.

VINCENT:

> I know this is out of the blue, but I was talking with Chris today and he told me in detail why you won't talk to me even after all these years. Chris probably already told you, but I'm telling you directly because you deserve it: I'm deeply sorry for how I treated you. It was thoughtless and insensitive of me. I had no right to get involved in your business and didn't respect your boundaries. Since my recent cancer diagnosis, I've had to really think about and re-evaluate how I've treated other people. I'm sorry for what I did. I'm sorry for how I made you feel, and I'm sorry it's taken me this long to apologize.

I put my guitar down and read his message multiple times. *He actually has cancer?* I thought. *What the hell? That seems way too ironic to be true.* I checked his Facebook timeline to see if he was telling the truth. A few minutes later, I found his public post from last November about his hospital stay in Milwaukee, expressing gratitude for the doctors catching the cancer early and getting countless support comments and love reactions and care emojis from friends and family. I felt a lump in my throat, a huge sense of guilt for the times I wished he would actually get cancer.

I started typing, but I then instantly remembered how he treated me years ago. Remembered how he tried to force his advice down my throat and made me feel worthless. Remembered how he humiliated me in that Facebook group. Remembered how he went around telling others how "worried" he was I would yell and scream at Ana. Remembered how he told others I wanted to sexually control her. Remembered all the times I struggled to talk to Ana because I was scared I would prove him right.

I started over, rewrote, and sent a message.

ROB:

> I really appreciate this. It means a lot. I do wish I had reacted to what you did better than before, and for that I'm sorry, too. I'm also sorry to hear about your cancer diagnosis. My grandma had it and I wouldn't wish it on even my worst enemies. I hope you kick cancer's ass.

I stopped, taking a moment to think carefully what to type next.

ROB:

> But while I acknowledge your apology, I do not forgive you. I'm not in a place in my life where I can forgive you. I think it's better for the time being you live with what you did so you can grasp just how awful your actions were. I don't want to hate you anymore, but I don't forgive you. Not right now. I hope you understand.

I leaned on my elbow, sighing as I heard Mom telling me it was time to go. One more message came through, and I looked down again at my phone.

VINCENT:

> I understand. I don't blame you. You had every right to be angry.

I stared at his message until Mom yelled for me again. I put my phone away and headed out.

July 20, 2022

I had been walking around my neighborhood for the past hour listening to music, something I hadn't done since getting COVID. I turned the corner and went down Armstrong street as it started to get overcast.

I walked until I saw a familiar boarded up house. Clothes, pictures, and other personal items laid out on the lawn as contractors went back and forth from the house to the truck parked in the driveway. I stopped to watch until I saw an older man with a somber look sitting on the lawn on the phone.

I only caught snippets of what he was saying before realizing who it was. He ended the call as he looked at everything laid out on the lawn.

I waved to him. "Excuse me. I don't know if you know me, but I'm Rob. I live around the corner. I was here when the fire happened, and I never got a chance to say how sorry I am about your house. I hope everything's okay."

The homeowner looked up at me. "I appreciate that. Thank you."

"If you don't mind me asking, do you know what caused the fire?"

The homeowner sighed. "So far they think it might have been some sort of electrical fire, but they're not sure yet of the exact cause. They're still working on it." He sighed as he looked over his shoulder to gaze at the house. "Right now I'm just going through everything since it's been a couple months. I remember the first time me and my wife walked inside the house so many years ago. It was the first house we ever bought, and while it always had problems here and there, it was our house, you know?"

I looked up at the house as the contractors did inspections outside.

The homeowner picked up a charred picture of a little girl with black hair hugging a puppy.

"Who's that?"

"That's my daughter Sarah when she was seven. Me and my wife . . . when we moved here from Taiwan, we wanted to give her a good life. We watched her grow up in this house. We saw her play around, throw extravagant birthday parties, get so excited for family gatherings—those were wonderful times."

"Is she still around?"

"She went to college in New Hampshire and never came back. We're lucky if we get a phone call from her. I still don't know what made her cut us out of her life, but I hold onto hope she'll come back."

"What if she doesn't?" I found myself asking.

"Then I have the memories. Yes, the house we made them in is practically gone, but I still have them. I will always cherish them. They make life worth living."

I looked at the house a little bit before saying goodbye and heading home.

I spent the next couple hours cleaning my room, pulling out all the posters Ana gave me as gifts from under my bed and reorganizing my drawers and shelves. I went through a plastic bin of trinkets, looking at each one, remembering the small little things she would give me whenever we would go to street fairs or take road trips. I dusted off a piggy bank shaped like a dog from the shelf, taking me a moment to remember she gave it to me when we went to the Asian American Expo.

Here, I remembered Ana saying as I looked at the piggy bank. *I want you to have it.*

Wait, are you sure?

Ana nodded, smiling. *I'm sure. It's for you.*

I put the piggy bank down and went through more trinkets, finding postcards she got me when she visited New York and Indonesia, and other trinkets she got when we went on road trips.

When I found a refrigerator magnet from Big Bear, I remembered us cuddling in the lodge we rented when we went up there sometime before Labor Day in 2020.

I'm sorry we weren't able to go boat riding, I said.

It's okay, she said.

I should've planned better.

People aren't really practicing social distancing anyway, so it's okay.

I smiled. *I guess I'm just glad to be here with you, away from everything then.*

Me too.

I put away the plastic bin and went through my shelf again to see if I missed anything, finding a black notebook covered in dust, hiding underneath a bunch of books I no longer read.

I really need to take better care of this shit, I thought.

I pulled up the notebook and glanced at the first page, thinking it was just some random scribbles. I stopped to read when I recognized my old crappy handwriting:

June 10, 2002

>*Hello, my name is Rob, and I'm 13 years old. I'm writing this journal because I have nothing better to do. Let me tell you something about myself. My full name is Robert Brian Sullivan, but I prefer to go by Rob. I live in San Diego, California and was born in Eugene, Oregon on September 14, 1988. I go to ~~Schwit~~ Schweitzer Specialized Education Center, though me and the other kids just call it Schweitzer for short.*
>
>*Hopefully someday I can go to a real school, away from*

Schweitzer forever. I wish I didn't have to go to a place like this where I deal with kids constantly having seizures and then come home to Jason throwing tantrums everyday, but I've gotten used to it. My school life is kinda the same except it's sad. I used to have a best friend named Tim Myers. We had been best friends during elementary school, but for some reason he became a big bully and ever since I've been a loner, mostly hanging around the house, but nobody at school knows about it.

That was the only entry. I couldn't recall why I didn't write more. I rubbed my eyes when I started crying, remembering all the years of feeling like they didn't care, angry for how they almost allowed me to fall through the cracks.

Then I met Kelly.

Then I found out Schweitzer wanted to keep me behind, and all of them—especially Maggie Richardson—blamed only me for it.

Then I fought like hell to catch up on high school credits.

Then I almost lost my mind.

Then I got my high school diploma and left.

Then after grad school I stomped on that diploma, screaming "go to hell" as I destroyed it.

I couldn't stop crying, sobbing uncontrollably in ways I hadn't in a long time.

I sobbed until slowly began to calm down when I remembered the night Ana comforted me when I told her what I went through at that place.

I'm sorry if I'm telling you too much, I mumbled.

You have nothing to be sorry for, she softly said.

I took a deep breath, putting the notebook down to go through my drawers. I went through each one until I found the Airpods Ana gave me for Christmas last year.

"I could've sworn I put these in the plastic bin," I muttered.

I picked up the Airpods, reliving the day she gave them to me in my head.

I know you like to use headphones all the time, so I thought these would be great for you, Ana said.

Now I can go on my walks or go to the gym and not get tangled!

Exactly.

I slowly put on the Airpods, syncing them to my phone so I could listen to music while laying on my bed, thinking about the years I spent with her.

August 15, 2022

I laid a flower below Dad's gravestone before kneeling down, staring at the inscription: *Brian Phillip Sullivan, US Army CPL, 1949—2001*. I placed my hand over his name as I remembered all the times I spent with him before he passed into the great unknown. "I know it's been a while," I muttered. "If you're up there, I hope you're doing well."

I kissed his tombstone before heading over to Grandpa and Grandma's graves. I tilted my head as I saw a figure standing in front of their tombstones, but as I got closer, I realized it was Alicia. She didn't say much when I asked her how she was doing.

"Where's Mom?" I asked.

"She's at home right now." Alicia placed bouquets of flowers next to Grandpa and Grandma's tombstones.

"I miss 'em," I said.

"Me too."

"I don't know about you, but I'm just glad I was able to spend time with them both. Wish they didn't have to go." I looked over at my sister as she stared at the gravestone. "It's kinda weird that we're not yelling at each other right now," I said.

Alicia shrugged. "I guess."

Neither of us said anything for a moment. "Did you see Dad's grave already?" I asked.

Alicia looked at me for a moment before looking back at our Grandparents' tombstones.

"Alicia?"

Alicia sighed. "I have. It's just hard for me."

I said nothing.

"I just can't get it out of my head what I saw when me and Mom went to see him," Alicia said. "You're so lucky you didn't see what I saw, Rob."

"I wasn't feeling well, so I stayed home."

"I know that, but what I'm saying is that you should be thankful that you didn't see it."

I sighed. "I'm sorry you had to see him decomposing."

Alicia straightened out the roses below Grandpa and Grandma's tombstones. "It is what it is."

I said nothing else for a moment as Alicia finished straightening out the roses.

"He loved you too, you know," I eventually said.

"I just wish he didn't go at a time when I really needed him, and Mom became so focused on taking care of Jason that I ended up having to fend for myself."

"What are you talking about?" I instantly asked. "You did much better than me. You got to go to a public school and have tons of friends and do so well. You didn't have to go to a Special Ed school your whole life that tried to fuck you over."

"You think you're the only one who struggled?" Alicia exclaimed, as if trying real hard not to raise her voice. "You think you're the only one who had to figure out how to grow up on your own?"

"No, that's not what I'm saying at all."

"Then don't make it seem like you are!" Alicia yelled.

I sighed again. "You're right," I mumbled. "I'm sorry. You don't have to yell at me about it, you know."

"You just frustrate me," Alicia softly said.

I sighed, neither of us saying anything for a moment. "Mom did the best she could, you know."

"I know."

I took a moment to figure out what to say next. "You know, from time to time I wish we had the same relationship we had before he died," I eventually said. "I just wish we didn't fight so much."

Alicia said nothing as both of us just looked at the tombstones.

"Does Mom know you're moving out?" Alicia eventually asked.

"She does."

"Make sure you still come by once in a while to check up on Mom and remind Jason that he still has his brother, okay? I know Mom can be a real pain in the ass and can be mean sometimes, but she still needs both of us. Please don't forget that."

"Of course," I muttered.

"By the way, before I forget, I wanted to say I'm sorry about you and Ana," Alicia said.

I looked over at Alicia, not sure how to respond. I didn't think she actually cared. "It is what it is," I said. "I'm better now. Grandpa really liked her."

"I know. He would always mention her in some way, even when you weren't there."

I didn't say anything else as I put a flower next to Grandma and Grandpa's graves before both of us took time paying our respects to them.

Alicia started walking away.

"Where are you going?"

"Heading home."

"I'll see you later then."

Alicia began heading to her car. I stayed behind, looking at Grandpa and Grandma's graves for a while before walking away.

I was halfway across the cemetery when I found myself drawn to a blank cement plaque in the ground, as if it was getting ready to be used soon. I looked down at it, not understanding why I stopped to stare.

But then I thought about Ana again.

I thought about everything we've been through in the past five years before we broke up. I thought about everything about her that annoyed the shit out of me, all the times she would make us late, the constant speeding, the moments when she would be so quiet it felt like I had to extract teeth to get her to talk to me, the times she would shut herself off from me.

But then I thought about all the things about her that made me happy. I thought about the sense of comfort and safety she used to create, the random gifts she used to bestow, the cuddles she used to supply, the stories and jokes she used to share, the love she used to give.

I thought about her smile.

I thought about everything that made her *her*.

I imagined words slowly swirling in the air before writing on the plaque below:

Ana Kang
October 4, 1994 — May 19, 2022
My Iron Man, I hope you won that invisible war,
for that's all any of us can try and do . . .

I knelt down and placed my hand on her name, the imagined inscription staying in my head as tears fell to the ground.

I stayed on the ground.

I could not stop crying.

March 11, 2023—Yesterday

I didn't have to go to campus today, so I spent most of the afternoon at my place grading papers and playing my guitar. The walls of the granny flat were mostly soundproof, so I didn't have to worry about making too much noise for my roommates on the other side of the house.

Even six months later, I still couldn't believe Aunt Judy helped me find this place.

Sitting on the bed, I did some light strumming before it occurred to me I never got around to mastering "Till Tomorrow." After not playing the song in a while, I thought it high time to try again.

I got my fingers ready and began the chord progression, only to mess up again.

"God you suck at this song, Rob!" an audience member shouted.

I kept trying to play, continuing to mess up as I saw myself on *the stage again.*

The audience coldly stared at me. "You're such a failure, Rob!" a portion of them shouted.

My fingers messed up on the fretboard *as someone in the audience threw a bottle at me, smashing into a thousand pieces against my head. "Kill yourself, you sack of shit!"*

I stopped playing and put the guitar down, taking deep breaths.

Later in the evening after dinner, I put Don McLean's "American Pie" on my dad's vinyl player. I felt immersed in the song until it reminded me of the night I listened to it with Ana when she asked me why I listened to music like this.

The way I see it now, I said. *The reason I listen to older music is because when I take the time to listen to the sounds of yesterday, they make me remember the promises of tomorrow.*

What kind of promises? Ana asked.

. . . the promise of a better future, and the promise that everything will be okay, no matter what . . .

I pulled out my phone and found myself looking at her photos. As the music played, snapshots of everything Ana and I have been through over the years flashed here and there in my thoughts. I saw images of us cuddling in bed laughing and giggling, of us going to the art festival by the waterfront, riding bikes by the beach, and taking selfies at museums. I saw flashes of restaurants we explored and trips we went on, an image of us together when we saw Poets of the Fall.

I couldn't stop thinking about the night I comforted her when she cried in my arms.

***

Today

Last night, I dreamt Ana and I watched the sunset at Ocean Beach Pier.

Has work gotten better? I asked.

Kinda but not really, she said. I'll tough it out, hope for the best.

Yeah. Have things gotten better with your mom?

Ana just shrugged, not saying anything as we watched the sunset.

When I woke up, I couldn't help but look at Ana's pictures again. I replayed those five years in my head before getting up, taking a shower, and having breakfast.

***

I finished grading papers for the day and began playing my guitar. I practiced a couple of easy songs before I started thinking about trying to finally master "Till Tomorrow" again.

I stretched my fingers, made sure my guitar was in tune, and started again. I did good in the first part until my fingers slipped on the fretboard.

"This again, Rob?" An audience member lectured. "Just give up!"

I took a moment to stop, Ana's smile appearing in my thoughts. I took a breath, got myself ready to try again, and began playing.

As I played, I *firmly stood center stage directly at the audience, the spotlight pointing directly at me.*

The audience threw every insult at me.

"You have no control over me," I asserted.

The audience continued to coldly stare at me. "Why should we believe anything you say, you disgusting idiot? You're a failure and you should stop pretending you're not a failure!"

They booed as I stood there, getting ready to walk away before stopping.

Ana's smile briefly flashed in my thoughts again.

I took a breath before standing defiantly, slowly taking off a mask replicating my face. I dropped the mask to the floor and kicked it to the side before staring directly back at the audience. "You have no control over me," I asserted again.

"Your existence is a mistake! Your mom should've aborted you, just like many Autistic Moms would have wanted to do if they could!"

"Bullshit!"

"You're a fraud! You're stupid! You don't know shit! Maybe if you weren't autistic, you wouldn't have so many issues! It's your fault Ana broke up with you! She broke up with you because you are so dumb and pathetic, and you should kill yourself right now!"

I stood firm. "You have no control over me!" I asserted once again. "You are all lying bastards!"

"Just kill yourself already!"

Someone in the audience threw a bottle at me.

I caught the bottle and held it straight up in the air.

The audience gasped.

"No!" I shouted. "I have a will to live! You have no. Control. OVER! MEEEEE!" I threw the bottle at the spotlight, smashing the bulb as sparks flew and glass shattered all over.

Everyone in the audience started to panic, scrambling to figure out what to do before they disappeared and the seats were all empty, the entire auditorium going dim.

"Rob?" I heard a familiar voice from behind.

I turned around to see who that familiar voice was several feet away. "Ana?"

I slowly walked up and hugged Ana. "I miss you so much," I said as she hugged me back.

We hugged for what seemed to be an eternity before letting go.

I held onto her hands. "How've you been?" I meekly asked.

"I've been okay," she mumbled.

I gently placed one of my hands on her cheek as I looked into her eyes, the somber look I'd seen so many times. "It's okay to not be okay, Ana." I took my hand off her cheek and just held her hands. "I've been thinking a lot about what happened since our last phone call. I replayed the entire five years of the time we spent together, trying to figure out why you ended everything. At first, I thought it was my fault. I blamed myself for what happened. But then I realized that, no, it's not my fault."

Ana closed her eyes and knelt her head down.

"At first I thought you hated me and thought I was a burden, but the more I thought about it, the more I realized that wasn't the case either. I realized that there were things going on with you in ways I didn't understand, and for that I'm sorry for not understanding better."

Before I could say anything else, a flying race car landed next to us as the ceiling of the auditorium opened slowly up to reveal a night sky full of stars.

"What's this?" I asked.

"It's my ride to the stars," Ana said. "To my special place."

"Can I come with you?"

Ana slowly shook her head. "I'm sorry, but I'm afraid you can't."

"Can I at least say something before you go?"

"Sure."

I held Ana's hand again. "A friend of mine once asked me if I had to relive the five years I spent with you all over again but not have the ability to change the outcome, would I do it? I thought about that question for a long time and the more I thought about it, the more I would say yes. Absolutely yes! I would do it all over again! In a heartbeat! Take the great and the not so great things about what we've been through because love is about working through the friction, and the friction I had with you, no matter how much it pissed me off sometimes, was worth dealing with because YOU are worth it! No matter how you feel about yourself or how others feel about you. You are worth it, Ana!"

Ana gave a faint smile. "You've always been so sweet."

My eyes started to water. "I still to this day don't understand why you chose to walk away from us. I often wondered what I could've done differently to get you to stay, but it really does feel like you died and I'll never—EVER—see you again. I'm trying so hard to wrap my head around it that it hurts. I just don't get it. First my dad. Then my grandma and grandpa. And now you! Why? Why did you feel the need to shut me out so much? Why did you feel like you had to cut me out of your life? Why didn't you feel like you could talk to me?"

Ana said nothing.

"Can you at least tell me why you didn't tell me you weren't happy?"

Still no words from Ana.

I looked at her, finally accepting she was never going to tell me. "I guess this is goodbye then?"

No response as Ana had that somber look on her face again.

We hugged. "It's okay if I don't ever know why," I said. "I just want you to be happy and that's more important than anything in the world."

I looked into her eyes.

"It's okay," I tearfully said. "You can go."

I gave her one final kiss before we let go. Ana looked at me and for one last time gave the radiant smile she always had when I first met her. She slowly got into the race car and hovered up into the air before flying towards the sky, leaving me to watch as she disappeared forever into the stars.

I dropped to my knees as the ceiling closed up tight. I saw each light of the auditorium go out, one by one. I couldn't stop crying as the auditorium slowly went dark. And when it reached the final light, I braced myself for pitch blackness.

But instead I stood in light, looking up to see a ghostlight standing tall above me. "What's going on?" I muttered.

As I stared up at the ghostlight above me, I slowly stopped crying.

Then another ghostlight appeared on stage left, this time shining light on my guitar on a stand. I went over and slowly picked up the guitar, inspecting it to make sure it was in tune and ready to perform.

I put on my guitar strap and moved center stage.

A voice blasted from the auditorium's speakers. "Everyone, give it up for Robert Brian Sullivan!"

I turned to see the audience filling all the seats again, all cheering for me. I held up my guitar, smiling as so many people held banners with my name on them and clapped for me. "You got this, Rob!" Someone in the audience shouted. "We love you, Rob!"

I did a practice strum, causing the crowd to go wild. "That was just a warm-up. I want to start us off with a song called 'Till Tomorrow' by Don McLean."

The crowd cheered again as I began playing. As I played, a group of kids stuck their tongues at me while a few people egged them on, only for some security guards to start escorting them out of the building. Once I finished the song, the crowd gave a massive round of applause and threw roses and bouquets at my feet.

I raised my fist in the air as I finally saw the light.

The Sounds of Yesterday
Rob and Ana's Playlist

1. "Sounds of Yesterday" - Poets of the Fall
2. "Into You" - Arianna Grande
3. "Diamonds for Tears" - Poets of the Fall
4. "Piano Man" - Billy Joel
5. "And I Love You So" - Don McLean
6. "The Night We Met" - Lord Huron
7. "This Happiness" - Of Monsters and Men
8. "Perfect" - Ed Sheeran
9. "Landslide" - Fleetwood Mac
10. "Ain't No Mountain High Enough" - Marvin Gaye & Tammi Terrell
11. "Wasted Years" - Iron Maiden
12. "Carnival of Rust" - Poets of the Fall
13. "Dancing on Broken Glass" - Poets of the Fall
14. "Wish You Were Here" - Pink Floyd
15. "Cradled in Love" - Poets of the Fall
16. "Waltz of the Snowflakes" - *The Nutcracker*
17. "American Pie" - Don McLean
18. "Dreaming Wide Awake" - Poets of the Fall
19. "Late Goodbye" - Poets of the Fall
20. "Yesterday Once More" - The Carpenters
21. "Kathy's Song" - Paul Simon
22. "No Surprises" - Radiohead
23. "The Scientist" - Coldplay
24. "I Will Follow You into the Dark" - Death Cab for Cutie
25. "Silent Night" - Frank Sinatra
26. "Black Hole Sun" - Soundgarden
27. "It's Too Late" - Carol King
28. "Into the Unknown" - Idina Menzel
29. "Till Tomorrow" - Don McLean

A MESSAGE FROM THE AUTHOR
JACOB HUBBARD

It is recommended this message be read after reading the book as it contains spoilers.

I began writing *Sounds of Yesterday* in early August 2022 to help me process my own grief. I didn't really have a clear-cut idea of what my writing goal was, let alone an idea of if I would even finish it in the first place. I didn't have a title or what direction I wanted to take the story. I wasn't even confident I would finish, considering how I've attempted (and failed) book projects in the past. I just knew I was heartbroken after a devastating breakup, and writing about it was my form of therapy. The breakup had happened months prior, so it was fresh in my mind when I started writing. I struggled at first to figure out if this was a story worth telling, especially considering breakup stories have been done countless times before. It wasn't until I listened to the Poets of the Fall song of the same name for the umpteenth-millionth time that the title and the general direction for the book finally clicked: yes, this was a story worth telling!

Early on when I started writing, I watched the film (500) *Days of Summer* for the first time since college. Watching it again helped clarify my ideas for this book. I was surprised by how put off I was by its ending, particularly the famous park bench scene many people would praise. The film did many things right, but then we get to the end where they're both sitting at that bench talking about why they didn't work out and something about it just didn't sit right with me. Summer directly gives Tom closure, but who gets clear-cut closure like Tom does? How in the world does the breakup Tom experienced not reopen so many of the traumas and insecurities he had growing up? And why in the world does Tom just throw a plate on the kitchen floor? That joke aside, despite its good intentions, I was put off by many things about the film itself, so I decided early on to try and do the opposite of what that film was doing. In a way, this book serves as a strong critique of that park bench scene since closure rarely happens in real life like it does in the movies. My hope with this book is to explore the question, "How do you move on and heal when you don't get that cathartic sense of closure?"

Grief was what kept me going with *Sounds of Yesterday*. During the grieving process, I found myself forced to confront many topics regarding neurodiversity, lingering trauma, mental health struggles, memory, the nature of empathy and sympathy, and (most importantly) coming to terms with my own internalized ableism. Seeing much more clearly on paper just how deeply ingrained my internalized ableism was helped me better understand how my experiences going through the Special Education system in the 1990s-2000s mentally affected me going into my adult life. Even years later when I've finally escaped the Special Ed environment and worked hard to get where I am professionally, the lingering fear of feeling erased again doesn't truly go away. The story presented in this book *is* based on actual events I lived through, though as with many works that are semi-autobiographical, plenty of creative liberties had to be taken for reasons that I hope are obvious. I've been told by some of my beta readers that the idea of a neurodivergent relationship story is under-explored territory in today's fiction, though that was not something I initially set out to do. As mentioned already, the main driving force for writing this book for me was simply grief.

I think a lot about grief because in many discussions I've seen about breakups, I saw a constant downplay of how emotionally devastating a breakup can be. This is not to say it's not acknowledged that people get hurt from them, but rather the cultural perception about breakups is that they are somehow different from deaths. If you ever experienced a devastating breakup, how many times have you had someone say something to you along the lines of, "There are plenty of fish in the sea," "You two were not made for each other," or "You will find love again someday"? There is a major contrast between the cultural perception about breakups and the reality of the emotions and heartbreak that come with them. Think about it: you spend so much time with someone (four years, five years, etc.), only for the end of the relationship to feel like the person you loved for so long suddenly died, like they've become a ghost and rode that flying race car to disappear forever into the stars. We (rightfully) express our condolences to someone whose partner passes away, yet we don't usually express a similar level of condolences when a breakup happens. You have the pictures and mementos and videos and music (the "sounds of yesterday," if I may) that remind you of happier times, but they also remind you in a bittersweet way that things in the future will be okay if you allow the emotional scars to help carry you forward, rather than allow them to destroy you.

These ideas were constantly in the back of my mind throughout the writing process, but it also reminds me how crucial it is to think about not just *what* this book is about, but *who* it is about. Is it about Rob? Sure. That makes sense. I mean, he is the point of view character after all. We learn who Rob is, his upbringing, his traumas, insecurities, and mental health struggles. But this book is also about Ana. It's about Rob _and_ Ana. The Ana you read in these pages is the closest you as the reader will get to knowing the woman I spent five years of my life with from 2017 to 2022. One of the goals for writing this book was to pay tribute to her. I wanted to honor her memory by attempting to show both the great and the not-so-great things about Ana to demonstrate why her real-life counterpart was such an important person in my life. Unlike Tom from (500) *Days of Summer*, I do not believe love is about ignoring the imperfections of that person or about how they are supposed to compliment *your* happiness because to do so would be to romanticize them and put them on a pedestal, for to romanticize them like that isn't truly loving that person. Rather, to truly love someone is to embrace both their strengths and their complexities. I think about those five years I spent with the real-life Ana, remembering all the great times we had and the tender moments we shared, but also the emotional struggles and communication issues we faced that gradually led to us growing apart.

But I think about who she was as a person. Her likes. Her dislikes. Her mannerisms. Her quirks. Her habits. The small things about her that annoyed me or got on my nerves but also all the small things that made me fall in love with her. I think about how introverted and reserved she was, how quiet she could be but also how funny she could be, the laughs we had, our in-depth conversations, the stories we shared. It's weird to talk about her in the past tense as if that makes me some type of a widower, but I don't think grieving the passing of a relationship is any different from grieving the passing of a loved one. I grieve for someone who meant so much to me, but I also express joy that I got to know someone so wonderful and so wholesome. She came into my life at a time when (as the cliche goes) I needed someone like her. She was there for me. She allowed me to be myself. She created a space for me to feel like I could finally start healing and moving on from my experience with the special education "school" represented in this book.

But it would be a mistake to assume she saved me, similar to how I think it would be a mistake to assume Ana saved Rob. I think about what Rob's sister asks him near the end of the book: about whether he thought he was the only one who struggled in life, and in many ways she is right to ask that question. As readers, we have a natural tendency to empathize with the protagonist as a novel progresses, but this can come with the risk of not taking the time to also empathize with other characters. My hope with this book is that any empathy you potentially gained for Rob, you also worked to extend that empathy to Ana as well, for this book is, in a way, about empathy. The struggles many people face is something we don't always see; we often only get glimpses of that struggle through breadcrumb trails they leave behind, since we don't have direct access to the invisible wars that go on in their heads.

But that doesn't mean we should just walk away or never take risks with love if that is the case. Rob's decision to try again with

Ana is a direct reflection of my own experience with her real-life counterpart. In the face of adversaries like Vincent Smith who attempt to control our decision making through peer pressure and gaslighting, I learned (and by extension Rob learns as well) just how crucial it is to stand up for your emotional autonomy with all your might, even when it doesn't align perfectly with neurotypical norms and expectations. Vincent was wrong when he tried to pressure Rob to "run for the hills" and that he should "only listen to his worried voice," not just because it attempts to take away Rob's freedom to make choices about his life but also because it completely misunderstands the nature of love in the first place.

Near the beginning of the book, I've included a quote from the Lebanese-American poet Kahlil Gibran that spoke to me quite strongly. I think about that idea of joy and sorrow being two sides of the same coin (or as Gibran says, "Your joy is your sorrow unmasked"), and that's true for how I view the themes of *Sounds of Yesterday*. Vincent's real-life counterpart made the mistake of assuming that his relationship or breakup experiences were universal and that one must always walk away from a "transparently bad situation" because there is nothing to be learned from a "playful roll of the dice." In a lot of ways, Vincent's actions mirror the harmful ways many people try to "help" those with disabilities, neurodivergent differences, or mental health struggles based on superficial and self-serving attempts at empathy. The arrogance of this mindset only perpetuates the ableist notion that somehow we need to be saved from the supposed consequences of our own life decisions, or that we are somehow "delusional" for going back to a "bad situation." The systems that are in place (as represented by Maggie Richardson) and the societal norms that inadvertently continue those systemic practices (as represented by Vincent Smith) only serve to perpetuate the harmful assumption that we don't really know what's best for our own lives, as if we need to be talked down to because we supposedly don't understand the potential risks for our choices.

But when we talk about love, love does not mean no risk at all.

Love does not mean we go in expecting no pain to happen. Love means knowing the risk for pain but taking the risk anyway. That's a major reason why Rob's decision to try again with Ana was not only the right decision, but the *only* decision that would've made any ounce of sense given what he went through in his life. From Rob's point of view, she was worth that risk, regardless of how others view her or how she views herself. Relationships don't have to last forever for them to be meaningful. It would've been a terrible decision to take Vincent's unsolicited "advice" and avoid taking a risk with someone again simply because it could cause pain, no matter how great that pain may be. What life lessons would Rob have been deprived of if he had blindly followed Vincent's unsolicited advice? What real, serious regrets would he have to live with for the rest of his life if he didn't take that chance, even in the possible face of heartbreak and suffering? As a good friend of mine once told me after she finished reading a draft of this book, "We don't get to know when love ends, right? So love. Love with everything in you as often and as much as you can." I resonate with that with every fiber of my being.

As I think about all these, I think again about Poets of the Fall's "Sounds of Yesterday," the song that helped me see that this was a story worth telling. I think about what that song means to me and how it relates to my story (and in the off chance Marko Saaresto or any other member of the band is reading this, I cannot thank you enough for your music inspiring me to keep writing). I think about the dynamic I had with Ana's real-life counterpart and the emotional journey I spent with her that led to the creation of this book. I think about all this to emphasize just how important this story is to me.

And if Ana's real-life counterpart is reading this, I want you to know that it still hurts that you are gone, but I am no longer mad at you for ending things. I still don't really understand why you decided to end things or why we couldn't have worked things out, but I've grown to accept it's okay to not ever fully know. Your happiness is more important than having all the answers, and I likely will go to my grave someday never fully understanding why. But that's okay. I still love you, and I hope this book honors your memory. The pain of losing you is an emotional scar that will take a lifetime to heal, but as Gibran said, you cannot have joy without sorrow. You brought so much joy into my life at a time when I needed someone like you that the sorrow I have due to your absence is absolutely worth the chance to have experienced that joy. Many people in my life have come and gone, but you made an impact on me in a way I will never forget. You made life worth living, and I hope you will continue to go out there and live a life filled with nothing but peace and happiness, even if it's without me, for your happiness is more important than anything in the world.

I write all this to explain my reasons for writing *Sounds of Yesterday*. I do not expect every person to resonate with this story, but I hope there is something here you can take away with you or will give you something to consider. This is a neurodivergent story through and through told by a neurodivergent author, warts and all. I did not write this book for money or fame. I wrote this book as a form of therapy. While I recognize that writing a book by itself won't provide immediate healing, it can absolutely be part of a larger process of working towards that healing. And this can be something that would benefit not only myself but also you as the reader. This book has been nothing but a labor of love for me, for it is just as much as *her* story as it is mine. The story ends in heartbreak, but it's a heartbreak that can, paradoxically, bring joy as well for it shows how beautiful love is. It's the kind of heartbreak that can remind you just how worthwhile life can be.

I know this book won't bring her back. No book can. My biggest hope though is that this book will be a force for those who are going through things similar to what what I went through. I hope this book will also encourage other neurodivergent people to tell their stories to the world. I hope this book will be a reminder that you are not alone in your grief, whatever pain or heartache your are going through. There is so many things I could say, but I feel the best way to end this message is to expand on what Rob imagined he saw in

the cemetery when he thought about Ana and apply it directly to
her real-life counterpart:

My Iron Man,
I hope you won that invisible war,
For that's all anyone can try and do.

Grief is a winding path of emotions.
Tears will shed.
Tears of pain.
Tears of joy.

My Iron Man,
I hope you found true happiness,
For that's all anyone can try and do.

Love is a tightrope, a balance of joy and sorrow.
Love is saying the ever classic four-lettered words to
*   anyone who cuts you down or says I deserved*
*   better than you.*

Love is holding both your joy and your sorrow.
Love is letting you disappear forever into the stars,
No matter how much it bleeds.

My Iron Man,
I hope you conquered the world,
For that's all anyone can try and do.

I love you and miss you every day.

- Jacob Hubbard
November 19, 2024

ACKNOWLEDGEMENTS &
THANK YOUS

Writing this book took a lot out of me, having spent an entire year working on this project while teaching full time and another to get it edited and out there into the world. Whenever I'm not working, I would go to a Starbucks or Lestat's to write, even when I'm tired and so desperately want to sleep. I'm proud this is my debut novel, but it would not have been possible if I didn't have help along the way.

I first want to thank my colleagues at San Diego State University, starting with my (now former) department chair of the Rhetoric & Writing Studies (RWS) Department Glen McClish for all the years of guidance about writing that gave me the confidence to take on a book like this. I cannot thank you enough for your unwavering support for this project to succeed so it can spread more awareness for neurodiversity. I want to thank my RWS colleague Lea Baker for her meticulous feedback, providing me wonderful suggestions I believe helped strengthen different aspects of the book itself. I want to thank Jess Whatcott from the Women's Studies Department for the critical feedback I needed to clarify my ideas and to make the book's themes more prevalent. I want to thank my office mate Betsy Robertson for all the conversations we had about topics related to this book as a way to help me overcome the occasional writer's block.

I want to thank so many of the people who agreed to take time out of their busy schedules to be either beta readers or just be a sounding board for ideas I had during the drafting process. I want to thank Phil Godshall, Joe Florence, Dave Brown, Roberto Valenzuela, Emily Davis, Janel Spencer, Randy Helzerman, Jonah Schwartz, Stephanie Morse, Garret Merriam, Brandon Hill, David

Shih-wei Chang, and Sebastian Certik for providing their honest thoughts and suggestions (whether reading over the whole manuscript, bits and pieces, or just helping me clarify my ideas I wanted to put on paper even if they didn't read the manuscript itself).

I want to thank my aunt Pam Peabody for taking time to read each chapter and being one of my first readers. I want to thank my editor and dear friend Amber Rodenbo from River City Siren Press, for collaborating with Celestial Seaside Publishing to help edit and promote this book. Thank you for taking time out of your day to go through this book line by line to make it the best it can be, being its champion. I want to thank my partner Erin for reading over every draft of each chapter, providing thoughts and feedback, and being there when I needed someone to help stay motivated to write.

I want to thank Monét Nyree Panza for creating such an amazing cover for the book and to Doan Trang for the fantastic interior artwork. The styles of both are different but they compliment each other in ways that really help bring this story to life, and I cannot thank both of them enough for their hard work.

Finally and most importantly, I want to thank Diana, for without you this book would not have come to be. I still love you and will miss you everyday until the moment I take my last breath, but I hope with your ride to the stars, you are able to find peace and happiness . . .

. . . wherever you are.

ABOUT THE AUTHOR

Jacob Hubbard is a neurodivergent writer and college writing teacher living in the San Diego Metro area. With a Bachelors in English and a Masters in Rhetoric from San Diego State University, Jacob has developed a love of writing in all its forms, being drawn to stories about very real human experiences, even ones rooted in the fantastical.

As an advocate for the neurodiversity movement, Jacob has made neurodiversity an important theme in his writing and teaching to help spread awareness of neurodivergence within a neurotypical world. When he is not writing or teaching, Jacob loves hiking, traveling, browsing his local indie bookstore, and playing video games like *Elden Ring* and *Dark Souls*.

Sounds of Yesterday is his debut novel.

Find out more by scanning the QR code